Please return/renew this item by the last date shown
on this label, or on your self-service receipt.

To renew this item, visit **www.librarieswest.org.uk**
or contact your library.

Your Borrower Number and PIN are required.

Libraries**West**

STONE

KEEPER

THE BOOK OF EARTH

BETH WEBB

MHM
March Hamilton Media

MHM
March Hamilton Media

www.marchhamilton.com

*

For Tom

a painter of dreams

Acknowledgements

with special thanks to:
Dr John A. Davies,
Chief Curator Norwich Castle Study Centre
and **Dr Paul R. Sealey,**
Curator of Archaeology, Colchester and Ipswich Museums
For their invaluable help and advice about Boudica and the
British rebellion against the Romans.

Also to Andy, Chloë, Lucinda, Philippa, Charlie and Yael
and all my friends and family for
their unfailing support.

*

THE STORY SO FAR ...

It is the end of the Iron Age and the Romans have invaded Britain. The druids are looking for a 'Star Dancer', a warrior-mage who will bring hope in the midst of despair.

Desperate to find and train the boy, they overlook the birth of an insignificant girl –Tegen.

As she grows, her wild, untutored magic attracts two archenemies: the scheming Gorgans, who longs to be the Star Dancer himself, and Derowen, a malicious witch with dark powers.

With the help of Griff, her 'half head' foster-brother, Tegen begins her training as the Star Dancer and a druid of the Winter Seas, but she is tricked into poisoning Gilda, the kindly midwife who believed in her from the moment of her birth. Tegen's confidence is further crushed when Gorgans steals the green silk shawl that she believes holds her magical powers.

Derowen and Gorgans raise a cave demon to destroy Tegen, but they have summoned more than they can control and are killed by their own warped magic.

Tegen brings the catastrophe under control. At last, the druids recognise her powers and offer her a place of honour amongst them. She refuses, believing she must fulfil her destiny on Mona, the druids' sacred island.

On the way she meets Owein, a young ovate travelling in the opposite direction. He has a past he's trying to hide, and an uncle, Admidios, who is hell-bent on vengeance and power. Against her will, Tegen becomes entangled in Admidios's dark plots, beginning with the murder of Owein's foster father and ending with betrayal and the destruction of the stronghold at Sinodun.

But Tegen has learned one important thing from Admidios: that she has the power to summon fire, and in those flames to divine the future.

As Sinodun burns, Tegen flees, once more determined to reach Mona. She has with her Epona – a white mare, Wolf – her dog, and Kieran – a boy she helped to rescue from slavery.

But Tegen has not left everything behind.

She is being watched. The cave demon is still alive ... And it's following her.

Kieran leads Tegen to his own home in Y Fenni, but the Romans who are systematically devastating the lands of the Cymru have destroyed the town. Kieran agrees to take Tegen as far as the House of Bera at the foot of Cadair Idris, but the demon follows them, first as a mist, then in the body of a half-dead bear. They find refuge in Bera, where Tegen makes a friend and learns wisdom, but the demon's lust for Tegen's powers brings betrayal and hatred in its wake, and once more she is forced to flee.

She reaches the sea, where Brigid, the Goddess' daughter puts her into a boat. But the waves take Tegen to Ériu, not Mona. Ill and alone in the stronghold of Tara, she is controlled by the well-meaning but unwise queen Étain, and is married to Étain's youngest son, prince Tonn.

Together they sail to Mona, only to witness the slaughter of the druids by Roman troops. Tegen is convinced she has failed in her life's work to save Britain. The few remaining druids decide that one of them must become a human sacrifice to rid the land of the Romans, once and for all.

The lot falls on Tonn, and despite Tegen's arguments that to live and fight takes more courage than to die as a sacrifice, he submits to the ritual knife.

Tegen is left bereft and alone, her faith in the Goddess destroyed – and she is pregnant.

She longs to return to Ériu, but the druids insist she joins Queen Boudica of the Iceni. It is time for her to take her place as the Star Dancer and become the battle druid for the great rebellion.

Tegen knows she'll have no peace until her destiny is fulfilled, so she agrees – but on her terms.

NOTES ON WHO'S WHO IN TEGEN'S WORLD,
ANCIENT FESTIVALS, GODS AND GODDESSES,
HISTORICAL CHARACTERS, PLACE NAMES AND
PRONUNCIATIONS, CAN BE FOUND ON
PAGE 362

1.   THE GAME

The Gaming Board was spread out in the late summer sun: square brown fields and green woods, crisscrossed by bright dividers that sparkled towards the sea.

The demon had chosen and placed its pieces with care.

In the top western corner, a war-maker raged amongst the mountains. He commanded an army that carried out his cruelty without question. His bloodied armour matched his scarlet cloak.

This one pleased the demon.

It cast its gaze towards the marshy islets in the east. There, a proud queen stoked the furnaces of vengeance. Her wind-tossed hair tangled in her golden jewellery, as knots of grief strangled her reason. Her minions were ageing and battle weary, but fired by her molten hatred.

And the demon lusted after her madness.

Around both these pieces, warriors gathered like flies on corpses. Soon town streets would echo with wailing, and fields would be drenched with gore. Both leaders would betray their own with unforgivable wounds.

The demon surveyed the board again.

Riding towards the queen was the game piece he wanted most: a druid girl on a white horse.

But without a hold on her spirit, or a physical host to follow her, she was insubstantial and intangible. The demon could only catch an occasional whiff of her presence.

Before the end, it swore, *she will crawl to the gates of Tir na nÓg begging for power to contain the horrors I will unleash. The cost will be exquisite. Her compassion for humans will compel her to agree to my terms. Her obedience will bring the Time of Stone to her world.*

A winter of death, emptiness and fear – with no bright spring to follow.

The demon did not care which pieces won the coming battle. Victory was simply a lull between cycles of mayhem, slaughter, hatred and revenge.

And soon the Star Dancer would become the demon's own hands and feet.

Bringing all to pass.

2.   THE SOOTHSAYER

A deadly miasma drifted eastwards on a steady wind. The demon would arrive before the girl. But without a physical presence it had no voice to speak, it needed a messenger with plausibility – and drama. Swathed in mist, the demon sniffed its way through the fenland marshes. At last it found the partly rotted corpse of a fisherman and donned it like an old coat.

Manipulating the cadaver was not easy. The demon struggled to grip unwieldy bones and sinews with spirit-fingers. At last, it hauled the stinking puppet to his feet. The dead hand pulled his hood low. Unsteady legs stumbled through peaty waters.

Marsh birds screamed and flapped in panic. Somewhere, a dog howled. Step by dragging step, the demon found an island camp hidden by sedges and scrub.

The place was bustling with warriors, smiths and horses. The savour of oily roasting meat hung in the air.

Away from it all, a cloaked woman stood alone on an outcrop of rock with the wind tossing her red hair like a Samhain blaze.

The demon-corpse drew closer. The reeds rustled.

The woman turned, knife in hand.

A chill wind caught the torches. They guttered and went out. Night was closing in.

Boudica shuddered. Behind her, the fire gave little light. She squinted into the dark. Was someone there, or was it just one more shadow against the shifting gloom of the fen?

'Show yourself.' She raised her blade. 'Your tribe? Your name?'

The corpse jerked his limbs up the muddy bank. The demon's spirit-tendrils were slipping on the slimy bones and rotting flesh. It would have to be quick, before its host fell apart.

The cadaver swayed before the queen. Mist seeped from its mouth. 'Aah ... I am a friend, lady. I bring good news.'

Retching at the putrid stench, Boudica forced herself to peer under the messenger's hood. White orbs gleamed back at her.

The dead fisherman stretched out a pale hand. 'A white-robe is coming to stand at your side, an advisor of kings and queens.'

'I *know* that,' she retorted impatiently. 'The wise ones promised me a battle druid three moons ago. I've been waiting ever since.'

'This one has untold power. Stronger than any other.' The demon worked at the dead lungs, struggling to form the words, 'You must not trust. Must *control* ... her. '

Boudica gripped her knife, staring with disgust and fascination. Who, or *what*, was this creature?

The demon was losing its grip on the corpse. It heaved the soggy lungs and the voice bubbled. 'Take ... my spirit in ... to yourself. Control ... druids ... win victory ... you

4

crave …'

The corpse staggered.

Boudica's mind swam. 'How do I know you're speaking the truth?' she demanded.

The demon opened the dead mouth. A tiny trail of mist wound towards Boudica, sniffing, sensing and learning her fears.

The corpse cracked his spine upright and whispered, 'Your daughters suffered … Unless you obey me, it will happen again. But *worse*.'

Then he collapsed at Boudica's feet.

And the spirit oozed free – towards the camp.

Moments later, a girl's screams pierced the night. Boudica span around. '*Megan!*' she gasped, holding her arms wide. 'Not more nightmares!'

A slim figure darted between the warriors, past the campfires and flung herself into Boudica's arms. 'It's those men that did nasty things to me,' she sobbed. 'I dreamed they came again.'

She paused, looked down at the mottled waxen corpse. Then with a shaking hand she pointed, 'Lead by *him*!'

Hugging her distraught child, Boudica did not notice the trickle of mist that drifted away into the darkness.

The moon was just rising in the southeast. The night was noisy with bitterns booming above the perpetual hissing of the reeds.

'No one threatens my children,' Boudica told the wind.

3. CLAUDIA PRIMA METELLA

Leaping flames – frayed, tossed and tattered by the wind. Gold and red, yellow, with sparks of blue. Spangles, crackling and spiralling into the midnight sky.

They weren't the fine, gauzy tongues of a campfire; these were huge, towering and intense – smoke-laden and filled with fear – blocking out the stars beyond.

Tegen shielded her face from the raging heat and fought to breathe. She knew she was dreaming, but there was no way to struggle through the unbreakable silken web that held her strung between her own world and the mystical realms of Tir na nÓg. What were the spirits trying to tell her? Was this a warning or advice?

Or was something evil tormenting her?

Lady Goddess, she prayed, what is going on?

Then she remembered: she was no longer sure the Goddess existed. But the spirits of fire were real enough. Tegen held her breath.

From out of the flames, a charcoal shadow strode towards her. It was roughly human-shaped, but bigger and made of charred wood, ash and soot. As it moved, its fragile skin cracked, exposing the crimson heat that raged beneath.

It stood before Tegen, bowed, opened its red maw and …

'Excuse me, Miss,' said a small voice.

Tegen opened her eyes and was blinded by the late afternoon sun. She sat up and rubbed her face.

Kneeling before her was a skinny girl a little younger than herself, maybe fourteen summers old. Behind her, seven or eight Roman soldiers waited with drawn swords.

'Sorry to wake you, Miss …' the girl spoke British, but with a heavy accent.

Tegen sighed. She shouldn't have rested by the roadside in broad daylight, but sleep had overtaken her – she'd been unable to resist. It happened a lot since she'd become pregnant. She glanced around. Epona, her white mare was grazing close by. She ought to just get up and go.

The girl touched Tegen's arm timidly. 'Please?' she began again.

'What do you want?' Tegen demanded, more curtly than she'd intended.

The girl looked nervously over her shoulder. 'It's my Lady, Miss; she's in that litter. She wants to speak with you.'

Tegen followed her gaze beyond the cordon of soldiers to a canopied bed slung between four broad-shouldered slaves. The curtains twitched and a hand appeared, made an impatient gesture, then withdrew.

'Mistress doesn't like being kept waiting,' the girl urged.

Tegen's heart sank. 'What's your name?'

'Ula, Miss.'

'Very well, Ula, please tell your lady, that I regret that

I'm unable to speak with her today, but I wish her a safe and pleasant journey.' She stood, brushed herself down and stepped around the soldiers towards Epona.

Ula leaped ahead and grasped the horse's reins. 'Don't say that, Miss, please. I'll be beaten, *hard*.' The girl's cheeks bore old purple-yellow bruises and her white linen veil only partly hid three vermilion scars.

The soldiers laughed. Obviously they understood.

Tegen considered the bulging muscles of the litter-bearers. She sighed. This foreign girl had done nothing wrong except become a slave of a cruel Roman matron. 'Very well.' She touched the girl's hand. 'I'll talk with your mistress.'

Ula bowed and stepped aside. At a sharp command from behind the curtains, the slaves lowered their burden to the ground. The men eased their necks and backs as the fine drapery was drawn back and an eerily white face looked out.

She said something in Latin and when Tegen did not reply, Ula translated, 'Miss, my lady wants to know who you are and where you're going?'

'My name is Tegen of the Winter Seas and I'm searching for lost relatives. I've heard they're trading with the Iceni, so I'm going east.'

Ula translated, then her lady spoke again.

'She asks why are you riding a Roman horse with a military saddle?'

'I bought it from a man who didn't need it anymore,'

Tegen replied. It wasn't far from the truth.

The mistress clicked her fingers at Tegen. 'You will bow whilst addressing me,' she demanded in British. Her voice sounded younger than the heavily made-up face implied.

Tegen bit back her anger. As a druid, she was equal to royalty and this stranger should bow before *her*. But if the woman so much as suspected the truth, Tegen knew she'd be dead within moments. Only three moons before, the Romans had slaughtered nearly all the British druids on the isle of Mona. Now they were scouring the land for any survivors.

Tegen was wearing druid's white, but the gown was not embroidered and she wore no amulets to betray her. She hoped she looked like a lady of status, no more. Pulling her green silk scarf over her tattoo, Tegen approached the litter and lowered her head. 'Greetings, lady,' she said quietly. 'How may I be of service?'

'I'm bored.' Ula's mistress yawned. 'I want someone to talk to. Have you dined?'

'No, my lady.' Tegen's empty belly rumbled.

The woman nodded. 'Good. You will follow and share my repast while you tell me your story.' She drew her curtains closed and clicked her fingers. 'Lift!' The silent slaves bent their backs and obeyed, followed by the soldiers, two in front, four behind, with two more walking either side of a baggage cart at the rear.

Sighing, Tegen mounted Epona and followed the swaying litter. How could she excuse herself? She considered the soldiers from the corner of her eye. She had seen the work of their short, stabbing swords. Even if she kicked Epona into a gallop, she could not outrun their javelins. She was trapped. But her rumbling stomach warned that she needed food. For the sake of her baby she must eat as well as possible.

Damn! Tegen swore silently. It's my own stupid fault. I should've travelled on ancient trackways, whatever else these bastards have done to my beloved land, their roads *are* superb. Too tempting to use!

Tegen leaned over Epona's neck and whispered, 'From the smoke above the trees I'd say there's a settlement ahead. That means good fodder and a rubdown for you. We'll tolerate this woman for one mealtime, and then we'll get on the road again. We may have to sleep rough tonight, but that doesn't matter. We've done it before.'

Epona snorted and tossed her head as she trotted sedately behind the litter.

The land on both sides was flat and becoming progressively marshy with smallholdings dotted across the scrub landscape. As the crimson sun lowered on their right-hand side, dark clouds swept from the east, bruising the sky purple. The wind blew cold and Tegen shivered, but at last, the long straight road brought them to a low hill with a garrison and its small township.

The procession slowed. 'Where are we, Ula?' Tegen called out.

'Colonia Lindensium. I think you'd call it Lindum.' She

pointed towards a white-walled, red-roofed inn built in a u-shape around a courtyard near the road. 'That's where we're staying tonight.'

Tegen had never been inside a Roman building before. She was intrigued, but worried too. She twisted Epona's reins around her fingers. How would she be treated? Was this a trap? Had her dress betrayed her?

At the entrance, slaves took charge of the animals and baggage. Tegen surreptitiously wove a spell of protection over her beloved horse as a boy led her away.

Epona would be safe, but what would happen to *her*?

They were led to a rectangular room. Tegen's jaw dropped; she'd never seen such opulence before.

She put her bag in a corner and tentatively stroked the smoothly plastered walls, admiring the red and yellow painted panels. Several spoon-backed wicker chairs were placed around a low table in the centre. Against one wall stood a large wooden cupboard and a long couch with red woollen cushions.

Slaves brought warm water. Ula helped her mistress wash and change into a clean tunic. Under the woman's too-white make-up was a pretty young girl with olive skin and dark eyes.

'My name is Claudia Prima Metella,' she said as the slave worked. 'My father is Julius Claudius Metellus. He was a terribly important commander in the twentieth legion, based in Deva. He's retired now and he's been given land in Camulodunum in the east. He's there already, supervising the building of our new villa, and I'm on my way to join him. I'm a widow you see.'

Tegen was about to add that so was she and to extend her sympathies, but Claudia made it quite clear that her guest was not expected to do more than listen attentively. 'I was married last Inuius, but within two weeks my husband was killed in an awful battle in the land of the Ceangli in that unholy mountainous region where the barbaric Cymry live.' She rolled her eyes in horror. 'There were all these *demons* on an island and they slaughtered *everyone* – well almost everyone. Certainly my husband killed his fair share of barbarians before he had his throat ripped out by those ghastly wizards ... what do you call them? *Druids*, that's it!' She spat and swatted Ula for spilling a drop of rose water on her dress.

When the washing was complete, Claudia sat by a wind-eye, looking out onto a courtyard garden, while Ula combed out her mistress's hair.

Tegen touched the shaggy tufts on her own head. Hot tears burned her eyes. Once more her mind replayed images of Tonn lying unburied in the mud ...

But Claudia was still rambling on about how bravely her husband had fought alongside the noble, most glorious governor of the Britannic Isles: Suetonius Paulinus.

Tegen pulled her green silk shawl forward and hung her head. Her eyes stung with tears, remembering the cruelty, the slaughter, and how her beloved Tonn had mercifully sent so many of the badly wounded of both sides to Tir na nÓg with his knife.

Her blood boiled. These are my friends she's insulting! She wasn't *there*; she doesn't *know* what it was like! Tegen's cheeks flared red, but she could say and do nothing. It was too dangerous! If only she hadn't fallen asleep by the roadside she wouldn't be in this mess. And why was she so cowed by this invader? She was just a girl of her own age.

Tegen sighed. All her courage had left her since Tonn died. She kept her eyes downcast, examining the minutiae of the magnificent mosaic floor, a circle of flowers in tesserae – tiny stones of blood red, cinder black and bone white.

Then she remembered another stone with those colours – Tonn's last gift to her – a smooth white marble egg with blood-coloured veins. 'Keep this to remember me,' he'd said. 'It's my druid's egg. No one can gainsay you while you hold it.'

Tegen opened her waist pouch and touched the stone's cool smoothness. She *should* be stronger, but she was so heart-weary.

Just then, Ula interrupted with fresh water and offered to help Tegen bathe.

'I'll see to myself, thank you.' She smiled and took the linen towel from the slave's arm. It was only then she let the silk shawl fall, revealing her shaggy hair and the dark tattoo on her face.

Ula's eyes opened wide. 'You're a ...' she began, but

Tegen put her finger to her lips. The slave's hands shook and the washbowl slipped and shattered. Hot water spilled everywhere and Claudia laid about Ula with her fan.

Tegen leapt to her feet. '*Stop!*'

Claudia and Ula both gawped open-mouthed at their guest.

'It was *my* fault. I knocked the bowl,' Tegen announced.

Claudia lowered her head and flared her nostrils. 'She's *my* slave, how dare you interfere?' she began.

Tegen raised her hands and spread a spell of calm across the room. 'You will be still, Claudia,' she said firmly and quietly. 'I smell food coming. Now, sit, eat and I will tell you my story.'

At that moment the door opened and slaves entered with omelettes, fresh cabbage leaves wrapped around olives and duck breasts, little dormice stuffed and roasted on a spit and brown sticky fruit.

Tegen sat at the table, but Claudia stared at her, wide-eyed in disbelief.

'I *said* sit and eat.' Tegen repeated.

Timidly, Claudia obeyed.

Tegen loaded her plate and between mouthfuls she told her tale. 'I was born in the west country, on the Mendip hills, overlooking the Winter Seas. I travelled with friends who were salt merchants and when I had the chance, I studied a little herbal medicine.

'I've also been married – twice. The first time to a fine man who was killed by a cave demon (*dear Griff, I still miss you!*) and then to a man from another land who was a healer. He drowned (*was murdered, sacrificed, betrayed by his friends for no good reason, my poor beloved Tonn*). 'I cut my hair in mourning.' Tegen ran her fingers through her untidy mop.

Claudia sneered. 'Hacked your hair more like! *Ula!*'

The girl, who'd been clearing up the mess, bowed before her mistress.

'After we have eaten, you are to take the shears to Mistress Tegen's hair and style it as best you can. Now, we are thirsty.'

Ula piled the shards of bowl in a neat heap and poured purple liquid from a jug into red earthenware cups.

'Is that wine?' Tegen asked hopefully.

'Goodness no!' Claudia snapped. '*Ladies* don't drink wine; it's not seemly. This is grape juice. Now, you may continue with your tale. I am interested.'

Tegen sipped the dark, sweet liquor. 'Now I am alone again, I am searching for relatives to take me in.'

While Tegen spoke, Claudia wriggled uncomfortably in her chair. 'You'll have to excuse me,' she said, dashing out of the door, her retreating sandals tapping urgently along the corridor as she ran. 'Where's she going?'

'Madam has a weak stomach,' Ula giggled. 'She often needs the *lavatorium*. But while she's gone let me cut your hair. Please come and sit by the wind-eye.' Ula draped a cloth over Tegen's shoulders, then taking a comb and shears from her bag, she began to cut.

As she worked, Ula leaned close to Tegen's ear and whispered, 'You're a druid, aren't you?'

Tegen sensed she could trust this girl. 'Yes.'

'Then I have *secrets* I need to tell you …'

'Go on, I'm listening.'

'Later. Madam will be back at any moment. Stay still please, or I might cut badly.

Tegen obeyed. 'Where are you from Ula? How do you know about druids?'

'I'm Gaulish. My father was a great warrior and my mother and I were enslaved after his defeat.'

'I'm sorry. Did you teach Claudia to speak British?'

Ula leaned across the shears and laughed. 'Her father was indeed a great general, but her mother was a Gaulish slave like me – although she'd rather cut out her own tongue than admit it. She's her father's only living child and the apple of his eye. When she reaches Camulodunum, she's to be betrothed to a British nobleman, then married next summer. It's hoped their union will be politically useful.'

'Are they in love?' Tegen asked.

Ula snorted and tried to comb what was left of Tegen's hair into a pretty shape. 'They haven't even met. I pity whoever marries *her*!'

Just then the door opened. Claudia reappeared, whey faced and clutching her stomach. 'Did you say you studied medicine?' she asked. 'My father would never trust a woman healer, he says they're witches and should all be put to the sword. But I like you, can you help me?'

'I'll see what I have in my bag. I know I have chamomile,' Tegen replied, and then they returned to their meal, which was now cold.

As they ate, the skies lit up and thunder roared. Rain lashed and Ula closed the clattering shutters. All the rain in Taranis' vast stores was pouring to earth at once. There was no way Tegen could sneak away. She would have to stay the night.

More importantly, she hadn't yet had a chance to hear Ula's secrets. The girl was frightened.

Tegen resolved to find a way to be alone with her.

4. ULA'S SECRETS

After dinner, slaves brought in clay oil lamps and bedding. Claudia chose the softest blankets and stretched out on the dining couch.

Tegen pulled her straw mattress near the wind-eye and lay awake, her mind churning with all that had happened. Less than half a moon before she'd been with the other eleven druids, possibly the only ones left in the whole of Britain. They'd sacrificed her beloved to the gods to drive the Romans out: Tonn, prince of Ériu, druid, healer, and father of her child. Without being allowed time to mourn, she'd been forced to make her way alone to the lands of the Iceni to stand as battle druid by the side of Boudica.

Boudica! Tegen tossed on her bed. The queen had once supported the Romans.

'Don't make judgements,' she whispered to herself. 'She's learned, and now she's doing the right thing. Because of her, Britain is raising its spears against the invaders and it's my duty to help. Defeating Rome is the only thing that'll make sense of Tonn's stupid, *stupid* death.'

Tegen stared into the dark, remembering her darling lying face down in a bog. She had buried him with her own black hair and the water she'd dragged from the earth by the fiercest of spells. She'd ruined the crops by that storm and flood. She'd slashed at the sacred web of magic and abused it cruelly.

Hot tears streamed down Tegen's cheeks as she sobbed. The noise of her grief would never be heard above the battering rain that lashed the inn.

The following morning was bright and fresh. Tegen woke and breakfasted while Ula washed and massaged her mistress with scented oils, then plucked any stray hairs from her body with tweezers. Throughout it all, Claudia screamed and swore. At last, draped in a towel, she bolted out of the room. 'A curse on this place for not having a bathhouse. It's *uncivilised*!' she yelled, and slammed the door.

Tegen glanced at Ula. 'Now, tell me your secrets.'

The slave spoke softly as she tidied up. 'You know that Boudica is no longer a friend of the Romans?' she asked nervously.

'I do.'

'But do you know *why*?'

Tegen shook her head. So much had happened to her in the last few moons, she hadn't given the question much thought. 'I'd assumed the queen had decided to do what was right?'

Ula folded her mistress's clothes and packed them into a basket. 'You know of course that Boudica was married to king Prasutagus. For many years he'd been hand-in-glove with the Romans. Whether he was a traitor, or simply thought it was his best chance for peace, I have no idea. But he did well out of it. The Romans gave him huge gifts of money and left him pretty well alone. But when he died last year, he willed his kingdom to be split, half going to his two daughters Megan and Oriana and the rest to the Emperor Nero.'

'That's a very odd thing to do,' Tegen put in. 'Why didn't he leave everything to Boudica?'

The girl leaned forward and whispered, 'Roman law dictates that the Emperor's agreement was with Prasutagus, *not* his wife or descendants. In fact, in Rome, women aren't allowed to inherit anything ...'

'That's ridiculous!' Tegen scoffed.

'That's the way it is.' Ula shrugged. 'Strictly speaking a woman may only own half a gold piece. Anyway, the Roman procurator Catus Decianus ignored the will and immediately marched into Iceni territory. He said all the gifts of money to Prasutagus were loans and had to be repaid immediately, *and* he demanded the whole Iceni kingdom to be gifted to Nero! Decianus then made the kings' relatives captive, threw all the chieftains off their lands and parcelled everything out to his favourites. Soldiers looted the royal house and ...'

Ula stopped and hung her head. She was blushing under her veil.

'*What?*' Tegen demanded urgently.

'He had Boudica dragged into the street, stripped and publicly flogged. And the girls, Megan and Oriana, they were only ten and twelve years old.' Ula looked up, her eyes red and her face taut. 'He let *slaves* rape them!' Then she burst into tears.

The blood roared in Tegen's ears and she felt sick. How could she have tolerated being the guest of a *Roman*? She should've used magic, her druid's egg – *anything* to get away before now. She stood. She had to leave.

But before she could gather her thoughts, Claudia returned and launched into a stream of orders for Ula. Tegen tried to help, but Claudia was disdainful. 'Anyone can see you are of noble birth; it's not your fault you're a pagan. Anyway, Ula is lazy; I'll get one of the men to whip her later. *Be careful!*' she roared as the exhausted girl almost tripped with a tray of perfumed oils.

Tegen was determined to distract Claudia from her bullying. She had to slip away unnoticed and without Ula being blamed. 'How do you feel this morning? I fear the chamomile I gave you last night wasn't strong enough for what ails you.'

Claudia leaned back on a pillow and allowed Ula to apply her dead-white makeup. 'I feel dreadful. I never sleep and my guts are agony. This imbecile of a girl does nothing to make things easier for me, have you seen the way she treats me?'

Tegen's temper snapped once more. 'I've seen she works very hard and without complaining. I've also seen the bruises you inflict on her for nothing. However, I suspect your temper is foul because you're ill.' Tegen turned to Ula. 'Give me that face cream, do you make it up yourself? What's in it?'

Claudia sniffed derisively. 'I wouldn't trust *her* to do something like that. It's made by no less a man than the apothecary to the Governor himself! What's in it? I don't know, why should I?'

Tegen took the small enamel pot, touched and smelled the white paste, then licked it. 'Claudia, if you keep using this preparation, not only will you continue to be ill, but you may well die. It has lead in it.'

'Oh, everyone knows *that*!' Claudia sniffed. 'I thought you meant what *secret* ingredients did it have? Lead is what makes the face so pure and white. I can't risk being seen in public as hideously dark as the gods have seen fit to make me. Heavens, I'm almost as brown as Ula!'

The slave blushed and hung her head.

Tegen persisted. 'Lead may make your face white, but it also prevents you from sleeping and stirs up the spirits in your bowels.'

'*Rubbish*!' Claudia snapped, then with a groan she made another dash for the lavatorium.

Ula left the room on errands for her mistress. Tegen wondered whether this was her chance to flee – but she had no idea where Epona was. What if Claudia sent soldiers after her?

Think, she told herself. Claudia's 'collected' me like a plaything. She's nothing but a spoiled brat. She'll soon get bored and she'll send me away.

For the moment, Tegen was glad of the silence. She would never cease to grieve for Tonn. The anger at the stupidity of his death raged inside her. Her old mentor Gronw would say she mustn't let her feelings overwhelm her – the anger would damage the balance of right and wrong in the world. If she couldn't control her own emotions, how would she defeat the demon that still pursued her?

On the other hand, Ula's story filled her with rage. For the first time, Tegen was glad she'd been sent to be Boudica's battle druid. She'd ensure justice for those who'd suffered because the Goddess was asleep – or dead.

Since Tonn's death, nothing made any sense.

Tegen looked out at the rain-drenched road and fields beyond the inn. Morning sun bathed everything in gold and shivered the air above the distant marshes. The speedwell-blue sky was noisy with birdsong and dotted with white clouds scurrying eastwards.

The morning looked so serene.

Tegen pressed her hot forehead against the metal grill across the wind-eye. Her thoughts were in turmoil. Why don't I just run away *now*? she asked herself. Epona can't be far. I might get past the guards with a spell.

'I think – something's telling me to stay.' She stroked her belly. Her pregnancy didn't show, but it made her weary and she was still vomiting in the mornings.

'Or maybe,' she whispered to herself, 'I'm just exhausted. I need friendship – even if it is only for a day or so, and from a slave and foul-tempered Roman girl.'

5.   BOUDICA

On a low hill hidden by high reeds and treacherous marshes, a fire sent sparks and dark ashes dancing into the glowering sky.

Boudica was pleased; at last she had a war council she could rely on. Four tribes had sent their leaders: Venutius, the deposed king of the northern Brigantes who was also her uncle, three chieftains and a spell-caster from the Trinovantes whose territory bordered the Iceni lands to the south. Half a dozen weary-looking men from the Catuvellauni had joined them and, most heartening of all, Sabrina, queen of the Dobunni had sworn loyalty.

In all, there were twenty worthy men and women gathered around her, swatting mosquitoes and talking loudly above the evening chorus of frogs and crickets.

Servants brought dishes of roast waterfowl and baked fish to the tables, followed by heaped bowls of steaming bulrush roots and barley loaves. Torchlight danced on the queen's golden torc as she took her place with her guests. Tossing back her waist-length plaits, she raised her drinking horn and saluted the company.

'Welcome to my island of council. Here we may talk openly without fear of betrayal. When my new druid arrives, we'll have our discussions in earnest. Meanwhile, eat, drink and be exceedingly merry.'

Everyone cheered and a servant refilled the ale pots.

Sabrina covered hers with her hand. 'Is heavy drinking wise, sister? Shouldn't we keep our heads clear?'

Boudica wasn't used to being contradicted. She glared at the Dobunni queen. 'Strong drink puts strength in our hearts. We need it.'

'That's right!' several voices yelled.

Sabrina stood, her dark hair like a summer storm. 'Ale puts *anger* into warriors' heads. Tonight we must put all quarreling aside. Solidarity is our only hope!'

Venutius poured half of his drink into Sabrina's pot. 'C'mon girl, we need some fun. We've all fought long and travelled far.'

Sabrina pointed at Megan and Oriana eating huddled in the shadows. 'We must win this fight. Drink will only make us piss and vomit. For your daughter's sakes we must be sober – and united.'

Venutius gripped Sabrina's elbow and pulled her down. 'Yes, my lady, and if my children had been raped by Roman slaves, my blood would boil too. Tomorrow, we'll be wise. Tonight we'll get drunk.'

Boudica stabbed the roast heron in front of her. Steaming juices trickled down her knife as she hacked two slices off the breast and dropped one in front of her uncle, and the other before Sabrina. 'We already have unity. Now *eat!*' she ordered, looking from face to face in the torchlight. 'All of you – you'll need your strength.'

'So will you, my Lady,' her uncle replied with concern. He pushed a basket of bread towards her.

She ignored him, but took her ale and limped across the damp grass. Her back still stung from ulcerated wounds – nine months after the flogging. She squatted next to her children. The firelight scarcely reached them and they stuffed their mouths as if they might have to run at any moment. Megan and Oriana were now so terrified of men they'd never look up, even if an old friend came near.

Boudica stroked their dark hair. 'All shall be well, my little birds,' she sighed, wishing she could believe her own words.

When the meal was over, Boudica sat chewing the meat from a bone and surveying her guests now slumped over the tables, snoring in their own vomit. Was Sabrina right? Should they be as sober and controlled as the Romans? They all needed courage if they stood a chance of winning. Strong drink made the weakest warrior brave.

She closed her eyes and lay along her bench. The time for vengeance was very near.

In her mind she counted her stocks of spears and swords. They'd all been made in secret, for the Romans only allowed one eating knife each – not even a boar spear on pain of death.

Boudica had always told her husband the Romans weren't to be trusted. 'You don't understand politics!' Prasutagus laughed as he ran his hands through his hoards of Roman-gifted silver.

'Neither do you!' she'd retorted. And she'd been proved

right. The Iceni had been faithful for twelve long years. Now they were being treated like mutinous slaves, and all because of a will!

He'd thought he'd been so clever, bequeathing half his kingdom to Nero. 'That will appease the Emperor,' he'd promised, 'he'll leave you in peace. But just in case, I'll give the other half to our girls. You can handfast them to strong chieftains when they come of age and the Iceni will be safe. If I leave everything to you and the girls aren't old enough to lead the tribe or to marry by the time you die, then everything will be lost.'

That memory seared Boudica's mind. She flung the bone aside and jumped to her feet. Striding up and down, her mind churned. How could her stupid husband have trusted Catus Decianus? Why had he died and left her to sort out the mess?

She fingered the delicate designs on her ancient golden torc. It lay heavy about her neck – like her leadership. She'd show the foreign bastards that British women weren't to be ignored or abused. She would have vengeance!

And she would give anything … *anything* to win.

She swigged from her ale horn and walked out to the mud bank where she'd met the hideous soothsayer. He'd looked more dead than alive. She shuddered as she recalled the way his eyeballs rolled back as he wheezed: '*Take … my spirit in … to yourself. Control … druid's powers … Win victory.*'

She hadn't trusted the creature, but he had warned her

the girls were in danger once more. Would his spirit really help?

Last Beltane she had sent a messenger to Mona to beg for a battle druid to stand at her side. The man had returned with news that the white-robes had been slaughtered. He'd said a few had escaped and one was even now riding to stand at her side. An important one – with a title.

'I'll make up my own mind about this druid when he arrives.' She decided. 'The soothsayer could have been mad – or setting a trap.'

6. BLESSINGS

At dawn, Tegen was woken by Claudia yelling at Ula to get packed. Slaves brought fruit, bread, oil and cheese, and the three girls ate hurriedly. Messengers had come in the night from Julius Claudius Metellus. He had sent a new escort to relieve the men from the IX Hispaniola who had brought Claudia from Deva. He wanted to know why his daughter was being so slow and demanded her presence with him in Camulodunum immediately.

Tegen had been glad of the rest and good food, but she was relieved to be on her way again. Quietly, she packed her things, then poured a little leftover breakfast oil into a jar of crushed herbs and stoppered it. She took it to Claudia who was reclining on the dining couch, complaining of a headache.

'Use a little of this on your face every night. In about two moons your skin will look paler so you won't need your old make-up. I've shown Ula how to prepare it.'

'She's *useless!*' Claudia rolled her eyes. 'I wouldn't trust her with anything!'

Tegen pushed Claudia's feet aside and sat next to her. '*I would!*' she replied firmly. 'Ula is a good girl, she works hard and tries to please.'

'How *dare* you have an opinion about my slave?' Claudia raised her hand to strike.

Tegen narrowed her eyes. 'Ula is the nearest thing you have to a friend in this land. You're frightened and lonely. You need her. And furthermore,' she took a deep breath. Dare she say what was in her mind? She may betray herself as a druid – but the words spilled out anyway.

'Furthermore, one day Ula will save your life, I have seen it.'

Claudia stared open-mouthed.

Tegen stood. 'Now, I'm going out to find the remedy for your lead poisoning. I'll be back very soon, and if you have to leave before I return, I'll find you on the road. If Ula has fresh marks on her face or arms, I won't give it to you. Is that understood?'

Claudia nodded. 'Yes,' she murmured.

'Good.' Tegen snatched up a basket. 'I'm borrowing this. I'll see you later.' With that, she stormed out of the door and let it slam behind her.

Ula tried to hide a smile as she wrapped her mistress in a cloak.

Relishing her freedom, Tegen ran down the low hill to the surrounding marshes where she cut several slices of peat and squeezed them dry. When her basket was full, she returned to the inn. Outside the gates, Claudia had settled in her litter, but was waiting for her baggage to be loaded.

When she saw Tegen returning, she sat up and pulled the curtains wide. 'Have you got it?' she asked, a little more politely than usual.

Tegen presented the dripping basket. 'You may not like

this, but it does work.'

Claudia peered at the soggy mass of dark brown peat. 'Yuck!' she sneered, pushing it away. 'I'm not eating *mud*!'

'It's not mud,' Tegen replied. 'My father was a silver and lead worker, he used to chew a little of this every day. We all did. Look!' She tore off a piece and put it into her mouth. 'It doesn't taste too bad. The mosses trap the evil spirits then you spit everything out. Try it. You'll feel better in half a moon, I promise.'

'Oh very well. Give it to Ula.'

Just then, the captain of escort stepped forward and saluted, speaking to Claudia in Latin. She nodded and replied.

'He says we must hurry.' Then she added with a half smile, the first Tegen had seen, 'He doesn't want you to travel with us. He doesn't trust you.' She hesitated, then added, 'I know we're on different sides, but I hope, if we ever meet again, that we'll be friends?'

Tegen closed her eyes, then replied, 'I think we shall. May the road rise to meet you!'

The slaves pulled the litter straps onto their shoulders and marched past Tegen, Claudia's thin hand waved from between the curtains, then pulled them shut.

The soldiers and the baggage cart trundled past, leaving Ula with her veil pulled low over her forehead. She bowed to Tegen. 'A blessing, lady?' she begged.

Tegen glanced at the retreating party to make sure no one was watching them. 'Tell me first, what these scars are on your face?'

Ula pushed back her hair and revealed the dark red marks. They formed the letters, FUG.

'What is that?' Tegen asked, 'I don't read.'

'It means I'm a fugitive,' Ula replied. 'I ran away. Branding was part of my punishment.'

Tegen touched the scars, tracing the letters. 'One day, you will be free.'

At that moment, Claudia's screeching yells for her slave made Ula gather her skirts and run. 'Thank you,' she called back, her eyes bright.

Breathing the fresh morning air, Tegen guided Epona away from the Roman roads and Lindum, then southeast across the flat landscape. Together, they squelched the lonely paths across the marshes, trudging through hissing forests of rushes, resting on small islets inhabited by chattering reed buntings and statuesque herons. The sun rose higher, and then began to sink. They were getting nowhere.

Weariness dragged at Tegen's body and soul. 'The Iceni lands can't be far, I'll be with Boudica soon,' she told herself firmly. Her back ached. 'I don't know if I'm really up to being a battle druid, I hope the fighting's over before the baby's bump shows.' She tugged at the front of her white robe. 'When the weather gets colder I can wear shawls and overdresses. No one will notice. I'll fulfil my destiny as the Star Dancer and send the Romans away forever. Then I can rest.'

She closed her eyes at the delicious thought. She loved Epona, but riding all day was wearisome – for them both.

Two days later, Tegen chose an ancient muddy trackway that snaked between small fields. Everything had been harvested a moon before and the furrows lay darkly waterlogged after the rain.

With a surge of joy, Tegen spread her arms and proclaimed to the muddy fens, 'This land may not be the sacred body of a goddess, but it is *beautiful*! I will fight, I promise I will.'

Her shout scared a lapwing in her path. Epona stumbled and Tegen slid off sideways. 'Oh dear,' she groaned as she picked herself up, 'Gronw would tell me off for being noisy, but sometimes I just have to shout. When I go to Ériu I'll dance and sing and be really happy. I'll deserve that when this is over.'

The only answer was a straggling arrow of honking geese flying eastwards against the grey washed skies. 'I know,' Tegen sighed, 'I've work to do before I think of having a home. I'm coming. I only rested at the inn for a short while – because of my baby.'

By noon she could see where low hills rose beyond the fens. Boudica's armies were gathering somewhere there – but how would she find them? The interminable marshes were impassable. Way-finding magic had never been Tegen's strong point.

She asked directions from eel fishermen and bird trappers. Some were helpful, others slid away between the towering reeds, quicker than otters. Tegen didn't blame them. They weren't to know which side she was on. Just because she was dressed in druid's white proved nothing. Neither could she be sure whom *they* served – willingly or otherwise. She dared not betray Boudica by asking too many questions, so she thanked those who offered help and made her way forward on foot, leading her mare along rickety trackways that disappeared into quagmires as often as they led to lonely settlements.

For three more days, Tegen and Epona pushed onwards, suffering leech and gnat bites. They cut themselves on the buff-coloured rushes that hissed and swayed above their heads. Now and then, soft splashes hinted at unseen creatures hopping and slithering out of their way.

Tegen's boots were wet, her skin itched and her hair was tangled.

At last they reached a small rise covered in scrub oak. Tegen could go no further. She dismounted and let Epona graze. Exhaustion and despair washed over her until she fell asleep in the late summer sun.

A twig cracked nearby. Tegen's heart thumped. She opened her eyes and saw a pair of boots at her side. *British* boots made of heavy leather tied with thongs and caked with mud. By the right foot was the point of a heavy spear.

Without moving, she said, 'Good day,' in a quiet voice.

'Stand up!' a man replied, pressing the spearhead into her shoulder. She obeyed and looked into the face of a warrior – weary, grey, and scarred.

'Who are you and what are you doing here?' he demanded.

'I am Tegen of the Winter Seas, from the Dobunni tribe in the west.' She took a deep breath, 'and I am a druid seeking Queen Boudica.'

'Oh are you?' he sneered. Pushing two filthy fingers into his mouth, he gave an ear-splitting whistle. Epona whinnied and sidestepped as three men and a woman slid out between the reeds, swords and knives at the ready.

The woman took Epona's rein and started to lead her away. 'Hey!' Tegen protested, 'You can't take my horse!'

'No good where you're going!' she growled.

Then everything went dark as a sack was thrown over Tegen's head. It had been used for flour and made her sneeze, but she could breathe and see specks of light.

Strong hands took her shoulders and steered her downhill, where peaty mud sucked at her feet. She sensed fear and suspicion rather than outright hostility from her captors, so she didn't struggle. She needed to listen and think, rather than to lash out with power.

Her instincts told her they were Iceni, rather than Roman spies. She prayed she was right and that they'd take her to Boudica. I'll wait and see what happens, she thought. If I smell treachery, I'll do something. They haven't tied my hands so they aren't afraid of me. The hood must be for secrecy.

Just then, strong fingers grabbed her elbow. 'There's a

coracle by your feet,' said a voice, 'Step forward.' Tegen did as she was told. The little craft rocked and hands pressed her down. 'Sit. Don't move, or you'll have us over!'

Tegen settled on a rough woven framework of hazels covered by tarry hide. The boat rocked away from the edge and swayed into the current of a small river. By the steady splash and tug, Tegen could tell someone was poling, rather than rowing, the little craft along.

'Where is my horse?' she asked.

'She'll be safe.'

'Where are you taking me?'

'Somewhere.'

Tegen sighed and made herself more comfortable. At last the boatman called with the rising notes of a snipe, and was answered by a fox's bark. The coracle bumped and scraped against a bank, then Tegen was hauled out and marched uphill.

The hood was pulled off; she blinked and rubbed her eyes. A low mist drifted between the rushes and scrub. With a quick gesture, Tegen wove a spirit shield around herself. The islet did not feel safe.

The warriors marched her up a muddy path to a circle of huts. In the middle were three large trestle tables around which a group of British nobles and warriors were seated.

A tall woman stood and came forward. Long flames of hair spread over her embroidered dress and enamelled brooches. She was no longer young, maybe thirty or even more, but her proud face was strong.

'What is your name?' she demanded.

'Tegen, druid of the Winter Seas,' she answered. 'Moryn, chief druid of the Ordovices sent me to stand at the side of Boudica, Queen of the Iceni. I am her battle druid.'

The company started to talk excitedly, but the woman raised her hand for silence. Frowning, she stepped forward and grabbed Tegen's chin. 'I am Boudica. How old are you?'

'Sixteen.'

'How can you be a trained druid in so short a time?'

Tegen shook her head free and met the woman's gaze. Her fingers curled around Tonn's stone egg. 'I may not have years, but I have a title and the blessing of the spirits. That will be enough.'

The woman raised one dark eyebrow. 'Oh will it? And what is this *title* that puts you above those with years of experience and wisdom?'

Tegen swallowed hard. 'I am the Star Dancer,' she replied.

Boudica stared blankly and shrugged. 'Never heard of you!' She turned to the others. 'Anyone here heard of a Star Dancer?' They all shook their heads. One elderly man seemed thoughtful but kept quiet.

'It'd be nice to have a bit of dancing,' a young chieftain leered. 'Be a change from watching bloody frogs all day.'

They all laughed.

Tegen shuddered as pale threads of mist crept across the islet. She raised her hand to turn them back, but Boudica grabbed her wrist.

'You're not a druid! You're a *spy*! My scouts saw you several nights ago with the Romans at Lindum, in Corieltauvi territory! Take her away and beat her. Find out who she really is and why she's here!'

'But ...' Tegen began. She'd guessed the queen wouldn't be easy to work with, but she hadn't envisaged things would be this bad. 'Let me prove it,' Tegen began, 'I shall summon fire.'

Two warriors grabbed her outstretched wrists, dragged her to the side of a hut and tied her hands to the supporting posts. With handfuls of withies, they began their work.

Stripes of fire raged across Tegen's back as they lashed her again and again.

Her soul curled inwards, wrapping around her unborn baby.

The ropes cut her wrists and she screamed.

Just then, someone yelled. 'Stop that you *stupid* morons! *Tegen*! Are you alright?' Heavy boots stamped closer.

The voice swam in and out of pulsing pain. Tegen turned her head and winced. '*Sabrina*! ... *Ouch*!'

The Dobunni queen drew her sword and held it to the throat of the nearest man. 'Cut her down before I slice your head from your imbecilic neck!'

He glanced back over his shoulder. 'My lady, Boudica?' he called out.

Sabrina pressed her sword into his neck. '*Now*!' Blood trickled thickly down the edge of her blade.

Boudica lifted her skirt and ran. 'What's going on?' she roared. 'Sabrina, you can't interfere. We caught this lying bitch skulking around. We've got to know who she's working for.'

Sabrina, as tall as Boudica and with a will to match, did not take her weapon from the man's throat. She smiled, showing her missing teeth. 'I will vouch for this young woman with my life!'

Reluctantly, Boudica nodded at her men, who drew their daggers and cut Tegen's bindings. Sabrina sheathed her sword. Scooping Tegen up as if she were a child, she carried her into her own hut and placed her on her bed.

Boudica followed. 'Are you sure? She travelled with a Roman woman and slept in one of their inns.'

'I'm sure,' Sabrina roared. Then pointing at Tegen's torn dress and bleeding back she added, 'And if this young woman is not in the mood for forgiveness, you are dead, as is our cause. What were you thinking? A girl like this isn't built to take a beating! You of all people should know!'

Boudica crossed her arms and scowled. 'My scouts say she's a spy!' Then she yanked one of Sabrina's plaits. 'And what about you? Maybe *all* the Dobunni are in the pay of the enemy?'

Sabrina grabbed Boudica's ears and pulled. The two queens stood nose to nose, breathing heavily.

'You, *sister*, are a fool!' Sabrina sneered. 'This is Tegen of the Winter Seas, the Star Dancer, the most important and powerful druid in these islands. Without her, Britain will fall and so *lady*, will you!'

Boudica paled, hesitated, then looked down at Tegen. 'I'm sorry, forgive me,' she muttered through clenched teeth.

'It is forgotten,' Tegen gasped. 'But I beg you, get someone to wash my back and give me willow bark to chew. I'm in agony.'

Boudica nodded tersely and snapped her fingers at a servant. 'Do it!' she said, then strode outside to stand amongst the reeds.

The afternoon was growing chilly and the fog was thickening; mist droplets veiled Boudica's hair. She swung her seven-coloured cloak around her shoulders. Not far away, the warriors she had called to council were eating and discussing the events.

The queen's mind was a turmoil of embarrassment, anger and pain. She liked Sabrina and trusted her: they'd make things up later over a flagon or two of mead, but this *child* with piercing green eyes, how could she be a *druid*? Boudica snorted derisively.

And she didn't need a soothsayer to tell her what to think – she knew already that she hated the girl.

7. COUNCIL OF WAR

Washed and dressed in a fresh gown and shawl, Tegen walked towards the cushioned chair on Boudica's right, wincing as she sat.

The queen turned and bowed. 'Welcome my lady,' she said coldly, then raising her drinking horn, she stood. 'A toast, to Tegen of the Summer Seas, the Star Dancer and druid amongst druids who has been sent to bless us!'

The war council rose to their feet. 'Tegen of the Summer Seas,' they roared.

'*Winter* Seas,' Tegen muttered under her breath. She guessed the mistake was deliberate to unsettle her. But she would ignore it. Sabrina sat on the far side of the table, smiling warmly as she raised her cup and cheered more loudly than the rest. Tegen was relieved to have one true friend, but she didn't have time to worry, for the first cut of meat was being presented to her as the guest of honour.

As she ate, she considered the woman she had come all this way to stand beside: tall, strong, trained for war and used to leadership. She could feel bitterness and anger raging in Boudica's spirit. It was hardly surprising, after what she and her children had been through.

But it was how that anger was *expressed* that worried Tegen: some who suffered became more sensitive and kind; others took their spite out on everyone else.

Boudica was one of the latter.

Worst of all, she could sense something she had hoped not to meet in a British war leader. The demon was here. Not in great strength, for it didn't inhabit the Iceni queen, but Tegen suspected it was close, maybe feeding from her fears and hatred as it had done with Enid on Cadair Idris?

Tegen's thoughts were interrupted as Boudica stood and everyone fell silent. The flickering lanterns painted the queen's chin and cheeks yellow, dark shadows hollowed out her eyes.

Boudica pushed back her stool and paced to and fro. 'We have one chance to strike at the heart of the Romans,' she began. 'Our target is Camulodunum, in the Trinovantes' territory. This city has been built by the sweated slave labour of our brothers and sisters – and at their expense. It is the Roman's pride and joy – it is where they reward their old soldiers with land and wealth.'

Here she stopped pacing, then added in a low voice, 'And it is virtually *undefended*.'

At this the listeners cheered and hammered their knife handles on the table.

The queen held up her hand for silence. 'It's late in the year, but the timing is perfect. The so-called 'Governor of all Britain', Suetonius Paulinus, is still on the island of Mona, beyond the northern mountains of the Cymry. The main legions are concentrated in the northwest in Cornovii lands, at Deva, and in the southwest on the great river that divides the Dumnonii from the Durotriges. The garrison at Lindum is six days away, but we have warriors watching them and ambushes set up all along the road between here and there. Otherwise, there are no significant forces less than twelve days' march away, and that is only if the men are not allowed to rest. If they travel at that speed they'll be exhausted and unfit for battle by the time they arrive, so we can bring down our revenge before the Romans know what's hit them!'

Boudica thumped her fist on the table making the plates and knives jump. Everyone cheered.

The queen waited, then smiled and spoke again. 'And that is only the *beginning*. The Romans are too spread out – if we move swiftly, we've almost a whole moon to crush these foul cockroaches once and for all. Let us fall on the major towns and *destroy* this cancer! Britain will be ours again!'

The cheers were deafening. Despite her pain, Tegen got to her feet and joined in. This woman was a stirring orator. No one could hear her without being inspired.

The queen signalled for silence. 'Tomorrow, we leave this camp. Gather your warriors and meet at my royal house at the bend in the southern river at nightfall the day after tomorrow.'

The cheering resounded once more, then Boudica leaned forward, resting her knuckles on the table. The firelight glinted in her eyes and on her golden earrings. No one stirred or spoke.

She gestured towards Tegen. 'A soothsayer visited me

recently and prophesied my new battle druid would have untold power and sway each battle for us. Now she is here. Together we will wrest Britain back from the invaders. We will be strong and free again!'

The council clapped and raised their drinking horns to Tegen.

Boudica smiled and drank.

Tegen returned the toast, but a chill passed down her aching back. A soothsayer? Could it have been the demon in some guise or another? What was it playing at by flattering her powers?

There will be neither peace nor love between Boudica and I, she thought. The demon has already touched her somehow. This battle will be harder than I ever imagined. I will be an enemy to the one who should be my greatest friend.

Boudica was speaking again. 'Although our plans are sound, we have a major problem with supplies,' she explained. 'Last year's harvests were a disaster. This year's weren't much better because of torrential rain at harvest time. Furthermore, many families sacrificed sowing their crops to spend the summer making weapons to replace the ones the invaders confiscated.'

There were murmurs of agreement. A man with heavy moustaches and a plaited beard raised his dagger in salute to Boudica.

She nodded to him. 'Chieftain Daig, how are things with the Trinovantes?'

He shook his head as he looked around. 'Our people have not sowed this year either. We want our fields left bare so there'll be no pickings left for *them*!' he spat. 'We're moving away – going north to the mountains. It's said the land there is impenetrable for the Romans.'

Venutius stood. 'Aye, indeed, the soldiers have tried in those parts but are beaten back every time. The Picts and the Old Ones work together and they're deadly. Though what sort of welcome you'll get, I can't say.'

Daig sat down again. 'We'll risk it. We'll help the tribes fight, then we go, there's nothing for us here. You can share what food we have, but there's no more. A curse on this land, I say!' He paused and glared straight at Tegen. 'There is no Goddess, or she would have defended herself – and us!'

Some people gasped, casting worried glances in Tegen's direction, but her thoughts were elsewhere.

Harvest was when Tonn had died.

It was *me* who called down the terrible rains and ruined the crops, she thought. My anger and thoughtlessness has done untold harm and endangered our cause. I owe it to these people to fight with them, even though I cannot trust Boudica.

Suddenly she realised that silence had fallen and everyone was looking at her. What had been said? For a moment she wrapped her fingers around Tonn's stone egg and caressed it, then, with the drying scabs pulling mercilessly across her back, she hobbled towards the great hearth beyond the feasting tables.

Every fire-lit face turned to her expectantly, waiting for her words. Would she call down the Goddess' vengeance on Daig's blasphemy?

Instead, she beckoned to the nearest slave. 'Bring me ale and bread.'

The man obeyed, handing Tegen a brimming tankard.

Gripping the handles, she walked in a wide circle, enclosing the men and women of the council, pouring the drink in a tiny trickle onto the ground.

Next, Tegen took a large bannock and broke it into pieces that she shared around. 'By the pouring of the ale, I have made a protective wall,' she explained. 'Now eat. By the sharing of salt and grain, we will become one. I make my blessing on you all, and especially on queen Boudica of the Iceni, our chieftain of chieftains. I promise you my prayers, night and morning, and my spells on all your shields and spears.'

At that, cheering broke out, but Tegen held up her hand and examined each face that stared at her from the darkness. Her gaze fell on Boudica who was staring at her chunk of bread on the table as if it were poisoned.

Tegen went on, '*But* in return, you must trust me and do as I say. If you don't, your spirits will go to Tir na nÓg without me to guide you. You will be on your own.'

Sabrina cheered loudest of all, then she grabbed her bread and chewed it. Raising her horn, she called out, 'To Tegen of the Winter Seas, battle druid of Britain! Long may she stretch her hands over us!'

The responding roar was deafening. Shouts, whistles, cheers mingled with the sparks and pale smoke that drifted from the hearth fire into the starlit canopy above.

Tegen looked up at the constellation of the Watching Woman. For the rebellion to succeed, she would have to talk as if she believed the wise mother Goddess was real – and with them.

Boudica worshipped Andraste, the bloodthirsty war-goddess. Were Andraste and the Lady two faces of the same being? If not, the two deities were probably at loggerheads – if they existed. That would explain Boudica's instant mistrust.

From the corner of her eye, Tegen saw the queen stand and leave the table.

By her empty place was an untouched piece of bread.

Late into the night, each of the chieftains and kings explained their situations to Tegen. By the last of the candlelight, maps of Roman roads and garrisons were drawn in ale on the wooden table-top. Distances between tribal strongholds were calculated and travel times added up. Strategies, tactics, troop movements and land formations were meaningless to Tegen, but she listened intently to how people spoke and tried to learn what spirits ruled them until her head ached.

When everyone was asleep, she took a torch and sat alone on the edge of the marshy night listening to the noisy chatter of crickets and frogs. 'Come all good spirits,' she called out softly, 'whatever you are called, I need wisdom.'

The wind stirred the rattling rushes and Tegen shivered. She wished she could dance, but her back hurt too much. Instead she pushed her torch into the soft, muddy ground and crouched down to watch the flames.

'All my spells must be made with the web of magic, just as Gronw taught me,' she whispered. 'I mustn't act in anger again. The rains I summoned after Tonn died caused too much suffering – as did the fire I started at Dorcic. I'll have to listen and be patient.'

In her mind she pictured each of the faces of the men and women she had met that night. Some she instinctively knew she could trust as friends, others she wasn't so sure about, especially Addedomaros, the Trinovantian chieftain and his brother Aodh the spell caster.

And Boudica – she worried Tegen more than any of them.

'I must find a way to get her to trust me,' Tegen told a large brown toad that hopped out of the mud. 'She doesn't have to like me – just work with me. If we are divided, the revolt will fail before it begins.'

Tegen sighed. Being a battle druid was going to be hard work. As Owein had said, the tribes were too busy fighting each other to co-ordinate their tactics. At least Boudica understood that.

Lost in her thoughts, Tegen did not hear footsteps approach. Someone touched her shoulder; she jumped, and found herself looking into the weary face of the queen.

'Thank you for your blessing this evening,' Boudica said. 'In the morning we'll go to my royal home where the warriors are mustering.' Her words were flat and without emotion.

Equally impassively, Tegen responded, 'I'll be ready.'

'Good.' Then the queen walked away between the darkened huts.

The old raven bite on Tegen's finger ached. She wished she still had Goban's ring to warn her of unseen danger. 'I need sleep,' she told herself. She threw the remains of the torch into the campfire, and went to Sabrina's hut.

As they readied for bed, Sabrina wrapped Tegen in a warm hug.

'Ouch!' Tegen squealed.

'Sorry, I forgot your sore back.' Letting go, she took Tegen's hand. 'It's wonderful you're here – how are you? Where is Tonn? Did he stay with the other druids? I thought you two were handfasted!'

'He died,' Tegen said simply.

Sabrina's jaw dropped. 'My poor dear! That's terrible, what happened?'

Tegen held her breath. Sabrina didn't deserve her venom. None of it was her fault. She kissed her friend's cheek. 'I – I'll tell you another time. Right now, I'll fall asleep on my feet if I don't lie down.' Then she curled up on her straw-filled sack. She longed to tell everything – especially that she was pregnant, but it was too dangerous.

No one must know. Not even Sabrina.

At dawn, Tegen walked beyond the camp. There was a narrow strip of land with a hurdle walkway that led between the reed beds and alongside a stretch of open water. Following it, she came to harvested fields and a settlement. It reminded her of her childhood home. She had danced for pleasure in those days. It had given her joy.

She needed joy now.

Kicking off her boots and stockings, she smiled as meadow peat squelched between her toes. The scars on her back hurt, but she didn't care. Closing her eyes, she thought of Griff, her foster brother. The villagers had called him a 'half-head,' but he had been kinder, wiser and more honest than the druids. She thought of her father, dirty from the metal work he loved, and her mother who was always so frightened for her.

Most of all she remembered Tonn, her beloved, who had followed her to a foreign land – and his death. Her tears flowed. She longed to feel their spirits close. 'Come to me, Griff and Tonn,' she murmured. I need you both, my brother and my man.'

But there was no whispering answer in her mind, no ghostly touch of love. Only the images of how they had both died: in darkness, water and blood.

Tegen stopped dancing. Her heart pounded and pain wrenched at her skull. Crouching down, she curled into a tight ball.

I mustn't let anger take a hold of my spirit, she told herself, or I won't be of any use in the battles to come! I must celebrate what's been good, or I'll become as warped as Admidios and as vulnerable as Enid.

Taking a deep breath, she danced a blessing on the past and everyone she had ever loved. Swaying to the music of the reeds and the calling of the wading birds she leaped like a green frog and greeted the clouds like a silver birch in the wind.

And Tegen remembered joy.

'Now,' she said aloud, 'I will dance a blessing on the future, then all shall be well.'

She imagined her baby in her arms and the land at peace once more. But in her mind there were only flames, terrible screams and a lumbering grey shape made of ash and embers.

8. THE MUSTERING

Two days later, Tegen sat in the sunlit doorway to Boudica's royal longhouse. It was built on a high hill in the south of the Iceni lands, overlooking a wide, shallow river that glistened as it curved its way between the fields.

Sabrina and the other tribal leaders were inside, making final plans for the onslaught. Tegen half-listened to their voices as they demanded, cajoled and argued.

In her own mind, she sorted through all she had ever heard her mentors say about the role of a battle druid. In theory, she should meet the opponent's representative before conflict began – to try and find a solution that gave honour and satisfaction to both sides without bloodshed.

She sighed. She doubted whether Suetonius had trained his legions to respect such overtures. She had seen the Romans advancing as one relentless mass behind their shield walls, fire glinting on their eagle-headed standards, and demonic determination in their eyes.

The slaughter of her fellow white robes at Mona still haunted her at night, and flickered through her consciousness by day.

But she also remembered the extraordinary weave of magic that the druids hung in the air above the battle. It had *almost* worked. If only she'd been there to help create it, things might have been different.

Tegen shook her head. Maybe she could have stopped that false thread worming its way in, but she had not arrived in time. Was that her fault or a malign fate? Because of her lateness, she was still alive while hundreds of good men and women were dead. Why had the Goddess allowed it …?

No. Tegen rubbed her face. There was no use wondering. The past was sealed. She was a pawn on the gaming board of fate, no more. There was no Lady. All she had on her side were her wits and maybe a few spirits she had honoured in the past.

But there *were* lessons to be learned from that awful day. How had that weaving been made? Could *she* make and hang one in the air the same way? Were there any more druids left who could help? Even if they were old or infirm, she'd be grateful.

Then a voice calling her name made Tegen sit up.

Sabrina's hair danced wildly over her leather jerkin as she strode out of the royal house. A new sword hung by her thigh. 'Come on daydreamer!' she teased. 'Time to go.'

Tegen hugged her. 'We're not leaving until tomorrow, surely?'

'Today's the mustering!' Sabrina's blue eyes sparkled as she tossed her dagger in the air and caught its handle deftly. 'And we have a surprise for you! Hurry!'

Bemused, Tegen followed her old friend down the hill towards the stables just inside the main gate of the palisade. Sabrina spoke to a scruffy boy who was currying a small pony. He went inside and brought out the most magnificent white mare Tegen had ever seen. She was freshly shod, her coat brushed to perfection and her mane and tail plaited with bright ribbons of yellow and green. On her back was a new tasselled saddle painted with swirling red and blue designs.

The mare stood at fifteen hands, much taller than any British horse. Her step was spirited but she followed the boy gently.

And as soon as she saw Tegen, the horse nickered and stamped.

'Epona!' Tegen squealed as she ran, flinging her arms around the animal's strong neck. 'I don't believe it! They've looked after you so well, I didn't recognise you. Rhiannon of the old stories would have been proud to ride you!'

Then she turned to the stable boy. 'Thank you for doing such a magnificent job, a blessing on you!'

He shrugged and wiped his nose on his sleeve. 'T'weren't me Miss! T'were 'im!' He jerked his thumb towards the smithy on the other side of the gate.

Tegen's heart stopped. There, standing by the fire in the open-sided shed, was a tall man with a thick black beard and a leather apron. '*Goban*?' She gasped. Could her old friend, the god of smiths be *here*? She leaped towards him, but the sound of wheels rattling on cobbles and the clattering roar of a carnyx made her turn.

Boudica was driving her own chariot drawn by two roan stallions. She was dressed in red with a heavy golden torc around her neck. A seven-coloured cloak flowed from her shoulders fastened with huge bronze pins. At her wrists, an assortment of thick golden bangles jangled.

With shouts and whistles, several more chariots drew up, all with chieftains at the reins. Sabrina laughed and leaped up beside her driver. 'We're off!' she whooped and the parade moved through the open gates.

Tegen turned to wave to Goban, but so many people were milling around, she had lost sight of him. Silently she sent him a blessing. If he's truly here, she thought, then maybe all *shall* be well. She smiled, grabbed a saddle-horn and swung herself onto Epona's back.

Her horse's withers were scarred. 'We've both had too many cruel adventures,' Tegen whispered, and stroked her mane.

Epona tossed her head, and then trotted behind the others.

The procession made its way north for about a hand span of the sun. Just before noon they rode towards a long, low hill crowned with a towering palisade, but strangely, no smoke drifted up from roundhouses inside. The road was thronged with men and women who raised their swords and cheered. As Boudica approached the gateway, a guard of warriors blew deafening horns and carnyxes.

Tegen was amazed to see that despite the vastness of the palisade, there was no village or oppidum inside, only endless regimented rows of wooden piles driven into the flinty soil – a daunting, branchless forest.

On all sides, the crowds roared and whistled. Some bowed, others threw small bundles of herbs in tribute and blessing.

Boudica's chariot rattled ahead; followed by her uncle Venutius, Sabrina and then Tegen. Behind them came the other warlords, all dressed for battle and glittering from head to toe with pins and brooches, torcs and armbands.

At last the procession reached the rectangular heart of the enclosure – wide enough to hold a very large village and still be completely surrounded by the serried lines of stark posts.

Tegen urged Epona forward to ride beside the queen. 'What is this place?' she asked.

'It was built by my husband's druid,' Boudica replied. 'When Prasutagus decided it was prudent to accede to the Romans' demands,' she spat and made the sign against evil, 'the druid Devin had this erected. These posts are spirit-walls that prevent the invaders from knowing what we're saying. It's always been a sacred space for our people to gather and take council.'

'Then why did you spend so long in the marshes?' Tegen asked. The midge bites she'd collected there still tormented her.

Boudica glanced scornfully at Tegen. 'I had to ensure that the bodies of any dissenters were never found. These are dangerous times. Accidents happen.'

Tegen's spine chilled at the queen's ruthlessness, but

now was not a time to argue. They drew up at the threshold of a small wooden building at the far side of the enclosure. Here, Boudica turned her chariot and signalled for Tegen to join her. The rest of the chieftains and warlords arrayed themselves on either side, facing the huge crowd.

The people were still coming, pressing more and more tightly together, men, women, and children. Some were ready for immediate war, their hair plastered white and spiked, their skin painted with blue spirals. Others huddled together, pale and frightened.

As the sun reached its zenith, Boudica raised her arms. The light glinted on her golden torc; the wind billowed her red and green cloak and tossed her auburn hair. She raised her spear and an immediate hush fell over the gathering.

Tegen held her breath. Whatever her personal feelings about this woman, she was magnificent. She *was* Britain. Her name, Boudica, meant 'Victory', surely the spirits would bless her? Fleetingly, Tegen wondered whether to offer Epona to the queen to ride in triumph – the living image of the Goddess amongst her people?

It didn't matter that the Lady wasn't real; the picture would put heart into the crowds.

But she had no time to think; Boudica was speaking.

'My friends,' she began in low, rich tones that rippled in the air. 'Men and women of *all* our tribes, today we are united as brothers and sisters, all sheltering as one in this sacred space. The Iceni people open our arms and bid you welcome!'

The crowd roared and Tegen smiled as she covered her ears. Her old friend Owein would have approved; Boudica was achieving what he had always longed for – the unity of the tribes!

'Today, we see the beginning of the end of tyranny!' The throng erupted into deafening applause. Boudica held up her arms for silence. 'Tomorrow, we march on Camulodunum and take it back. We will destroy its unholy filth and restore the land to our good friends, the Trinovantes, so a wholesome settlement may be built there once more!'

Struggling to be heard above the adulation, Boudica went on: 'Then, the day after, we march on the place our oppressors have built at the White Hill by the Tamesis. They call it Londinium. The "governor" Suetonius Paulinus is twelve days away in the lands of the Ceangli. It will take more than a moon's waxing and waning for a messenger to summon him and his armies. By then, every Roman settlement in the east and south will be nothing more than ashes in the wind!'

The cheers and applause were thunderous. Tegen felt her heart swell with pride. Maybe her doubts about Boudica were unfounded? This was a great woman who loved the people and the Land. Waving her arms, she yelled with the rest.

Boudica looked at Tegen and smiled. 'And what is more, Andraste, the Goddess of Victory has sent us a new druid.' She beckoned Tegen closer. 'Do not look at her youth, for her body holds the spirits of generations of the wisest, most powerful druids, and her great grandfather was Bran the Blessed himself!'

This time the crowd gasped and raised their hands in awe.

Smiling, Tegen returned their warmth, trying not to wince at the outrageous claims.

Then Boudica made a signal. Two men dragged a boy from the wooden house behind them. He was Tegen's own age and bound in chains. Whey-faced, he looked up at the queen and fell to his knees without being told.

Boudica turned to Tegen. 'He's all yours,' she said.

Tegen was puzzled. 'What for?'

The queen raised her eyebrows. 'You *are* going to augur his guts, aren't you? The people are waiting to hear your predictions of victory. Give us courage and certainty!'

When Tegen did not respond, Boudica drew her dagger and offered it handle first. 'You have no knife? Borrow mine.'

'W … what has he done to deserve such an end?' Tegen stammered, as the boy's shirt was stripped from his shoulders.

Boudica laughed. 'You are such a *child*, Tegen of the Summer Seas. He's *Roman*! Now, we're all waiting.'

Tegen slipped down from Epona's back, the handle of Boudica's knife warm in her hand. She took one step, then two towards the boy. His head was bowed and he was trembling.

'No!' She turned back to face the queen. 'This is all wrong, human sacrifice never …'

But before she could finish, there was a harsh sound, a cry and a gurgle. The boy slumped forward, blood pumping from his throat. Dark crimson sprayed up the guard's arm and down his tunic.

The man kicked his victim over.

The youth's eyes flickered, his arms twitched. Then he lay still. The man plunged his knife into the boy's belly and ripped the blade upwards. Gleaming intestines spilled into the pool of blood.

Tegen gagged. This must *stop*, she told herself. As soon as we have victory I will speak with the queen.

Unwillingly she looked at the sacrifice. Instantly, her head filled with the noise and smoke of raging fires. Shielding her face with her arms, she stepped back. Out of the angry red and white heart of the inferno stepped a looming figure, its skin was blackened charcoal, and its blood was flames …

It opened its maw …

'*Well*?' Boudica's voice rammed through the vision. 'What do you read?'

Dragged back to reality, Tegen stared up at the queen, imperious on her chariot. Sabrina and all the other war-leaders crowded around, craning their necks to see and hear everything.

'Victory,' Tegen whispered, despite herself. 'There will be victory at Camulodunum.'

9. THE CURSE

Flies were already spreading neat ranks of white eggs across the boy's gaping wounds. The salt-sweet stench of blood and the senseless death were too much for Tegen. She swayed and stumbled.

Sabrina leapt down and heaved Tegen onto the back of her own chariot. 'She needs to rest; the spirits have worn her out!' Then she yelled at a servant, 'Take her horse, make sure you *lead* – don't ride her or you're dead!'

'Just hang on tight,' Sabrina said, taking the reins. With a crack of her whip, she drove her two piebald ponies through the grove of wooden piles, forcing men and women to stagger back, trampling each other as she passed.

Tegen stretched across the chariot platform, wedging herself between the basketwork sides. She gritted her teeth and dug her fingers around the poles that made the frame. Slowly they jolted through the crowds. Some people threw curses for being crushed; others sent blessings to the poor druid girl whose divinations had taken such a toll.

At last, with a whoop and a yell, Sabrina burst through the great gateway and onto the open heath beyond. She gave her horses their heads. Behind her, sparks flew as iron-shod wheels and hooves cracked against the flinty ground.

Tegen's teeth jarred and her bones shook. The journey wasn't long, but she was sick and exhausted by the time they came to the gates of Boudica's stronghold.

Sabrina threw the reins to a boy, then eased Tegen onto the ground. 'Come on, let's sit in the shade by the river. You're as white as wool!' Together they walked to a shady bank and dangled their feet in the river. 'Have a wash,' she said, 'you'll feel better.'

Tegen obeyed, then lay staring up through the canopy of late summer leaves, viridian against the woad blue of the sky. There, she allowed the stream's song to soothe her.

'Now, talk to me,' Sabrina ordered, settling herself beside her friend. 'What happened to Tonn and why did you disintegrate when you were given the boy to sacrifice? What sort of a druid are you? You must've done that before!'

Tegen sighed. Her throat was too tight to speak, but at last she managed to whisper, 'Tonn was chosen by the druids to be a sacrifice to appease the gods and free Britain from the Romans. He died – horribly.' Then she fell silent, remembering how she'd lain like this on her wedding day and seen the raven in the branches above her head. It had warned her …

Sabrina shrugged. 'Surely it gave you pleasure to get your own back today?'

Tegen glared up at her. 'Don't be *stupid*! I didn't get *anything* of my own back! Is Tonn walking here? Can you see him?' She ripped up handfuls of grass. 'Vengeance breeds more vengeance. Hatred breeds more hatred. I know you're a warrior, not a druid, but I thought you'd have understood that at least. Didn't Owein's beliefs mean *anything* to you?'

Sabrina pushed her curly mane back and laughed. 'He had some strange ideas. I sometimes wondered whether he really was British. I secretly suspect he was part Roman!' She tossed a stone into the river.

Tegen thought for a long moment and closed her eyes. 'My instincts say that Owein had a genuine vision of the future. His Roman education gave him some rather strange ideas – but maybe a single nation is what we need?'

'Boudica wants that.'

Tegen stretched her sore back as she considered what she'd seen and heard in the last few days. The hypnotic effects of Boudica's speech had worn off and left a chilly void in her soul.

'Boudica doesn't care about what's wise,' she said at last. 'She'll do *anything* to win, and she'll cause more hatred and division before it's done. Owein stands for a different sort of unity – one based on respect. I wish I knew where he was.'

Sabrina nodded and stood. 'I miss him too – but we've no time for wishing, we have to deal with what's in front of us. I must go; I have to meet with the queen before the sun's mid-haven. Tomorrow we ride.'

She grasped Tegen's hand firmly and met her eyes. 'Will your whole spirit be with us Tegen? Without your magic, all is lost before we begin.'

Tegen returned her gaze. 'You will have my all. This is

what I was born to do. The stars danced at my birth, and I will make the Land whole again. You have my word.'

For a long time after Sabrina left, Tegen stayed where she was, watching the sunlight playing on the river as it swept its lazy way around the stronghold mound. She longed to doze in the midday warmth, and to nibble the peppery cresses that grew at the water's edge. She knew a rest would be good for both herself and the baby. Things were about to get very difficult indeed and there'd be little respite in the future – she had seen it.

But she was too agitated to sleep. She slid down the bank and paddled in the gravelly shallows, scattering dragonflies as she moved. She scooped up cool mud and started to play with it. Soon she had an array of little clay figures drying in the sun. She gave them reeds for spears and swords, and sticks with small leaves for standards. As she worked, her anger and grief slipped unnoticed through her fingers into the ranks of little soldiers, fully armed and staring up at Boudica's longhouse.

Tegen's words of peace slid away with the river, and thoughts of vengeance took their place.

As the sun begun to sink in the west, Tegen surveyed her handiwork.

Then it happened.

Hatred and grief overwhelmed her. Her throat tightened.

She hacked a stick from a nearby willow and stripped away the side branches. Raising the switch above her head, she smashed it down, shattering her work, grinding her teeth and cursing.

'Thus will you die! *All of you!*'

She raised her stick and struck again. 'I hate the Romans, I *DO!*' And with her bare feet she pulverised the figures back into the riverbed. 'Mud you were and mud you shall be again!' she cursed through clenched teeth. 'May you rot in outer darkness! If you hadn't come to conquer and steal, we would be at peace.

'If you hadn't come, my Tonn would still be alive!'

She slammed the stick so hard it flew from her grip and span away down river. Wading waist deep after it, she slapped at the water with her hands. '*I demand vengeance!*' she sobbed.

'This river will run red with Roman blood! So will it be!' The final spell-seal was spoken.

Exhausted and panting, Tegen staggered and fell. Neck deep in the chilly water she sat for a long time, amazed at the strength of her vehemence.

Shivering, she made for the bank. 'I must've been bottling all that up for ages – but I feel better now!' She wrung out her hair and dress as best she could.

Deep down, her soul twisted into nasty, unpickable little knots, but her mind was whirling with the strength and potential of her powers.

'I still have one more curse,' she told the trees as she ran towards the longhouse. 'I'll bring vengeance on the druids for Tonn's death – and do you know how I'm going to do it?' she asked a wren that swooped across her path. 'I'm going to do exactly what they asked of me: I'll help Boudica however I can. I'll strengthen her hatred and vengeance until she destroys everything – including herself! There'll be death and destruction. But when it's all over, the kites will pick the bones of British and Roman alike.

'And the Land will be left in peace to rebuild itself.

'There'll be no druids, no Romans – just ordinary people getting on with their lives. 'And I shall go to Ériu, have my child and forget everything!'

Tegen threw her wet shoes in the air, laughing as she caught them. She felt light and happy as she climbed the mound to Boudica's stronghold.

All would be very well indeed, but not as anyone expected. This would be a Great Cleansing – like winter, before the New Beginning.

And she, Tegen, the Star Dancer and druid of the Winter Seas, would be the one to usher in …

The Time of Stone.

10. THE GIFT

Inside Boudica's Longhouse, Tegen changed into dry clothes and lay on her bed, staring at the ceiling. Beyond the woven screen that gave her privacy, voices murmured over plans and plots.

Tegen's head ached. She closed her eyes. If only she could sleep.

As the shadows lengthened, she thought about what she had done and began to cry. She wiped her eyes with muddy hands. 'I let anger rule me – but allowing both sides to exhaust themselves is the only way to end this – isn't it?'

At last she slept, but in her dreams a voice whispered: *I have a gift for you, would you like it?*

'What is it?' Tegen asked aloud.

Something you want. Very much.

Tegen remembered Angor using similar words when he gave her the leeches that destroyed Eiser. 'Who are you and what is your gift?'

I am one who longs to see you become the most magnificent druid this land has ever known. I will give you the power to contain the horrors that are rising like a great tide on all sides. You will be a saviour.

'And what is your price?'

Nothing. You merely have to ask.

Tegen imagined herself on a beach, arms raised towards the water. 'Go back!' she commanded. 'This Land is sacred.'

And the sea obeyed.

But the waves were made of blood.

Tonn's blood.

He was the Strong Wave that was meant to heal the Land. In her mind she saw his kind eyes and heard his lilting voice: *Be careful Tegen,* he said. *You are not the Goddess – just her hands and feet for the little while you're in this world. Don't forget the web of magic – power is never for free. Don't let my death be in vain.*

She felt Tonn curl his cool fingers around hers and she felt stronger.

'I promise, beloved,' she answered. 'This fire has to burn itself out, but I will try to bring hope to the people who are left.'

Then to the voice in her head, she replied, 'No gifts, thank you. My task is to steer Britain through these evil times, not to rule.

'The Land must heal itself.'

CAMULODUNUM

11. SPYING

The warriors set out at dawn. Tegen led the procession dressed in fine white robes. She'd allowed her face to be painted with ochre spirals and her hair spiked with lime. Between her breasts clinked talismans of each tribe's deities. She would pray to them all for the peoples' victory – whether they were real or not. Sitting tall and proud in Epona's saddle, she smiled sadly as she thought of her plan.

Both sides would get what they longed for – and what they deserved.

That's what magic was for – gaining ends. Who dared to say what was right and what was wrong? No one ever agreed; that's why there were wars.

To bring peace, she must become a knife – deadly, amoral – and loaned to both sides.

Once Suetonius Paulinus and Boudica were dead, the Land would recover – and she'd be a mother with her own hearth in Ériu.

The morning was beautiful. The servant at Tegen's side spoke little, leaving her to her thoughts.

Boudica rode ahead on her chariot, with Sabrina and Venutius alongside in theirs. Bronze fittings gleamed with red and blue enamel, and brightly painted reins guided the war-horses with their tossing manes. Behind them, the ranks of lesser nobles lead their bands of warriors. At the rear trundled baggage carts loaded with the elderly and infants who could not be left at home alone.

Tegen turned in her saddle. The endless stream of people, waggons, carts and chariots, wound its way between the hills and woodlands, back along the road as far as she could see. Spears, helmets and swords glinted in the sun. The road shook with the tramp of boots and hooves and the air was heavy with song.

The servant saw Tegen staring. 'Seventeen thousand men, women and children so far, lady,' he said. 'We'll collect more on the way.'

By the time Bel's course was in the east, the army reached an open heath. Boudica's chief steward called a halt.

'But we've hardly come any distance,' Tegen protested. 'Can't we ride further?'

The man shrugged. 'It'll be almost dark by the time the last stragglers arrive and cook a meal. Camulodunum isn't far, but it'll take five or six days because we're so many. Suetonius is too far away to harass us, even if a rider was sent this morning, which I doubt, the town is ours!' Then he turned to organise the pitching of Tegen's tent.

Frustrated, Tegen found fodder and water for Epona and watched the setting up of the camp. Although she longed to be on the move, she was weary. Carrying a child, even one that still didn't show, was hard work. Spreading her cloak under a cart, she lay down and slept, ignoring the call to supper.

As her servant had predicted, the journey was slow, but at noon on the fifth day, they camped just below a rise.

Tegen walked a little ahead and saw Camulodunum nestling in the valley below. She recognised the strict pattern of a Roman garrison, softened here and there by the informality of civilian houses and shops. In the centre rose a vast building, its terracotta roof supported by white columns. Next to it ran a sweeping, curved wall. Although too far away to be sure, it looked like the circus where she had danced for the Romans and Sabrina had fought as a gladiatorix.

Tegen strolled away from camp and chose a sheep-path, avoiding the fields and settlements scattered on the higher slopes. Apart from the fact that many of the farms boasted new rectangular buildings with tiled roofs, all seemed normal.

The hedges were cut and tidy, the fields had been harvested and some had even been ploughed. Crab apple trees hung heavy with ripe fruit and brambles still carried fat purple berries.

Then, on the hillside opposite, Tegen spotted movement. Two grey-haired men were crouched by a wall, scanning the heath and Boudica's camp.

Tegen slid behind a gorse bush and waited for them to go. So, Camulodunum wasn't entirely asleep. The men looked too old to offer much of a threat in battle and Tegen sensed their fear as they trudged back towards the town. She glanced at the sky. There were many hand-spans of daylight left. Plenty of time for what she needed to do.

Back at camp, she washed and changed into a brown dress and shawl. Taking a basket of herbs she made her way to Boudica's tent where the queen was huddled over a sand-map with her advisors.

Tegen watched. I will support Boudica, I will give her my all, she vowed silently, but she must die before she destroys Britain. She is so full of venom she will poison herself in the end. And I am glad. She *deserves* it!

Then Tegen noticed Oriana and Megan huddled on a rug at the back of the tent.

But I will try to save her children, she promised, laying her hand on her own belly. They've suffered enough.

Just then, the queen looked up. 'Ah, my druid, will you join us?' She smiled, but without warmth.

Tegen shook her head. 'No, thank you. I wanted to tell you I'm going down to Camulodunum. I need to know about their temples and gods and to discover what spirits they may have arraigned against us. I need to put my own spells in place to make the taking of the town easier.

Sabrina jumped to her feet. 'I'll come with you.'

Tegen shook her head. 'No. Thank you, but this is secret magic. I need to be alone.'

'But you can't go unguarded,' complained Daig. 'We'll send warriors with you at least.'

Tegen was adamant. 'If I have guards, it'll be plain that I'm a spy.' She held out her basket. 'Dressed like this, they'll only see a herb seller.' Then she ran from the tent. She had no idea why she needed to be alone so badly, but she did.

At a signal from Boudica, two men followed her.

Pulling her shawl over her too-short hair, Tegen chose the road to the west gate of the town. Boudica was right – it was undefended. There was a shallow ditch that ran around the perimeter and a temporary-looking palisade; strong enough to deter wild animals, but that was all.

Nervous urgency crackled in the air. Men and women were stacking thorn bushes against the flimsy stockade and children were gathering pebbles for slings.

Just then, a group of boys passed her, carrying bundles of spear-length ash and hazel saplings.

The gates stood open and a steady trickle of handcarts and waggons were leaving the town loaded with household goods, women and children.

Tegen resisted the urge to curse them as she approached the gate. None of this is their fault, and we'll need to build a new population, she told herself. They may be Roman or British now, but we'll all be one tribe in the end.

Just then, two guards raised their spears and blocked Tegen's way. 'Where do'ye think you're going?' one snarled in reasonable British. 'Don't recognise you.'

Slipping her hand into her pouch, Tegen touched her stone egg. Help me now, she prayed. I must get inside.

She bowed to the men. 'Sirs, I'm Mirna, a herbalist.' She smiled sweetly.

'Not a good time for selling,' the other one jerked his

head towards the hills. 'Trouble brewing, see? Now run along home like a good girl.'

Tegen took a big breath and a bigger gamble. 'Claudius Metellus' daughter summoned me.' She tapped her basket. 'Poor girl's got stomach cramps something awful. I've got her tisanes here.'

The guards exchanged glances and nodded. 'Very well. Do you know the house?'

Tegen peered around as if looking for someone. 'I was told a slave would meet me.'

The first man pointed along the road that led from the gate into the heart of the town. 'Straight along there, you'll see the temple on the left and the house of Metellus is to the right. Anyone'll show you. But don't stay long, that rabble on the hill look angry. Not that they're any match for our soldiers!'

Then he snapped to attention and saluted as a young man in a toga rode past on a cream-coloured pony.

The rider turned and stared at Tegen, but she ignored him.

'Thank you.' She smiled flirtatiously at the soldiers. Behind their hard eyes there was fear and weariness. Neither of them was young. If they were the best that Camulodunum offered, Boudica's battle would be easy.

If only they didn't have to die.

She strode past them into a long, straight street of open-fronted shops, but few were trading. A man was selling sheep's milk from a barrel on a cart. Tegen bought a beaker-full and sat on a bench to drink. Up and down the street, worried looking citizens were erecting barricades or scurrying towards the gate clutching bundles and babies.

To be able to cast her best spells and bring about defeat, Tegen needed to understand who these people were and why they were here. As she watched, she found she could not distinguish between Roman and Briton. Children with blond and dark hair played together in the late summer sun. The few soldiers striding past weren't all dark and long-nosed. The civilian men were old or war-wounded, slow and infirm. The women were just women, some pregnant like herself.

Was it *right* to destroy these undefended people? Once again she regretted the spells and vows she had made by the river.

Just then a voice called her name. Tegen looked up.

There was Ula, smiling, but with a fresh bruise on her face. 'I'm so pleased to see you.' She gave a little bow. 'Madam'll be pleased as well. Shall I take you to her? Our house isn't far ...'

Tegen looked at Ula's cheek and anger welled up inside her. 'She's hit you again?'

Ula laughed. 'Oh no, I tripped. It was my fault entirely.'

'You can tell me the truth.'

'Honestly ...'

Tegen pursed her lips. Why was she covering up for Claudia? These Romans *weren't* human – they were monsters. They had to be got rid of, exterminated like rats!

'Will you come?' Ula gestured along the street to a fine house at the far end.

'No, thank you.' Tegen daren't get involved with them again. Not now. 'I'm on an errand. Do you have time to sit and drink milk with me?'

'I'm in a hurry too,' Ula replied with genuine excitement. 'Claudia's new husband has arrived and they're to be betrothed tonight. We have a feast to prepare – if I can find any shops open, that is!'

Tegen's mind was in turmoil. How do I tell Ula to get out of the town? She wondered. What if she's faithful to Claudia, even after all the abuse?

Tegen smiled. 'If … if you can, slip away for a while before dawn tomorrow, maybe go for a walk in the hills? It'll be good for you. Give your mistress my greetings and tell her I send my blessings for her future happiness. Farewell.'

Before Ula could reply, Tegen got up to go. Her conscience roared at her. *What* happiness? *What* future? There were *some* good people in the city. Could she do nothing to help them without betraying Boudica's army? Were they all doomed, good and bad?

Tegen grabbed her basket and ran, pushing her way through the crowded streets. Who was good and who was evil? Who had a right to live, and who to die? Who was she to decide anyway?

At last she came to an open square. All along one side were wide steps leading to the white columned building she'd seen from the hill. It had to be the temple.

In front, high on a pedestal, stood a white-skinned woman with vast spreading wings and arms outstretched towards the city. Tegen stood agape. It could almost have been Boudica ... but she wore only a loose shift ... and why was she all white? Why didn't she move? Was she a goddess?

'Hello?' Tegen ventured.

No response.

None of the passers-by seemed to take any notice of her at all. Gingerly Tegen sidled closer and placed one hand on the woman's foot. She was made of stone, superbly crafted yet so very, very nearly alive. Tegen shuddered.

An old man surreptitiously spat against the base.

'Excuse me, what is this?' Tegen asked.

He made the sign against the evil eye and muttered, '*They* call it "Victory"! Phah!' Then he leaned closer to Tegen's ear and whispered, 'It's said that *she* is just over the hill. When *she* comes, we'll be free again. We'll show 'em what "Victory" looks like. She won't let us down. By tomorrow, us slaves'll be proud to be British once more!' And he straightened his old back.

Recoiling at the smell of stale garlic on his breath, Tegen thanked him and went to sit on the steps, exhausted and angry.

'Victory,' she mused. 'Boudica'll like that – a statue to herself and she hasn't even crossed the outer ditches!'

12. VICTORY DEFEATED

Tegen sat on the temple steps, staring dully at the passers by until late in the afternoon.

The sight of ordinary, frightened people milling around her, crumbled her resolution to steer both sides to their fates.

If Huval was right and Rome was not the enemy, was it right to kill any of them?

Should she fight for peace – or victory?

As she cradled Tonn's egg, she wished that she too could become stone, then she wouldn't have to care.

Just then, a deep, melancholy horn bellowed in the temple behind her. Within a few heartbeats a crowd was pushing and shoving up the steps.

Curious, Tegen roused herself and crept cautiously amongst them. Under the portico, she leaned against the plinth of a towering column and listened. From somewhere, a man's rich voice led a solemn chant and the people sang responses while spicy incense filled the air. Everyone bowed and then the song began again.

Tegen couldn't help but be fascinated. I wish I could understand their rituals, she thought to herself. I'd like discussions with their druids; if I could understand the way they thought, then might be able to come to an agreement. That is the first duty of a battle druid after all.

But the little she knew of the Romans assured her they

wouldn't talk to a mere girl who didn't even speak Latin!

Wriggling her way through the people, back to the steps, Tegen sat and stroked their pristine whiteness. Tears streamed down her face. In her mind's eyes she could see the marble streaked with blood. 'If I support Boudica, then Britain will win, but the cost will be awful. If I leave her to her own devices then there will still be slaughter.'

She pulled out Tonn's stone egg and examined the glistening red streaks.

I was born to *avert* evil – not to cause it! she told herself. Now I'm forced to make war magic for a queen I neither like nor trust! Boudica cannot be the spirits' tool to bring healing to our Land. And with all the anger and fear inside of me, I'm not much better. I must get a grip on myself. I shouldn't have sworn to leave the two sides to their own devices. I shouldn't have made those curses with the clay soldiers – but if I undo it, will I unleash mayhem on my people?

I wanted vengeance for Tonn. I was wrong. There has got to be a middle path. There has got to be hope somewhere in all this mess. If only I could be certain the Goddess was real and still cared …

In the temple behind her, the townspeople were probably praying for deliverance from the coming battle. Back in Boudica's camp, her friends were doing the same.

Tegen closed her eyes. Are you real Lady? Are you listening? A lot of people believe in you – they need your help. Don't you think it's about time you answered some of these prayers? If you're so powerful and great, can't you deliver *both* our peoples and help us live in harmony?

Silence.

Tegen scowled at the overcast skies.

What if you're there – but just one spirit amongst many? She wondered. You're all scratching each other's eyes out to get as many worshippers as possible? Is that it? You and Andraste and Taranis and whoever they're worshipping in there – are you all sitting in Tir na nÓg tallying up headcounts?'

Then an even worse thought crawled into her aching head, Or are you playing a game with us? Are we just pieces you're shoving across a board for your divine amusement?'

The desperate prayers behind her, swelled into a crescendo.

'I'm listening!' she called out.

Still nothing.

Then came the soft, persuasive voice inside her head once more – *I will give you the power to contain the horrors that are rising like a great tide on all sides. You will be a saviour.*

Tegen rolled her stone egg along the steps. White and red on red and white.

Blood on white marble. Two colours, one stone.

Did she have the power to contain these horrors? Was *she* the hope? Was this her destiny? 'I do not trust you, Whisperer,' she said aloud, 'but I must find the magic that will contain what is to come.'

'May I be of assistance, lady?'

Tegen jumped. She'd been so lost in her thoughts she hadn't noticed a thin, grey man standing by her side. Every part of his face was tattooed with mystic spirals and symbols with meanings that Tegen could only guess at. She blinked. She had seen him at Boudica's secret camp in the marshes. 'You're Aodh, aren't you? The brother of Addedomaros?'

The man bowed. 'A simple spell-caster at your service my lady. And if I may mention,' he coughed deferentially, 'containment spells are my speciality.'

Tegen narrowed her eyes. 'What kind of containment spells?'

Aodh put his head on one side and licked his pale lips. 'I have a spirit that serves me. It does my bidding. It will do yours also.'

'What spirit?' she asked.

Aodh made her feel nervous. What's he doing here? She wondered. Is he following me? Did Boudica send him or is he on his own creepy business?

As if he could hear her thoughts, Aodh flared his nostrils and straightened his back. 'My spirit is one who wishes you well. It longs to work with you and to see you succeed.'

Tegen scratched the itchy scar on her finger. If only she hadn't lost Goban's ring ... 'What is the spirit's price?'

Aodh shrugged. 'Why should there be a price? Don't we all want the same thing?'

'I need to think.'

'Of course, my lady.' The spell-caster tucked his hands inside his sleeves. He bowed, and then turned to watching the steady stream of people still arriving at the temple.

Tegen walked down the steps and leaned against the statue. *Think!* She urged herself. All of my training has come to this moment. If the Romans aren't the enemy – what is? My own indecision maybe? *Someone* has to do something ...

Tegen held her breath as she remembered being too scared to dance in the funeral caves at home. Then she'd allowed herself to be delayed in Tara and arrived at Mona too late to save her fellow druids. 'I mustn't hesitate again,' she muttered through gritted teeth. 'If I don't act, then more will die.'

'Aodh,' she called out.

He stood before her, as dull and featureless as a tree in winter. 'My lady?'

'How does this magic work?' she asked.

'Just imagine – and all will come true.'

'How ...?'

But Aodh just smiled, then he strode across the square and disappeared in the crowd.

Hot anger welled up inside Tegen. 'Just *imagine*? What is that stupid man talking about?'

She kicked at the steps but the evening light on the white marble glinted back at her – unmoved, unscathed.

Then she stopped and thought. 'Gronw would say I must stop and listen – but to what?' Then she raised her chin and called out to the sky, 'Lady Goddess, this is the last time I'm asking – are you there? Do you care?'

There were no comforting words in her mind. No miracle. No omen to read.

'Pull yourself together,' she told herself firmly. 'I'm the only one who can act. The web of magic is here and I must *use* it! It's impossible to know and follow every thread.'

More and more frightened worshippers were gathering on the temple steps. The daylight was already fading. In a few hours the town would be rubble.

'I just don't have time.'

She looked at her hands and remembered throwing fire at Suetonius and his men. Her vow not to do that again had been weak. What if she threw flames now, at everyone? British and Roman alike! Would that make them stop and *look* at the stupidity of what was happening?

She was the Star Dancer, the wielder of the greatest magic Britain had ever known. The demon that pursued her was hatred and vengeance. With or without divine help, she would stand against it, once and for all.

Very well, she decided, I *will* imagine, but I'll use the power to contain the horror and prevent as much innocent death as I can. Firstly, I want these people out of here …

She closed her eyes and saw the streets of Camulodunum deserted.

And to make them run away, I'll bring down their 'Victory'.

Tegen climbed the temple steps and raised her hands.

Cracking stone rumbled like thunder. The ground shook

and the winged statue rocked. Tegen's palms itched as she sent power from her fingertips. 'Damn you! *Fall*!'

With a deafening blast, the statue toppled. The wings smashed into clouds of dust. The head snapped, then rolled. Shards of stone flew like knives.

Screams. Silence.

As the air cleared, Tegen sprang forward and kicked the head until it stopped – facing Boudica's army.

'Victory' had surrendered.

Tegen curled up small against the statue's plinth as surging waves of people ran from the temple, weeping, pushing and howling.

'Good!' she whispered. 'Victory is ours and it *shall* be so! Now get *out* of the town you stupid, stupid people!'

Then she closed her eyes and imagined ghouls and tormented spirits.

A strangled, terrified wailing sobbed through the streets.

'Ghosts in the theatre!' screamed a panicking woman, pushing her way through the melee.

'It's a warning!' 'An omen!' yelled two men shoving in the opposite direction. '*Flee*!'

Arms waved, hands clutched, eyes stared in horror and dread. 'It's the British, they're coming!'

People tripped, shoved, elbowed, trampled.

'Attack! Attack!'

'My babies!'

'Save us!' The turmoil grew worse by the heartbeat. No one knew where to run.

Trying not to be swept away, Tegen clung to the plinth and gritted her teeth. Part of her longed to flee like the rest, but deep down, she wanted to stay and relish the chaos.

She had done it! *She* had cast a great spell that would change the course of this stinking war. This was her first battle and it was a glorious triumph. Britain would be free because of her. The curse of the Romans would be broken.

Just then, a small child fell screaming at her feet.

Instinctively Tegen grabbed and enfolded him against the terror. His small fingers clutched hers and his sobs subsided.

'But I will try to keep *you* safe,' she murmured.

13. COLLABORATOR

'*Sedate*!' a stern voice bellowed. 'Calm down!'

The crowd froze.

The man roared again, his words echoing between the houses.

Still clutching the child, Tegen ran up the temple steps, slid behind one of the columns and watched.

In the gathering dark, flickering torches and stamping boots heralded a dozen legionaries marching into the square.

The terrified people drew back.

The men formed a circle around the smashed statue, facing outwards, shields raised and swords at the ready.

An eerie silence fell.

Then came the clatter of horse hooves and two men in togas rode into the square.

The circle opened, allowing the riders to enter. One dismounted by the decapitated Victory. Reverently, he picked up a carved finger and shook his head. He replaced the piece gently, as if it were alive. Then he spoke in clear, loud Latin. There were murmurings of assent and a few people slipped away.

The speaker nodded to his companion who turned his cream pony to face the remaining crowd.

From her hiding place, Tegen caught sight of the man's face and gasped. '*Owein*? It can't be! He wouldn't ...?'

Owein spread his hands to the people, then in British he proclaimed, 'My friends, do not be alarmed. You have seen the tribes in the hills and believe the fall of Victory is an omen of war. This is not so. The statue fell because too many people pressed around it. There is no reason for fear or panic. We do not know why the tribes have gathered. They have luggage, women and children with them, so they may simply be looking for new homes. To reassure you, Claudius Metellus has requested reinforcements from Lindum. I give you my word; they will be with us by dawn. We are safe. What British warrior would raise his hand against his own people? Go home, be at peace.'

No one spoke or moved, so the young man went on: 'There are as many people of the Trinovantes tribe as Romans here in our town, so have no fear!'

'Yes, but we're only here as slaves!' a voice yelled from the back. 'Given the choice we'd be up on the hills with the others!'

'But you are still British, no one will hurt you. As many of you know, I am British myself ...'

'*Collaborator*!' someone screeched, throwing a shattered fragment at Owein.

'*Traitor*!' Stones and horse dung flew in earnest.

The grey haired man remounted his horse and snapped an order. Three soldiers pushed through the crowd until the troublemakers were backed against a wall, sword tips pressed firmly against bellies and throats.

'*Go home*!' Owein shouted. 'In the morning, we will be

defended and all shall be well.'

Then the yelling began again. In the end, it was swords not words that emptied the square, leaving only the youth astride his mount amidst the ruins of the statue.

Tegen released her grip on the terrified child. 'Find your Mam,' she whispered, and he ran.

Anger welled up inside Tegen as she strode into full view on the Temple steps. Hands on hips she yelled, 'Owein *Sextus*! You vowed to defend Britain with your last breath ... *You*, the son of Caractacus, king of the Catuvellauni. You swore your Roman education meant nothing! Look at yourself: collaborating! Betraying!'

She began a spell to blast him from his saddle, but without flinching he urged his pony towards her. She lowered her hands and went towards him.

The thickening evening shadows hid his face, but torchlight glimmered on his auburn hair. 'Hello Tegen,' he said calmly. 'I saw you earlier – talking to the guards. Will you meet me tonight? *Please*?'

Her eyes opened wide. She hadn't expected him to say that.

Owein leaned forward and whispered, 'There's a deserted mill by the river, a short walk from the eastern gate. I need to talk to you urgently.' Then turning the mare's head, he trotted her out of the square.

Tegen was left alone in the semi-dark, with wisps of mist curling cool fingers around her face and arms. She looked down at her hands. She was holding horse droppings, ready to throw. She tossed the stinking, sticky mess away, took a torch from its socket, and picked her way gingerly across the square.

The streets were slowly filling with people pushing heavily laden handcarts towards the gates. For those who were able to leave, the exodus was almost complete.

Tegen had imagined an almost empty city so few would be killed when the attack came – and now it was coming to pass. She had scared them off with the falling statue and the ghostly wailings.

She allowed herself a glow of pleasure. 'I can do this. I can save Britain! To keep the people together, I must still speak as if it's the Goddess, but it's *me* that has the power! … What shall I imagine next?'

Her foot kicked against something that rattled. It was a lost wooden doll. She set it upright on the ground. 'Stand!' she commanded. It stood. 'Walk,' it walked. 'Fall on your face before me.'

And it did.

Tegen shuddered, suddenly afraid of what she could do. She closed her eyes. In her mind she saw the town with spitting fire blossoming up the walls and into the roofs. People were running and screaming in dreadful terror.

She remembered the river by Boudica's longhouse. The water had sparkled in the sunlight, but the image shifted. Now it flowed red, the colour of blood. Just as she'd said it would.

But was all this her doing, or was she just seeing the

inevitable future? She didn't hate the people of Camulodunum. She almost wished the Roman troops would come to their aid in the morning, then Boudica might be persuaded to think twice about attacking.

'Where are they?' she whispered, 'the men of Lindum?'

Tegen crumpled as a ghastly image seared into her brain: a cohort of fully armed men lying hacked and stiff, while dogs, wolves and birds shared the spoils. They were in a wood, not far away. A couple of British warriors had fallen there too, but Tegen understood.

They had been ambushed, as Boudica had promised.

Tegen swung around on her heel and surveyed the town's proud, straight streets and fine houses – now empty and silent. She had seen many people leaving, but her spirit could still hear terrified prayers whispered in dark corners.

'Get *out*!' she yelled, to the empty pavements and the loosely banging shutters. 'Get out, *tonight*!'

She stamped her foot until the ground shook. A few buildings swayed, stones shifted and fell, then a scream echoed into the dark.

'I don't want anyone to die – not really. If anyone's still here, you must *leave*! *Now*!' Her voice echoed in the deserted streets.

Wiping her eyes on her shawl, Tegen pulled it tightly around her head and dodged between the half a dozen men and boys who guarded the western gate.

Once outside, she trudged up the hill towards Boudica's

camp, praying the people of Camulodunum would heed the earthquakes and ghostly wailings – and leave.

'But Owein can stay!' she growled as she kicked a stone, 'he's a traitor and deserves to die.'

With scarcely a nod, she marched past the guards at the camp entrance and followed her nose towards the smell of cooking. She was ravenous.

'Tegen!' Sabrina yelled. 'Wait!'

Tegen stopped. She didn't feel like talking to anyone, even her best friend, but she was too tired to think how to avoid her.

Sabrina's boots thudded through the mud. With a whoop of glee, the Dobunni queen flung her arms around Tegen's neck. 'We heard what you did, smashing the statue like that! You were magnificent!' She laughed, slapping Tegen on the shoulder. 'Boudica's looking for you, come and eat!' She steered her into the queen's tent, where a trestle table was spread with a linen cloth and bowls of stew and bread.

Tegen's head ached, but there was no escape.

Boudica rose unsteadily to her feet and raised a mead horn. 'To the arch-druid of the Winter Seas!' she called out. 'The men I sent to guard you told me everything. You're a battle druid above all battle druids! I'll command songs in your praise that'll be sung for a thousand years. Come, sit by me!' And she pulled a golden bracelet from her arm and pushed it over Tegen's wrist.

'We need music!' Boudica yelled, clapping her hands.

'Send in a bard!'

With gritted teeth Tegen submitted to a kiss on the cheek. The gold felt like the grip of dead men's fingers. She longed to fling it away, but she needed Boudica's trust. If the queen could be persuaded to listen, then the revolt still might succeed.

She mumbled thanks and shovelled food into her mouth as Boudica continued, 'Tomorrow will be a great battle. Eat, drink and celebrate. Thanks to this woman at my side, Andraste has ensured we shall win! Their Goddess of Victory is already smashed before my feet. My chariot wheels will grind the town to dust with the morning light. To Andraste – the *real* Victory!'

Everyone cheered. Despite herself, Tegen drank and the honey sweetness seeped into her aching body and mind.

As the celebrations waned, Tegen rose, thanked the queen and went to her own tent.

It was cold and damp. The chilly mist had crept through the oiled linen tent flaps and into her bedding. For a long time she shivered in the dark silence, then, without really knowing why, she pulled on her cloak and boots and went outside.

The guard turned at the sound of her step. He raised his spear.

'I'm Tegen the druid,' she told him. 'I need to cast spells.'

He lowered his weapon and bowed his head.

Guided by starlight, Tegen made her way across the

open heath and around the outside of Camulodunum's walls to the eastern gate. Keeping low between the gorse and scrub, Tegen watched the armed guards, silhouetted against bright watch fires. They stood staring out into the darkness. They had not heard her.

To her right was the faint sound of water. Following the noise, she came to the river and followed it upstream until the black shape of a ramshackle building loomed ahead. To one side, the starlight showed a pale pony.

Tegen hesitated. Why had she left the safety of camp and her bed? Was she just cold and lonely? The Owein that Tegen had once loved and cared for had been a good soul, whom she could trust with her life. What had happened to him? Why had he donned the toga? Was she here to rescue him?

But Owein had never been the sort to need rescuing.

The mare nickered softly as Tegen approached.

No going back now, she told herself. Owein will have heard that. I won't stay long. If he doesn't have anything useful to say, I'll just go. It'll be easy to disappear in the night. Owein can't follow with that gammy leg of his.

She crept forward and rubbed her hands over the pony's neck. 'Hello, Heather old girl. How've you been?' The mare pushed her velvet nose under Tegen's chin. 'I've come to see your master – I've got to know why he's betrayed us all.'

There was a shuffled step, then another.

Tegen didn't look up. What was she going to say?

'Hello,' Owein said softly. 'I hoped you'd come.'

His warm voice filled her with a squirming confusion of love and hatred. 'I ... don't know why I did. You're a collaborator and an oath breaker. I hope you die and come back as ... as a *toad*!' Tegen's fury swelled in her throat. 'No, wait, you're already a toad. Well come back as a *slug*, then I can stamp on you!' And she turned to go.

Owein's shadow stepped from the deeper darkness. His strong arms caught her. 'You'll do no such thing, at least not until we've talked. I thought you trusted me – I thought we were friends?'

She tried to wriggle free, but his grip was too strong. 'That was before you sold your soul to those thugs and murderers!' She tried to spit but he put a hand over her mouth.

'And you're quite certain that everything Boudica does is clean and pure? And I suppose her thugs aren't bent on slaughtering everyone, whatever their tribe or nation who happens to be in the wrong place at the wrong time?'

Tegen shrugged. 'This is war.'

Owein sighed. 'I've seen what Boudica can do. There's not much to choose between Suetonius and your precious queen. Now come inside. There's a chilly wind and we don't want to get caught by spies.'

'Whose?' Tegen demanded, refusing to move.

'Either.' Owein sounded exasperated. 'Well, if you don't want to talk, what are you doing here?'

'I don't know,' she muttered as she followed him into

the ramshackle mill. Everything was pitch black. 'Perhaps I'm just curious how a good man can become a traitor?'

Owein grabbed Tegen's hand and led her to a slanting wooden beam. 'Take a seat. Let's at least give each other a chance, shall we? I presume there's going to be an attack tomorrow?'

'At dawn.'

'I thought so,' Owein replied. 'We've just heard that the relief troops from Lindum were ambushed in a forest on the way here. We'll be completely undefended.'

'Then why did you tell everyone not to be afraid and go home?' Tegen snarled. 'At least I tried to scare them away!'

'Oh, so that was what the ghostie-noises and statue-toppling theatrics were about?'

'They weren't theatrics! I was simply trying to warn people.'

'There are simpler ways.'

'So, what would happen if I stood up and told them straight? Boudica sent spies to follow me – they'd have slit my throat as soon as I opened my mouth. And would the good citizens have believed me anyway? *Women* have no standing in your wonderful new Roman society!'

'You're right,' Owein replied. 'The truth is, until now, the Roman officials have been confused as to Boudica's motives. Spies have watched the tribes gathering for months, but they cannot understand why the warriors are bringing whole families and all their possessions with them. Is it war, or mass migration?'

'It's both in a way,' Tegen replied, calmer now. 'Many are planning to go north once it's over. Those planning to return are scared to leave their loved ones undefended at home. Whether the British win or lose, there'll be Roman repercussions – the warriors will come home to fly-blown corpses.'

'That makes sense.' Owein leaned close and whispered, 'I guessed it was war and I've sent word to all the British homes to get out tonight.'

'And the Roman families?'

Owein's dark shape shifted uncomfortably. 'There's nowhere for them to go. If they flee, they'll be dead. If they stay they'll be dead. Stores are being put into the temple of Claudius, where you were today – food, water, blankets. It's a very strong building; it should withstand the onslaught. It'll just be the elderly, women and children. All the men will have to fight.'

Tegen was silent for a moment, then she asked, 'And you? Who will you fight for?'

Owein took a deep breath. 'I have a fiancée now and she lives with her elderly father. I will have to do my best for them, it's my moral duty. But I will never attack, only defend.'

Tegen's anger flared once more. She sprang to her feet. '*Moral duty*? What do you care about what's right or wrong? Why are you working for those … those *vermin* anyway? What happened to you Owein? What happened to your vows to restore Sabrina as queen of the Dobunni and

97

to keep up the fight for our sacred Land?'

With difficulty, Owein also stood. His voice was level and cold. 'When you left me at the burning of Sinodun, I was captured by the Romans. They knew who I was. I had a simple choice – either to serve them as I had been trained to do – or die. With Admidios dead, I could see working for the Romans would help our cause ...'

'Oh yes, I can see that!' Tegen sneered, 'A nice villa and a cosy Roman wifey to warm your bed? Very convenient! Plenty of money, slaves and a nice pension when you're old!'

'I was *going* to say ...' Owein continued patiently, 'an advantage for us British. I could make sure that laws were applied fairly and justly and explained in a way that our people can understand and relate to. I have also been spying for chieftain Daig of the Trinovantes and helping some of his people to escape. If it wasn't for me, the lives of the British in Camulodunum would have been much, much worse!'

'You sound like Admidios.' She spat. 'I should've known you'd have a good story all worked out!'

Owein heaved from his good leg to his crutch. 'Well, if you don't care about the truth or about working together, then I'm off. Goodbye!' He stomped out of the door, mounted Heather and pointed her nose towards the town gates.

'*Good riddance*!' Tegen muttered.

Pulling her cloak around her, she set off for Boudica's

camp. With any luck she'd still get some sleep before dawn. The next day was going to be long and painful.

Back in Camulodunum, Owein did not think about sleep. Instead he stabled his pony, then crept through the town, sliding quietly between the guards and nervous refugees.

At last he hobbled up a flight of stone steps to an impressive house, knocked and was admitted. Inside he was greeted warmly by the grey-haired citizen he had accompanied in the square.

Owein bowed his head. 'Forgive the unseemly hour; this is urgent.'

The old man smiled and slapped Owein on the back. 'You're always welcome. When you marry my daughter, this house shall be yours. Have some wine. Catch your breath. Will there be a battle?'

Owein flopped in a chair and rested his aching leg. He accepted the drink, draining it in one go. 'You must leave. The British are attacking at dawn. I expect you've heard the relief cohort from Colonia Lindensium was ambushed? None survived.'

'I heard.' The old man shook his head sadly. 'But why should we flee? What can a woman and a few rabble peasants do to us?'

Owein leaned on his crutch and stood. 'Father in law,' he said carefully, 'The British women aren't like your women, they are trained to war, and this one is exceptional. Camulodunum has no real defences and we're guarded by a few elderly soldiers. Even if Boudica wasn't anyone special, her "rabble" can still do severe damage. Because of her, many good men are now feeding carrion crows. Please, let me find somewhere safe for you and Claudia to hide until this all blows over. What do you say?'

The old man laughed and patted Owein's shoulder. 'Son, many would say that Julius Claudius Metellus has lived too long already. I have commanded the twentieth legion in Deva, I have served in Gaul and Egypt; I've never run away yet. I'll take what's coming. The gods hold my life in their hands. What will be will be. But,' he sighed, 'I would like you to take my daughter and her slave to safety. Look after her well. Be a good husband to her. *Vale.*'

He gripped Owein's arm, and left the room.

Just before dawn, Owein mounted Heather and led two more ponies, each laden with a rider and baggage. They made their way across the heath and along the muddy edges of the water until at long last they came to a shepherd's hut.

There, despite shrill female protestations, they made themselves as comfortable as they could, and waited.

14. DAWN ATTACK

In the deep blue of pre-dawn light, Boudica's warriors crept around the town's barricades, stealthily choosing hollows or patches of scrub to hide and wait for the signal. The soft clink of armour and weapons was scarcely audible above the first hints of dawn chorus.

The eastern sky paled. Epona's white coat almost shone with a light of its own as Tegen rode towards Camulodunum's northern gate. Her heart drummed under her embroidered robes and Boudica's bracelet weighed heavily on her arm.

Tegen had risen early and completed as many rituals as she could think of. Then she found a grassy bank. There she sat, closed her eyes and breathed deeply.

Using her new powers, she imagined the town's street quite empty. Her mind's eye saw a few guards, of course that was unavoidable, she told herself. Next came a battle. 'It will be short,' she whispered, 'and afterwards there must be a cleansing fire, like at Samhain. That will make way for a new beginning.'

Tegen stood, brushed herself down, and beckoned to her servant for Epona.

Mounting, she rode towards the town and the red glow of the watchmen's braziers. 'Have I really done my best to warn people?' she wondered. 'Could I have sent secret messages? But how, and to whom?'

Owein was right; she'd dabbled in theatrics. She should take up juggling, not druidry.

She wished she'd tried harder to speak with Goban at Boudica's stronghold; she shouldn't have let herself be distracted. He'd have told her what to do.

The morning sky was bleeding crimson. It was all too late now.

Everyone was waiting for Tegen's signal. Even Boudica.

Ahead, the gateway was blocked with wooden planks. Behind it were terrified men and boys. Tegen could sense their fearful prayers. She could imagine their sweat, their shaking hands and dry mouths. Why had they stayed? Duty or love?

She summoned up a picture of the last defenders fleeing, but the image was dull and flat. It was not a true seeing.

'This magic must obey me. It's *got* to ...' she whispered.

On the eastern horizon, a tiny glimmer of golden light told her it was time. Tegen rode to the northern gate. There she dismounted.

Holding a small yew branch high, she split the wood with her knife and tore it into two. Laying one piece each side of the road, she called out, 'The way to Tir na nÓg is open. Warriors of the Goddess, I command you to become the *cŵn annwn*, the hounds of death. It is time to drive these unclean souls home!'

And may their journey there be swift, safe and sure, she muttered under her breath. May they be reborn in happier times.

She nodded to her servant who lifted a ram's horn and gave three blasts. There were answering calls from all around the city, a thousand shouts and Boudica's first wave of warriors swarmed down the hill with bloodcurdling cries.

Just then, an arrow-flock of geese flew across the reddened sky. The billowing smoke from bonfires at the gates made them scatter, honking angrily.

'That's a good sign at least – the enemies will soon be dispersed,' Tegen said.

Closing her eyes, Tegen's mind watched as Boudica's warriors, hair limed and faces painted with woad, flung themselves on the defenders' spears and gladii. Brave young boys with sharpened spikes stabbed at their enemies, but they were no match for the flood of full grown men and women who came on and on in relentless waves.

I must end this slaughter quickly, Tegen thought, opening her eyes once more.

She had chosen the northern gate because it symbolised stone and death. It was also on the lower slopes of the city. Behind her, the river ran seawards – a strong path for dying souls. She looked up at Camulodunum and imagined the great curved theatre walls and the red roof and white columns of the temple where the women and children were hiding.

For now, they were safe.

But their menfolk weren't.

Tegen straightened her back and tried to shut out the bellowing screams as the battle raged on only a few arrowshots away. 'I must concentrate,' she told herself as flashes of axes, slings and stones streamed into her head. Then she saw stumbling old men and wild-eyed grandsons fighting with anything that came to hand. Blocking, flinging, jabbing.

On and on stormed Boudica's warriors, breaking bone and ripping flesh.

'May you all be safe in the arms of your gods,' Tegen prayed, but her mind knew differently. She vomited and spat bile.

She hated 'seeing'. She was beginning to realise that Aodh's magic of 'imagining' only applied to death and destruction.

It was not a gift she relished, but now she had it, she must learn to control it and use it for good.

More unbidden images swarmed into her mind – women and children dragged from basements, their throats cuts.

Tegen clutched at her eyes. '*No!*' she yelled. 'Stop thinking like that and it won't happen! Concentrate on the city being empty, imagine it – everyone fled, except maybe a few brave souls left to make a show. Imagine *that* and all will be well.'

But it was not so, and could not be so. Even *her* powers could not change what was already happening ...

The chilly dawn wind brought her back to her duty. Best

to finish everything quickly. Tegen sighed and unhooked a basket from Epona's saddle. Inside was everything she needed to perform the ritual she dreaded.

She clicked her fingers and her servant boy placed a pot of hot charcoal and a bag of dried moss by her feet.

The sun was warming the day, but Tegen's teeth chattered as she drew a sacred circle with her staff. At the northern edge she placed a skull. In the east she tipped a little incense over the hot embers. For the south she placed a candle, flint and tinder, then in the west, she poured water into a silver bowl. Standing in the centre, she closed her eyes and breathed deeply. This was her first real trial as battle druid. She must dance the Star Dance. She must not fail Britain.

She imagined the countryside green, with crops growing and good weather. She saw plump, healthy children, happy parents and the elderly still strong enough to work. She thought of traders, visitors, and marriages with handsome men and women from other tribes and countries. That was good – that made stronger children and brought new skills.

But no more invasions, no more death.

Tears trickled down her face. The imagining was stiff and flat. Some things simply could never be.

Tegen did not notice the thin wisp of early morning mist drifting across the heath land, but her mind heard the soft whisperings: *Imagine the figures you made and crushed. Imagine death. Imagine fire! Make it come to pass.*

Without meaning to, she remembered the flames of

Sinodun and Dorcic.

Close by, something crackled. A hot cinder pricked her hand. Tegen smelled burning.

The fire pot had tipped on its side and the red-hot charcoal had spilled on the moss. Yellow tongues of flame licked the dry heather and fern. Fanned by the wind, the fire was spreading.

'Damn! Look what my imaginings have done now! I haven't even finished my ritual,' she muttered.

She shoved the boy back. 'Run!' she yelled. 'Back to camp.' Then pulling off her cloak, Tegen whacked at the flames, but they raged hot and high, hungry for the gorse and scrub. Sparks leaped, catching quickly.

Tegen sprang back to the road and watched as the wind swirled the roaring inferno towards the town.

Black smoke curled into the pale sky. Epona whinnied and Tegen coughed. She couldn't breathe. Glowing ash scorched her skirt and hair. She had to run, but where? The way back to the camp was already alight, as was the road to Camulodunum. There was only the river ...

The river! That was it.

Tegen faced north, pulled her cloak over her head and crouched down low.

'Fire will bring an easy victory,' Tegen told herself, 'but only by making a pyre for British and Roman alike.' She gritted her teeth. 'The only fire must be afterwards – to cleanse.'

Tegen took a deep, choking breath and then she blew,

long and hard.

In that moment the wind changed, sweeping the scarlet flames towards the water. Tegen watched until she was certain that the blaze had moved away, leaving the heath blackened and sour.

15. TEGEN'S REWARD

Tegen grabbed Epona's reins and ran uphill across the hot, blackened ground. At last she reached the charred gates, defended only by a few blackened corpses. Inside the wrecked palisade, the houses were untouched by flames but ash swirled in the air, falling as grey snow.

The streets were empty. Here and there, a few Romans were lying dead, but that was all. She had saved the town, but had her most important spell worked? Had the townspeople fled? Ahead and to her left, she could hear shouting and cheering. Passing the high-walled theatre to her right, she came out onto the temple steps.

Below, the square was packed with warriors and chieftains.

Two men were lifting Boudica onto the plinth where Victory had once stood. Her great cloak flapped like a single dark wing. She spread her arms wide and her warriors cheered.

Tegen shook her head. 'She's the same as the old "Victory" – just different robes!'

From the back of her mind crept a picture of the queen lying spread-eagled face down, where the cold marble now lay shattered. She will die before it's over, Tegen thought, but for now, I must imagine her triumphant, laden with gold and silver, surrounded by exultant crowds.

Just then, Tegen's thoughts were interrupted by Sabrina,

her face flushed with excitement. 'There you are! The queen wants to honour you. Come.' Taking her friend's hand, she led her towards the plinth.

Boudica looked down. 'All hail the battle druid who brought us this victory,' she proclaimed.

Tegen was lifted onto burly shoulders. Underfoot, the pavement shook with cheering.

For good manners' sake, Tegen smiled and inclined her head.

Boudica went on: 'The place is deserted! Our warriors have searched every house and killed the few that remained, but they were weak and elderly. What did you do with the vermin that lived here Tegen? Have they been spirited away? Where could so many people hide? Our patrols picked off those who tried to flee last night, their corpses are feeding the crows this morning, but there must be more! Use your skills, find the people so they may take the taste of British iron to the Otherworld!'

Tegen's mouth went dry. She must distract the queen from the temple where she knew so many had been herded in the dark hours. 'I will walk though the town and read the signs the spirits have left,' she answered. 'May Sabrina, Queen of the Dobunni accompany me? Anyone else who wishes may come also.'

Soon Tegen was leading Boudica's warriors along the streets. 'Search each house again,' she ordered. 'Enjoy whatever loot you find there, it's your just reward.'

Then maybe you'll be distracted by drink and forget

what you're about, she reasoned silently.

The men smashed at doors without even trying them, then the ransacking began.

'Look at this!' someone shouted, flinging crockery into the street.

'Wine in this one!' a man hollered, and there was a stampede for a share.

Tegen ignored them, stepping over debris and the few corpses: trying not to throw up when she slipped on the guts of a disembowelled woman, or accidentally kicked a loose head.

Sabrina was full of chatter about how the fight had gone. 'There were a few old men at each gate,' she said, 'We burst in like a great wave on the Rearing River! We were magnificent!'

'Did you have to fight like heroes?' Tegen asked quietly.

Sabrina scratched her chin thoughtfully. 'No ... I suppose it was a bit disappointing really. All we found were the sick and a handful of boys with sticks.'

A young man ran past carrying an oil jar in his arms. Sabrina grinned cheerfully. 'But the looting's been good.'

Sabrina was a warrior. This was her life; this was who she was. Tegen tried to share her friend's delight, but her stomach churned at the stench of death and faeces. She would never get used to it.

They tramped the whole town, street by street. All around, the warriors were smashing and stealing. From time to time Sabrina stopped to examine bodies that lay in the street. If life was still lingering, she sent each soul on its way to rebirth, Roman and British alike.

'You're a true warrior, Sabrina,' Tegen said, adding prayers and blessings. 'The spirits will repay your kindness.'

Her friend nodded. 'One of them might be my brother in the next life, I don't want to make trouble for myself!' Then she laughed and helped herself to a handful of fruit from a spilled basket. She offered some to Tegen, but she refused.

'There's to be a feast tonight, once we're sure the place is clear. Boudica has ordered that everyone in the camp may come and help themselves. You can sacrifice some animals for us and do your augury, then we'll eat until we burst.'

Tegen shuddered at the thought of more killing – even of animals. The way the hot blood spurted made her long to eat only bread and parsnips for the rest of her life. 'What then?' she managed to say.

'After the feast? Oh, then the fun begins, Addedomaros, the Trinovantian high chieftain, has asked for the privilege of opening up the temple and taking the first loot.'

A picture of women and children lying slaughtered on the white marble steps flashed into Tegen's mind. 'That must not be!' she told herself as she struggled to turn the image into a scene of warriors laden with gold. But she knew what she had seen.

She swallowed hard. 'Why does the privilege belong to the Trinovantes?'

Sabrina laughed, showing the gaps in her front teeth.

'Because their taxes paid for the place – and their slave labour built it. It's only right they should take it all back!'

Tegen understood the justice, but her mind floundered to think of how to save the people she knew were huddled inside.

All around, the streets were filling up with hangers-on from the camp. The bustle and shove made walking uncomfortable. 'I'm going back to the temple square,' Tegen said. 'I left Epona there, and there's something I need to do.'

Sabrina smiled and jumped through an open shop front. 'Here,' she called out, 'catch this!'

For one awful moment, Tegen thought she was being thrown a human head, but it was a whole cheese. She didn't want it. She couldn't eat knowing the slaughter that was about to happen. Handing the food to a pregnant woman who was rummaging amongst some broken jars, Tegen strode back to the square.

I should have *noticed* they hadn't touched the temple, Tegen berated herself. But it's not too late …

She pushed and shoved through the assembling crowds until she reached the temple's polished bronze doors. Breaking them down wasn't going to be easy.

Maybe high chieftain Addedomaros won't get in, she thought hopefully. Then when we've gone, everyone will escape.

She knew that was wishful thinking, but until her vision became reality she'd fight with everything she had.

For the first time in too long, Tegen stood still.

I need somewhere to be alone, she thought. I need space and quiet to create a proper image. I have to prevent this slaughter.

At last Tegen found a small garden at the back of a shop. Vines heavy with purple grapes hung over a small pool. She sat on the parapet and closed her eyes. Concentrate! She told herself. *Make* a good outcome happen. You have the gift of imagining, learn how to use it. Don't let it use you!

Sitting quietly, she replaced the picture of slaughter on the temple steps with a new scene – a glade of trees where the prisoners sat quietly.

When Tegen returned, Boudica looked up from examining a basket of treasure by her knee. She broke into a welcoming smile and handed Tegen a second golden bangle. 'And your rewards will be greater than these,' she said, 'take what you like. The rumors about you weren't exaggerated. You were magnificent!'

Tegen did not want to offend, so she slipped the gift onto her wrist and kissed the queen's cheek. As a druid she was equal to nobility and had no need to show deference, but what she was about to ask would need all the flattery she could manage.

'Madam, there is one thing I really would like …'

'*Anything*! Just name it!' Boudica smiled with genuine warmth. The morning light glinted on a circlet of blue and red stones in her hair. She was queen of everything and she owed it all to her druid.

Tegen turned to face the crowded square. She tapped a large warrior on the shoulder. 'I need to speak,' she said.

'Silence for the druid!' the man bellowed.

Tegen took her place beside Boudica. She raised her arms so her golden bangles glistened in the sun.

Silence fell.

'By the powers of the Lady Andraste, Goddess of the Iceni, this city has been delivered into the hands of Boudica, and indeed,' she paused and bowed to the gathering, 'into your hands also. This is your day of triumph. I bless your victory and I give you this town!'

Everyone cheered and Tegen waved for silence. 'It has been justly decreed that the temple and any treasures found within it, belong to Addedomaros and his people. They paid for it, they built it with their sweat and toil.' There were more cheers. 'And I bless that too! *But* ...' she paused and looked around, 'Queen Boudica has graciously granted me that I shall take what pleases me as my share of today's riches.'

The crowd hooted and whistled heartily. Tegen took a deep breath. 'The spirits have revealed to me that if anyone should be alive inside the temple, they belong to the Goddess and to her alone! So for her honour, I claim any souls found alive within that place.'

There were more raucous cheers. Tegen glanced back at the queen, but she was talking with an aide and hadn't even been listening. Thank goodness for that, she thought. She won't argue. Now at last I can relax and enjoy the party. Everyone will be safe, but goodness knows what I'm going to do with them, I've never had captives before!

16. TEMPLE TRIBUTES

Boudica and her warriors feasted in the temple square that night. Tables were dragged from the houses and piled with looted food. The nearby farms yielded cattle and goats for roasting; all washed down with Roman wine.

Tegen ate at Boudica's side on the Temple's top step. From time to time she thought she heard a child crying from beyond the bronze doors at her back.

'It won't be long now,' she whispered into the fire-lit darkness. 'When they open the temple, I'll make sure you're safe.' For the first time for many, many months, Tegen ate, drank, and after several horns of mead, she even danced.

At midnight, Tegen and Sabrina staggered wearily back to camp, arms round each other's necks.

'You enjoyed yourself tonight, that was good to see,' Sabrina commented as they approached Tegen's tent. 'You need to laugh and dance more often.'

Tegen hiccoughed as she uncurled herself from Sabrina's support. 'I like it when people don't die.'

Sabrina kissed her cheek and shoved her inside. 'This is war. Your soul is too gentle to be a battle druid. Goodnight.' And she closed the tent flap.

When she was alone, Tegen tugged off her boots and pulled her blanket over her shoulders. 'I'm not too gentle,' she whispered into her pillow. 'I just do things differently.

Tomorrow, everyone in the temple will be led to a sacred grove where they'll be under my protection. If the rest of the campaign can be like this, then I will have a clear conscience.'

But Tegen could not sleep. She wished she could have shared the left over food and drink with the prisoners in the temple. 'They've been in there for a whole day and night,' she mused. 'Conditions must be awful – stinking, longing for water and light ...'

She sat up in bed and imagined a sacred grove – there had to be one nearby.

In her mind, two or three hundred people were lying quietly in groups, glad to be in the sun and air once more. But she was worried about what she was going to do with them. Should she sell them as slaves? They'd never survive a British winter if she just set them free to roam. Slavery was better than destitution.

She yawned and lay down. Tomorrow would be another long day.

At dawn, the horns sounded and Tegen woke with a hangover. She tidied herself and stepped out into the early autumn air. A mist lay in the valley, making the town of Camulodunum look like an island floating between the hills.

Taking her staff and her ritual gear, she made her morning offerings to the spirits. 'Show me what to do with the people that come under my care today,' she prayed.

Then she followed Boudica's warriors as they marched into the town to begin their second day's work.

Most were busy with heaping oil, wine and bright woollen blankets onto carts. Unwanted furniture was dragged into the streets and piled against the house walls. Children climbed onto the thatched roofs and threw straw down to their parents who stacked it between the houses. Mattresses, clothes, everything was heaped outside.

But a deafening banging and crashing drowned out the shouts and chatter. Tegen hurried along the straight streets to the temple. As she entered the square, she saw men with hammers and large pincers stripping bronze from the Temple doors and loading it onto waggons.

On the top steps, high chieftain Addedomaros and his cousin Daig were directing operations. Larch trees had been lashed together to make ladders, and lengths of rope were being handed out amongst the crowd of excited Trinovantian warriors.

At last Daig shouted, 'Pull the carts back! Pile kindling against the doors – no, not like that, leave room for them to open a bit.'

Then Addedomaros, his hair freshly spiked with lime, raised his hands for silence. 'My brothers and sisters of the Trinovantes, this day is yours. This temple is yours. The glory is yours. *TAKE IT ALL!*'

With an answering shout, the crowd drew back and the ladders were raised. The younger, lighter men scaled the walls. Taking hammers from their belts, they smashed the terracotta tiles. Soon there were a dozen large holes in the roof.

Tegen could imagine the stench of urine and fear inside, and the prisoners' mixture of relief at the fresh air and dread of what was coming. 'If only I could tell them it'll be all right,' Tegen whispered. She closed her eyes and reminded herself of the terrified people lying on the grass in the fresh air.

The picture was clear. It would come true.

All will be well, she promised silently. Your souls belong to the spirit of the grove.

The holes in the roof were growing. The young men uncoiled ropes from their waists and tied them to exposed beams, then dropped the free ends down the outside of the walls.

Tegen elbowed her way through the cheering crowd. What was going on? A faggot of dried wood was tied to each rope and then hauled up. Tegen's heart missed a beat. They were going to use fire!

She tried to get through to speak to Addedomaros, to warn him that no lives must be lost, but the excited crowd took no notice of Tegen's shouts. She was just a small young woman drowning in a sea of large, excited men.

Suddenly there was a scream, and a boy on the nearest ladder swayed, toppled, and fell back. An arrow in his chest.

The people inside were armed! The boy had scarcely landed on the ground, before another took his place, hauling firewood up behind him.

More arrows flew. More of the climbers fell. But that only made the crowd nastier. Young men and a few girls were queuing for their chance to scale the walls. More and more wood was tossed inside, followed by small baskets of burning kindling.

Tegen bit her knuckles. The Trinovantes had betrayed their promise. Thick smoke was already billowing from between the roof tiles, carrying screams of terror and agony.

Then one great door creaked open to thunderous applause from the onlookers. The prisoners staggered from the fire into the light.

Tegen elbowed her way to the front of the crowd, then sighed with relief as she saw men binding the captives' hands and looping ropes around their necks.

So maybe this was what Addedomaros had planned? Using small fires to make sure the prisoners came quietly? That's not so bad, Tegen thought. She looked for the little boy she'd shielded from the riot only two days before and wondered whether he was safe.

In the fire-lit gloom of the temple stood the ominous figure of their god, a stone figure in Roman clothes. Tegen turned away in disgust.

A new surge of warriors, forcing their way into the temple, shoved Tegen against a sooty wall. Once more she had to fight her way forward. Breathless and bruised, she managed to stand beside Addedomaros at last. 'What d'you want done with the vermin?' he yelled over the noise.

Smoke filled Tegen's mouth. She spat. 'Take them to a sacred grove,' she shouted back. 'I'll deal with them there.'

The chieftain put two fingers in his mouth and gave a piercing whistle. A man dressed in a plain grey robe came and stood by his side. His ashy hair was tightly bound in a single plait. 'You know my brother, Aodh? He'll see to everything.'

Then Addedomaros turned away to supervise the final destruction of the temple, which was already burning nicely.

A smile flickered across Aodh's face. 'My lady,' he said. 'I trust your new gifts serve you well? What is your will for the prisoners?'

Tegen beckoned him to move away from the noise, but just as they were about to speak, a boy came running up to her.

'Are you the druid lady?' he panted. 'Boudica wants you. *Now!*' He pointed to the front porch of a tavern where the queen sat drinking with Sabrina, watching the Trinovantes' triumph.

'Tell her I must finish one sacred duty, and then I will come.' Tegen turned back to Aodh. 'Take them to the grove of Andraste, feed them and give them water. Have them well guarded. Spill no blood. Their lives are sacred to the Goddess.'

'Your will is my will.' The spell-caster's face was unreadable under his dense tattoos. He wove a blessing above Tegen's head, then added, 'As you must speak with Boudica, I will send a servant to show you the way to the grove later. Everything will be done.'

Tegen thought she saw a glint of pleasure in the man's eyes but she had no time to wonder at it. Boudica would be angry if she delayed.

As she approached the tavern, the queen greeted Tegen with a kiss and a drinking horn. 'Swallow it all,' she laughed. 'I like the Romans' wine, but they drink like girls in their prissy little cups. Now, the temple's destroyed and the looting's almost finished ...' She smiled and waved a hand towards the heaps of furniture and straw. 'The bonfires are ready to light. When will you perform the final ritual?'

Tegen pretended to drink the blood red liquor as she tried to concentrate. Images of the prisoners being led away crowded her head. She could think of nothing else. Something was wrong, but what?

'I will destroy the town at sunset,' she replied handing the horn to a servant. 'Will that be enough time to clear the booty and make sure everyone has gone?'

Boudica nodded. 'Do you need anything? Would you like some of the prisoners for sacrifices to seal your curses?'

Tegen shook her head. 'I have all I need, thank you. There'll be no moon until the middle of the night, so we'll light the fires at moonrise when the magic is strongest. When I have finished, the Time of Stone will be proclaimed. Everything must be left empty until Imbolg, then the town will be cleansed and ready to belong to its own people once more. Meanwhile, I need to rest and prepare. Will you excuse me?'

Boudica gripped Tegen's hand. 'When I first met you ... I misunderstood. I was terribly wrong and I'm sorry. Now I trust you above all my counsellors.'

'Thank you,' Tegen said. 'I swear I will do my best for Britain.'

She walked back to the western gate through the streets, weaving her way through the stacks of thatching, beds and chairs. Now and then the sight of a doll or a toy horse bought tears to her eyes. But she had no time to be sentimental. These fires would destroy everything and wipe the slate clean, then everyone could begin again without the past dragging them into the mire of memories.

At moonrise, Camulodunum would burn.

17. THE BURNING

At sunset, Tegen woke and dressed in her white robe and Boudica's bracelets. As the sky darkened and the stars came out, she made her way to the northern gate of Camulodunum.

In her mind's eye saw the sun rising on a charcoal barren waste. She knew it would be so.

Once more she split a yew branch into two and laid it either side of the road. She wanted to ensure that whatever spirits were left would have a safe passage to Tir na nÓg. There must be no malicious ghosts around to pursue the warriors and their families, or to haunt the town's remains, terrorising any Trinovantes who chose to rebuild. Picking her way across the dark, flint-strewn moorland, she walked widdershins to the western gate, then the south and finally the east. At each one she laid a spell that forbade any except the living to pass. No spirits could escape into the surrounding countryside.

Tegen raised her staff and entered the town, summoning any lost souls and showing them the way they must go. A cool breeze sighed through her short hair as the dead brushed past her, drifting away in the starlit darkness.

She stood, head bowed, unmoving. 'May you be born again soon,' she called after them. Then, weaving a spell of closure, she shut that way to Tir-na-nÓg.

The night was silent. Not even a birdcall to break the emptiness: only the shattered gates creaking uselessly in the wind.

Tegen took a deep breath. It was safe to burn the place now. Everyone had gone. 'One day, you will be rebuilt,' she promised. 'Perhaps with another name, in another time, with green fields and no need for gates and walls?' She couldn't be sure, the image was misty, difficult to fix and far off.

Anyway, she had other matters to attend to.

Grasping her staff, Tegen walked carefully along Camulodunum's cobbled streets, wary of debris and bodies in her path. The starlight only gave a very pale impression of where to put her feet. The pungent-sweet smell of smouldering wood drifted down from the temple.

At least I prevented that massacre. She smiled. I'll just have to be careful what I imagine. I must rein in my anger and bitterness. No curses where they aren't deserved.

The town square was lit by red and gold light from a bonfire where a few warriors were on guard. Deep shadows danced on their cloaks and the woad on their faces swirled. Those with limed hair looked like surprised skulls hovering in the dark.

Boudica was there as well, seated on a carved wooden throne. Imperious and drunk.

Tegen faced the queen across the fire. The gold on her wrist jingled and glowed as she raised her staff. 'Hail Victory!' she called loudly.

'Hail Boudica!' the warriors roared their reply.

'Hail to the Goddess Andraste,' Tegen continued. She was uneasy about Boudica's bloodthirsty goddess, but now was not the time for discussion.

'Hail Andraste!' came the reply.

Tegen stared into the crackling flames, and watched. In their bright tongues she saw darkness and ashes where Camulodunum now stood. It's probably for the best, Tegen thought. Now is the Time of Stone – a spiritual winter. Wipe the Land clean and start again in the spring.

She raised her head and her voice. 'I see these streets as ashes, and the houses will blow as dust in the wind,' she proclaimed.

Everyone cheered.

Using her staff, Tegen wove a spell in the air above the fire, and then calling for drum music, she danced widdershins against the sun's path. Her movements were sharp and brittle as she span in an ever-widening spiral, unwinding magic behind her, undoing everything that the Romans had ever made in this place. At last, in her mind's eye she could only see emptiness.

She stopped, stamped and held her pose.

That is sufficient for now, she thought. Spells for rebuilding will be the task of another druid. Not me.

She didn't like leaving a sacred pathway open, but she knew a culvert had to be left in place to drain all hatred and bitterness from the town. Without it there would be a wound in the Land that would fester and rot, spreading a gangrene of hatred and revenge that would curse the living for generations.

'I'll come back and close the spiral when the fire's cooled,' she promised. Then with the heel of her shoe, she marked the ground with an entry-mark, ensuring that the door she had made to the spirit kingdom would only be an inward portal. Nothing could escape from Tir na nÓg into the human world.

Tegen turned to the assembled crowd. As she had hoped, the moon was just rising in the southeast. It was now time to begin the cleansing and healing. 'The spell is complete,' she announced. 'Set fire to the town, but leave quickly.'

Horns winded and the assembled warriors lit torches from the bonfires. Brandishing their flames, they ran from street to street, whooping and shouting as the piled kindling caught. Red, gold and yellow leaped up into the night sky. Smoke rose to smother the stars and red cinders winked and span away.

As Tegen's widdershins spiral uncoiled its sacred path, the gates of Tir na nÓg opened to admit the remaining spirits.

The demon heard the spells and followed the stench of mage-craft.

At the gateway, Tegen's entry-mark blocked its escape.

The demon clawed and whimpered, but it could not pass the seal she had made in the dust of Camulodunum.

Tegen was alone in the square. She sighed and blessed the fire. 'May you cleanse this Land,' she said. 'Make it new so we may live again.' Ashes floated like crows' feathers, black on white in the moonlight.

Trapped so close to its quarry, the demon's fury exploded into flames and earthquake.

As Tegen turned to go, the walls of the nearest house burst into woven fire. With a crash, a roof beam fell into the street, smashing into a thousand flaming daggers.

Tegen staggered back, struggling to breathe. She sank to her knees, remembering the sacred fire spiral she had walked a year before. 'The flames shouldn't have caught this quickly,' she gasped. 'I must keep low and stay calm.'

Another beam crashed by her head. She rolled backwards, sparks in her hair and clothes. Hot and singeing. Soot caught in her eyes and throat. She was choking ...

'*Tegen*!' a voice yelled. Strong hands caught her.

As she was dragged clear, her left foot unmade her spell.

In the sour, stifling smoke she did not notice.

And the demon danced free in the fires of the town.

18. THE GROVE OF ANDRASTE

Cool dawn air soothed Tegen's exhausted lungs and the chilly damp of the ground seeped through her robe, cooling her skin. She opened her eyes. She was lying on the blackened heath. Above her flapped a cloak woven with dark and light green, crossed by blue, gold, yellow and black.

She knew those colours had meant something to her once …

'Thanks,' she said quietly. 'I owe you my life.'

The cloaked figure turned, crouched down and smiled. 'Once again – yes.' It was Owein.

Her heart missed a beat.

'I always seem to be pulling you out of fires,' he said gently. 'You should make your offerings to the spirits of the south more carefully.' He plucked at her white robe. 'Especially as you're a full druid now.'

Tegen winced. He was a traitor and the last person she wanted to see, but she was too dazed to move. 'Why are you dressed as a Briton?' she seethed.

He handed her a leather water bottle. 'Because I *am* British, as you well know!' he retorted. 'And if you'd listened last time we met, you'd know that I've been a double agent for the Trinovantes for many moons.'

Tegen sat up and drank. 'What about your precious new

129

Roman family?'

'Some are dead and the rest are safe. There are none you need worry about.'

She narrowed her eyes. 'So why did you decide to join us all of a sudden? Scared?'

Owein raised his eyebrows. 'Because I don't want the Romans here any more than you do, but while they *are* here, I'll use my Roman upbringing to help my people in any way I can. *Any* way, do you understand that? If sometimes I have to wear a toga and recline on a couch at dinner, I will. If I have to don my cloak and take up a long-sword I'll do that as well. You'll just have to trust me, Tegen.'

'Why should I?' she scowled.

'Quite simply - if I wanted the Romans to win, I'd have let you die under that burning wall,' Owein replied. 'The death of the Star Dancer would have demoralised Boudica's rabble and this rebellion would have fallen apart by dawn.' Leaning on his crutch, Owein got to his feet and offered Tegen a hand up. His face was solemn and pale.

'Why don't you just thank the Goddess that Heather and I were there to save you?'

'I don't believe in the Goddess. Or if she's real, she can't be bothered to help.'

Tegen struggled to her feet and hobbled over to where Owein's pony was cropping grass. She stroked her nose. 'Thanks Heather,' she said. 'I owe you some crab apples.' Then she bowed formally to Owein. 'I offer you my thanks,

Owein Sextus. Now I must get back.'

'Wait, I'm coming with you,' he said.

Ignoring him, Tegen strode away towards Boudica's camp on top of the hill.

Owein called after her, 'Before you go running back to that carrion crow, I need to show you something. It's important.'

His voice was heavy with what sounded like grief.

She stopped and looked into Owein's eyes. He was once her dearest friend, someone she had trusted – and loved too, in a way. Old emotions of warmth, stirred once more. He used to make sense – she owed him the courtesy of a hearing at least.

'I'm sorry. I was rude. It was just a shock seeing you yesterday all draped up and with that other … Roman.'

'His name was Claudius. He never hated our people. In fact, he encouraged me to stand between the British and Romans and broker some sort of understanding,' Owein replied quietly. He swung himself into Heather's saddle. 'And … if he'd lived, he'd have been my father in law.'

Tegen stared at him open mouthed. I mustn't jump to conclusions, she reminded herself.

After several heartbeats she took a deep breath. 'I do trust you,' she said. 'You've saved my life twice, for which I give you every blessing and thanks. And I really am sorry for my rudeness. You're right. It's time we talked – properly.'

'Apology accepted.' He bowed formally.

'I still think you'd have been a splendid king.' Tegen smiled. 'Now, what do you want to show me?'

Ignoring her comment about kingship, Owein kicked Heather's flanks and they set off through the woods.

'So, tell me about how you got engaged?' Tegen asked.

Owein shook his head, and replied 'Later,' rather tersely. Then he rode on in silence.

Tegen walked a little behind him, confused and worried. Why did he want to talk to me, now he's saying nothing? She wondered. Then she noticed how stooped his shoulders were. It's as if he's carrying a great weight, she thought. The grief of the battle? Is his fiancée really safe?

Soon they came to a small valley with a spring and a stream at the bottom. Here the scrub and undergrowth had been cleared, revealing a sheep-nibbled lawn edged by oak trees. A druid's grove.

Owein dismounted and gestured Tegen forwards. 'You need to see this, better than me telling you,' he said quietly.

Gathered in small groups around the grove were about two hundred people. Some were elderly, the rest women and children: the temple prisoners. Their clothes and hair were sooty and unkempt, but just as Tegen had imagined, they were peacefully leaning against trees or lying on the grass. By each group was a water bucket and the remains of a meal.

'Oh! My captives!' Tegen gasped, delighted. 'Thank you Owein, I'd wanted to find them this morning. I don't know what I'm going to do with them, but I saved them by dedicating them to the Goddess. I didn't want innocent people to die!'

Owein went very pale, then he sighed. 'Stop talking Tegen – just look – and listen.'

No one was moving. All were silent and still.

'Are they all asleep?' Tegen asked.

'What do you think?' Owein raised an eyebrow.

A chill ran down Tegen's spine. 'What's wrong with them?'

Owein pointed to the closest group. 'Ask them.'

Tegen ran down the slope and put her hand on the shoulder of a woman to wake her, but she was cold and stiff. Tegen turned to a small boy curled up with his brother. Their waxen faces had a bluish tinge around their lips. There was vomit on the grass.

With tears in her eyes, Tegen walked from group to group. Mostly it was the same story. They had been poisoned, although here and there a throat had been cruelly bruised. Probably those who hadn't died quickly enough.

'Who has done this?' she demanded, clenching and unclenching her fists. 'I'll personally poison whoever's responsible! My prisoners' lives were sacred!' She threw back her head and bellowed, 'Come out you murderers … NOW!'

But there was only the rustle of frightened birds rising from the branches above.

Owein limped painfully to Tegen's side. His eyes were red and wet.

She grabbed his tunic and shook him. 'Tell me! What do you know about this? Who did this?'

He pointed to a baby lying in its mother's arms, dried milk crusted on its lips. 'In a way, this was your doing.'

Tegen stepped back, eyes wide in horror. '*Me*? What are you talking about?'

'This is the Grove of Andraste: the Goddess in her guise of war. By dedicating the prisoners to the Lady, the guardian of the Grove would automatically have assumed you meant them to be sacrificed to her.'

'But I gave clear instructions no blood was to be spilled.' Tegen choked as bile rose in her throat.

Owein took her shoulders and looked into her eyes. 'And no blood was spilt. That's why they were poisoned. When I found this grove, I thought it was a sick joke of Boudica's. I wanted to show you what she's really like. You've got to believe me Tegen, the queen is not a good woman.' He waved his hand across the scene. 'I know you would have meant kindly bringing these people here. Whoever had charge of them knew exactly what you meant, but chose – or was told – to do this anyway.'

Tegen closed her eyes. Her voice was choking. 'It was Aodh,' she said. 'He offered to look after them. I thought he had a funny smile when he took them away. I should have thought – he's Trinovantes – and Addedomaros's brother. He'd have been longing for vengeance. I'm so sorry, I didn't mean …' And she began to cry.

Owein put an arm around her. 'I have heard of Aodh,

he's not to be trusted. 'Now, you've had an awful shock, I will take you back. Bel's chariot is high and Boudica will be wanting you to concoct another curse or something.'

'First I must pray for the souls of these poor people,' Tegen said. 'Lend me your water bottle.' She filled it from the spring, and trickled a few drops on the heads of each of the victims. 'May the spirits of the west take you home, may you be reborn soon in a happier place,' she whispered as she worked.

At last she followed Owein as he hauled himself up the hill and through the woods to where Heather was waiting. They made their way back to the camp in silence, but at last Owein asked, 'You really didn't know what was happening to those people, did you?'

'Of course not!' Tegen snapped.

'Haven't you *seen* what Boudica and her people are like?'

'I have. I don't like them.'

'Then why do you work for them?'

Tegen shook her head. 'The same as you, I suppose. I'm hoping to bring some sort of sanity into the madness.' She paused then thinking of the clay figures she had made and smashed, she added, 'As well as that, I'm very angry and I have made curses, terrible ones. Do you mind if I tell you … things?'

Owein reached down and took Tegen's hand. As he rode and she walked, she poured out her heart about Mona and Tonn's death, but she didn't mention her baby. She wasn't quite ready for that.

'I wanted to go back to Ériu,' she said at last, 'But I have a destiny to fulfil, and unless I complete what I was born to do, I shall never find peace … So, I became Boudica's battle druid.'

Owein nodded sadly. 'I understand. We are all playing parts we would never have chosen for ourselves in this deadly game.'

Too soon, they realised they were close to Boudica's sprawling camp. Owein dismounted and they sat by a steep sided rill and let Heather drink.

At last Owein said, 'I understand why this revolt has happened. The people are angry: it isn't just Boudica who's been deprived of her kingdom, been publicly flogged and watched her girls raped by slaves. The injustices are endless and I want to fight to make things right, but not by slaughtering women and children. Do you know why she ordered the burning of Camulodunum?'

'I agreed with that – it was to cleanse the Land,' Tegen replied.

Owein laughed. 'You are such an innocent Tegen! No, she was doing what she had learned from her Roman friends. If you want to destroy a place you make it uninhabitable. That breaks the people's spirit. Winter is coming; the solstice is in half a moon. Then Samhain – then winter. You've seen how it works. This is not the season for campaigning: it is the time for destruction and making people lose heart. She's forcing a Time of Stone onto Britain and Imbolg is a long way off.'

Tegen picked up a stick and threw it into the stream by their feet. She had thought a Time of Stone would be good – rest before rebirth. She hadn't seen it from the other point of view. In her heart she could hear old Gronw ticking her off for not listening to the Goddess – but she'd tried that and the Lady hadn't answered.

She longed for the luxury of time to feel the weave of magic in the air, to understand its patterns and to unpick any threads that were awry. But everything was unfolding too fast. Gronw would say there was always time to listen; she just had to make room for it. She buried her head in her hands and sighed.

Putting his arm around her, Owein said, 'I pass equally well as a Roman and a British nobleman. Bring me into camp with you. With your magic and my Latin, we will work together to control Boudica's madness and free Britain. Persuade her to let me mediate or at least spy. Daig and Addedomaros will vouch for me.'

Tegen shook her head. 'It won't work. Her spies will know about your Roman fiancée. She'll have you killed.'

He took her hand and squeezed it. 'Tegen, the evil you were born to avert is here. How many people can you really trust? Vouch for me before the queen. Let me help.'

After a pause, she nodded. 'I will. Now, if you have your Roman clothes with you, I'll need to hide them with a glamour. If they are found, we'll both be dead.'

19. A SECOND DRUID

Tegen and Owein picked their way through the outer ring of carts and waggons, where warrior families were sorting through heaps of booty. Loud arguments were raging over clothes, pottery, jewellery, mirrors, and even Roman couches.

Tegen winced as she passed a row of war chariots sporting severed heads impaled on spears. Late flies swarmed on the blackened stumps and crawled over dully-staring eyes.

In a clear space, children were kicking a skull around while parents watched, drinking and boasting about their part in the battle.

At last, Tegen led Owein to her tent, a fine ridgepole structure with sides and ends. Behind it, Epona chewed contentedly at a heap of hay. They tied Heather next to her and dragged Owein's panniers inside. He sat on one, while Tegen knelt on her bed of furs.

'It's quite a change from some of the places we camped!' Owein said with admiration.

'Being Boudica's battle druid has its advantages.' She smiled as she passed him bread, fruit and water. 'We'll have to think up a reason for you to be here otherwise you'll have to sleep where you can with the hangers-on. With your bad leg, no one'll mistake you for a new recruit and a wounded warrior is worse than useless here.'

'Tell the truth: I'm an old friend who's offering his services as a druid,' Owein suggested. 'And if any spies have been watching me they'll know I was captured at the sacking of Sinodun and forced into a Roman marriage because I'm a minor nobleman. Addedomaros will vouch for my usefulness.'

Tegen nodded as she ate. 'Good. Sabrina is here as well, so with three leading chieftains on your side, you might even get Boudica to listen to your ideas. We'll go and see her when we've eaten. How shall I introduce you to Boudica? Shall you be Caractacus's son?'

Owein's face broadened into a wide grin. 'Sabrina? How wonderful, I can't wait to speak with her. But just introduce me as Owein, of the Catuvellauni. I'll wear a plain cloak. I'd rather be incognito until I have my bearings in this game.'

They found the queen seated outside her tent, receiving tributes of gold, silver and spices from the chieftains. A small man at her side was making a tally with a knife on a strip of wood. When Boudica saw Tegen approaching, she jumped to her feet. 'My battle druid!' she laughed, slapping her on the back. 'Who's this? Have you found yourself a new man?'

Tegen smiled. 'No, this is Owein, an old friend and a druid-ovate of the Catuvellauni. He begs leave to join us, my lady.'

Boudica clapped her hands. 'Bring wine and meat. This is excellent news. I love magic. The more workers of wonders I have on my side, the better!'

'I specialise in law and poetry, madam.' Owein smiled as he accepted a cup of wine. 'And should it be any use, I also have a smattering of Latin,' he lowered his voice, 'I had an uncle who taught me. He said it might be useful one day.' He spat and made the sign against the evil eye.

Just then, Sabrina came running, her dark curls flying. 'Tegen!' she yelled, 'I thought it was you! Splendid curses over the last few days! Will ...'

She stopped as she saw Owein, her breath caught in her throat.

Boudica saw the stunned look that passed between the two and gripped her dagger hilt.

But Sabrina flung herself at Owein and hugged him. 'You're *alive*!' she squealed.

He hugged her back. 'We must talk,' he whispered.

Sabrina kissed him on the cheek and then gave him a playful slap. 'That's for making me worry about you.'

Boudica leaned back in her chair and watched in amazement. 'So,' she began, 'how do you two know each other?'

'This is my foster-brother, Owein, he's ...' Owein shook his head at her, so she added, 'by the gods, man, you're almost as bald as a Roman, what happened to your gorgeous hair?'

Owein smiled. 'It's a long story, I'll tell you later.'

Just then a servant joined them. 'Lady,' he said, 'a chieftain from the Cornovii has arrived with a war band wishing to join the rebellion.'

'Bring him here and feed his warriors.' Boudica waved her hand at Sabrina and Owein. 'You three obviously have much to catch up on, you are excused.'

'Come to my tent and drink wine,' Sabrina said, catching hold of Owein's hand and tugging him playfully.

He pulled her towards him and hugged her waist. 'No,' he murmured in her ear, 'tents make voices louder. I have secrets to tell, let's go for a walk. Tegen, you must come too.'

'Don't you two want to be alone?' she hesitated, thinking that fur might fly when Sabrina discovered he was betrothed to someone else.

'No!' Owein said firmly. 'We must work together. There must be no secrets between us.'

They chose a track that lead up onto the heath and walked slowly enough for Owein to keep up on his crutch.

Sabrina spoke first, telling Owein of her capture after Admidios's trap, her life as a gladiatorix and how she'd met Tegen and Tonn after the slaughter of the druids on Mona. 'So when I heard of the rebellion, well … ' She slapped her sword, 'It was obvious I had to stand with my sister-queen!'

When Sabrina finished, Owein described his capture after Sinodun's destruction. 'I realised that with Admidios dead, I was in a good position to work with the Romans to ensure some sort of justice for the British.' He shrugged. 'It was collaborate or die, really. I chose to try and do some good.' Then he turned to Sabrina, and with an apologetic look he added, 'I had no idea you were still alive. I have promised to marry a Roman girl, the daughter of an important man. She was his only child and I was to become an administrator – a *quaestor*. I don't care for titles or money, as you know, but it was a good opportunity to fight for justice – and for spying. Over the summer I have been helping the Trinovantes as much as I can. I believe I've saved some lives.'

Tegen held her breath and waited for Sabrina to explode. Her father, King Eiser of the Dobunni had betrothed her to Owein, hoping an alliance between his daughter and the only surviving son of the great Caractacus, would bring a lasting peace between the tribes.

But Sabrina laughed and punched his shoulder. 'That's why I could never marry you! Our ways are too different. You marry your Roman girl if you think it helps and I'll die fighting. You'll always be my favourite brother!' Then she hesitated. 'To be honest, I'm worried about what'll happen when we rid our land of these bastards. I can't see Boudica being strong enough to keep peace between the tribes. We'll need to unite properly to defend ourselves in the future. When that happens, then us kings and queens will count for nothing. There's bound to be Romans left behind with nowhere to go. Britain will have become home to them, they'll think they have a divine right to rule. You understand both sides, Owein; we'll need you to make sense of the mess we're left with.'

Tegen hung back, only half listening to the conversation.

'Hey!' Sabrina called out, 'Don't worry Tegen, we'll always need good druids – whatever happens, you'll have a place in my hall.'

'But I may not be here …'

Owein swung around. 'What do you mean? Have you seen your death?'

'No … It's just that, well, I'm pregnant. When this is over, I want to go back to Ériu with my child and raise him or her amongst Tonn's people. I felt I could belong there. I was almost happy – for a while.'

'You're *pregnant*!' Sabrina gasped. 'I don't know much about babies and things, but shouldn't you be resting?'

Owein eyed Tegen with concern. 'I thought you didn't seem quite yourself. Sabrina's right, you shouldn't be here.'

Tegen shook her head. 'After Tonn's death, the druids tried to make me take herbs to kill my baby, but I refused. It has its own destiny in Ériu. But if I don't fight here, then Rome might cast its shadow there as well. I can't deny I'm the Star Dancer, I have to avert evil – but the spirits have seen fit to give me a child … So, I fight on.'

'I'll tell Boudica, she'll send for someone else,' Sabrina began, but Tegen rounded on her.

'You'll do no such thing. I have new magic that'll work. At last I'm doing what I was born to do, and I will finish it.'

She paused and looked back towards Camulodunum. The red and grey smoke billowed in the afternoon sun. 'I won't be free until the rebellion is over. As soon as the fires cool, I must go back to the town. I have some spells that I want to make sure of. But for now, I'm going back to my tent.'

'I'll come with you,' Owein offered.

'No,' Tegen replied. 'I need to rest and think. You two will fuss like old women. I'm sure you've both got plenty to talk about.'

With that, she strode away downhill.

20. GOLEM

Three days later, the shattered pavements of Camulodunum were almost too hot to walk on. Here and there, fires still burned. Charcoaled posts and pillars pointed skywards like fingers accusing the gods. Collapsed buildings clawed at the sky.

Tegen crouched on the scorched turf inside the ruined palisade and cried for the people and the homes that had once been there, for the murdered victims in the grove, and for herself and her baby who'd be born into a world of war.

Her tears weren't the heart-rending grief and fury she'd wept for Tonn – tears that gouged water from earth and sky.

This time she felt only compassion.

She imagined Camulodunum's heat cooling as springs and wells ran again and grass and weeds sprouted from cracks and corners. As she worked, clouds gathered in the evening sky, and rain fell like divine tears, turning smoke to steam, washing black cinders between red shards of tile and plaster.

Picking her way along the roads, Tegen reached the temple's scorched marble pillars. They stood like giant bones scoured of their flesh. As she crossed the square, shattered roof tiles cracked under her feet. She stared around in horrified awe. The silence was terrifying, broken only by an occasional groan or crash as the town fell apart.

The rain was flecked with ash, filling the air with smoky haze. In every shadow, dark spirits hovered, ones that should have been banished in her sacred spiral.

Why are they still here? Tegen wondered.

She stood amongst the debris and closed her eyes, trying to understand. Owein had been right: the burning had done nothing to cleanse. It had only broken the hearts of those who had once lived here. That's why the spirits had remained. Vengeance had invited them back.

Had that been Boudica's doing or her own? She couldn't remember. The burning had seemed the right thing to do – like the Samhain and Beltane fires.

Did good intentions justify the action?

Did Boudica's vindictiveness turn good to evil?

Or was all of this the result of her curses on the mud soldiers? Everything she'd imagined had indeed come true, like the prisoners in the grove, but at what cost?

Could she really control the chaos as she'd been promised? Her flesh began to creep as she asked herself who – or what – had *made* that promise?

Tegen rubbed her aching head as she made her way back to the temple square. There she commanded fire to re-ignite the ashes. A spiral path of flames without heat gleamed instantly. Fighting despair and weariness, she danced deosil around the pattern. She closed the gateway to Tir na nÓg that she had left open for spirits to retreat.

Maybe that had been the mistake?

Round and round she reversed her steps, but this time her movements were fluid and healing. She leapt through the final circle of fire, and in the centre she knelt on the shattered wing of Victory. There she stared into the curtain of flames.

For the first time since Tonn's death, she found she was really praying. 'Lady Goddess, give me wisdom and inspiration. Show me the weave of the magic that is hanging in the air in this place. Show me *what* I am fighting and what I must do.'

A chilly, rain-laden wind tossed the flames wildly. She was not alone. In the heart of the magic a shape shifted and shimmered. For a moment it was her old enemy Derowen, then it became Gorgans, then Admidios.

The flames danced. Now Tegen saw Enid as she was on Cadair Idris, then Boudica. The wind blew, and there was the form of Suetonius – or was it a huge bear?

The crackling fire laughed.

'How did you get here?' Tegen demanded. 'I made a mark to prevent you ...'

You set me free, the voice whispered. *Anyway, I am not subject to such minor magics. I can be wherever and whatever you want me to be, I will become whatever you imagine. I am your loyal servant,* the voice mocked. *I can show you how much more you can become ...*

Rooted to the spot, Tegen was both horrified and fascinated. 'No,' she answered quietly. 'Go away, I'm not interested.'

But you summoned me, the voice persisted.

'I wanted to know what you are. Now you must go.' She waved her hand. The flames died, but the presence did not.

But I am your own imagination. If I go, so will your powers.

Tegen lifted her chin. 'So be it. For then you will be destroyed. This awful war will be over and my land will find peace. That is all I want.'

The demon sniggered as it shifted through a thousand eerie colours and shapes. *You will never destroy me because there is nothing to destroy. I am pure spirit! I will pursue you through life and death until you serve me!* The voice changed to wheedling: *Let there be peace between us and I shall reward you with riches and unimaginable power.*

'I don't like imagining.' Tegen retorted.

The demon's presence swelled. *But you will love power – once you have tasted it.*

Tegen stepped back and her foot kicked the statue's foot. Of course! she thought. The walking doll, the mud soldiers by the river! I know what to do. It's as clear as day! I'll contain the demon. This'll be the most dangerous spell I'll ever make. If only I could be certain that the Goddess is real and will help me. If she exists, then maybe she will help. But faith in goodness is all I've got. That will have to do.

'Very well!' she said aloud. 'I'll do some imagining and I'll use some power. I'm going to make you a body – one that contains you and your chaos!'

The shimmering shape divided, whirled like autumn leaves and scattered. Was it afraid?

Not stopping to wonder, Tegen took a roof tile and scraped ashes and blood-soaked dirt into a large heap. But the clumps fell apart; it was too wet to use. She ran to the western gate where the fire had not scorched the heath. There she gathered heathers and bracken, withies and hazel switches and brought them back. Ignoring hunger, cold and wet, she worked long into the evening; twisting and weaving a life-size figure of a man around a spine of charcoaled wood.

As she worked, Tegen uttered every entwining, enclosing and capturing spell she knew. Finally she daubed muddy, bloodied ashes into the gaps and smoothed the sooty paste into skin.

This was a golem: the creature that had haunted her dreams.

It had ears and eyes, but no mouth. It was animate, but forbidden speech or independent thought so it could never rule itself. To ensure it couldn't make or handle weapons, she gave it only a plate-like hand. To slow any escape, its feet were mere lumps.

In her mind she saw it standing, walking and silently obeying her every word.

I'll force the demon to inhabit it, she thought. I'll know where it is and what it's doing at all times. I am its creator. It *must* obey me. The demon will be caged. It will do no more evil.

Lastly, she plucked a hair from her own head and pressed it into the mud where a heart would have been.

'You are carrying all the anger and hatred of this war,' she whispered. 'But you will obey me and only me. Remember that.'

The rain, torrential now, hissed and spat against the creature's skin. Tegen stood back, wiped the water from her eyes and smiled at her work.

What are you doing? nagged the voice in her head.

'Don't you know?' she replied.

You have made me a body – if I step inside, you will never control me. A body without animal frailty is exactly what I crave.

'Then you won't object to stepping inside?' Tegen spread her hands and gave a mock bow.

Not at all.

There was a rush of wind and a swirl of mist …

The golem twitched, and moved.

'Are you comfortable?' Tegen enquired sweetly, weaving a locking spell with her hands.

The creature twisted its head but no sound came, either in Tegen's mind, or from the golem itself. Only its eyes glowed with crimson fury.

Excellent, Tegen thought. With swift dancing steps she span a deosil circle around her creation. 'Hold fast! By the power of life and death, I command that you be my slave and obedient servant forever.'

The golem glared at Tegen, unable to protest.

'Stand,' she said. Struggling awkwardly, it clambered to its feet.

'Now walk.' Shuffling on legs of slightly uneven length,

the creature obeyed.

'Stop!' It stopped.

'Bow to your mistress!' It bowed.

As it moved, red-hot gleams of fire sizzled through its cracked skin, but it didn't disintegrate. It was truly alive, standing at about Tegen's own height.

Her smiled broadened. At last, she thought, I have used my powers properly. I can keep my enemy where I can see it. It'll do nothing without my knowledge. When this hideous time is over I shall take it back to the Winter Seas and turn it to eternal stone, deep in the caves it came from.

'Follow!' she ordered.

As Tegen and the golem approached the camp, warriors gathered, spears at the ready. Most made the sign against the evil eye, some ran screaming, all held their breath in dread.

The creature sloshed awkwardly through the mud, its sooty skin steaming in the rain.

Tegen pointed to a rock. 'Sit!' she commanded. 'Wait. Do not move. If you see anyone attacking this camp, wave your arms to the guard. Do you understand?'

The golem nodded slowly, then sat, staring into the evening sky.

Weaving one last spell of binding, Tegen strode away.

The crowds fell back, eyes and mouths wide in awe.

Tegen's heart sank at their terror. She would have to earn their trust all over again. Now they'd see her as a weaver of dark spells. Owein was right; she could be naïve at times. She should at least have warned the guards that this creature was coming.

But now she needed food, then sleep. Tegen beckoned to the nearest guard. 'Call me if you're worried, but it'll do nothing until I say. You're all quite safe.'

Owein pushed through the throng. 'Tegen!' he called urgently. 'What's happening? Are you all right?'

'Come and eat with me and I'll tell you.' She took his arm and led the way to Boudica's feasting tent. Rain thundered on the awning as she chose a bench as far away as possible from the queen. Sabrina spotted them, and with her mead horn in one hand and a half a leg of pork in the other, she sat beside them.

As soon as they were all seated with bread and meat, Tegen began. 'As you know, when I first became the Star Dancer, a demon was released from the funeral caves near my home. I thought I'd put it back, but it followed me. It was the power that Admidios served.'

'And his ghastly raven?' Owein asked. 'That was demonic if anything was.'

Tegen shook her head. 'No, that was an old witch called Derowen – reincarnated, to help Admidios ensnare me.'

Sabrina looked puzzled, 'I thought humans only came back as humans?'

'They do normally,' Tegen replied. 'But with this particular demon, anything's possible. I suspect Derowen had been his slave for many years, so he controlled her rebirth. In raven form it was easy for her to follow me. Anyway, as I travelled to Ériu and Mona, I was followed the whole time – usually by a sort of fog. I often heard sniffing, as if something was *tracking* me.' She shuddered at the memory. 'Once it took the body of a wounded bear. That was horrible. Dear Epona saved me from it, twice.'

'But what's this got to do with that hideous *thing* just outside our camp?' Owein interrupted.

'Because I'm still being followed. That demon wants me, but I don't know why. An old woman once prophesied that it'd come after me "because it didn't make sense".'

Sabrina choked on her ale. 'What a useless sort of a prophecy!'

'It seemed so at the time, but now I'm beginning to understand.'

'How do you mean?' Owein asked.

Tegen lowered her voice. 'Nothing to do with this demon makes any sense: its *essence* is chaos. It doesn't seem to be on any side. I'm sure it's driving Boudica as much as Suetonius ... It's relishing the mayhem. But at the same time it's after *me*. I'm scared Owein. I don't like being pursued by an unseen enemy, so I made a golem out of the blood and ashes of Camulodunum and commanded the demon to enter it. Now it's trapped – not all of it of course, a spirit like that can't ever be totally contained – but it's diminished and I now know where it is and what it's up to. There's an old saying, "keep your friends close and your enemies closer," and that's just what I'm doing!'

Just then, Boudica stood and banged loudly on the table with a spoon. She flung her arm towards Tegen and bellowed, 'I have news! Our noble druid has captured a monster. Let's all go and look at it!'

The feasting tent fell silent. All eyes were on Tegen.

She rose to her feet. 'Very well,' she replied. She had hoped to wait until morning when the creature would not glow so fiercely. She pushed back her stool and led Boudica and her retinue outside.

In the darkness beyond the camp, sat the black shape of the golem, outlined in flickering fire.

'Torches!' Boudica bellowed as she strode right up to it.

'Don't look into its eyes,' Tegen warned. 'Although it obeys me, it's still dangerous.'

Boudica strode around it twice. 'What is it?' She asked.

'A golem. It's made from the mud and ashes of Camulodunum. It will walk with your warriors and strike fear into your enemies.'

Boudica whistled. 'They'll run like children! Is it safe?'

'In my hands, yes – and if it's treated with respect.'

'What if you die?'

'It will do nothing for ever.'

The queen nodded, satisfied.

Just as she turned to go, Tegen noticed that the golem inclined its head slightly in Boudica's direction. That tiny action sent a chill into Tegen's heart. Had she imagined it, or had she missed a part of the spell?

21. SHADOWS OF BEYOND

Tegen was roused early to attend Boudica's war council. The queen looked exhausted but elated as she spoke.

Sabrina poked Tegen in the ribs and whispered, 'She sat up all night next to your *thing*. I think she's in love!'

'Let's pray to every god that she's not!' Tegen replied.

'Are you two listening?' The queen roared. 'As I was saying, with the golem at our head, we'll march to the Roman trading post of Londinium. That's south west of here and very near to our settlement of Lundein on the river Tamesis. The town is small, but our spies say there are warehouses stacked full of grain, wool and metal.'

She opened her arms. 'And it's *British* wool and grain – so we shall take it back!'

The gathering cheered heartily. Generosity kept the tribes faithful. Boudica raised her hand for silence. 'Now, gather round this sand map and learn it with me.

'This pebble north of the river is Londinium. It was built to handle reinforcements as well as goods, so once it's smashed, Suetonius and his men will be cut off.'

Addedomaros laid down several twigs, spreading out from Londinium like wheel spokes. 'These show the roads they have built, making Londinium the hub for the whole land.'

Boudica pointed to one that ran northeast. 'This leads to

Deva, where Suetonius will be gathering his troops for retaliation. But we also can use these roads to our advantage. From Londinium, warriors can wade across the Tamesis and go south, ambushing the roads that lead to their Isca Dumnoniorum and Isca Silurium in the west. That'll cut off any legions attempting to join Suetonius.'

'Brilliant! Caught in their own net!' Venutius punched the air. 'We have them!'

Boudica smiled as her chieftains applauded loudly. 'Camulodunum was the head of Rome's monster. Now, to make sure it's dead, we need to hack off its arms, legs – and balls, if it has any!'

The tent erupted into yells and whistles.

Boudica gestured towards Tegen. 'And now we have our *own* magnificent monster on our side, this war is won! We merely have to dismember the Roman corpse. Now, we set off in one hand span of the sun. You are dismissed.'

Sabrina and Tegen exchanged worried glances.

'She's too confident,' Tegen whispered. 'She hasn't even let me explain properly about the golem.'

'But it can't move without your command, so what's the problem?' Sabrina asked, bemused.

Tegen rubbed the scar on her finger. 'I don't know,' she replied. 'It's just a feeling.'

Before noon, the carts and waggons were packed and the trek towards Londinium began, but even slower than before because of all the extra loot.

Tegen was edgy. Early one morning, she took Sabrina aside. 'I have been weaving magic to ensure victory in Londinium, but I sense something is unravelling my magic as fast as I make it. Can we hurry up? I have this strong feeling that Suetonius is going to be ready for us.'

Sabrina laughed. 'We're quite safe. The only way anyone could be there before us would be riding non-stop. And armies – even Roman ones – can't travel that fast. I was with Suetonius's men for long enough to know how they move. Even if he rode like a demon through the mountains and picked up fresh troops at Deva, we'll still arrive in Londinium first.'

Sabrina took Tegen's arm. 'Now, stop worrying. Will your golem walk with us? We ought to give him a name.'

'It'll walk, but absolutely no names.' Tegen scowled. 'It must remain what it is: twigs, ash and mud. Nothing more. You mustn't tell it your name either.'

Sabrina's eyes widened in dismay, 'But why? He's magnificent!'

'Because *he* is an *it*. Mud, ashes and fire. Names mean building a relationship with it, and that's dangerous. Just believe me, please! Now, Boudica's already left, and I want to keep up with her. Are you riding with me?'

'I want to be near your creature, it's the finest warrior I've ever seen – real or magical.'

Tegen sighed as she led Epona towards where the golem sat, staring towards the ruin of Camulodunum. Standing before it, Tegen raised her hands. 'Up!' she commanded.

The creature obeyed.

Sabrina walked around the figure, admiring every aspect of its physique. 'Can I train it to fight?' she asked.

Tegen shook her head. 'No. It's like wildfire; it could turn on us. I'll make it walk with you into battle. As Boudica says, with any luck the Romans will just drop their swords and run.'

'But we don't want them to flee, we want to kill them and grind their bones into the mud ...' Sabrina licked her lips. 'There wasn't any real fighting last time. To be honest, it wasn't that much fun.'

'Tough,' Tegen replied tersely. Then she turned to the golem. 'We're moving on today. You will walk with us. You will keep me in sight at all times.'

The golem stared at her.

Tegen mounted Epona. 'I'll see you this evening, Sabrina.' Then kicking her mare into a trot, she led the golem along the road.

Horses reared and fretted as they passed, carts gave way and warriors pushed their families behind them. But they all watched the creature's every step with fear and fascination.

Tegen found Boudica waiting in her chariot.

The queen pointed her whip along the Roman road. 'We'll travel more quickly this way than on the old tracks. We'll put some of our best warriors at the rear, so any pursuing troops will get a nasty surprise. Tegen, you and your creature must stay at the front to ward off evil and to show the world we mean business.'

Once more, a look seemed to pass between Boudica and the golem.

I don't like this – it's almost as if they *recognise* each other! Tegen thought. I must watch out, or Boudica will try giving it orders.

But something else gnawed at Tegen's mind as her creation lumbered along the road: its cracking, smouldering skin dripped charcoal with each step, yet she was certain it was *growing*.

Later that morning, Owein sought Sabrina out. She was easy to find, riding high on her war chariot, her dark hair streaming in the wind. 'Want a ride?' she asked, offering him a hand up. Owein tied Heather's reign to the horses' harness and clambered up beside his foster sister. 'I need to talk to you,' he said. 'About Tegen's golem.'

Sabrina smiled warmly. 'Magnificent, isn't it? I just wish I could find a live warrior like him – I might just be tempted to fall in love!' She glanced at Owein, her dark eyes twinkling.

But he wasn't amused. 'I'm worried,' he said. 'Something's wrong. I don't think Tegen knows what she's made – not really.'

'How do you mean?'

Owein shrugged then grabbed the sides of the chariot as the wheels hit a bump in the road. 'I'm not much good at magic as you know, but that thing's incredibly powerful, and Tegen isn't well – *vicious* enough to control it.'

'I'll take it on any day!' Sabrina laughed.

Owein's eyes remained cold.

'You mean it, don't you,' she asked nervously. 'You're really worried?'

'I am,' he replied. 'But we'll just have to see what happens.'

Smirking broadly, Boudica drove her chariot behind the golem. That hideous soothsayer had been right about Tegen – this Star Dancer or whatever she called herself had incredible powers. The defeat of Camulodunum had been so easy, and no booby traps, just a couple of hundred soldiers who didn't stand a chance, a few pot-bellied old men and a handful of women and farmers. The British slaves had been freed, and the Roman whores and bastards all sacrificed to Andraste.

She liked that touch, what a magnificent offering to the Goddess of War! Now Andraste owed her a favour. She *had* to bless the rest of the campaign. But why had the old soothsayer warned her not to trust the girl? It didn't make sense. This latest ploy – this animated *thing* was brilliant! And what perfect justice: from Camulodunum's ashes, a supernatural fighting machine to make *more* ashes! And her chieftains approved too. They were totally united for once.

Boudica admitted to herself that even she would be unable to raise a spear at something that had so blatantly come from the Shadows of Beyond. Surely those eyes of fire were gateways to Tir na nÓg? Anyone who saw it would be terrified.

And it was strange, thought the queen, but there was something familiar about the creature, although she'd swear on any oath she had never seen such a thing before.

Suetonius Paulinus, the Governor of Britain was worried too. He was laid up in the barracks at Deva with vomiting and diarrhoea he could not get rid of. The doctors had prescribed potions and poultices, even leeches, but to no avail. He was getting worse, not better – and he needed to get on the road.

Shivering and sweating, Suetonius yelled for more blankets as he rolled off his mattress and laid his hot head on the cool floor. Images of a girl with long dark hair and green, green eyes slipped through his feverish mind.

In his clearer moments he knew he had spent too long subduing the people of Cymru. He had dealt with the pestilential druids on the island of Mona just after midsummer, and then stayed to destroy everything that smacked of their superstitious claptrap, groves, altars, the lot. That had cost time too. Messengers had warned him of mischief in the east, but he hadn't believed a mere woman was capable of anything other than being a nuisance.

He'd ordered the IX legion from Durobrivae and sent word to the praefectus Poenius Postumus in Isca Dumnoniorum to send the II Augusta to quash the revolt.

But the IX had been ambushed, and a message had come back from Poenius saying he was too busy. All this had taken one and a half precious months.

Suetonius spewed bile into his bucket. The staff in Britain were all fools. Heads would roll for this incompetence – he would see to it – literally and personally.

Autumn was passing and the new garrison on the druids' island was far from ready. This irritating rebellion meant he'd left Mona in the hands of his subordinates. At least they were men he'd trained himself. He'd enjoyed taking his cohort of cavalry through the mountains. They'd arrived at Deva by the solstice, travelling faster than anyone had thought possible. Only yesterday, or was it last week? His head ached, he couldn't remember – he'd ordered a full detachment of the XX Legion, the Valeria Victrix to follow him to Londinium, where the infernal woman seemed to be heading.

Delirium toyed with the Governor's mind. He should be on the road right now. He *was* on the road, he was riding a horse, but why was he lying down?

His head was a jumble of images.

He had underestimated the revolt. Boudica was obviously just a figurehead; the British had a weak spot for females. Beautiful and desirable they may be, but they were also vicious and unreliable little schemers. He stroked the burn scar down the side of his face. Some girls could fight like badgers given a chance. An angry woman might inspire a rebellion with some balls – but who was the *brains* behind it all? It smacked of a powerful man, and maybe a druid. They were the nearest these savages had to intellectuals. He'd had a notion they'd not all been killed on the island raid: that idiot of a *pularius* had let several go.

Once more he saw the dark haired girl. She was dancing, wildly. Dangerous dancing, with magic in it. She swam in and out of focus. Sometimes she was far away swaying to a drumbeat, but then she came close, too close and had fire in her hands …

Suetonius tried to rip the scar from his face. His dreams made him afraid. More afraid than he'd ever been. He hauled himself back onto his bed and flung his blankets to the ground, knocking his sick bucket over.

His skull rattled with an inhuman voice – the same one that had spoken to him on Mona.

I'm your servant, sent by the gods it reminded him. *But in exchange, you must bring me the dancing girl.*

Suetonius pulled a pillow over his ears. 'Shut up, can't you see I'm ill?' he groaned. 'I'll hand her over when I find her, I swear!'

… After I've had some fun making her suffer for what she's done to me, of course, Suetonius vowed silently.

Then he remembered the promises this eerie voice had made …

He sat up in bed and yelled, 'Hey! You! Servant! Remember, you swore I'd have victory! Here I am sweating like a pig. *Do something useful!*'

Silence. He was dreaming again. Was this voice part of

his fever? By all the gods, he hoped he wasn't going mad.

Suetonius looked out of his wind-eye at the gathering clouds and shuddered. How he loathed this chilly, miserable land. The voice had once prophesied he'd become Emperor of the north, but that was only the beginning. Once he'd recovered and taken control of Britain, he'd prove his worth.

He'd become Emperor of Rome.

His stomach threatened to invert itself once more.

'*Servant*!' he yelled at the voice in his head, 'You'd better repair my body or both our causes are lost. The longer I lay here, the more damage that wretched woman Boudica can achieve. You want that girl? I want the rebels crucified. Make me better or you won't get anything! Do you hear?'

At once, slaves came running in the door with fresh water and clean buckets. 'Sorry master, who was it you wanted?'

Suetonius just glared at them. 'Idiots!' he spat. 'I wasn't talking to any of you!'

And from far away, the demon did hear. But it was confused. It wasn't used to healing, only causing chaos and destruction. However, the human had a point. Something had to be done.

By noon, the governor was sitting up and drinking broth.

By nightfall, he was bellowing orders.

By dawn, he was on the road.

LONDINIUM

22. ARGUMENTS

Tegen was frustrated and angry. For the third time that morning, a troop of thugs left the phalanx of warriors to raid a farmhouse. She rode Epona through the throng until she came alongside the queen's chariot.

'This isn't right my lady, you're stealing from your own people.'

'It's plain you're new as a battle druid,' Boudica sneered. 'We need supplies. Look behind you – how else are my loyal followers going to be fed? We're simply requisitioning what we need to liberate the very people you're whinging about.'

Tegen narrowed her eyes. 'I have heard, my lady, that you have the farmers and their families put to the sword.'

Boudica shrugged. 'They're collaborators. If they weren't they'd have joined us by now. Anyway, if we take their food, they'll have nothing to eat, so it's for the best.'

Tegen's fingers twitched to weave a curse, but her good sense told her to wait. Britain needed Boudica in revolt, but in peace she'd be a despot.

'Beware,' Tegen warned. 'The Goddess won't be pleased if you act without mercy. There will be a reckoning.'

'After your wonderful sacrifice in the sacred grove?' Boudica laughed. 'I think we have the Goddess in the bag;

she'll do whatever we demand of her. She owes us!'

Tegen ground her teeth with rage, but before she could reply, she noticed the golem stumble. The creature never faltered. What could be wrong? She rode over to it.

'Stop!' she ordered and it obeyed. Tegen dismounted and walked around the ashy figure. Perhaps the spells that kept its feet intact were crumbling?

All seemed well. 'Walk on!' she commanded. Remounting Epona, she followed, watching closely.

The creature was still growing. Tegen didn't like that, but it was better than the whole structure crumbling apart.

Just then Sabrina's chariot rumbled alongside. 'Not far to Londinium,' she announced. 'Come up and ride with me for a while?'

Tegen shook her head. 'No thanks, I need to think.'

'Come on, you're always "thinking", you need to relax,' she persisted. 'Tie Epona to the chariot.' She stretched down and offered Tegen a hand up. 'Would you like to have a go at driving?'

Maybe I do need company, Tegen thought, allowing herself to be hauled up.

Standing in the basketwork box beside the Dobunni queen, Tegen took the reins. The power of the harnessed horses thrilled her, but her mind couldn't rest. 'Do you know Boudica's ordered the slaughter of the farmers whose crops we steal?' she shouted.

Sabrina nodded. 'Yes. I'm not pleased, but she's got her blood up these days. Her temper in council last night was appalling. I don't know what's got into her of late. Oh, but there's good news as well.'

'I could do with some,' Tegen replied, struggling as the chariot began to yaw.

'Our spies say that Suetonius has beaten us to Londinium.'

'Why's that good news?'

Sabrina leaned over and tugged on the left rein. 'Careful or we'll end up in the ditch. It's good because Suetonius was in such a hurry he only had a few men with him. He decided the town is indefensible: it's only a trading post, no proper ditches or palisades, just a few river landing stages, a crossing point, some shops and warehouses, a few inns – nothing much there at all. He's evacuated everyone except the infirm and a few women who got all weepy. It's in the bag – Londinium is ours for the taking without a battle!'

Tegen's eyes widened. 'Are you serious?'

'Absolutely.'

'And it's not a trap?'

'No. This is a reliable source.'

Tegen frowned.

'What's bugging you?' Sabrina was bemused.

'It's too easy, something's wrong. Is war usually like this?'

'No, but then this isn't a normal war. In military terms the answer's simple. The Romans have overstretched themselves; their troops are spread too thinly. If there's a big demand for men at one end of the country, it leaves a gap at the other. Suetonius lost hundreds of men and horses at the battle of Mona, then he set up a new garrison to subdue the "ungrateful natives". That's left a huge deficit of manpower in the northwest. They're stretched in the southwest too. I've heard the Dumnonii have rebelled too. In the north, the Picts are fighting hard, probably helped by a few Old Ones who fled that way. So, towns like Londinium have no garrisons. It's a gift!'

'Like the web of magic,' Tegen murmured, 'tug at one end and it pulls at the other.'

Sabrina slapped Tegen on the back. 'Cheer up! Celebrate! Thanks to you, the Goddess is giving us our Land back.' She jerked her thumb towards the golem. 'And with *that* thing on our side, who can stand against us?'

Tegen watched her creation striding dumbly along the grassy verges, only half a stone's throw away. 'You're right.' She smiled and straightened her back. 'How long before we arrive?'

Sabrina pointed her whip at a glimpse of silvery ribbon that wound across the valley below. 'That's the Tamesis, do you remember it?'

'The same river that flows past Sinodun?'

'That's right, only a lot further along. Londinium is built on its banks, near old Lindum. Most of Rome's supplies come through there, so once that's destroyed we've a strangle hold on Suetonius's troops. In two days, it's ours.'

The next evening, Boudica's war bands camped around

Londinium's small settlement on the banks of a wide marshy river.

Hardly a soul moved in its streets as it huddled, waiting for the inevitable.

The queen summoned Tegen and Owein to her tent. A feast was spread on the table. Venutius, Addedomaros, Daig, and Sabrina were already seated and deep in conversation.

'Come and join us,' Boudica called out. 'We're honoured to have *two* druids to lead us into battle. I am sure Tegen's magic will be as spectacular as before.' She clicked her fingers and servants passed platters loaded with meat and bread.

Tegen took a deep breath. 'No thank you.'

Boudica raised an eyebrow. 'Fasting? You must keep your strength up.' And she bit into a leg of goose, letting the golden juices trickle down her chin.

Tegen shook her head. 'No. I won't eat food that's been stolen from murdered farmers.'

Everyone fell silent and stared.

Boudica narrowed her eyes, then laughed harshly. 'Where else will you get food, my dear? This is war. You can't afford to be ruled by a girl's conscience in times like these.'

Tegen slapped the table. Glaring at the queen she roared: '*You* are destroying your own people! How will you rebuild this land if the farmers are dead? It's *you* who's being naïve!'

Boudica wiped her mouth on her sleeve. 'What did you say?' she asked quietly.

Shaking with rage, Tegen raised her right hand and pointed at the queen. 'You are abusing your people. You have gold and silver enough to pay for food.' She pulled her golden armbands from her wrists and flung them at Boudica. 'Here, have these back in case you get peckish before breakfast!'

The queen reddened. 'The farmers were collaborators! We found Roman furniture in the houses.'

'Like the chair under your own backside, my *lady*? Anyway, as for collaborators – what were you before your man died? Heh?'

Boudica's knuckles whitened on her dagger.

Owein shuffled beside Tegen and touched her arm gently. 'Calm down. This won't do any good!'

She shook him off. 'I'm going.'

'*Wait*!' Boudica roared.

Tegen's face tightened as she turned back.

'What if I agreed to look into how we get our supplies?' Boudica smiled, but her eyes had a cunning glint.

'I will eat with you when the food has been paid for.'

'Very well. I agree. But right now, your friend is right. Arguing won't help our cause.' The queen gestured towards a stool by her side. 'Sit. Eat or not as you please, but I must talk with you.'

Tegen stood where she was, her eyes flashing. 'I'm listening.'

Boudica sighed. 'Tomorrow we attack Londinium. As you know it isn't a big place, but it is Suetonius's umbilical with his homeland. We must make the Romans too scared and disheartened to return or they will simply rebuild. I understand you've never been a battle druid before Tegen, but this is how things must be. And I've an idea you can help me with.'

I'll never trust this woman, Tegen told herself, but if I understand how she thinks, I'll know how to fight her without destroying our cause.

She sat, then replied meekly, 'I apologise for my outburst. Please explain.'

'It's your creature,' Boudica began. 'I want it in the front line when we attack in the morning. At dawn you will do your ritual curses on the town, and then you will order your creature to obey me in battle.'

Tegen gasped. 'I can't … I mean, it won't …'

Boudica's face reddened and her guards drew closer.

Tegen looked up nervously. 'However, it shall march with you tomorrow. Concerning the rest, I'll need to speak with the spirits. Please excuse me, this will take time.'

The sky was clouded and a chilly wind blew. Tegen wrapped her cloak tightly around her shoulders and went to sit beside her silent golem.

Its hideous fiery eyes stared unblinking into the dark.

Her mind was a-whirl, had she done wrong making this *thing*? How else could she have kept the demon within sight? The situation was turning very nasty. She should have guessed Boudica would want to control the golem … What should she do now?

Limping footsteps approached from behind.

Tegen looked up. 'Hello Owein. Thanks for coming, I hoped you would.'

He sat beside her. 'You're shivering,' he said. 'Do you want to share my cloak?'

She hesitated.

He laughed. 'You aren't scared of me, are you?'

'I am cold but … Is sitting so closely a good idea?'

'How do you mean? Are you sick?'

'In Sinodun you said you were in love with me. I've been handfasted twice and both men have died. I don't think I could face it again, not even with you.'

'I understand,' Owein replied. Sitting next to her, he wrapped his cloak around her shoulders. 'Don't worry. I've decided to go through with marrying the girl I'm betrothed to. This is just for warmth and companionship.'

Tegen looked up. 'Your woman survived Camulodunum?'

'Yes. In fact she's here.'

'How did you manage that? I thought she was Roman. Boudica will torture her horribly if she finds out.'

Owein laughed bitterly. 'Thankfully this young lady is only half Roman, she speaks British well, and so does her slave. I told Boudica they're both Gaulish and I said we're already married.'

'I'd like to meet them,' Tegen replied. 'But tonight I have other things to worry about. Since Tonn died, I've lost faith in the Goddess, and yet I really need her. Dancing under the stars used to help, but it's too dark tonight.'

Owein put his arm around her. She laid her head on his shoulder. It felt like old times.

She sniffed back a tear. 'Everyone expects so much of me, but I've got nothing more to give.'

He squeezed her shoulder. 'I understand how you feel and I'll help you however I can. Right now, we have to think about Boudica's demand for the golem.'

Wriggling free of Owein's comfort, Tegen stood and approached the creature slowly. Spreading her fingers before her, she felt for the protective threads of magic she'd cocooned around it.

'What are you doing?' Owein asked.

'Something's wrong,' she replied. 'I'm sure it's growing and it keeps stumbling.'

Owein considered the fiery outline in the darkness. 'Isn't that because it's got flat feet?'

'Not necessarily. I think maybe someone else is trying to control it – and two masters pulling in different directions make it unsteady.'

'But isn't it protected from that?' Owein asked. 'I mean, you must have used some very powerful spells. Even I can feel the magic barriers.'

'I'd thought so, but maybe it's not enough.'

'Why did you make it?'

Tegen hesitated. 'The demon wants me and I have a suspicion that I allow it to come closer when I get angry. I made the golem to keep the demon where I can see it – and maybe control it a little. Also I needed to be reminded what anger looks like,' she replied quietly.

'Do you think that was wise?'

'You mean making it was a stupid idea?'

'Possibly.'

Tegen shrugged. 'What would you have done?'

'I don't know,' Owein replied. Then he added, 'I know you have a bit of a temper, but it's not bad enough to have created *this*.'

Tegen shook her head. 'My anger's getting worse. It makes me do unforgivable things. You saw the way I brought down fire at Dorcic – and I caused the terrible rains that ruined so many crops at Lughnasadh.'

'How was that you?'

'I was torn apart with rage that Tonn had been sacrificed to save Britain. What was worse, he died willingly. He wouldn't believe that the most difficult and important sacrifice was staying alive to fight for what is right.' She glanced across at the heavily armed guards. 'I don't mean a *war* sort of fighting – I mean, I don't know, standing up for justice.

'I have a suspicion that all that's needed for evil to triumph, is for good people to do nothing.'

'Which is exactly why I decided to work with the Romans,' Owein replied. 'I hoped my skills with the law and my understanding of both sides might ameliorate things.'

Tegen sighed. 'I can see that now. I'm sorry I didn't listen.' She walked around the golem. 'But as to this creature, I'm very worried. When it was new, it was my own height. Tonight it'd scarcely fit into Boudica's tent ...'

'Is your anger feeding it?' Owein asked.

'In theory it's possible. I'm livid with Boudica, but that's a good sort of anger; it's inspiring me to keep fighting. Even my longing to repay the druids for sacrificing Tonn has lessened. Inside, I'm grieving rather than raging.'

'So what *is* feeding it?'

Tegen spread her fingers again. There's another magic here, it's been cleverly inserted. I've felt it before but I can't remember where.' She turned to Owein, her voice trembling in the dark. 'I think someone is trying to use my golem for their own ends. This is very, very dangerous.'

'Is there anything I can do?' Owein stood beside her in the dark and put his arm around her again.

Tegen leaned against him. 'I could use your spying skills to find out who's behind this and what they're up to.'

Owein had a smile in his voice when he replied. 'Excellent. It's us working together again. Just as it should be. I'm sure Sabrina will help too – she doesn't like Boudica's methods any more than we do.' He pulled his cloak more tightly around his neck. 'Shall we go back in now? I'm freezing.'

'I'll be in soon, I just want to stay here a little longer.'

In the stillness of the night, Tegen closed her eyes and imagined Tonn, strong, safe and loving. He sat by her side and held her. Then she thought of Griff with his big smile and huge heart. His sticky hands clutched adoringly at her fingers.

'Speak to me, please, both of you. Tell me what to do,' she begged.

23. LONDINIUM

At dawn, Tegen began her ritual war-curses by the northern gate of the town. This time she was careful with her fire, but the damp, yellow clay sprouted only rushes and scrub willow, so there was little danger.

The chilling wind whipped at Tegen's cloak as she opened the gateway to Tir na nÓg for the fleeing spirits. She shivered, not from the cold, but from the feeling that someone was watching her out of sight and silent in the half-light. Perhaps it was a soldier with a javelin, waiting to kill her? Of course she had guards hidden nearby and she'd created a strong spirit shield before she started to work, but was that enough? Had the golem followed her?

She had left the creature ready to march with the warriors; she hoped the shock of its presence would terrify the people of Londinium into a bloodless surrender. It had strict instructions of when and how to move, and was tightly cocooned in fresh spells in case it developed ideas of its own.

But she would never quite trust it.

As soon as this is over, I'll find a way to unmake it, I'll cast the demon to the lowest, foulest parts of the Otherworld, Tegen promised herself. I can't wait.

She split the yew branch and placed the halves either side of the road so the dead souls could flee safely to Tir na nÓg. She secured that part of the spell with knotted grasses and branches of rue, no longer trusting a mere mark in the dirt to guard the world of the living from malice.

Only when all was complete did she risk looking around.

There was someone – a grey-haired man dressed in black, watching silently at a respectful distance.

Aodh! The spell-caster who had murdered her prisoners. Tegen's heart faltered. But she had to concentrate.

The trading post was built on the banks of a river and Tegen had no boat, so she could not do a ritual at the southern gate. Instead she walked to the western end and threw three gold rings into the swirling water. Each piece splashed bright against the murk. 'An offering to the spirits of the West and to the god of this river,' she said aloud, then she bowed, scooped up some of the water in her hands and let it trickle back. 'Convey my blessings to the spirits of the south. Tell them that Tegen of the Winter Seas greets them.'

As she worked, her unease increased. She could not help watching Aodh from the corner of her eye.

He did not move. He simply stood. Watching her.

Suddenly there was a thwack by Tegen's side.

A spear!

She gasped and ran. A hail of pebbles clattered behind her. Someone was firing catapults.

'Get *down*!' Aodh yelled.

Tegen sprawled flat.

Aodh ran and flung himself across her back.

From all around came shouts and yells as her guards returned fire.

'Keep low, I'll lead the way.' Aodh rolled aside and crawled between the tussocks towards the trees.

Tegen was angry as she wriggled like an eel through the mud. Damn, *damn*! Now I'll have to be grateful to this ghastly man!

Soon they stood together in the shelter of a small wood, watching both sides drawing closer and yelling abuse.

Tegen worried at the scar on her finger. 'This shouldn't have happened … I hadn't finished.'

Despite the bitter wind, many of Boudica's warriors were running into battle naked, their skin painted with blue spirals and their hair limed. Soon screams from the dying and wounded rose above the noise of swords on shields.

'This is disastrous!' Tegen gasped. 'I thought the town was almost empty and undefended?'

Aodh peered through the trees at the melee. 'Who knows how many people are still inside? Maybe a hundred, maybe a thousand.'

Tegen climbed up a tree and looked back towards the camp for the golem. 'Do you know where my creature is?'

Aodh stared up at her. 'It's with the queen, my lady, as you left it.'

Tegen jumped to the ground and brushed herself down. 'Something's wrong. I must go back. I told the golem to walk with our warriors to terrify the enemy. It's not there.'

Aodh pursed his bloodless lips. 'I believe the queen

spoke of that idea, but her chieftains were hungry for battle themselves. Many haven't had a real fight yet!' his dark eyes narrowed. 'Our warriors get twitchy if they don't have a spear in one hand, a sword in the other and their boots soaked in blood! Rest assured lady, your creature will be waiting quietly. I don't believe you're needed.'

Ignoring him, Tegen crept to the edge of the trees. The battlefield was a writhing mass of blood, and clashing shields. The fighting was almost over. 'I didn't finish my rituals at the gates. They'll be inside within half a hand-span – but I don't know how safe they'll be. Unfinished magic is worse than none.'

Beside her, Aodh bowed his head slightly. 'Lady, please don't be angry, but I took the precaution of laying a few small spells of my own before dawn ... Just in case things didn't go according to plan.'

Tegen clenched her hands. She'd had just about enough of this man's false subservience. Interfering bastard! she thought. His 'magic' could throw everything I've done out of balance!

She made her way to the far side of the copse to watch the road for a sight of the golem. At last she spotted it, a dark shadow loomed over the brow of the hill, followed by a second wave of warriors. The creature was tall as a young sapling now and heavy in arm and leg. Tegen swallowed hard. Now she stood so close to Aodh, she recognised the other spells she had sensed on the golem, they were *his*.

But right now, there was nothing she could do about

Aodh. Hitching up her skirt, she climbed an ash tree and made herself comfortable in a fork. From there, she wove spells to bring the fall of Londinium to a speedy end. 'May the suffering of both sides be short,' she prayed.

But as the fresh warriors arrived, the noise of the fighting started up again. From inside the town, women's screams and terrified children's wailing jarred with chilling battle cries. Flames gobbled the flimsy palisade and its gates. Choking smoke billowed from the rows of wooden houses that lined the wharfs.

Downstream, a dozen or so small boats crammed with huddled figures, were floating away. A cargo ship with fire in its prow, drifted lazily on the current, unmanned except for a bleeding corpse hanging over the gunnels.

'May you all be born again soon in happier times,' Tegen whispered.

Then she gripped the branch she was sitting on and stared.

The golem was moving – without her command! To left and right, warriors scattered before its lumbering gait.

The creature's fiery eyes flashed and flames and smoke seeped through the cracks in its charcoal hide. Slowly and purposefully, it strode towards the remains of the town. As it reached the burning gates, it ripped each leaf off its hinges, raised them above its head and flung them down.

The screams inside rose higher. Then there was silence.

Tegen jumped down and pushed past Aodh. Blindly she ran along the road, leaping bodies, sliding in pools of blood and sidestepping hands that stretched for help. At last she plunged through the burning gap and into the fiery streets.

Wooden houses sagged and creaked as fire and smoke darkened the skies and devoured the town.

Tegen pulled her scarf over her face and ducked down, keeping as low as she could under the pall of ash.

Ahead, the golem was darkly silhouetted against the flames, calm and unmoving. Its back was towards her. Could it sense she was there?

Tegen crouched down and watched as warriors brought maybe twenty or thirty people to the town square. Everyone was coughing and struggling to breathe. The bitter wind shifted. The roaring flames were getting louder. And hotter.

Coughing warriors fled, but the golem stood solidly between the prisoners and the last path to safety.

Tegen sprang forward and waved her hands at her creation. 'Get them out of here!' she yelled. 'Lead them!'

The huge creature turned and lumbered impassively away.

Tegen picked up a terrified child and grabbed an old woman's hand, signalling for everyone to follow.

The marsh wind blew cold. After the intense heat, the prisoners shivered and wept. Dereliction hung over them as they huddled together. Above the roars of wind and flames, drifted the thin, piercing wails of the babies.

The golem stood over them, staring down with its

burning eyes.

'Move away!' Tegen commanded. 'You'll frighten them.'

What could she do to protect these people?

Just then, Aodh appeared at her side once more. 'Is it your wish to dedicate these souls to the Goddess also?' he asked in a soft, chilling voice.

Tegen shuddered. 'No ... thank you,' she replied tersely. 'You have done more than enough for me today.'

Looking around she found one of Sabrina's older warriors. 'Chieftain Gwier, will you take my prisoners somewhere safe, feed them and give them water, but do *not* kill them. They are sacred, but the Lady hasn't yet revealed to me what their fate must be.'

Gwier bowed his head. 'Very good, Lady.' He strode away to yell the orders to his men.

Coughing and spitting the soot from her lungs, Tegen signalled to the golem to follow her. Together they stumbled back towards the town. I must make sure there are no unfriendly spirits on the loose, she told herself. I can't risk things going so badly wrong again.

Just then, one of Boudica's bodyguards rode up to Tegen. 'The queen says to come back Miss. It's getting dangerous down here. The fire got going quicker than we meant, it's going to be a hot one. There must have been a great deal of grain and cloth in the warehouses. Pity we didn't get to empty them first.'

Tegen shook her head. 'Tell the queen I will come as soon as I have fetched my creature.'

The man bowed and rode away.

With a shawl pulled over her face, Tegen picked her way to within an arrow shot of the inferno. The heat seared her skin. She'd have to wait for the ground to cool before she could get any closer. This wasn't safe even for a fire-walking druid.

The golem was staring hungrily at the raging flames.

She yelled, 'Come!'

Either it didn't want to obey, or it simply didn't hear, but it ignored her and lumbered right into the heart of the fire. Although it had no mouth, Tegen sensed it was *smiling*.

Just then, chariot wheels rattled behind her.

Tegen turned. It was Boudica. 'Come up beside me,' the queen called out. 'We need to talk.'

Tegen hesitated, looking anxiously back at her golem.

The queen stretched her hand. 'Leave it – it's safe in there, surely?'

Sitting by Boudica's side in camp once more, Tegen watched as the queen drank mead, then wiped her sooty mouth on her cloak.

'That wasn't much of a fight,' she announced. 'Scarcely a hand span of the sun and it was all over. Mind you, it's much smaller than Camulodunum. They had a guard of two hundred there, this place just had a few women and a couple of boys – not much of a challenge.' She thumped the table loudly. 'We've got to find something for the warriors to get their teeth into, they're raring for a proper battle.'

Tegen sipped water; she still refused to feast at Boudica's table. 'Is that why the skirmishes into the countryside are continuing?'

Boudica shrugged. 'It's difficult to hold our warriors back – they're bred and trained to fight. It's in their souls.'

Tegen was about to protest when the queen leaned across the table and gripped her hand. 'But that's not what I wanted to discuss. Today, fighting with your creature, was *brilliant*! You must name your reward!'

'The lives of the prisoners,' Tegen replied without having to think.

Boudica raised an eyebrow. 'Don't you want gold? Jewels? How about a couple of dozen slaves?'

Tegen shook her head. 'Justice for a few people will do for me.'

'Very well. Now, how much do you want for it?'

'What?'

Boudica pursed her lips. Her look was harsh. 'Don't play silly games Tegen, you know perfectly well what I mean – your golem, how much do you want for it? I want to own it, for it to obey only me. Watching it striding into battle was the most thrilling moment of my life. With that creature at my side, I could rule the world! I could even become Emperor of Rome!'

She laughed coldly as she gripped Tegen's hands, her eyes bright with madness.

Tegen pulled away. '*No!*' she snapped, and stood to go. 'I can let it walk into battle with you, but you wouldn't be strong enough to control it. It's not a toy!'

'But you could teach me!' Boudica wheedled, 'You're so clever, I know you could ...'

Spinning on her heel, Tegen strode out of the tent, right into Sabrina and Owein. 'She wants to *buy* the golem now!' she snarled. 'I've had enough! I'm going to destroy it. But I'll have to leave as well. The demon inside it wants *me*. Tomorrow I'll take it somewhere it'll do no more damage!'

Owein grabbed her arm. 'But you *can't* go Tegen, you're the Star Dancer. We need you!'

Tegen shook her head. 'But it's the only option.'

In the middle of the night, two of Boudica's guards shook Tegen awake. 'Come,' they said. 'You're needed urgently.'

Heart in her mouth, Tegen dressed and followed the men to the queen's tent. Lying on the floor in the shadows were two figures, both tied and gagged. One was squeaking and wriggling vigorously, the other was silent and passive.

With a blast of cold air, the tent flap opened and someone else entered, also accompanied by guards. It was Owein, demanding loudly to know what was going on.

He was soon followed by a stormy-eyed Sabrina. 'What are you up to Boudica?' She roared. 'It's the middle of the night. There's no counter-attack. I need my sleep!'

Boudica was reclining on a Roman dining couch, her arms heavy with gold and silver bracelets. Her ears dripped with blood-ruby earrings. She smiled at her visitors, but she did not invite them to sit.

Boudica dipped her hand into a dish of grapes and played with their green globes. 'There has been treachery in the camp,' she drawled.

Owein looked nervously at the bound figures.

Tegen caught the look and gulped. That's his *wife*. Boudica's caught her!

The queen leaned forward and pointed a sticky finger at Tegen. 'And *there's* the traitor!' She hiccoughed and smirked, then swigged from a golden goblet.

Tegen slipped her hand into her pouch and stroked Tonn's stone egg. Don't let me down, whatever is coming! Give me your power.

There was no tingle of magic – just coolness.

'How am I a traitor?' Tegen demanded. 'I've never let you down, you yourself congratulated me, you said my magic won Camulodunum.'

Boudica shrugged. 'Maybe. Your magic is very good, but you are holding back on me. You won't give me control of that creature. I am the high queen. I am the battle Goddess incarnate. It must serve *me*!'

'No.' Tegen crossed her arms and scowled.

Boudica flung the fruit bowl across the tent. She stood, her fiery hair wild, her blue eyes boring into Tegen's spirit. 'You will *make* it obey me!' she roared.

'But lady, it cannot be done,' Tegen replied mildly. 'It's too dangerous. Even *I* have difficulty with the magic that controls it.'

Boudica glared at her attendants. 'See? She wants to be

my equal. *She* wants my throne – can't you sense it?'

Sabrina strode forward. 'No! she wouldn't.'

'She's not like that!' Owein protested. 'Magic is dangerous stuff ...'

Boudica snorted. 'Ah! as I guessed, you're all in this plot together!' she clicked her fingers and four of her guards dragged the wriggling bundles into the centre of the tent. 'If you don't comply, druid, then Owein's woman dies.'

Hoods were pulled back from the prisoner's faces.

Owein went pale and swallowed hard.

Tegen gasped. '*Claudia? Ula?*'

24. THE NECKLACE OF HAIR

Sabrina drew her dagger and pointed it at Boudica. Guards stepped forward to disarm her, but the queen raised her hand.

'She won't harm me,' she sneered. 'She needs me to get her own kingdom back.'

Sabrina kept her blade drawn but lowered it. 'Don't be so sure, *lady*! I prize loyalty and honesty above being a queen – something you know nothing about, it seems.'

Boudica's nostrils flared. 'I can have you killed at any moment.'

'And you think I can't do the same?' Sabrina responded, with her gappy smile.

Rolling her eyes, Boudica glowered at Tegen. 'This is all beside the point. This so-called *druid* is not putting all her magic at my disposal, which she swore she would do. A soothsayer came to see me before she arrived. He told me not to trust her. After my initial misgivings, I thought he was mistaken – her powers achieved two easy victories. But now I know better. This female ...' Here she kicked Claudia who tried to head-butt her back, 'was the Roman Tegen was seen consorting with on the road to Lindum. Now I discover that Tegen's "friend" is married to her.'

'She's Gaulish,' Tegen put in quickly. 'Raised by Romans, it's not her fault.'

Claudia's eyes opened wide in silent thanks.

Boudica snorted. 'Who knows what tales a whore will use to get into my camp to spy?' She swung her vicious gaze on Owein. 'And where, Owein ap Caractacus, king of the Catuvellauni, did you spring from? You were thought to have died in the fires of Sinodun a year ago. You must hve been playing at being Roman to get yourself a Roman slut!' Boudica ground her teeth as she paced the tent.

At last she stood before Tegen, nose to nose. 'If you won't give me the golem, then these women die. Here and now. You choose. What's it to be?'

'It's not as simple as that, I can't just give ...'

Boudica raised one finger and a guard pressed the tip of his knife under Claudia's chin. A trickle of blood appeared. She whimpered and screwed her eyes shut.

'So, to whom does the golem belong?' the queen demanded.

Tegen worried at the scar on her finger. I'll tell the truth, she decided. Maybe that'll scare her. She took a deep breath. 'The golem is much more than just fire and charcoal. It has a demon in it. If it's anyone's, it belongs to Gwynn ap Nudd, lord of the Otherworld.'

'Aah ...' Boudica sat back on the sofa and put her feet up. 'Even better. If I have death on my side, who can stand against me?'

Tegen ignored her question. 'And if you don't let all of us go unharmed, then I won't curse your next town and I'll no longer stand at your side.' She glanced across at Owein, 'and neither will any other druid. I will see to it.'

Boudica laughed and emptied her drinking horn. 'So what? When I have the golem, I'll rule everything. Anyway, *druids* are dispensable.' She clicked her fingers once more, and out of the shadows at the back of the tent drifted a grey figure.

Aodh.

Tegen hissed between her teeth. She should have seen this coming. 'Give me a short time with my golem,' she said, 'I will have to raise strong magic to communicate with it. But in the end, I cannot promise whom it will choose to obey.'

Boudica dismissed them with a flick of her ring-laden fingers. 'Very well, but Aodh will go with you, just in case of any *errors*. If he's not satisfied, then when you return, Owein's women will die.'

Tegen stormed out of the tent and down the slope to where the golem sat, unsleeping, staring at the smouldering remains of Londinium. Sabrina strode beside her, and Owein hobbled behind as fast as he could.

'What are you going to do?' Sabrina asked.

Tegen looked up at the stars, it was a bright night and the Watching Woman sparkled almost overhead. She stood still. 'I have an idea. Is that ghastly man following us?

Sabrina looked around. 'I can't see him.'

'Good. Distract him if he comes, will you? A sword thrust in the throat will do nicely, if you can get that near.'

Glancing back at the stars for comfort, Tegen walked

over to her creature. 'Stand,' she commanded.

It obeyed, towering taller and stronger than before – but clumsier too.

'Owein, I need you,' Tegen called out.

'How can I help?' He came to her side.

'I know you don't enjoy magic,' she began, 'but you do understand things most people miss. Why is the golem growing, and why is it so clumsy? Is it feeding on Boudica's anger? Any thoughts?'

'I agree with your idea about it being pulled in several directions at once,' Owein replied. 'It's got too many masters.'

Tegen nodded. 'And you've noticed it seems to have some sort of link with the queen?'

'Unfortunately, yes.'

'We must find what that connection is and break it. We must search the golem – it must be wearing a trinket or something personal of hers.'

Owein shook his head. 'Can you make a light? It's too dark to see.'

Pulling a dead branch from a woodpile, Tegen commanded it to burn and held it high.

Together they walked around the golem. 'It's no good,' Owein said at last, 'it's all charcoal and fire to me.'

'You're right,' Tegen agreed. Then she called out, 'Sabrina? Is there any sign of Aodh?'

A raised sword glinted in the firelight. 'Not yet,' she replied.

'He's somewhere close by,' Tegen murmured. 'The back of my neck is prickling.' She took Owein's torch and stared into the flames. 'Show me where Aodh is,' she commanded.

The fire spat. A grey cloak flickered in the darkness.

Tegen span around. 'There!' she yelled.

Sabrina leapt towards him, sword in hand.

'*Karshta-bahona*!' Aodh screeched, flinging blue sparks from his fingertips.

Sabrina yelped, staggering back.

Tegen threw a spirit-shield over her. '*Fiend*!' she yelled, blasting orange flames.

Aodh slunk aside, a shadow amongst shadows. 'You want to play games?' he sneered. 'How about – a little contest? You and me. And the prize will be ... the golem.'

Sabrina was back on her feet. 'Don't Tegen! Aodh's blood is mine!'

'Catch me first,' Aodh laughed, from behind her.

'Catch me first,' Aodh laughed, from the trees beyond the camp.

'Catch me first,' Aodh laughed, from inside the golem.

'Catch me first ... *Catch me first* ... *Catch* ... *me* ... *first* ...'
Endless voices jeered from every direction. In the darkness, twenty or thirty Aodhs were closing in on Sabrina and her friends, eyes glinting, skeletal hands outstretched. The darkness beyond was filled with a thousand more.

Wide-eyed, Sabrina swung her sword in a full circle. '*Coward*!' she yelled. 'Stop playing tricks. Fight like a man.'

Grabbing her torch, Tegen nodded to Owein. The three

stood back to back, facing the tightening circle of eerie figures.

Suddenly, Sabrina lunged, piercing one of the Aodhs in his heart.

He shivered into mist. Two more shades took his place.

On all sides, the Aodhs pressed closer.

Again and again Sabrina's sword hacked and swiped. 'Some help would be nice,' she called out.

'The real one's between you and the golem,' Tegen shouted back. 'Watch his feet.'

Sabrina swung to where Tegen was waving her torch.

Only one of the wraiths cast a shadow on the grass.

Sabrina sprang forward, but stumbled amongst the tangle of avatars.

The spell-caster slid away, his fellows swirling after him.

'No!' Owein yelled, hurling his crutch like a javelin. It cracked on the man's skull.

Aodh howled and stumbled against the golem.

The air filled with the stench of singeing flesh and hair. One by one, the other Aodhs snuffed out like embers.

With a whoop of glee, Sabrina drew her dagger and sliced Aodh's throat.

Blood spurted and gurgled, pooling in the mud.

Grabbing the brand, Owein limped across to Aodh's lifeless form. Between the corpse's fingers was a razor-sharp dagger.

'I don't like the way things are going,' Owein said quietly.

'Neither do I,' Sabrina answered. Then she gave a loud whistle. After a few heartbeats, two Dobunni warriors ran to her side.

Sabrina kicked Aodh's corpse. 'This demon tried to murder our beloved druid who's brought us so many glorious victories! Throw him in the river.'

The men grasped the body. Aodh's head fell back, his eyes staring blankly up at Tegen as he was hauled away.

Sabrina cleaned her knife on the grass and slipped it back in its scabbard. 'What're we going to say to Boudica?'

'I'll think of something,' Owein replied, 'although I don't think Boudica will believe whatever we say.'

Tegen stood in front of her golem. Pulling herself upright, she spoke to it: 'Did Boudica give you something to keep?'

The creature nodded.

'Give it to me.'

With its flat hand it reached to its neck, broke what looked like a string, and handed it to Tegen. She examined it in the torchlight. 'It's a necklace of plaited hair,' she said. 'Probably Boudica's. It's not enough to control it completely, but it would make it confused and hesitant.'

'Treacherous witch!' Sabrina shook her head. 'But what do we do now? Owein's woman will die if Boudica doesn't get her way.'

Tegen beckoned Owein and Sabrina closer and whispered, 'Firstly we need a new hair necklace so Boudica doesn't notice hers is missing. Mine is too short, Sabrina's is too dark. It's a shame you cut your hair Owein, it was almost the same colour as the queen's.'

He laughed. 'I know you'll think me vain – but I did keep a plait, just to remind me of who I really was – in case I became too Roman.'

'Can you get it?'

Owein nodded and left.

Tegen turned to Sabrina. 'Tell Boudica I'm preparing spells to transfer some power to her. Explain it's going to be a slow process, but by dawn, she will be able to give her first command … But not until Claudia and Ula stand at my side, alive and well.'

When Tegen was alone, she looked up at her creature. 'It will be light very soon. When the sun has risen completely, queen Boudica will give you orders. You may obey three of her commands and three only. Do you understand?'

The golem nodded. Crackling fire glimmered beneath its charcoal. The demon understood. And it was pleased.

By nightfall of the next day, the tall woman with the big voice would be the one doing the obeying.

25. A DEAL IS STRUCK

When Owein returned with a handful of long red hair, Tegen plaited a new necklace, then made the golem bow low so she could replace it. 'You must never reveal that this is not the queen's hair, do you understand?'

The golem raised its head then with glowing eyes it spoke, very clearly into Tegen's mind. *You made me,* it jeered, *so remember, everything I do, whoever gives the order, will be your fault. Shouldn't you destroy me now?*

'You can speak?' Goose pimples prickled Tegen's back.

Only those who love me can hear me.

'Who are you talking to?' Owein asked.

Tegen flapped her hand at him. 'Ssh!'

Turning to the golem, she searched his face for signs of a mouth. There were none.

'When did you learn to speak?' she demanded.

I always could, but chose not to, it replied. *I wanted you to think you were in control. Now you're in a fine mess – what are you going to do? Isn't it time you begged for my help? So many innocent people are suffering …'*

'Who *are* you?'

You know perfectly well.

'No I don't!' Panic rose in Tegen's throat.

I am you. I'm not you. I am everyone you've ever hated and every one you've ever hurt …'

'You're not making any sense!'

I never do. That's the point. Remember?

Owein stood beside her. 'What's happening?' he whispered.

'It can talk into my mind,' she replied softly, not taking her eyes off it. 'I ... I have no control. It's beyond me!'

The golem threw back its head and its body shook, racked with silent laughter.

At that moment Sabrina returned, closely followed by Boudica. A little way behind, Claudia and Ula stood with their hands still tied and gags in their mouths.

'Where is Aodh?' the queen demanded.

'He died,' Owein replied.

The queen just shrugged. 'Stupid man. Still, it doesn't matter. The creature will make me all-powerful. I don't need witches *or* druids.'

Tegen narrowed her eyes and considered Boudica carefully. *So, she's been conversing with the golem? How long? Since I brought it into camp? That would explain the looks and small bows. I wish I'd never made this thing. It seemed a good idea at the time.*

'Give me the women,' Tegen demanded.

Boudica crossed her arms. 'When my first command is obeyed, they're all yours.' Claudia wept into her gag, but Ula's eyes widened and she shook her head frantically.

Ignoring them, Tegen replied coolly, 'Magic takes time, especially complicated spells like these, but I will begin.'

As she spoke, Tegen stroked the stone egg in her pouch. Although she felt no spark of power, it gave her courage.

'Very well,' the queen replied, 'bring me food and ale, I'm hungry!' Servants bustled about fetching a chair, a table and food. Boudica made herself comfortable and ate as she admired her latest spoil of war: the golem.

Tegen busied herself with binding spells and incantations; by the time she had finished, the camp was flooding with early sunlight.

Praying her own hair was still in place where the creature's heart should be, Tegen stood before the queen. 'My lady, the golem is yours until sunset, but it will only obey three commands. You may try more, but I have no idea whether it will obey – or turn on you, so make your choices wisely!'

Boudica walked around her prize, admiring its grey, cracked skin, its burning red eyes and smoking veins.

Just then, a small puppy ran past and Boudica pointed. 'Kill it!'

Without hesitation, the golem grabbed the little brown and white bundle and squeezed it. With a flick, it shook the slimy corpse onto the grass. The golem's hands sizzled with the puppy's blood.

'That leaves two commands, my lady,' Tegen said quietly. Then she nodded to Sabrina who stepped up to the hostages and cut their bindings.

Claudia fell whimpering into Ula's arms and Owein led them both away.

Tegen turned her back on the camp and strode towards the ruin of Lundinium and the silvery river. She wished she had time to listen to its song and learn its wisdom; but that would have to be another day.

Sabrina walked at Tegen's side. 'You took a risk letting Boudica loose with that thing – she could command it to kill you.'

Tegen shrugged. 'I don't think so. She says she doesn't need me, but when she discovers it really will only obey her three times, she'll want me back. Furthermore, Owein has a small power over it now with his hair around its neck.'

'Won't it just do what it wants anyway?'

'I don't think it can – not completely. But with any luck I'll have destroyed it before things go too far.'

'But how? I watched it in battle, and swords and spears go right through it.'

Tegen sighed. 'I'm not sure … I've got to work something out today, before she demands more power.'

They turned at the sound of clattering hoof-beats. Owein was galloping his pony as fast as her short legs would go. He slowed as he came alongside. 'I've hidden the girls with the Dobunni as you suggested, Sabrina.'

'Good, they should be safe for a while. With any luck, Boudica's got other things on her mind.'

Tegen looked back at the camp. The giant figure of the golem was sitting exactly as they had left it.

'I hope Boudica chooses sensible commands,' Owein muttered.

Tegen smiled. 'Well, actually, I'm rather hoping that they aren't. The nature of the demon is that nothing about it makes sense. With any luck, things'll go badly wrong and she'll be only too pleased to give it back to me.'

Suddenly an awful thought struck her. 'Oh, Owein, I'm so sorry. You gave your hair to the creature, I'd been thinking you could give it orders if anything happened to me, or maybe together we could rein it back, but what if it uses your hair to hurt you?'

Owein laughed. 'Actually, the same thought struck me. In the end I raided the tail of a rather elderly roan mare pulling a baggage waggon. If the demon tries to reverse the spell, it'll mean pots and pans everywhere. Nothing worse!'

'You're so clever! Well done!' Tegen hugged him. 'I did think the hair felt rather coarse, but I didn't like to say anything.'

The three friends walked on. 'We've lost Boudica's trust,' Sabrina said at last.

'I'm not sure we ever really had it,' Tegen replied. 'She said a soothsayer warned her about me, and we've never seen eye to eye about anything. But I can't leave – I have to perform the Star Dancer's duty to Britain. I must stick to my part of the bargain. However, today I need somewhere with trees and some sense of peace so I can think.'

Owein pointed to a low, chalky hill with a few round houses huddled near the water's edge. It was only a short walk across the marshes. 'That's Lundein, the old settlement. I've heard it's deserted.'

'Let's try it,' Tegen said. 'Will you two come? I'd be glad of protection, Sabrina. I don't quite trust Boudica not to send prowlers around, and Owein, if Claudia doesn't need you I'd be grateful for your advice.'

Sabrina exchanged a glance with Owein. 'We'll come. I don't think the queen will miss either of us today,' she said.

26. THE WHITE HILL

On the hill of Lundein, autumn winds span golden leaves in a dancing frenzy. The rotting thatch on the scattering of tumbledown roundhouses showed the place had been deserted for several winters.

Sabrina went to gather firewood while Owein led Tegen inside one of the stronger looking buildings. From his satchel, he produced bread, mead and handfuls of little yellow apples.

When their midday meal was finished, Tegen sat staring into the fire. 'I see danger coming,' she said at last. 'Suetonius is far from defeated.'

'I don't think even Boudica would argue with that.' Sabrina replied, heaving another log into the flames. She dusted off her hands and sat beside Tegen. 'To be honest, I've a mind to assassinate her.'

'*What*?' Tegen gasped.

Owein crossed his arms and scowled. 'Don't.'

'But she's ruining everything. We could finish Suetonius off now,' Sabrina urged. 'Boudica says the time isn't right. If she was out of the way and we sent a few crack warriors like me and that hulking giant from the Durotriges after him, this'd be over in half a moon. We've got good spies along the route, we know where the troops are …'

Tegen snapped a twig irritably. 'Then why doesn't she

just get on with it?'

Sabrina rolled her eyes. 'Because she's after a glorious showdown that bards'll sing about for years to come. I can understand how she feels, but a decisive victory is what really matters.'

Owein threw a rotten apple into the ashes. 'I can see your point; she has no chance of winning a head-on battle with the Romans. She doesn't bother to understand how they fight! She's drinking too much and alienating everyone, but it would do more harm than good.'

Tegen looked at Sabrina thoughtfully. 'Would you really do it?'

Sabrina and Owein exchanged glances.

She nodded.

He shook his head.

'If Boudica dies, then the alliance will fall apart overnight,' Owein warned.

Sabrina's fingers played with her dagger. 'But with her out of the way, our Catuvellauni and Dobunni warriors combined can finish the job. We can worry about tribal in-fighting once Suetonius is carrion.'

'But you'll be put to death before Boudica's corpse is cold,' Owein warned. 'It'll cause mayhem.'

Sabrina sighed and slid her blade back into its sheath. 'What do you see, Tegen? Would it help to kill Boudica?'

Tegen rested her chin in her hands and stared into the fire. 'Do you see that log in the middle?' She pointed. 'The one that's almost burned through? That's the British alliance. The root end is holding it together, that's Boudica. We need her a little longer. But she will die, of that I'm certain.' Tegen looked up at Sabrina. 'How long before Suetonius can get enough troops to face us?'

'The biggest garrison is Deva,' she replied. 'He's probably nearly there. He'll have sent the people he rescued to friendly villas, then ridden like a hellhound to pick up more troops and return.'

Owein nodded in agreement. 'We have wasted three days since the fall of Londinium, Suetonius has a five day start. We don't have long – maybe a half moon at most.'

Sabrina scowled. 'I've told Boudica all of this. She just laughs. She really believes the golem will make her invincible.' Sabrina got to her feet and leaned against the roundhouse door. 'Look out there.' She waved her hand towards the sprawling British camp. 'There's thousands and thousands of us now and it's getting worse by the day. We've got more children and elderly than warriors.'

'We ought to build base camps for the families and keep our warriors moving,' Owein suggested.

Sabrina shrugged. 'Boudica won't do it. In fact, she's actively spreading rumours of families being raped and murdered if they're left behind. I suspect she likes having handy hostages to threaten, should anyone argue with her – like she did with Claudia and Ula.'

Tegen sighed. 'So we go more and more slowly, and meanwhile Suetonius can build up real strength at his leisure?'

'It's worse than that,' Sabrina warned. 'As Owein says, in a face-to-face battle, we'll not stand a chance. We fight best in ambushes and short forays: chariots in, drop the warriors, fight, then substitute fresh muscle. The Romans tire but we don't. We dart from flank to flank, picking off troops at the rear with surprise attacks.'

Sabrina shook her head. 'One day we'll meet a whole cohort of Romans in deadly formation in a terrain of their choosing. Our tactics won't work and we'll have to protect the hangers-on as well. It'll be like fighting with the whole of Britain strapped to our backs. It'll be slaughter, not glory.'

'What do the other chieftains think?' Tegen asked.

Owein laughed wryly. 'They are too busy squabbling over loot. At this rate, we'll have destroyed ourselves before Suetonius throws the first pilum. But I agree with Tegen, assassinating Boudica now will leave a deadly vacuum.'

Sabrina stood tall. 'I'm happy to die to save our cause. If we get rid of Boudica and proclaim Owein as king of the Catuvellauni the people will flock to Caractacus' son.'

He threw up his hands in horror. 'You *know* I'd be useless. Anyway with my bad leg the tribes would never accept me. The body of a king has to be perfect.'

'Times are changing,' Sabrina urged.

Tegen looked up from prodding the fire. 'No, Boudica has to live – for now.'

Sabrina rolled her eyes in despair. 'We have to do something, this rebellion is falling apart.'

'What else does the fire tell you?' Owein asked, peering over Tegen's shoulder.

A twig crumbled, scattering embers on the edge of the hearth. 'I'm not sure, maybe …'

'It's too late for maybes,' Sabrina snapped. 'You have to be *sure*. Tell us what to do.'

A second crack of a burning branch sent more sparks flying. 'If we sent a fast group of warriors towards Deva now, we still might win,' Tegen replied. 'But I don't know how we persuade Boudica.'

'Could we make the golem tell her? She'd listen then!' Sabrina suggested.

Tegen buried her face in her hands. 'No, it must *never* speak aloud. That'll make it truly alive – and free. That's why I gave it no mouth. Anyway, I can't control what it says – it's the demon speaking.'

Owein shrugged. 'Maybe you could tell her what you have seen in the fire – you're still her battle druid after all.'

'She doesn't trust me.' Tegen sighed. Then joining Sabrina by the door, she looked across at the camp.

Owein scratched his stubbly beard thoughtfully. 'As there are so many people here, would Boudica know if a few Dobunni warriors slipped away after Suetonius?' He winked at Sabrina.

She grinned back at him and clapped her hands. 'I don't think anyone would notice at all. What do you say Tegen?'

'I think you must hurry!' she smiled. 'And may the Lady Goddess go with you.'

Bowing formally to her friends, Sabrina strode cheerfully back towards the camp, singing a battle song at the top of her voice.

Owein poured a beaker of mead for them both. 'I need to talk to you Tegen – about this hill we're sitting on.'

'It's Lundein? The ancient settlement that was here before the Romans came? It feels very magical.'

Owein nodded. 'It's also called the White Hill where the head of Bran the Blessed is buried. As you know, his head will still give wisdom to anyone who asks. Perhaps he can tell you how to get rid of the demon once and for all?'

Tegen's eyes brightened. 'Do you know where Bran's head is buried?'

'No, but when Sabrina returns, we'll stand guard if you want to stay here for the night and dream, like you did in the wight-barrows.'

'But,' Tegen frowned, 'won't she have gone after Suetonius?'

'No, Boudica would miss her and smell a rat. Sabrina will probably send a war band discretely, then feast with the queen and slip back here this evening.'

Tegen looked around the warm, fire-lit roundhouse. 'Then when Sabrina returns, I will sleep here – and dream of Bran.'

27. THE THIRD COMMAND

That evening, Lundein glowed in a blood red sunset.

At the top, Tegen made a circle of pale stones and danced her evening ritual.

Owein poured the fresh spring water into the sacred bowl and lit the holy incense for the spirits while he intoned the prayers in his rich, melodious voice.

At the most northerly point, Tegen laid her stone egg and blessed it. They bowed to the four quarters and closed their circle.

'You've got a druid's egg!' Owein exclaimed looking back. 'It's a nice one too!'

'Tonn gave it to me, it's meant to enable me to argue in a way that no one can gainsay. I'm not sure it works though,' she grinned ruefully. 'Either that, or Boudica has a stronger one.'

At that moment, hurried footsteps scuffed through the long grass. It was almost dark, Owein swung around nervously. 'Who's there?' he demanded, one hand on his dagger.

'It's me!' Sabrina called back breathlessly. Moments later she stood inside the round house, her face as white as ash. 'Can you hear screaming?'

Owein and Tegen ran outside.

Somewhere nearby – women were howling.

'I must try and help.' Tegen snatched up her cloak.

'You go ahead!' Owein said. 'I'll come at my own speed.'
Sabrina grabbed Tegen's hand. Together they made for
the woods beyond the camp. The screaming intensified.
Heart-wrenching wailing became a jagged wall of
anguish.

Tegen felt sick and dizzy, but Sabrina's steady pace
urged her on. More and more screams tore at the evening
air, mingling with the sour stench of burning flesh.

As they got closer they heard words – begging, pleading
for mercy, answered by angry shouts.

The trees grew closer, tangling branches with Tegen's
hair. She tripped, then gasped. 'Must stop … got a stitch …'
Tegen folded.

Sabrina ran on. 'Catch up when you can,' she yelled
back, ploughing on through brambles and ferns.

The screaming dwindled to exhausted sobs, then a new
voice rose in agony.

Sabrina stepped forward, dagger drawn and wary.
Between the wet, dark branches firelight flickered and a
dark, fiery shape strode to and fro.

Sabrina trod carefully on the wet leaves, working her
way silently closer, then she retched and turned back.
Holding her arms wide, she caught Tegen's shoulders.
'Don't look. It's too awful.'

'I've *got* to look. I must know …'

'No you don't.' Sabrina tried to turn Tegen around, but
she wriggled free.

'I'm sorry Sabrina, but it's my duty to know.' She

glanced into the clearing, swallowed hard and whispered, 'Stay out of sight unless I'm in trouble. Better she thinks I'm alone.' Then Tegen ran into the torch-lit clearing.

Under the shadowy branches hung twenty or thirty mutilated, crucified woman.

Between them strode the golem, glistening with blood.

And by its side, swaggered Boudica.

The queen saw Tegen and sneered. 'Ah, my druid. Welcome.'

Tegen gestured towards the dying women. 'Those prisoners were dedicated to the Goddess, you had no right ...' Tegen fumed.

Lifting a torch high, Boudica stomped through the red bracken towards her. 'But I *have* given them to the goddess, and I am certain she is very, very pleased with my sacrifice.' With wet, red fingers, she pinched Tegen's chin. 'This is what happens to collaborators. Did you imagine we'd allow your little pets to escape? How sweet!'

Tegen jerked her head aside. 'You were a collaborator once!'

Boudica slapped her, 'That's a lie.' She clicked her fingers.

The golem's eyes glowed white hot.

Tegen stared at her creation in disgust. 'Why does it obey you? I bound it.'

'Dear child, you have such a lot to learn about real magic ...' Boudica held up a short, dark hair. 'My second command was to give me what controlled it.' She returned the hair to her waist pouch.

Tegen's eyes widened in horror. She had never imagined Boudica would have the magical knowledge to be so cunning. There were a few witches and spell casters in the camp, but no one with *these* powers. 'Who helped you?'

Boudica turned and nodded.

Tegen peered into the gloom and saw a shifting dark shape. Aodh's pale lips smiled cruelly, matching the dark slash of dried blood across his throat.

'You didn't think he was *dead*, did you?' Boudica sneered. 'You saw him bleeding, and thrown into the river, but that doesn't mean a *thing*. I have so much power now, I don't need you … In fact, maybe I'll hang you up with those other sluts?'

Tegen took a deep breath. It's not Aodh, she told herself. It can't be. It's just a shade,

'What was your third command?' she asked aloud.

Boudica laughed. 'That it should obey *all* my commands, of course!'

Tegen ducked away and fled.

'Run!' she yelled at Sabrina as she burst between the trees.

Branches reached out like clawing witches' fingers, roots rose to trip them and the darkness blinded them.

With firm hands, Sabrina helped Tegen through the snagging brambles, over ditches, into the fields and towards the firelight on the White Hill.

Behind them, the golem crashed through the wood,

tearing down trunks and boughs, lumbering and smashing as it ran.

Tegen's lungs ached. Her stitch returned. Her leaden legs could do no more.

She stumbled and coughed as the stench of burning grass and wet wood caught in her throat.

Blistering hot plates grabbed her waist and swung her high.

Tegen gasped as smoke billowed from her woollen robes. Flames licked her arms and back.

Then she screamed and fainted.

28. BRAN'S RAVENS

Cold and wet, Tegen opened her eyes in the dawn light. Rain dripped through the remains of the autumn leaves above. Her hands and feet were tied, and a couple of old cloaks had been thrown over her. Her head ached. Where was she?

Twisting her neck she looked around. The sight of cold, mutilated figures on crosses made her vomit.

Boudica had threatened she'd be next.

Wriggling around, Tegen counted three guards – all slumped asleep.

All was still, except for the rough *kark-kark* as carrion crows circled.

Tegen began to compose a spell against her bindings, but she froze. Someone was creeping up behind her, soft footsteps on leaves. She held her breath.

'Don't move,' Sabrina whispered. 'We gave the guards drugged ale – not sure how long it'll last.' Drawing her knife, she sawed through the ropes.

Tegen clambered to her feet, swaying drunkenly.

Sabrina swung her over her shoulder and marched into the woods. 'Keep your head down!' The going was hard between the closely growing trees and the rough, marshy ground. Sabrina tripped. Tegen rolled into the mud.

'I'm sorry, 'Sabrina gasped. 'You'll have to walk. Do you

think you can?'

Keeping low under brambles and sedges, they crept on until they crested a hill. Below lay the corpse of Londinium and the vast sprawl of Boudica's camp. It was still early and only one or two wisps of smoke drifted between the waggons and tents.

The golem was nowhere in sight.

Sabrina pointed to Lundein's low hill on their left. 'Can you make it to there? Owein's waiting for you. I'll join you when I can.'

Thanking every good spirit for the dimpsy light, Tegen picked her way across the treacherous marshland. If she could reach Bran, he would protect her. The river's tide was high, leaving silver-mirrored pools reflecting the pale sky at her feet. There was no direct path and the way was slippery and treacherous. The White Hill lay just ahead – always just ahead. Never any closer. Tegen struggled to breathe. She stopped on a hillock to rest her aching limbs and clinging wet skirt. If only she could be safe and warm.

She tried to imagine warmth, maybe she could magic her clothes dry again?

Then warmth came, sudden, hot and very close …

She rubbed her eyes. Trees. Burning trees … *Walking* burning trees …?

She leapt to her feet and ran. The two stout trunks were the thick legs of the golem, pounding in her direction. Why hadn't she heard the thudding steps, or the hiss of water boiling on its skin …?

There was no time to wonder. Tegen flung herself pell-mell onwards. Slipping, sliding, grabbing at tussocks of grass, hauling herself along. Chilled. Soaked. Too scared to breathe. She willed herself to reach the sanctuary of the White Hill.

She had no breath to call for help. What could Owein do anyway?

The ground shook. Scorching smoke billowed. The golem was gaining, unperturbed by water or mud.

Tegen tripped and fell. Clutching her sodden skirts, she ran again.

A sizzling charcoal fist snatched for her head.

She ducked.

The golem swayed and lost its balance. With a hissing splash, it fell. Black waters boiled as it sank.

'Keep it there, good spirits! *Please!*' Tegen begged as she sprinted on. But slopping and gurgling, the golem rolled over and found its feet. It was gaining on her once more.

Tegen skipped to her right, slid down a small slope and hauled herself upright just out of reach.

Trying to turn, the golem swayed, and fell again.

The mud shivered and wading birds rose screaming into the sky.

Then from high above came the slow beat of raven wings. At least a dozen birds were circling and tumbling in the grey skies above her head.

'Oh *no!*' she sobbed. 'Not them too! Now I really *am* lost.'

Her lungs hurt, her head swam and the golem was

almost on its feet once more. The birds closed in, scolding as they swam the air.

'Go away!' she gasped. 'Leave me alone!'

They dived closer.

She ran.

The ground rose steadily. This was Lundein's hill – she'd soon be safe.

Then she tripped, falling face down in the reeds. Her chest wheezed. She could not get up.

A pang shot through her belly. Her hand cradled her belly. 'My baby,' she breathed. 'Oh, my baby!'

'Tegen!' a voice yelled. She raised her head. Owein was hobbling towards her.

Behind her, the golem was still struggling through the quagmire.

Owein thumped closer, holding out his hand. Tegen grabbed it. Together they climbed the final slope.

But the ravens followed.

'Make them go away!' she sobbed, 'They're worse than the golem!'

Owein raised his crutch and swung it at the birds, but more and more came tumbling out of the skies, screeching their cacophony of noise.

After a few moments, Owein laughed. 'They're not hunting you – they're *protecting* you, *run!*'

Panting painfully, Tegen forced herself onwards with Owein struggling on behind. Only when she was at the top, standing in the centre of her ring of stones, did she dare to look back.

Owein was right. Now Tegen was safe, the birds were diving at the golem, driving it towards the river.

Caught in the sticky marshes, the hideous creature waded the incoming tide. As the waters swirled around it, they boiled, cloaking the golem in steam.

29. THE HEAD OF BRAN

When Tegen woke, it was late morning and all was silent. She sat outside the roundhouse and looked back towards the woods where the prisoners of Londinium had been massacred.

How could I have been so stupid? She groaned. I forgot all about the poor prisoners. I summoned this evil – then handed it over to Boudica. I thought I'd been clever, but I wasn't wise, and my magic wasn't strong enough. I don't know why I *am* the Star Dancer, I'm useless and naïve and causing terrible things.

Pulling out her knife, she stabbed the turf by her side.

If only I hadn't believed the voice that told me to imagine. I should've known it was the demon, but it seemed so logical – and simple. Too simple now I think about it. I wasn't listening to the web of magic.

The ravens gathered in the sky like huge black flakes of soot, then with the softest whisper of feathers, they settled around her. She stretched out a finger and stroked the breast of the nearest bird.

'Thank you,' she said. 'Did Goban send you, or was it Bran?'

The bird clacked its beak and bowed.

Just then, Owein's voice called out, 'Come inside. You need to eat. The people of Britain need our Star Dancer alive.'

'Are you sure?' Tegen muttered crossly.

'Yes.'

The ravens called *pruck pruck* and nodded, as if agreeing.

Tegen clambered to her feet and went inside. She ate the pigeon stew Owein had prepared, then accepted his offer of dry breeches and a shirt. She settled down on rancid straw next to the hearth, but lay awake listening to the calls of the water birds that sounded too much like the screams of the tortured women.

All around the White Hill, the gleaming coal-rainbow birds roosted silently, their jet black eyes watching for their enemy.

The next time Tegen woke, it was night. The Watching Woman's stars glittered brightly overhead. Tegen was stiff and aching as she walked to the sacred circle she had made the day before. At the northernmost point, she found Tonn's egg. She picked it up and held it at arm's length. If she screwed up her eyes, she could imagine the swirling colours made a face. This was Bran the Blessed, the Lord of the Britons who made the Cauldron of Re-birth and gave his life to rescue his people and his sister. His head was buried somewhere close by, ready to protect the Land for ever. Ready to give wisdom to all who sought it.

The features on the stone head were indistinct, but the eyes were alive and aware.

'Bran, tell me what to do,' she begged. 'I made this golem to try to contain evil, but I was unwise. Now it only serves Boudica and I don't know how to unmake it. I've brought the enemy within our camp – it's about to destroy us all!'

Tegen held her breath and listened.

Only the soft hush of the rippling water caressing the shore as it flowed between the black, low-hilled banks.

'Speak to me Lord Bran,' Tegen whispered again.

And the dark red streaks on the stone turned into eyes and nose and mouth.

Tegen found herself seated at a great feast. She was seated between warriors and bards in ancient dress, singing songs she didn't know. In the place of honour stood a throne piled high with cushions.

The heap was draped with a cloak as if it were a human torso. Settled between the folds at the top, was a head, crowned with silver hair.

There was no body, yet the face was fully alive, joining in the songs with a fine and hearty voice.

As Tegen stared, his dark eyes turned to her and he roared, 'Ladies, gentlemen, we have a guest. I give you Tegen, druid of the Winter Seas.'

The hall erupted with applause and cheerful shouts.

'Welcome to my Hall,' said the head. 'Eat, drink, rest, and then ask what you will.'

Tegen rose to her feet and bowed. 'Lord Bran, I thank you, I need to know …'

But a rowdy song drowned her out. A woman handed

her a mead horn and a thick slice of roast swan. 'Eat and drink first, my dear,' she whispered. 'Rest and laughter bring wisdom.'

So Tegen ate and sang and danced. One by one, the feasting companions fell asleep with their faces in their platters or curled up under the table where lanky dogs chewed on the last of the bones.

When the hall was quiet, Bran called out, 'Tegen, Star Dancer. Come and talk to me. Now you may ask what you will.'

Taking her mead horn, Tegen picked her way through the debris. She knelt before the throne and poured a little of her mead onto the floor.

'Hail Bran,' she said. 'A thousand blessings on your hall and your warriors.'

'And my blessings on you. Come and sit with me. Tell me your story.'

The head listened with attention to every word. At last he asked, 'And what do you need from me?'

'Huval the druid said my destiny wasn't to defeat the Romans.'

'So do you now understand? The Star Dancer's work is to prevent hatred and vengeance becoming the song and the life-blood of our country's future.'

'I do.'

'So, how will you make that come to pass?'

'I need to begin by destroying the golem. I know the demon would have wormed its way into the rebellion with or without it – Boudica would have made sure of that, but the creature was a deadly mistake, I cannot control it.'

Bran smiled through his white beard. 'And what is the golem made of?'

Tegen shrugged. 'Ash, mud – maybe with some blood in it, rain, tears, and a framework of heather and withies.'

'Then that is *all* it is – held together with intention and dreams. Nothing more. You have nothing to fear. Take courage Star Dancer. Your destiny is almost fulfilled, then you shall have the hearth and home you long for. Remember my head is buried here to protect Britain. For a short while, you are my hands and feet in the Land, but respite is coming. March on with Boudica a little longer. Your little girl will be born somewhere safe. You have my word.'

30. AODH

Owein woke Tegen in the dawn and handed her fresh bread and cheese. 'I heard you praying to Bran last night, did he speak?'

Tegen nodded. 'Yes, but I need to think about what it means before I try and explain.' She fell silent.

Owein sat down and cuddled her. 'I understand,' he said softly. 'You don't have to say anything, but I'm here when you need me.' He gave her a friendly peck on her cheek.

Tegen rested her head on his shoulder and chewed her bread. 'I must go and do my morning ritual,' she said at last. 'Will you join me? I need my magic to be strong now the golem serves Boudica.'

'I'll do anything to help. She's worse than uncle Admidios because she's clever and she has most of the tribes behind her. There'll be more bloodshed when they realise how badly she has let the people down. There are no homes or crops to go back to for the winter.' Owein stabbed his cheese with his knife. 'In some ways, she's destroyed our Land without the Romans having to lift a finger.'

Tegen nodded. 'That fits in with what Bran told me – he said my destiny is to prevent vengeance becoming the song and the life-blood of the future.'

'That's impossible,' Owein scowled.

'There … there may be a way but I need time to think.

I'll explain everything,' she promised, 'but right now, we need to prepare some very strong magic. I fear Aodh's spirit is walking.'

When they had finished eating, Tegen and Owein went to stand in the ring of pebbles. They drew sacred circles in the air with their staffs, then trickled fresh spring water on the grass. Tegen laid twigs end to end around the perimeter and commanded them to burn. Thus protected by all the elements, the two druids stood side by side, holding hands and looking towards Boudica's camp.

Tegen began:

'Lady Goddess and Lord Bran,
bring this terror to an end.'

'Bring peace to your Land,' Owein chanted in reply.

'Give us strength to work with your hands,' Tegen continued.

'May healing be our song
and reconciliation, our life-blood.'

The words hung in the air as they looked across the muddy margins of the river to where the British camp squatted, scratching irritably at itself like a mangy dog. Clouds scurried across the sun and a rain-laden wind threatened to drench them.

'I think that means go inside and get warm!' Owein laughed.

Tegen raised her right hand and her fire-circle went out. 'Enough. Let the flames rest until we need them again.' She turned to run inside.

It was then she saw him.

Aodh.

Standing, grey and silent, unbothered by the wind and rain that sliced right through him.

Tegen's blood roared in her ears. 'What do you want?' she demanded.

'Who are you talking to?' Owein asked, staring right at the apparition.

'Can't you see him?'

'Who?'

Tegen blinked. The figure was gone.

'You get warm, Owein, there's some dark magic going on. I need to face it.'

The rain lashed into Owein's eyes but he didn't move. 'I want to help you.'

'Then sit by the fire and pray for me.' She handed him her cloak. 'And warm this for when I come in.'

Alone within the circle, Tegen summoned fire in the twigs once more. Through chattering teeth, she called out, 'Aodh! Where are you? Let me see you!'

There was no reply.

Why was this shade calling for her, and then hiding? What did he want?

Tegen closed her eyes. 'Think: first I must protect myself, then seek wisdom. If one ghost has escaped Tir na nÓg, there'll be others close behind.'

Despite the rain, Tegen decided to dance. It would keep

her warm and she could work her strongest spells that way. Raising her arms and listening for the rhythm of the drummer boy in her head, she began to sway, slipping and sliding in the mud. A picture came into her head of the Goddess embracing the sacred hill. Spreading her arms wide, she did the same.

'I hope you're really here, Lady,' she prayed. 'Show me what's happening.'

When she opened her eyes, Aodh was standing just beyond the ring of stone and fire. His face was deathly pale, his eyes and clothes the yellow-grey of the swollen river.

Tegen kept dancing. 'Why are you here?' she demanded.

The figure leaned towards her and without a breath, he whispered, 'We are one, you and I.'

'No. That's not true.' Tegen straightened her back and with fierce gestures, she fended off the shade. Her hands and feet swept and sprang in time to the pounding of her heart. She had to imagine this creature *away*. It wasn't real, it couldn't be.

But every step she took, the grey figure shadowed and mimicked her beyond the circle. Knowing her next move before she did, persistent, closer than her own soul, leaping, landing, turning ... Around and around the sacred stone and fire they danced.

Tegen inside, Aodh outside.

Suddenly, Tegen twisted around and took a swipe at Aodh's face.

Her hand passed right through where a mouth should

have been. Tegen's momentum carried her forward. She slipped, stumbled and fell face down in the mud, sprawled across the magic flames, half in and half out of the sacred space.

The flames died, and Aodh was gone.

It is a ghost! She told herself, it *has* to be ... what else could appear and disappear like that? Bran had told her not to be afraid, and at Sinodun she had walked in Tir na nÓg and come to no harm. She lifted her head towards where the apparition had last been.

Her heart missed a beat, for there was Admidios, staring contemptuously down at her.

Rubbing the dirt from her eyes she sat up. 'Not you as well!' The shade shimmered and shifted, melting slowly into Gorgans with his long, white hair, still wet from the caves where he had died. The albino stretched out his thin hands as if to embrace Tegen.

Shivering from cold and wet, she stared in horror as Gorgans shrank into Enid, her dark eyes pleading and angry at the same time.

'Enid ...?' Tegen reached towards her old friend, but the woman's eyes hardened accusingly.

Then Aodh was standing there again, yellow-grey and ghostly as before.

He laughed and stepped inside her fire circle. 'Don't you realise what I am yet, *druid*?'

'You're a ghost.' Tegen stood. She raised her hand. 'Go back to the Otherworld, you have no place here.'

Aodh shook his head and smirked.

It took all Tegen's strength not to run to the warmth and security of Owein and his hearth.

I will not be afraid, she told herself firmly.

Her head swam as she tried to think, if he – *it* wasn't a ghost – then what? Lowering her head, she raised a spirit shield around herself.

With one step, Aodh melted through it. He stood so close to Tegen they would have shared a breath – if he had life.

Aodh shook himself and became a raven that rose screeching into the air, then plummeted, clawing at Tegen's face.

She screamed and hid her face.

The raven flipped a somersault and stood as Aodh once more. He pretended to brush dust from his robe. 'I'm rather good at imitating faces. Boudica is quite intrigued by me.'

Tegen steadied her breathing and made herself calm down. 'What does Boudica see?'

'Oh, lots of things, but mostly the men who raped her daughters and the soldiers who flogged her.' The shade span around, laughing in the rain that streamed right through his filmy body.

Tegen's eyes widened. 'You are my worst fears!'

Aodh bowed. 'At your service – forever.' The shade embraced Tegen and slid icily through her. 'You thought you were pregnant with a baby,' he taunted, 'but someone with your powers is giving birth all the time. It's in your nature. You have to create, to make – both good and evil. It's bursting out of you and there is no way to stop it.'

The figure of Aodh whooshed around her. 'And you will never destroy your creature or me because you can't. We are also your babies. We terrify you. You made us. You worship us!'

'That is where you are wrong.' Tegen wiped the rain out of her eyes and thought of Goban, Brigid and Bran. 'I have good spirits who love me and protect me. The golem will die, and you, *liar*, are not a part of me!'

Aodh looked shocked, then faded away.

'Good riddance,' Tegen muttered. 'I've had enough of being afraid.'

'Tegen?' Owein's voice broke in, 'you'll be catching your death of a cold. Hadn't you better …?' he broke off. '*Admidios*?' he gasped in horror. 'What are you …?'

Tegen span around. 'I said, *go*!' she roared.

Once more, the figure faded.

'What was that?' Owein asked, pale as linen.

'Nothing to worry about,' she replied. 'You imagined it.'

Owein rubbed his eyes. 'I am very tired,' he muttered. 'Listen, it's getting late, perhaps we should go back to camp after all?' He wrapped Tegen's warm cloak around her shoulders. 'Come inside, you're frozen.'

Tegen pulled the woollen folds closer as she followed him in. 'I'm going back to camp. Boudica will move on in the morning and I must be near the golem. I need to work out how to destroy it.'

Owein's jaw dropped. 'But she'll kill you.'

'It's what Bran told me to do. He has promised his help. I'll hide – I'll ride with the warriors' families, but I must go.'

In the doorway, a coal black feather fluttered. Tegen picked it up and stuck it behind her cloak pin.

Ravens are sacred to Bran, she told herself. This'll remind me of his protection. None of these visions can harm me – and nor can Boudica. I have Bran's word.

I must leave the good spirits a thank-offering, but what? She looked around. The fire in the sagging hut was fading. Owein was packing his panniers ready to leave.

'Is there any bread left?' she asked.

He pointed to a small lump on the edge of the hearth. 'It's a bit dry, you could moisten it with ale.'

'Perfect, thank you.' Tegen took the bread and the ale flask and went outside to the remnants of her stone circle. Standing in the centre, she poured ale over the bread and tore the sodden mess into small knobs that she scattered on the ground.

'What on earth are you doing?' Owein asked as he dragged his panniers through the mud towards his pony.

'Feeding the ravens,' she said with a smile. 'I pray there'll always be some living here on the White Hill of Lundein to protect our Land.'

VERULAMIUM

31. VERULAMIUM

After dark, Tegen and Owein slipped amongst the crowds of hangers-on at the back of the camp. They slept shivering under a cart, and at dawn, Owein slipped away.

'Be careful, keep out of sight,' he whispered, kissing her cheek.

As the sun rose, the army began its lumbering crawl northwest, led by thundering drums, shrill pipes and the clatter-blast of carnyxes.

Tegen worked her way towards the front and watched from a distance as Boudica mounted her chariot, her red hair flowing over her wing-like cloak. The crowds parted, allowing her to ride alongside the striding golem.

With shining eyes and a raised spear, the queen greeted her subjects.

They cheered and beat their swords on their shields.

Tegen worried at her sore finger. 'Everything's going her way,' she said to herself. 'The war, the magic, the adulation …'

Tegen looked around for Sabrina, but could not see her, so she slipped back amongst the crowds.

Sabrina was riding the other way, mounted on a fine chestnut stallion looted from a dead decurion. She searched for Tegen all morning, but Bel's chariot was high before she spotted Epona's white head nodding proudly between a waggon and a baggage mule.

Tegen was slumped in the saddle, her cloak pulled down over her face.

Sabrina wove her way between the clattering carts and screaming children, until she came alongside. 'Are you all right?' she asked.

Tegen started and rubbed her eyes. 'Sorry, I think I was asleep. The last few days have been exhausting.' She stroked her belly. 'But we are both well. Did you send the secret detachment of warriors to cut Suetonius off?'

'Venutius has chosen twenty of his best men and sent them in pairs "on scouting missions". No one will suspect. I haven't asked Daig or the Iceni chieftains. They think everything Boudica does is wonderful.'

'And Addedomaros?'

'I don't trust him.' Sabrina rolled her eyes. 'I've sent fifteen of my own warriors – men and women I can really trust – and the Parisii have sent another dozen or so.'

'Is that enough?' Tegen's voice was tense.

Sabrina slapped Tegen on the back. 'Suetonius's detachment isn't large, and keeping the war band small gives our warriors the chance to catch up. Hopefully they'll not be noticed on the road either. A few deadly spears well aimed between Roman shoulder blades will do more harm than this rabble ever could.'

Tegen nodded. 'I feel as if we're moving more slowly by the day.'

'We are, and at this rate we don't stand a chance.' Sabrina lowered her voice. 'I've a suspicion that mad spirits and wine have taken Boudica's mind – she's just getting worse.'

'Has she mentioned me?' Tegen asked.

Sabrina beckoned Tegen to lean closer. 'Not even Boudica would dare kill a druid, but I've overheard her saying that she's worried; apparently the golem doesn't always obey her. Now Aodh is dead, I think she'd be secretly relieved if she knew you were still around – just in case it goes berserk.'

'It might well,' Tegen warned. 'The demon isn't on either side – it could just as easily swat our warriors as trample a legion. I'd like to stay out of sight for a while. Will your people bring me news of what the golem does?'

Sabrina nodded. 'I will see to it.'

Tegen smiled wryly. 'It'll be a relief not to have to speak to that awful woman day after day. What do the other kings and chieftains think of me? Whom can I trust?'

Sabrina looked around carefully. 'Rumours travel fast: they've heard what happened to the prisoners of Londinium – they're afraid if they side with you, then the same will happen to their women and children. I'd say don't trust anyone until Boudica gets over her stupid obsession with the golem. When it doesn't do what she says, she'll be screaming for you, then you can demand what ever you like in exchange for your services.'

'It might not be quite that simple.' Tegen worried at her

finger as she watched children playing tag between the trundling carts. 'But you'll know where to find me.'

'But not *here*,' Sabrina spread her hands.

'Why not? No one expects a battle druid riding with farmers and fishermen.'

'But these are Trinovantes. They support Daig and Addedomaros. We must go to the Dobunni – our own people are honour-bound to give you refuge. That's where Owein has hidden Claudia and Ula.'

Tegen's eyes brightened. 'They're alive!' she exclaimed. 'I hadn't dared think that Boudica would keep her word.'

'She might change her mind if she finds them.' Sabrina shrugged. 'Boudica's word doesn't mean much these days. She thinks she's invincible: she believes the golem is Gwyn ap Nudd incarnate and she has Death at her command. That's why she's not bothering to hurry after Suetonius.'

Sabrina put her hand on Tegen's arm. 'Follow me. We've got to get you properly hidden. Epona shines like the sun on a rainy day. I'll make sure she's made muddy and walks well apart from where you'll be hiding.'

Sighing, Tegen stroked her swelling belly. 'I could do with a rest.'

For the next hand span of the sun, they wound their way between the marching crowds until the cloak colours changed and people bowed as Sabrina passed.

'We're home, with my Dobunni,' she smiled.

Dismounting, they handed their mounts and a few coins

to a boy, then Sabrina lead Tegen towards a covered waggon. She pulled back the oiled linen flap. 'Get inside. Keep your head down. Someone will bring your things, and I'll get back to you as soon as I can.'

Tegen clambered in. The waggon roof was made of leather stretched over wooden supports, making a dark tent on wheels. It was hot, stuffy, and loaded with bundles. She could just make out two cloaked figures at the far end, one lying down with her head in the other's lap. They were whispering quietly and didn't even look up.

Tegen was glad to be left alone. She made herself comfortable in a corner and thought.

I must use the courage and strength Bran gave me, she told herself. While that *thing* is leading Boudica's troops, we're all marching to our deaths.

She tried to imagine the golem dead at her feet, but the picture was faint and unreal.

'I'm too tired to think,' she murmured as sleep claimed her. She dreamed of throwing fire at Suetonius Paulinus, and wrestling with the demon when it inhabited Enid on Cadair Idris. Then she saw herself making the golem from the blood and ashes of Camulodunum. She had made it with such great care. Had it really been *loving* care?

Then the waggon jolted and woke her.

Aodh was right, she realised. I do love the golem – for its magnificence and power. But I loathe it as well.

If you kill our child, you will never come into your glory or have your revenge, came a whisper in her head. *Together we will be so powerful – we will rule the world.*

Then Bran's voice echoed in her memory, *Take courage Star Dancer … Remember my head is buried here to protect Britain. For a short while, you are my hands and feet in the Land, but respite is coming.*

Tegen breathed more slowly. Bran would protect her baby. He would show her how to destroy the evil she had also made.

'All shall be well,' she whispered; then she slept again.

But her dreams were of warriors trapped between Roman swords and fire. Mothers and children fleeing, their cloaks aflame. Then the image changed to Suetonius scowling under his thick brows, and he was searching – for her.

Just then, Owein climbed into the waggon with a clatter. He knelt beside her and wrapped a comforting arm around Tegen's shoulder.

She opened her eyes.

'You're shivering,' Owein whispered. 'Are you ill or just cold?'

Tegen leaned against him, tears wetting her cheeks. 'It's only a dream.'

'Do you want to talk about it? '

She shook her head. Until she knew what it had meant, she daren't say anything. It had all felt so real. Too real.

The women at the far end of the waggon were sitting up and watching her intently.

The nearer one made a gesture – Tegen guessed it was a

sign against evil. The figure that had been lying down wriggled forward. 'Sextus?' she asked, hoarsely. '*Tegen*?'

Owein knelt by her side. 'I have bought you some food.' He opened his satchel and handed out several packages.

Tegen stared. She'd forgotten about Claudia and Ula. 'You're safe! And we were hiding in the same cart. How long have you been here?'

Claudia crawled closer and touched Tegen's fingers. 'Since that night when your queen wanted to kill us. My betrothed is a good man and cares for us well. But why are you here?'

'The same as you,' Tegen replied. 'Now Owein and I are out of favour with Boudica, we must hide too.'

Claudia sat next to Tegen. 'So – you're that famous battle druid everyone's talking about! And I thought you were just some girl I talked to because I was bored.'

Tegen nodded. 'Ula guessed.'

Ula remained on the far side of the waggon, scowling. 'But I didn't guess you were cruel.'

'But I'm not ...'

'Why else would you give Boudica that killing-monster?' Ula raged. 'I'd rather die than have that *thing* running loose because of me!'

'Ssh! Keep your voices down,' Owein warned. 'It wasn't like that, Tegen thought she had outwitted the queen, but the creature chose its own mistress.'

'Pah!' Ula spat.

Tegen smothered a yawn as she took a piece of fish from

Owein's supplies. 'Look, I'm sorry you aren't happy about being alive. I'm very tired and hungry, can we discuss the rights and wrongs of saving your life another time?'

Ula turned her back, but Claudia stared with fascination as Tegen ate her food.

Out of sight, under her cloak, Tegen laid her hand over her growing child. 'You have been four moons growing inside me now, little one,' she whispered. 'Bran said you're a girl. I shall call you Gilda after my beloved friend.'

She let her fingers drift to Tonn's stone egg, stroking its reassuring coolness. Bran had spoken to her. What he had commanded must be done.

The golem must die.

The sack of Verulamium was worse than Londinium and Camulodunum. It was cruel and bloody. The daylight hours were filled with clattering, honking carnyxes mixed with weeping and yelling.

As before, the townspeople had seen the monstrous army lumbering along the road and most had fled. In retaliation, Boudica ordered the looting and burning of every farm and village along the way, whether British or Roman.

Tegen felt too exhausted to move. She lay in the back of the waggon, writhing with stomach cramps and praying she wouldn't start bleeding. She knew she'd lose the baby unless she rested.

What's more important? she asked herself, The birth of

my child who is the hope of Ériu, or miscarrying so I'll be strong enough to protect the people of Verulamium?

Too ill to think, she slept.

The fighting ended at sundown. Tegen was still asleep. The prisoners were slaughtered.

The next day, they set off once more. Tegen still lay, unmoving.

On the other side of the bumpy waggon, Claudia moaned about her lot, while faithful Ula tried to calm her.

Neither girl spoke to Tegen. Ula hated her, and Claudia feared her.

Sabrina and Owein brought food and news. Boudica was losing her grip; the tribes were fighting each other. Worst of all, the hand picked warriors who had gone after Suetonius on Sabrina's orders were found slaughtered, with British daggers in their backs.

'The only thing Boudica truly cares about is the golem,' Sabrina sighed. 'It's almost as if nothing and no one else matters. She doesn't even sit with her daughters any more. She's in a daze. She scarcely eats or sleeps. She no longer leads us. At this rate, the tribes will have destroyed each other by the next moon. '

Sabrina ran her hands through her hair. Threads of silver wound through her dark curls. She turned to Owein. 'I think we should pull the Catuvellauni and Dobunni away. I can't fight on in good conscience. This isn't war – it's mass murder.'

Owein chewed the end of his beard. 'If we did that, we'd be pursued and wiped out. She is merciless.' He turned to Tegen. 'Could you hold the golem back if she turned it against us?'

At that moment, Tegen felt a flutter in her belly. She laid her hand over the place. All she wanted was to go somewhere safe to have her child, as Bran had promised.

'Tegen?' Sabrina touched her shoulder, 'What do you think? Can you control the Golem for a short while?'

Tegen groaned. 'I don't control anything any more. I need sleep. I'll try and dream an answer.' She lay down, but every time she closed her eyes, she saw burning waggons and fleeing people once more. She sensed it was a warning rather than the inevitable – but how to avert it?

Tegen tossed and turned for half the night. The stone egg in her pouch dug uncomfortably into her side. Pulling it out, there was just enough moonlight to make out the features of Bran the Blessed.

Peace would come. It was just a matter of how to make it happen.

As the days passed, a rage like a red mist was infecting the camp. There was no sense or reason. Squabbles were turning into fights and suspicion brewed dissent. Owein rode up and down the straggling phalanx, reading the mood of the people and trying to calm the warriors who knew him.

One evening, two men galloped along the road, their

cloaks streaming behind them as they raced towards the tediously slow caravan of rebels. They reined their mounts at the sight of the golem. It was now as tall as a house with steam and smoke perpetually seething from the cracks in its skin.

They made the sign against evil and dismounted near the leading group of chariots.

'Where is the queen?' one demanded. 'We have urgent news.' They were quickly escorted to Boudica, who was reclining on a litter heaped with silk cushions and carried by slaves.

'Take me aside, I will talk to these men,' she commanded. Her bearers obeyed, leaving the golem and the huge army to march on, ponderous and relentless.

The travellers, grey with exhaustion, bowed their heads. 'Our chieftain Ninian sends loyal greetings, lady.' Then the eldest man raised his head and took a deep breath. 'And he also sends a warning. The self-proclaimed Roman Governor, Suetonius Paulinus has set up an ambush for you. It's two hard days' ride north from here. The road passes over meadows and a stream, then climbs uphill to a narrow wooded valley where they're hiding. It's a little beyond where their road from Sul's land joins this one. Spies say Suetonius has summoned reinforcements from the southwest; we'll be trapped between them.

The queen raised a heavily be-ringed hand and made a lazy gesture. 'How many are there?'

'Ten thousand men, my lady. All well armed.'

Boudica smiled slowly. 'And how many do you see with *me*?' She spread her arms wide.

The men exchanged glances. They knew her army was said to be beyond counting. The second warrior bowed. 'But they are a crack fighting unit, my lady. They are fresh and deadly.'

Boudica raised an eyebrow. 'Do you mean my fine war band are lesser warriors than a handful of Romans?' She spat over her shoulder.

The first messenger stared at the golem's back as it strode ahead. He shuddered. 'No my lady, that's not what I meant.'

'Good,' she replied. 'You will accompany us and point out where this puny little ambush is.' Then she turned to her aide. 'For now we will rest and make camp. Someone find me that awful druid girl. I know she's still around. I have a feeling we might need her, much as it galls me to admit it.'

Sabrina, who had been riding close by, heard Boudica's orders and slipped away through the crowds to the waggon where Tegen was hidden.

'Boudica is calling for you,' she whispered urgently. 'She's as angry as Andraste herself, you'd better come quickly.' She explained about the ambush.

Tegen gritted her teeth. 'Tell her I'll come when I'm ready!'

Sabrina's eyes widened, then after a few moments, a slow smile curved her lips. 'What are you going to do?'

Tegen thought for a moment, then her eyes twinkled. 'Sabrina, will you tell the queen that I will visit her soon. Tell her ... tell her I am currently in a trance speaking with the Goddess. Would you ask someone to groom Epona and make her look as fine as possible? Owein, would you mind being my acolyte? Can you borrow lamps and incense burners, anything to make a big religious show the queen won't forget? Get everything alight and piled with incense. Meet me in Boudica's tent in one hand span of the sun.'

Sabrina exchanged a look of amazement with Owein. 'What are you going to do?'

'I think ...' Tegen began, her face bright with mischief, 'I'm getting the hang of being a battle druid, and it's time Andraste took a leading role. Will you help?'

'At once, your holiness!' Owein laughed and swept a bow, then he and Sabrina climbed out of the waggon.

'What's going on?' demanded Claudia petulantly. 'I don't like all of this travelling and war. I want to go home.'

'So do I,' Tegen replied as she clambered across the baggage. Sitting by Claudia and Ula, she took their hands. 'I know you don't feel safe with me – what with the golem and everything, but I've never willingly hurt or betrayed anyone. The time has come for me to stop Boudica's madness. To make my plan work, I need to strike awe in everyone who sees me.'

She looked into each girl's eyes. 'And you are the people I need to make that work. Will you help?'

32. ANDRASTE SPEAKS

Tegen's hair had grown long enough to sweep her shoulders in a soft, black wave. Ula oiled and plaited it, adding gold thread and green ribbons as she worked.

Claudia painted Tegen's eyes, colouring the lids with powdered malachite and blackening the rims and brows with heavy lines of kohl. She painted Tegen's lips with carmine and smudged more of the same on her fingernails.

Then came the jewellery. Every bit of gold and silver that the three girls had was draped on Tegen somewhere. Lastly, she pulled on her white druid's robes and tucked Bran's raven feather under her cloak pin. Ready at last, she climbed down from the back of the waggon and mounted Epona.

Sabrina's servants had curried the mare and plaited her mane and tail with yellow ribbons that fluttered against her pure white coat.

As Tegen rode through the crowds, everyone gasped and stepped back in awe.

Slowly and carefully, Tegen made her way to where Boudica's personal waggons were drawn in a circle around the great and hideous golem.

This really is my moment, Tegen told herself. Bran commanded me to prevent hatred and vengeance from becoming the song and the life-blood of the future. After this I will have a home and a child. Bran has promised peace. I must make that come about. I can imagine good things; I must make those happen. Magic is about restoration and healing, not control and power.

As Tegen approached Boudica's tent, she thought of Goban the smith-god. His rich voice thundered inside her head, *'What you put into fire, and how long you leave it there determines what comes out ... be it gold, bone – or ash.'*

The golem is just ash, and Boudica is only a woman made of bones, she reminded herself. I have nothing to fear.

Tegen straightened her back. Pale fire crackled around her head. Her green eyes shone and the sun stroked her gold and silver jewellery with jealous rays. The crowds drew back and bowed.

Tegen's heart thudded with ecstatic joy. She was as beautiful as the wronged Rhiannon facing her accusers. She had the wisdom of Bran the Blessed on her tongue. Now was the culmination of all the old tales. They had come together in *her*. Each of the old ones was about to speak.

At that moment, Tegen *was* the Goddess, riding her white mare amongst mortals.

Boudica was still reclining on her Roman litter, her head lolling on a blue silk pillow. A goblet hung loosely in her hand, red wine spilled like blood over her dress. On either side, her finest warriors sat at council, helmets polished and cloaks lifting in the breeze.

Behind her stood the golem.

Sabrina and Owein were waiting for her. Sabrina wore the seven-coloured tartan of the Dobunni queen. Owein was dressed in his druid's robes and adding pungent incense to a bowl of charcoal. By his side, a youth and a girl carried beeswax candles in bronze holders.

'Excellent,' Tegen smiled. 'Sabrina, please lead my horse, and Owein stand by my side while I speak. I want to approach Boudica with the sun at my back so its rays blind her. When we are close, give her so much incense she can't breathe.

Owein bowed silently and with a wave of a finger, commanded the children to walk with him. Only his eyes betrayed a glimmer of delight. As he took his place before the queen, he opened the censer to billow dark clouds in Boudica's direction. The children raised their candles then stepped aside, allowing Tegen and Epona to approach.

'You requested my presence?' Tegen roared imperiously without dismounting.

Boudica blinked and coughed. She was very drunk, 'Who're you? What in the name of Skatha do you think you're up to? What's all this smelly smoke? Eh?' She swigged from the dregs of her wine, burped and lay back on her pillows.

Tegen raised one hand. 'Silence woman!'

Boudica sat up, sobering rapidly. She slid off her couch, took two wavering steps then glared at Tegen, first out of one eye, then from the other. 'I know you ...' she slurred. 'You're that druid nuisance.' She hiccoughed. 'Changed my mind. Don't need you any more, I've got this beautiful thing instead.' She jerked her thumb in the direction of the golem. 'My new champion. He'll scare the Roman scum back into the sea with no boats under them.'

'That's where you're wrong,' Tegen replied quietly. 'It *is* nothing. It can *do* nothing. Come and watch if you don't believe me!'

Boudica drew herself up, her auburn hair swirling over her shoulders. 'Do your worst. It won't listen to you. It's mine and it's *magic*!'

'Not as magic as I am.' Tegen raised her hands and called out, 'For *I am Andraste*! I made this creature and I will unmake it.'

She dismounted, strode over to the golem.

'*Ash you were, ash you are,*

and ash you shall be again,' she intoned.

The golem leaned forward and reached for Tegen.

Searing heat and choking smoke made her eyes water, but without flinching, she took a deep breath.

And she blew.

Ash and cinders flew and span as the great charred knees crumbled.

'Move back!' 'Run!' People screamed. 'It's *falling*!'

And Tegen still blew.

Hot embers spat and hissed past her ears, smoke stung her eyes as the colossus staggered … and fell.

A sour wind rose, swirling ashes into the sky. With a thundering roar, the golem sank, and crumbled.

People fled, screaming in terror. As embers fell, fires started in luggage, clothes were set alight, and the air choked with smoke, soot and heat.

Tegen pulled Tonn's egg from her pouch and held it high, then she pronounced,

'With fire you have killed and destroyed.

But fire is nothing in the face of stone!'

Boudica stared in horror as the creature's magnificence drifted away on the wind, leaving only its face staring blankly up at her.

Tegen blew once more and the head cracked. The golem's eye-coals cooled from scarlet to vermilion, then to dark blood … and black.

Howling with rage, the queen drew her dagger and flung herself at Tegen.

Sabrina leaped on Boudica, grabbed her hair and hauled her backwards. The queen staggered after her captor screaming, kicking and biting.

Sabrina twisted the dagger from the queen's hand and stood her upright. She waved her hand at the burned sticks on the ground. 'Look at what you've been adoring, *sister*,' she snarled. 'You sold the people's trust for a few handfuls of dust!'

Eyes bulging, Boudica swung around and slapped Sabrina's face.

Snatching the queen's wrist, Sabrina glared back. 'Grow up. Everyone is watching you!'

Boudica swung around. Crowds of astonished

spectators from every tribe were shoving and pushing to watch.

Tegen raised her arms and looked up at the sky. 'Taranis, bring rain!' she commanded.

And rain came. Large splashes pocked the hot cinders. Tegen stood like a standing stone amongst the wind, fire, smoke and water. Only her white robes fluttered against the chaos that raged about her.

Sabrina grabbed Boudica's shoulders and forced her to face Tegen. Glowering, Owein joined them, arms folded across his chest.

Boudica tried to wriggle free, but Sabrina twisted the cloth at the back of her dress so she couldn't breathe. At last the queen sagged and knelt in the mud, rain streaming down her magnificent hair, plastering it to her face, breasts and back.

Owein stepped closer and leaned down to Boudica's ear. 'Listen to your battle druid,' he advised quietly. 'If anything is to be saved out of the mess you have caused, she is the only one who can help you. It is that or death. You choose.'

With one gesture, Tegen commanded the rain to stop. With another she parted the clouds and the sun shone brilliantly on her white robes and jewels. When she spoke, her voice was deep and wild, with colours drawn from thunder and night.

'I am Andraste! You have defiled my name,' she roared. 'You have murdered and slaughtered without mercy. You have killed your own people as well as enemies who surrendered. You have defiled the holy name of war. Your war is not my war. You are not fighting for justice and freedom. Your heart-song is your own puny hatred and vengeance. You are without honour. I despise you.'

And she spat in Boudica's face.

Boudica struggled to get up, but Sabrina held her down.

The sun warmed the rain into a pale mist. The light made Tegen shimmer. No one dared stop her. She spoke again. 'Once you were my right hand and my daughter – now you are nothing but a rage-blinded puppet of chaos.'

Boudica stared up at Tegen, her eyes wide and red, her mouth hung open in horror. Then glancing past Tegen, she smiled slowly. 'I don't believe you!' she bellowed, jerking herself free from Sabrina's grip.

Tegen sensed a prickle at the back of her neck. She spun around to see a group of seven or eight Iceni warriors with spears and knives aimed at her heart.

With a sweep of her hand, Tegen flung fire at their faces. They fell back, howling in pain.

'Believe it or die, Boudica.' Tegen replied levelly. 'I chose you to be my weapon to free Britain of tyranny, but you betrayed me, and your people. You've become the worst tyrant of all. Choose now to serve me. Do what must be done, but without wine, cleanly and as a matter of honour. Leave your hatred behind. Worship me, and fight as a true warrior.'

Boudica pulled back her lips in a snarl. 'I refuse.'

The crowd gasped.

Boudica tossed her head and sneered. 'I say you're an impostor – a little girl in make up and sparkly things, trying to look like a woman!'

Sabrina wrenched Boudica's head back and pressed a knife to her throat.

Tegen shrugged. 'Very well – you've decided you wish to die. Then I decree that in your next life you will forget you were ever a queen. You shall be a slave – to a poor farmer.'

The crowd gasped. Boudica's eyes swept from left to right. The people were packed closely on all sides. She had no choice.

'I agree,' she muttered.

Tegen nodded to Sabrina, who let the queen stand. 'Then summon all the kings, queens and high chieftains here. We'll tell them what you've vowed, and you'll swear on the head of Bran to obey Andraste.'

33. THE OATH OF BRAN

A few nights later, Boudica's army camped on the southern slopes of a hill. Just as the spies warned, the Romans had taken command of the mouth of a narrow wooded valley, a short ride to the north.

Around their fires, the British warriors talked only of despair. Without the golem, what chance did they have of winning? The creature had been invincible, caring nothing about arrows and spears. Iron melted as soon as it touched that burning hide.

Whispers accused Tegen of witchcraft and treachery. But apart from making the sign against the evil eye, and keeping a wide berth, no one raised a finger against the girl who had destroyed the golem with her breath.

The chieftains of each tribe all came to meet with the queen that night. Boudica sat tense and terrified between her two daughters. She neither ate nor drank, but fiddled endlessly with a fragment of burned wood in her lap until her hands and skirt were black.

Still dressed as Andraste, Tegen stood behind Boudica with a tall ash staff in her hand. Her face was drawn, but her eyes burned. She had used every kind of divination – and she knew there was no hope for the following day. Suetonius would win.

He couldn't fail against such a disorganised rabble.

Tegen longed to avoid battle altogether – or at worst, to

make the Roman victory swift. That way, Suetonius's lust for vengeance might fade, most of the people could return to their homes unharmed and life could begin again – somehow.

She cast her eyes around the chieftains gathered for their last meal. By Tegen's command, the only drink was water. The food was finished in resentful silence.

At the end, Owein stood, leaning on his crutch. 'For those who do not know me, I am the ovate Owein ap Caractacus – King of the Catuvellauni.'

He gestured towards Tegen. 'Some have criticised our druid for destroying the golem. Half a moon ago on the White Hill in Lundein, I witnessed the head of Bran the Blessed tell her to do this. She acted in obedience to the god, for without his blessing, we have no hope.'

Owein's steady gaze compelled every man and woman to look at him. 'I may not take my rightful role of king because of my damaged leg,' he explained, 'but I speak with the heart of Caractacus. Apart from Boudica, my father was the only one who has put the invaders to flight – so *listen*.' Pausing, Owein held the moment. 'Unless we obey our druid tomorrow, there will be no more tribes, no more clans, no more kings – or even chieftains. Our way of life will be over. We must put aside our quarrels and desire for personal glory.'

'And roll on our backs and whimper?' sneered Boudica, bearing her teeth.

Scowling at her, Owein continued, 'Our actions have not

yet been determined.'

Mutinous murmuring broke out. 'Who the hell do you think you are?' roared a Parisii chieftain from the back. A tall Cantici warrior thumped the table. 'Caractacus had no sons. You're a liar!'

Drawing himself straight, Owein took a deep breath. 'There will be no shame if you go home without a battle. The fight for Britain will continue in other ways.'

Then he sat, glaring at the gathered leaders, daring them to argue.

Leaping to her feet, Sabrina drew her knife. 'You all know me, Sabrina, heir to King Eiser of the Dobunni,' she began, chin raised and eyes aflame. 'I don't do pretty speeches. I *fight*. And I will defend you all, whatever your tribe or rank.'

She drew the knife-point across her arm. 'Look, I shed my blood for you all. I am no longer a Dobunni: I am of the tribe of *Britain*. We share one sacred Land. Let us defend it together. However,' she plunged her blade into the table, making Boudica jump, 'tomorrow may not be the glorious battle you've been dreaming of. The gods may decree not to fight. Obedience will bring honour. Disobedience will mean disaster.'

'Run away?' sneered a grey-haired lord from the Trinovantes. 'I'd rather rot.'

The assembly clapped and cheered.

A chieftainess from the Parisii stood up. 'And what about that so-called druid? We've only got the cripple's word that Bran spoke to her. Without our golem, we're nothing!'

'Hear, hear!' There was more applause.

Tegen stepped forward. 'That golem was made for one purpose only, to contain the hatred we are all feeling – yes, even me. But the golem's magic was wrenched from me by the worst form of witchcraft. Remember how it destroyed your dignity and split your loyalty. Think of the women of Londinium …'

The room fell silent.

Tegen scowled. 'What had they done to deserve such an inhuman fate? Been born into slavery? Been forced to marry a Roman? Chosen to try and start a new life rather than see their children starve? Did that deserve crucifixion?'

Tegen rapped her staff on the table, making everyone jump. '*That* is not the way of Andraste. The Goddess fights without emotion, defending her people cleanly and honestly. If someone has to die, you send them to Tir na nÓg quickly. Fight to get rid of the Romans, fight for your families, your beliefs – but do it with honour and courage. Never pick on anyone weaker, never raid a farmhouse again, never rape, torture or hate.'

Heat and exhaustion began to overwhelm Tegen. She staggered, she had to finish … 'Hatred always breeds more hatred,' she urged, 'Then what happens? *Vengeance*! And who will avenge the revenged?'

Drawing the stone egg from her pouch, Tegen placed it in front of Boudica.

The queen stared at it in horror.

'Behold,' Tegen continued. 'The head of Bran. He will protect Britain as long as *we* act with integrity.'

She passed her hands over the white marble with its blood red streaks. As she moved away, the image shimmered and swelled into the head and face of Bran.

His blue eyes gazed steadily at Boudica.

Some screamed, some bowed or knelt, most stood stupefied with shock and amazement.

Tegen turned to Boudica. 'Now,' she said quietly, 'as you promised, you will place your hand on Bran's head and swear you will conduct tomorrow as the Goddess demands. If you fight, you will make it swift and fair. If the Goddess says retreat, you will obey.'

Boudica reached out and touched the stone with shaking fingers. 'I swear,' she whispered.

'Now, who will join our leader and share her vow?' Tegen demanded.

Sabrina wrenched her dagger from the table. 'I shall be first,' she exclaimed, 'and my warriors will follow me on pain of death.'

Then Owein stumped forward. 'And I shall swear on behalf of the Catuvellauni.'

One by one, a queue formed and men and women took their oaths. But many stormed away with thundercloud faces and tempers of forked lightening.

When all was done, Tegen returned the stone to her pouch. She beckoned Boudica aside. 'At dawn tomorrow, a female hare will be brought to your tent. Wrap it in your cloak, take it onto the field of battle and then release it. If it runs to the east then there will be victory, if it runs to the west, the British must retire without a fight. This is what the gods have decreed. You must accept what the hare shows you.'

'Very well. Now leave me in peace!' Boudica snapped. Then she turned aside to pull a cloak over her daughters where they'd fallen asleep by the fire.

'And make sure the girls are well away from here before dawn,' Tegen added.

Boudica straightened and frowned. 'I may be forced to listen to your self-righteous twaddle when it comes to battles and gods, but *I* decide what's best for my daughters.' She took a deep breath and jabbed a finger at Tegen. 'Megan and Oriana will be seated on my baggage waggon, watching me fight. They will tell their children and their grandchildren the story of how I saved Britain, long after *you* are dead!' And she spat.

Tegen shrugged. There would be no grandchildren. Megan and Oriana would be dead before the sun's midhaven. 'May you die quickly,' she murmured under her breath.

With a heavy heart, Tegen walked back to the waggon she shared with Ula and Claudia and packed her bag. 'You two must leave the camp, now, tonight. Things are becoming very dangerous. Travel back the way we've come and take the southwest turning. Go to a British settlement called Sul's Land, where hot springs bubble up from the mud. The first house inside the palisade on the southern side belongs to my friends Alawn and his woman. Ask if you can stay with them until I come.'

Ula started to pack, but Claudia hung back. 'Why now?' she moaned, 'it's dark ... There might be wolves. I can't go out there alone.'

Tegen tutted and rolled her eyes. 'You won't be alone. Don't you remember I told you Ula will save your life? Tonight will be the first of many times.'

Claudia shook her head. 'But I haven't eaten yet and it's cold outside. I'll go after sunrise.'

Tegen stared at Claudia. 'There'll be no escape in the morning. You will be dead before nightfall. What fate you choose is up to you.'

She turned to the slave girl. 'Do you have a sharp knife? Good. Wrap up well, take anything you need from the waggon and go.'

Tegen kissed them both, jumped down, then led Epona away through the nervous crowds.

Just because the golem was dead did not mean the demon had left.

Tegen could sense its malevolence sweeping through the camp, inhabiting all those who had refused the oath of Bran.

She also sensed its presence on the other side of the hill,

festering hatred amongst the Romans.

Especially in the heart of Suetonius Paulinus.

Once again, Tegen sensed that the Governor of Britain was looking for *her*.

34.   BEFORE THE BATTLE

Suetonius sat with his generals in his tent, a large sand map on the table between them. The battle site was excellent. He only had the XIV legion, and detachments from the XX. About ten thousand men in all, but they were well rested and equipped.

Suetonius jabbed at a deep valley in the map. 'Move the men into position below the trees, facing the open country at the bottom. In the morning, the British rabble will move north, straight into our trap. What's the state of that woman's "army"?'

A tribune handed Suetonius a wooden tablet with numbers tallied neatly in the wax. Suetonius thrust it back. 'Just tell me man!'

'Sir!' the tribune snapped to attention. 'Reports estimate over two hundred thousand, but in a hopeless mess. There are more women than men, and they've all brought their families and goods in the caravan. No discipline, no formation, no tactics and no perceived strategy. Sir!'

Suetonius nodded and drew a circle in the valley of sand. 'Then this is where we will contain them. The hills are too steep for them to avoid us and the woods will hide us if things go badly.' He placed pebbles at three points along the river. 'Their first offensive will use fording points. Break our army into equal sections to face them. Have your most experienced javelin throwers ready. Use a saw formation behind them, with auxiliaries on the flanks and cavalry on the wings. Any questions so far?'

'No sir!' his officers replied smartly.

'Good. Now, they'll attack just after dawn in their usual haphazard way. After the javelins, press on. The auxiliaries can take care of the first assault, then bring the infantry forward in tight formation. Drive the rabble between our wedges, funnelling them into small pockets so they can't fight or flee. Bring the cavalry in on the right and left to cut off any who try and escape. Don't even think of plunder. When we have won, you will have everything.' Suetonius scowled at them. 'Is that understood?'

'Yes *sir*!' came the reply.

'Good. They'll be moving uphill with no fall back position because of their carts and baggage which they will doubtless arrange like circus seating so everyone can watch! If they didn't carry so much loot and so many hangers-on, we might have reason to be worried. But as it is ...' The Governor of Britain smiled grimly. 'I won't pretend it'll be easy, these pagans have guts, I'll give them that, but our discipline will prove our superiority.'

Suetonius turned to where his oiled armour hung on the back of a chair, ready for the morning. He ran his hand over the eagle embossed breastplate. 'Tomorrow, my friends, sees the dawn of a new era: the complete, unconditional and eternal surrender of Britain.'

And myself proclaimed the Emperor of the North, he added silently.

'You are dismissed.'

The commanders stamped to attention and left the tent, talking quietly.

'You too,' Suetonius snapped at his slave. 'I need to be alone to think.' The boy bowed and withdrew. Suetonius blew out the oil lamps, leaving a trail of pale smoke in the firelight. He lay down on his camp bed fully clothed and pulled his fur rugs over his shoulders.

'Why do you want us to win?' he whispered to the demon in his head.

I don't. I simply want the raven haired one, and I am willing to help you if you will get her for me.

'She's yours, I swear.'

Then you shall have victory.

Owein and Sabrina sat by Tegen's side as she stared into a campfire. In the depths of the flickering flames danced the spirits of a million possible futures.

'It is Samhain tomorrow,' Tegen said quietly, 'appropriate, don't you think? A time for ultimate destruction of everything?'

Sabrina bit her lip and looked into the flames. 'Can't you see any hope?' she asked.

Tegen picked up a stick and poked at a heap of ash at the fire's heart. 'If my plan goes well and Boudica holds true to her vow, there will be no battle. The rebellion will fade away, and after the usual Roman repercussions, life will heal itself once more. But I don't trust the queen. The golem's spirit is embedded in her soul. I fear she'll choose battle, then vengeance will follow.'

Tegen turned to Sabrina. 'Listen, this is vital. If Boudica fights, then as soon as you can, take any who will follow you to the far southwest – where the land ends in the sea. Go by country roads and travel in small groups. There'll be no more war for a long time. You must never let vengeance take hold or the cycle will go on forever. Do you swear?'

Sabrina took Tegen's hand. 'I do. Will we meet again?'

Tegen frowned and shook her head. 'I don't think so, not after tonight. But if you live tomorrow, find a good man and marry him.'

Sabrina threw back her head and roared with laughter. 'Why, in the names of all the gods are you forever trying to marry me off and give me children? I'm a *warrior*!'

Tegen smiled as she stroked her thickening waistline. 'Because ... your descendants will be warriors too. One will be the greatest king that Britain will ever know. He must be born. Our land will depend on him.'

Sabrina stared at Tegen with her mouth open. 'You mean that, don't you?'

Tegen nodded and pointed with a twig at a roaring tongue of flame. 'He will be a great bear with your blood coursing through his veins and your own weapon in his hand. I have seen it.'

Sabrina drew her leaf-shaped sword. Its steel gleamed golden in the firelight. She was quiet for a few moments, then said, 'I had been determined to die tomorrow. I thought if we lost there'd be no point in living, but I will listen to you. I will keep my word and live if I can. You have my oath Tegen, and I will never forget you. If you are ever in need, look for me in the south west where the land ends.'

With that, she gripped Tegen's arms and then hugged her, tears streaming down her face.

Owein watched silently as Sabrina dried her eyes with the edge of her cloak. He had never seen his foster sister shed a single tear before. At last he said, 'don't tell me what becomes of me. I don't want fear to cloud my thinking … I have much to do tomorrow.'

'But …' Tegen began.

Owein raised his hand. 'Please, hear me out. Boudica was only putting on a show of agreeing tonight – to shut us up. We three have to know what to do when everything falls apart. I have an idea, but it will seal all our fates.'

The friends talked all night. Just before dawn, Sabrina hugged Tegen and Owein for one last time, then left.

Owein curled up in his cloak and lay down by the fire, but Tegen couldn't sleep.

She called out to a guard, 'Find me a bard – or a singer of some sort. I want someone to go through the camp and put heart in the warriors.' She threw another log on the fire. The branch was green and damp, making a thick, oppressive smoke. Tegen coughed. Her head ached and she was very tired, but it was too late for sleep.

Soon footsteps approached in heavy boots.

A red and black Silurian plaid swayed in the smoky firelight. 'Who's there?' she asked.

'I've come to sing,' announced a voice that sounded familiar.

'What's your name?' Tegen yawned and rubbed the ashy smuts from her sore eyes.

'The son of Cei,' the young man answered. 'Singer and poet, at your service.' He bowed.

'What songs do you know? We need something heartening, to give the warriors courage – and to strengthen those who must leave for Tir na nÓg.'

'I understand,' the young man replied.

Tegen squinted through the stinging smoke. 'I know your voice, but I can't see you. Are you a bard?'

'I am a warrior,' he went on, 'but I also make up songs. If you need a druid-bard, I cannot help ...' he hesitated.

'I'm sure you'll do very well. Let's hear you, I could do with hearing a cheerful song.'

The young man laughed and pulled out a small drum that had been slung across his back. He tapped a simple rhythm, then began:

> *'A rhyme's as good as me hat,*
> *It sits on me head*
> *and fills me like bread ...'*

'Kieran?' Tegen gasped, jumping up. 'Kieran ap Cei? Why didn't you say so? How long have you been with us?

Why didn't you come and see me before? It's wonderful to see you! Sit down with us. You remember Owein?' She shook his shoulder.

Owein, bleary from sleep gripped Kieran's hand. 'Last time we met, you were a scrawny little runt, bullied by your Mam and Aunt!'

'I'm a man of Siluria now!' Kieran announced proudly, puffing out his chest. 'Best thing you ever did, not letting me get on that boat with you Tegen!' he announced, puffing out his chest. 'That smith woman – she made me my sword and taught me how to use it, then she started on me singing and sent me back south to find the Silures again. I joined the rebellion a couple of nights ago, now here I am. At your service.' And he swept another bow.

Owein sat up and stretched. 'Then sing something to make us love our Land, something to make us fight for what we believe in!'

Kieran started to tap a cheerful tune. Despite her exhaustion, Tegen could not resist dancing. Drum music had always been special to her.

As she lifted her arms to sway, she could just pick out the constellation of the Watching Woman amongst the fading stars. She almost felt as if she could believe again.

'Forgive me for losing faith,' she whispered as she skipped and span, 'and for dressing up as Andraste. Boudica was in love with the demon, I had to do something.'

The stars twinkled back at her. Deep inside, Tegen knew

the Lady had approved, maybe even inspired what she had done. Now there was hope – just a little – that when the sun rose, there might be a way to avert disaster.

Suddenly, Tegen stopped dancing.

Kieran's fingers hesitated.

'Before you go, I want you to promise me something,' Tegen began.

He tucked his drum under his arm and laughed. 'Anything ... well, almost,' he added. 'I'm careful about rash promises to a bear-slaying golem maker!'

Tegen took his hands and looked in his eyes. 'This will be difficult. You mustn't stay for the battle. When you have sung for our troops, I want you to leave. Straight away, before dawn. You must travel on the southern road and find two young women. One is half Roman, Claudia, and the other is a Gaulish girl, Ula. They're both friends of mine and very important to how the future will be. I want you to protect them and bring them safely to Sul's Land, the village by the hot springs. Do you know it?'

'I do. Mam and Aunt came from near there. But I'm not a scrawny child anymore, I can fight and I want to fight.' He pulled away from Tegen 'Don't do this to me, please. You left me behind when you went on that boat, now you're sending me away before battle. Stop protecting me Tegen. I can look after myself.'

Tegen shook her head. 'Your father was a warrior, but he didn't fight on the battle field, did he?'

'No,' Kieran replied, 'he looked after travellers on

dangerous journeys. Didn't make him less of a warrior though,' he added crossly.

'Exactly. And you must do the same as the noble Cei. Now, it's getting light, you must encourage our people with song, then go … please. What I ask is more important than I can say.' Then she had inspiration. 'It's what Brigid the smith would want as well – I'm sure.'

Kieran nodded tersely. 'Very well.' Then he strode away through the sleeping huddles of warriors. As he walked, he tapped a steady rhythm and sang the story of Bran's cauldron of rebirth where wounded warriors were put to be healed before they were born again.

35. THE HARE

As dawn lightened the sky, Tegen undressed in her waggon, pushed her things into a bag, then handed it out to Owein who was waiting outside.

He slung the satchel over his shoulder. 'Tell me when you're ready.'

Shivering, Tegen looked down at herself in the grey half-light, her breasts were swelling and so was her belly, which was marked with a faint dark stripe.

That makes me feel like a wild animal, she thought. That'll help.

Then closing her eyes, she thought of Tonn who could turn himself into a hare at will. 'How do I do this, beloved? Help me,' she whispered. Breathing deeply, she remembered the scent of his skin next to hers and the soft lilt of his voice.

Remember how you became a fish, a river, a stone ...?

But did I really change, or did I just imagine it?

No time for questioning, just do it, Tonn's voice sighed like a breeze in her ear. *Crouch down; think of long furry ears, powerful hind legs, strong front ones. Your hair is spreading down your back as downy brown fur.*

She felt Tonn stroking her cheeks with his fingers. *Now give yourself whiskers, long, white ones. Spread them proudly. Now ... jump!*

She jumped, and landed with a soft thump. Shaking herself, she tentatively lifted a hind leg to scratch her chin. That felt good.

'Hurry up,' Owein called, 'it's almost light and the warriors are restless.'

There was no reply. He peered inside the waggon. Two jet-bright eyes peered back at him. 'Hello,' he said gently, reaching towards the hare, hoping she wouldn't take fright and run. But the beautiful creature only twitched her nose.

Owein wrapped her in his cloak and carried her to Boudica's tent. 'Good luck,' he breathed as they went in.

'You're late!' the queen roared, her eyes flaming in the lamplight. She shoved aside the maid who was painting her face with woad, and swaggered forward. 'Have you got it?'

Owein offered the hare. 'From the Druid of the Winter Seas,' he replied mildly. 'She asks you to remember that if it runs east, you may fight, but if it turns west you make peace – or flee, which ever you deem best.'

'Yes, yes, I *know*,' the queen snapped, buckling on her sword belt. 'Where is that wretched girl anyway?' She grabbed the animal roughly and stuffed her into the folds of her green and red plaid.

'Doing strong magic on your behalf, lady,' he replied. 'Now, I also have duties I must perform. May Andraste bless your endeavours.' He bowed and hobbled back through the tent flap.

'She'd bloody well better!' roared the queen. 'Where's my chariot?'

Owein mounted Heather and took Epona by the rein, then slipped out of the camp. The sun's first rays were gilding the horizon as he rode towards the western edge of the thick wood that spread its autumnal gold beyond the battle site. Between the safety of the trees, Owein found a place where he was hidden from enemy sight, but where Tegen would find him.

The Romans were already in place with their deadly wedge formation. Their ranks ranged the full width of the narrow valley mouth, the woodland at their backs and the stream before them.

As Suetonius had guessed, the British tribes were sprawled across the meadows with their baggage carts hauled into a tight semi-circle behind them. Warriors were still milling around, yawning and vomiting up hangovers from the night before as they waited for the great battle horn to blow.

Then, Owein knew they would all rush forwards, no discipline, no plan – all out for personal glory and head counts. Craning his neck, Owein could just see where Suetonius had arranged his troops. He'd hold them back, allowing the British to cross the water and come right up to their ranks.

Then they'd begin the slow march forward, javelins raised, ready for the slaughter …

By the time the sun was half up, the waggons were almost

all in place and crowded with spectators. Owein's mouth was dry. There would be no victory and no retreat. This was different from Boudica's other battles: those times she had taken towns that had been warned and were more or less empty. She'd simply walked in and taken over with fire and sword.

Today would be a *real* battle ending in disaster, unless Tegen's shape shift made Boudica relent. Owein guessed the queen would never keep her vow to obey the Goddess.

Owein bowed his head in respect. Good warriors would die today.

Dismounting, Owein hid Tegen's bag under leaves, keeping her cloak over his shoulder in case she transformed back into a human before she was clear of the camp. For now, he could only watch and wait. He pulled himself back into Heather's saddle and watched the sun rise.

Brilliant light gleamed on the Roman armour and sparkles danced on the stream that divided the armies. Across the meadows, endless crowds of British warriors waited, glorious in their rich coloured cloaks. Some were bravely painted blue and naked in the chilly wind. Other had spiked their hair with lime to terrify their enemies. But there was no sign of Boudica.

On both sides, horses pawed the ground, anxious to charge.

Suetonius's standard-bearer watched intently for his captain's signal. A drummer twirled his sticks, itching to strike the thudding call to war.

The dawn promised a magnificent autumn morning when the whole world is painted gold: the sort of day when cruelty and anger seem inconceivable.

Owein caught sight of the queen's chariot at last. Her matched grey horses swept in a neat curve across the field. Boudica stood beside her charioteer, the sun glistening on her bracelets as she raised her hand. The chariot stopped and she jumped down.

The Romans just watched.

Owein smiled. He knew they'd be intrigued as to what the queen was up to – they were every bit as superstitious as the British. They probably had their own augur strangling chickens at that very moment.

With a grand gesture, Boudica loosened her cloak and a hare leaped free, springing down to the grass.

In a wild panic, the animal darted east, then west. Then it returned, trembling before the queen's feet. It reached up as if trying to jump back into the safety of Boudica's arms.

The hare rose on her back legs and seemed to be growing tall – taller ...

'No, don't change back, not *now*,' Owein whispered, clenching his fists until his nails drew blood.

After a long moment, the hare sprang away through the long grass, only ears and the strong, leaping curve of her back showing her path.

'West!' she's gone west!' gasped the crowd. They looked around, disconcerted, uncertain ...

They hadn't expected the Goddess to say 'flee.'

Breathless, the hare dived straight towards the edge of the wood where Owein waited with her clothes.

Boudica watched the last flick of the animal's tail amongst the hazel and brambles. Her knuckles whitened and she ground her teeth. 'You think you can play the goddess and control me, druid girl? Well, two can play at that game!

She leaped back in her chariot and turned to face her warriors. 'My brothers and sisters!' she proclaimed, 'The Goddess has spoken! She has shown me that we must destroy these filthy invaders and drive them into the western mountains where they will starve or freeze. Any that survive will be hunted down by our good neighbours of Cymru. It's not just my kingdom and my daughters who will be avenged today – it is our sacred Land – and every child born here.'

She paused, took a deep breath and proclaimed, 'Today I shall win or die. You may follow my example – or become slaves. It is your choice.'

'Win or die!' the crowds roared thunderously. 'Win or die!'

Boudica brandished her sword. Her white teeth flashed in her blue-painted face. Golden sunlight set her hair on fire. She was magnificent. 'Then we shall *fight*! Hail Andraste!'

Boudica's words were met with deafening shouts of 'Hail Andraste!' and clattering spears. Horns and carnyxes bellowed as war drums boomed across the valley.

Just below the trees, Suetonius watched while his augurs explained the meaning of the hare.

So, Boudica had been warned, but she was fighting anyway. A cruel smiled curved his lips. He liked a woman who didn't know when she was defeated. He would enjoy crushing her under his boot. She had spirit. That made his blood race, but at the same time it disgusted him.

He would subdue her. He mounted his horse, straightened his helmet and gripped his baton, ready for the signal.

At that same moment Boudica turned towards him.

Across the stream and the grassy slopes of a soft valley, they were drawn to each other with the inevitability of lodestones.

Suetonius urged his stallion to the water's edge.

Boudica swung her wickerwork chariot around and drove to the opposite side of the stream. She faced him, chin raised and eyes narrowed, while her cloak flapped and cracked in the wind.

The two deadly enemies stared, brown eyes into blue. Lips tight. Each measuring up the other.

Boudica raised an eyebrow. 'You're the same as me,' she laughed scornfully. 'We're both possessed by the same demon. We will destroy each other. I don't need a druid-girl to tell me that!'

Suetonius leaned forward in his saddle and said, 'You have a druid girl? Does she have black hair like a raven's wing and stars here ...' He touched his right cheek under the eye.

Boudica's eyes widened. 'What if she has?'

'Bring her to me and I will let you live.'

Boudica spat. 'Come and get her. She's a nasty little witch. You can have her.' She nodded to her driver who swung the chariot around and whipped the horses into a gallop.

The queen's heart swelled with pride. The comforting arc of watching families on carts embraced the vast field of British warriors – a symbol of Andraste's protective arm around her people. It would also prevent any cowards from fleeing before the day was done.

Boudica took the reins from her charioteer and drove steadily along the lines of her warriors, sword raised. The cheering reached a deafening crescendo. A horn blew long and low. Boudica brought her blade down hard. The morning light flashing along its edge and, with a roar, the British pounded across the turf, each eager to draw the first blood.

Chariots clattered and bounced towards the Roman lines, the warriors leaping to the ground. Some ran along the shaft between the two horses, acrobatically flinging spears as their horses thrashed the turf. Shouting, swearing and raging, the British thundered onwards.

But not one piece of Roman armour moved. Even their feathered headdresses seemed cut from marble.

Then one single word was barked.

Scorpios twanged deadly bolts deep amongst the Iceni and Trinovantes who led the charge. The oncoming swarm of warriors stumbled over fallen comrades.

Next a rain of light javelins poured into the front lines. Once caught, the warrior's shields became unwieldy. They cast them aside and pushed on – undefended in the deadly hail.

Addedomaros called retreat, but discarded shields and bleeding bodies caught the warriors in a trap of flesh and wood and iron.

More barked commands. The Romans lifted their winged lightening shields, gladius points glinting.

Then their steady march began.

Sabrina's charioteer urged her horses alongside Boudica's, matching their pace. 'The hare told you not to fight,' she yelled. 'Are you mad?'

The Iceni queen glared back at Sabrina. 'You heard what the Goddess said through me! Her word is all I care about, what's a play-acting little girl in comparison to Andraste herself? All that showy stuff yesterday was rubbish and you know it. Now, it's time for action and *we* are the warriors. It is *us* who are Andraste!'

With that, her charioteer whipped her horses. Boudica held onto the rail as they ran pell-mell through the British lines. Her cloak spread like eagles' wings as she swooped.

'Fight! Fight!' she urged.

And they did. Screaming horses, yelling warriors and

shouting soldiers ripped and tore at the morning air. Spearheads and swords glinted, javelins thudded.

Blood pooled into red mud. The dying groaned and screamed. The dead stared blankly up at the chaos.

Tegen shivered with cold and fear as she dressed. Her limbs shook, her head swum and the baby kicked like a young bull in her belly. Worst of all, images of the golem, Aodh, Admidios and Derowen kept flashing through her mind.

They are just my fears, she told herself firmly. None of them exist, not really.

But she couldn't block out the sounds of the battle in the valley below.

As she pinned her cloak, she called to Owein, 'I've changed my mind. I'm staying, I want to try something.'

'What in the Lady's name can you possibly do apart from bring down fire and destroy everyone?' Owein scowled at her. 'This is no time for heroics. You have to leave. This is the end. You've done all you can. Now you must stay alive for the baby's sake.'

'There is one more thing I can try, and you must help me. We'll weave a web of spells.'

'A what? You know I'm hopeless at magic.'

Tegen rolled her eyes. 'I told you about it – the druids did it at Mona. It's hanging spells in the air like a great woven blanket. It almost destroyed the Romans last time. I think I can make it work. *Please* ...'

'Very well,' Owein sighed. 'What do you want me to

do?'

Tegen pointed to the sun, which was one handspan high. 'Fix that point in your mind, and imagine a really strong rope stretched from here ...' She swung her arms towards where the sun would set, 'to somewhere over there. I'm going to hang spells on it to confuse the battle so our people can win – or at least have time to escape.'

'So ...' Owein began, 'what do I do with this imaginary rope?'

'Just keep it taut, whatever happens. And sing something magical, something about the victory of the smallest over the greatest.'

Owein screwed up his eyes and imagined his mother's weaving frame hung in the sky. Then he began to sing.

'The birds they sought a king
to rule the air and sky
but who should be their lord?
He that would highest fly.'

As Owein sang, Tegen danced, fixing her thoughts on the Romans' accursed eagle standards hovering over the cruel battle below. In her mind's eye she turned the British warriors into wrens, thousands of them mobbing the great bronze birds.

'The eagle circled above
the lark and the raven black
but the little brown wren
he hid on the eagle's back.'

Each thought she turned into a coloured thread and

began to weave. *Fly! Fly!* she shouted in her head. Wrens, soar higher, win this battle. You can, by wile or wit. You are the true lords and ladies of this Land.

'So high the great bird flew
the birds proclaimed him lord
but as the eagle fell …
King Wren still higher soared.'

As Owein finished the last notes, he added quietly, 'Who's this?'

Tegen stopped dancing. Her concentration lost, the coloured spells unravelled and faded. She looked where Owein was pointing.

A thick set, bearded man was climbing the wooded slope. Dressed in a heavy leather apron and his face smeared with soot, there was only one person it could be.

'Goban?' she gasped.

'Some would say the wren cheated,' he called out. 'In the stories I know, the owl decided the eagle should be king because the wren hadn't flown so high all by himself.'

Tegen ran down the slope and flung her arms around the smith. 'Goban, can you help, please? Everything is falling apart – I've seen this end in slaughter and fire, I can't let it happen – I can't …'

He held her shoulders and shook his head. 'Like Sinodun, this is not to be, Star Dancer. You know you cannot save Britain from the Romans. What little is left to be done here, the Goddess has put into Owein's hands. You must go quickly; look down there, you've been seen and soldiers are on their way. The Lady will protect you.'

Shielding her eyes from the sun, Tegen saw a glimmer of armour moving through the trees below.

'But …'

Goban shook his head. 'Let go. This is not your fight. Your final battle will take place where you were born. Now *flee.*' And he pushed her firmly away.

Owein reached out and hugged her. 'Goodbye.' His voice was choked. 'Remember I love you.'

Tegen kissed his cheek. 'You were right about so much. Thank you for your love – and for everything. I'll never forget you.'

Owein wrapped Tegen in her cloak. 'Go my little blackbird. Find Ula and Claudia at Sul's Land.' He hugged her one last time. 'Farewell.'

He coughed and rubbed his eyes, then helped her into Epona's saddle. 'Keep the baby safe. She has a destiny too, remember? Go!'

He slapped Epona on the rump and she cantered away.

36. THE GOLDEN GOBLET

In the valley below, the fighting was in a lull, but under the pall of smoke, skirmishes still flared.

As soon as Tegen was out of sight, Owein pulled on a leather cuirass and covered it with his Roman tunic and toga. He cut a branch from a bush that still had a few green leaves, then holding it high in token of parley, he rode Heather into Suetonius's camp. He dismounted and made his way between the stacks of weapons and cooking pots to a large tent where he guessed Suetonius would be directing operations.

In Latin, he greeted the guards and asked politely, but firmly to see the Governor as he had vital intelligence.

The men kept their spears crossed. 'What sort of intelligence? We don't need lies from slimy Brits pretending to be Roman. We're winning anyway.'

Owein took a deep breath and bellowed, 'I am here to betray Boudica. Your commander will not be pleased if he hears you turned me away.'

From inside the tent, Suetonius's harsh voice yelled, 'Who's making such a bloody racket?'

'A Brit in a toga sir. He claims to have intelligence.'

'What's he doing here? How did a traitorous runt like him get so close? Has anyone searched him for his dagger?' Suetonius demanded.

'I am unarmed,' Owein replied, then repeated his offer.

'How do you speak Latin so well?'

'My uncle taught me. He lived in Rome for a while. Now, do you want Boudica at your mercy, or shall I go away?' Owein didn't feel comfortable trying to parley with a tent flap, but he had no choice.

Ignoring him, Suetonius yelled, 'Armourer! My breastplate won't buckle.' Then he called out, 'Boudica is good, but I also want a girl, got long black hair and dances, do you know her? Claims to be a druid or some such, but she's probably just a scabby little witch.'

'I know her. She's with the queen,' Owein lied.

'I want them both then. What are your terms?'

'If I deliver them, you must let the ordinary people go home. Disarm them if you must, but there's been enough bloodshed. Most of them don't want to be here, it's not the season for fighting. They were sworn to follow their chieftains and had no choice. Pull back your men and take Boudica, then they'll go quietly to their farms, I swear.'

'Bring me the dead body of the queen and the girl alive, *then* I will pull back the troops.'

Owein swallowed. How was he going to get around the fact that Tegen was already gone? He'd think of something. 'By noon. *Ave!*' he raised his arm in a smart salute, then leaning heavily on his crutch, he left.

It was only then that Suetonius strode out of his tent and watched his visitor mount a cream coloured pony, 'I'm sure I've seen that young man before,' he mused.

But just then a dispatch came from a cavalry officer

under severe attack on the western flank and he turned his mind to the battle.

Owein found the cramped waggon he had called home for a quarter moon. There he emptied a small pouch of black grains into a mortar. Taking a pestle, he pounded them into a rough powder. He wished Tegen was there, her skills with herbs were better than his own. This potion was not difficult: a small handful of hemlock seeds crushed and simmered in red wine with nutmeg and honey to disguise the taste.

Would the queen fall for it? What if he were caught? He laughed bitterly. Obviously he could never trust Suetonius? But if Boudica was dead, he might – just *might* pull back.

And if Boudica lived? Then this crazy war would go on and on, with vengeance killings and pointless skirmishes, slowly destroying his beloved land and its brave people. Boudica had been their best chance; but her paranoia and greed had ruined everything.

Now all that was left was hatred on every side. The demon was winning.

There had to be peace to rebuild and find hope, or the spirit of Britain would crumble forever. Suetonius was evil and cruel, but if there was no rebellion for him to quash, there was a chance that he might be content to simply rule.

It was worth the risk. Without a strong figurehead, the tribes' alliances would melt like ice by a fire. The people would go home. This was Samhain, a most inauspicious day for death and fighting as the doors between the worlds were wide open.

Owein was ready. He sniffed the brew. The steam was mouth-watering, but he knew better than to taste it. He poured the concoction into a golden goblet and commanded a boy to carry it while he hobbled alongside. Boudica's tent was empty. All able-bodied men were fighting. 'Set it there, on that camp table, then go back to your people,' he told the boy.

Once he was alone, Owein settled himself into the queen's favourite carved cedar chair and waited.

Soon he heard Boudica's angry voice bellowing, 'Change the horses. Those are tired. Bandage my hand, someone, I'm bleeding to death here!'

Entering the tent she reached for the goblet, drained it and wiped her mouth on the back of her hand.

Then she stopped and stared at Owein. 'What the hell are you doing here?'

'Bringing magic to aid our cause, majesty,' he said, modestly inclining his head.

'About bloody time!' she snapped. A servant bandaged her hand and offered her bread and cheese, which she brushed away. Ignoring Owein, she strode outside and was about to spring back on her chariot.

For a moment she hesitated and looked anxious.

Owein held his breath – the draught shouldn't have worked that fast. Boudica had to fall on the battlefield so no one would suspect foul play.

But the queen shook her head and took her usual place beside her charioteer. Taking a fresh spear from a rack, she yelled 'Death to the Romans, victory to Andraste!' And the horses pounded away.

Owein watched as the charioteer skilfully wound his way between the dead and the skirmishes. Then Boudica swayed and fell against her driver, knocking him off the platform. The chariot yawed from side to side. The horses tossed their heads and tried to rear as they realised there was no steady hand on their reins. The queen stumbled backwards onto the bloody field.

She did not get up.

From inside the tent, Owein watched in fascinated horror as the battle slurred into slow motion.

Then everything stopped.

Swords and spears were lowered. It was as if no one was sure what should happen next.

Suetonius must have been watching too, for he kicked his horse into a careering gallop, leaped the stream and pounded to where Boudica lay.

A crowd of whey-faced warriors was gathering around their dying queen. They drew back as the Roman Governor and his guard arrived.

Suetonius stared down at his enemy's twitching body.

The queen's hair was loose, her lips were blue and her eyes stared blankly up at her nemesis.

Suetonius dismounted and leaned over her. Then

drawing his gladius, he stabbed her heart.

A cheer went up from his followers who took this as a signal to swipe left and right at the gathered mourners, slaughtering everyone.

Then in all the mayhem, a separate detachment of infantry ran along behind the British baggage carts where the thousands of spectators waited and watched.

Thud! Thud! Burning missiles caught deep amongst the baggage.

Screaming and wailing, the onlookers jumped down, hair and clothes aflame. They ran straight into two flanks of cavalry waiting with drawn swords.

Men, women, children. It didn't matter. The orders were clear.

Rancid smoke swept across the churned field, smothering broken bodies, wrecked chariots, shields, javelins, blood and bone ... and here and there, a terrified soul.

Yelling, wailing, horses screaming, carnyxes clattering, trumpets sounding, spears hissing.

Death, death, death.

And all embraced by a raging serpent of flames.

The stores, the children, the old folks. All engulfed.

The smoke swept downwind.

Choking and spluttering, the last warriors turned to flee. But they were trapped, swords behind and fire in front.

Eyes streaming, Sabrina summoned as many of her people as she could find. The desperate few gathered in a huddle. '*Run!*' she commanded. 'Forget your loot and baggage. Just *go* – or no one will live to tell our grandchildren about today. There's no honour in that. Run through the woods, then turn southwest, until the sea binds the end of the land. I will meet you there.'

And in small groups, a few, a very few, managed to slip away.

Livid, Owein returned to the Roman camp. Brushing the guards aside, he bellowed imperiously for Suetonius.

The Governor turned at the sound of his name.

Owein dismounted and leaned on his crutch.

Suetonius stood, hands on hips, scrutinising Owein as if he were a slug. 'What do you want, cripple?'

'You broke your promise.'

'And where is the girl?'

'You've probably killed her in your slaughter – how should I know?'

'If she's dead then bring me her body.'

'Oath breaker!' Owein slid his hand under the folds of his toga and gripped his dagger.

Suetonius laughed. 'I took no oaths, boy. Now, bring me the girl alive or get out of my sight. I remember who you are now, the nephew of that obnoxious sorcerer. He couldn't be trusted either.'

'Then trust this!' Owein lunged, aiming his blade under the Roman's breastplate.

But his weak leg betrayed him and he fell on the point of

Suetonius's outstretched pugio.

Hot blood oozed around Owein as he lay staring at the Governor's hobnailed boots.

She's still alive, find her! whispered the demon in Suetonius's mind.

'Later, I'm busy!' the Governor roared aloud, to the amazement of those standing by, who hadn't heard anyone speak.

Seeing the puzzlement on their faces, he waved a hand at Owein's body. 'Get him out of here! I said, *I'm busy!*'

37. THE WINTER SEAS

Kieran moved his broken drum to his other shoulder, and wrapped his cloak tightly against the winter winds and the first flakes of snow.

He surveyed the bare moors that dropped through steep woodlands and rocky gorges. Below were grey, flat stretches of water dotted with marshy islets, and no real tracks to follow. This would be a difficult path. Could they all manage it?'

He looked back at Claudia who was moaning loudly. Ula had an arm around her shoulder and was cheering her on with kind words.

Tegen looked weary, even riding Epona was exhausting her.

He opened his mouth to suggest they gave up, but Tegen rode alongside him and shook her head.

'In case you're thinking of going back to Sul's Land,' she smiled, 'the answer is *no*. Too many Romans are wallowing in those hot springs and looking out for fugitives while they're at it.' She rubbed her aching back. 'The idea of lying in warm water is very tempting, but we're going on. It's not much further.'

Tegen pointed to her right. 'Just beyond that old stronghold on the hilltop, do you see smoke rising? That's the lead and silver mines. The Hill People do the actual mining. Da buys their ore, then he smelts and works it. Our house is just down that valley; we'll see the roof through the trees on your left soon.'

As they pushed through the brambles, Tegen pointed out small memories from her childhood. She knew Claudia and Ula were too cold and tired to care, but the excitement of coming home was bubbling up inside her.

Soon they arrived in the courtyard between the whitewashed stone house and the barn, with its little open-sided forge. The place felt neglected but a worn-out looking pony was tethered to a gate and something was clattering noisily.

'Mam?' she called, 'Da? I'm home.'

A tall young man with spiky red hair and beard came out and stared at the travellers. 'Clesek's not here!' he announced shortly and went back inside the forge.

Tegen slid awkwardly from Epona's back. She crossed to the forge and watched as the young man sorted out odd bits of half worked metal, stacking them in piles. The fire was out – it looked as if it had been cold for a long time.

'Where is Clesek? I'm Tegen, his daughter.'

The young man didn't even look up. 'I remember you. I'm Derren the potter's boy, remember? We were supposed to get married, my Da said. But ...'

Tegen was impatient. 'There was some talk, but I had things to do. Now, where's my Da?'

Derren jerked his thumb over his shoulder. 'Up at the mines. He works for them Romans now. They needed his know-how to run the works. He's got a new cottage and pay. He's doing all right.' With that, Derren picked up his sack and slung it over his shoulder. 'Your Da said I could help myself to the bits – thought I might have a go at working silver myself. Cheerio.' Pushing past her, he loaded his pony.

'Does Da still own this house?'

'Suppose so.' He shrugged and led his animal down the hill through the winter-bare trees.

Tegen stared after him for a moment, then turned back to her companions. 'Did you hear?' she asked, 'The Romans have taken over Da's mines. He didn't mention my Mam, I wonder ...'

'Come on Tegen,' Kieran urged. 'It's too cold to stand out here wondering. Let's get warm. We can worry later.'

With a heavy heart, Tegen pushed open the creaking door and stepped inside. The roof was still good, and she smiled up at the crook loft where she used to sleep. In the centre of the main room, the circular hearth was cold and forlorn.

Ula immediately rolled up her sleeves. 'Kieran, you stable Epona – there're plenty of outbuildings. Claudia, help me find firewood and Tegen, you curl up and rest. You look all in.'

Tegen didn't argue. She wiped the dust from her mother's favourite hearthside chair. Snuggled between its wide arms, she closed her eyes and dreamed of childhood ghosts.

Derren's gossip in the village soon spread back up to the mines. As soon as dark fell, Clesek filled a basket with food and hurried down to his old home.

The door opened and Tegen looked up.

There stood a man who should have been her father, but was not: he was grey, stooped and sad-eyed. Seeing his only child, he dropped his bag and wiped away a tear. 'Is it really you?' he whispered, holding his arms wide.

They hugged and cried and talked until late into the night, sharing bread, cheese, apples and mead that Clesek had brought.

'Your mother died last winter of the coughing sickness,' he said, stroking Tegen's hair. 'I moved up to the mines then. The Hill People disappeared about two years ago. One day they left their tools and went north. Quite eerie it was. About half a moon later the Romans came and announced that my mine and everything in it was theirs.'

'No!' Tegen protested.

'That wasn't all bad,' Clesek assured her. 'I had the choice to buy silver and lead from them and keep my own forge, or to work for them up there. They pay well. I'm old now, child. I get along, although I miss your Mam terribly. I know she could be grumpy, but I loved her.'

When Clesek finished, Tegen told of her adventures and how she had met each of her companions. She couldn't bring herself to say much about her beloved Tonn. She simply said he had died. The truth still choked her.

Meanwhile, Kieran found hay for Epona while Ula

swept the cottage, shook spiders from old sheepskins and laid them out ready for sleeping. Claudia did not try to boss her around, but neither did she offer to help.

As the night's chilly winds battered the little cottage, Tegen yawned, kissed her Da, then climbed the ladder to her old bedroom. In the dark, she felt her way past her little table to her old bed of straw and skins. She tried not to think of mouse nests as she crawled into the damp bedding and fell asleep.

In the morning, Clesek had gone, taking Kieran, Ula and Claudia with him. By sun's midhaven, the girls had returned with supplies of food and fresh straw.

Every evening Clesek came and helped to repair and restore his old home. 'It's yours now, my sweet,' he said as he kissed Tegen. 'It's for you and the baba, and your friends too, of course. When I'm too old to work, I hope you'll find room for an old man by your hearth?'

Midwinter approached and the hills were blanketed in white.

Villagers came once more to Tegen for spells and charms, but they treated her warily, as they had done before. Some even made the sign against the evil eye as they entered her home.

Tegen blessed them in return.

One by one, Clesek sold Claudia's gold bracelets. The money covered all their needs, but Tegen's mood sank as traders brought tales of vengeance killings and 'punishments' following the battle. There were rumours the Romans were seeking a witch with a tattooed cheek ...

Tegen stayed away from the village. She had not averted the great evil and, despite her friends, she was lonely. There were no more druids to discuss magic and stories with, so she taught Kieran some of the bardic songs.

Derren became less chilly, and often came to chat to Claudia by the fire. 'I think he fancies you!' Tegen whispered.

'I'd never marry such a common man!' she sneered, 'anyway, I'm betrothed.' Then she bit her lip. 'I often wonder ... is Owein alive? Will he find us?'

'I believe he was gravely wounded.' Tegen hugged her shoulders and rocked as she stared into the fire. 'He'll live, but you won't see him again. I'm sorry.'

Claudia nodded thoughtfully. 'I liked him. He was kind. I hope he'll be happy.'

The flames flickered through Tegen's mind and she found herself speaking again: 'Owein will go west into the mountains of Cymru and become the strong leader he was born to be. Many generations from now, a grandchild with his name will do great things.' She squeezed Claudia's fingers gently. 'You're free from your promise to wed, but you won't marry Derren, you have another fate. A good one.'

Claudia smiled. 'Thank you, but what about you and your baby? What do you see? Will you stay here?'

Tegen looked into the hearth's dancing flames, gasped, then held her breath.

'What is it?' Ula asked, squeezing her hand gently. 'You can tell us.'

Tegen shook her head. 'I'm too tired to see anything clearly tonight.' She kissed her friends and climbed to her nest under the thatch, leaving them staring after her in the dancing lights of the hearth-fire.

On midwinter's night, Tegen wrapped herself warmly and trudged up the hill to the clearing between the skeletal tress where Griff had told her to dance for the Goddess. It had been a night a little like this, with sharp, bright stars in the blackness above.

On an impulse, she threw off her cloaks and danced once more. Not as wildly as she used to, because of the weight in her belly and the grief in her heart, but she gave a graceful, courteous greeting to all the spirits.

'Tonight is the Time of Stone when death rules,' she told the winds, 'but like Rhiannon, in the old stories, I carry new life. Bring me to the Time of Air and re-birth.'

Then she sat on a fallen tree. 'What could I have done differently?' she asked the stars and shadows. 'I should've been firmer with Boudica. I should've saved Tonn. I should've prevented the slaughter of the druids – but I didn't manage to do any of it.'

The stars just twinkled back at her.

'What did Bran mean, I was born to prevent hatred and

vengeance?' Tegen went on. 'How can that ever be possible? It's just getting worse. How can our people forgive Boudica? How can we not hate the Romans?

'I've seen a bright future for my baby … in Ériu.' She wiped her nose on her sleeve and sniffed. 'But what about me? Bran promised I'd have my own hearth one day, but I see Gilda going to her grandmother's … without me. The vision is very clear, I must stay here, but I want to go. But then, Rhiannon gave birth to the Mabon, only to lose him. Must *I*? I can't bear it.'

She choked a sob. 'I *won't* bear it – I *can't*! I want to be with my child in Ériu. It's the only place I ever felt at home. We could have a future there. I might be allowed to take part in some rituals, not all the druids will be as harsh as Finglas.'

Tegen's teeth chattered as she studied the stars, scattered like ogham across the night sky. 'I'm sure your patterns have meanings. I wish Goban were here, he'd tell me what to do. But then I wish Owein, and Tonn and Griff were with me – and Mother Gilda and …'

Before she knew it, she was sobbing for all the people she had loved and lost.

For Tegen, the Time of Stone was cold and very deep.

★

BOOK 5
THE BOOK OF
SPIRIT

1.   THE REMAINS OF THE GAME

The demon was bored.

The clamour and stench of battle had barely faded. The drunken queen was dead, the last gaming pieces roamed leaderless and hungry across the chequered land. Fighting was sporadic and half-hearted.

It longed for chaos, sweet revenge and unbounded hatred.

Retaliation and bloodshed must be unleashed.

For that, it needed the female with more magic than any mortal deserved. But she had slipped its grasp – again.

The demon surveyed the wreckage of the gaming board.

Still under its command was the soldier dressed in red with plumes and armour. This one loved bloodshed and worshipped cruelty.

Aflame with hatred, the soldier also scoured the land for the girl who had dared to challenge him.

He would never forgive.

The demon valued this man. It would guide him to their quarry.

Together, they would break the Star Dancer.

2. A DIFFERENT DRUID

Spring came and Beltane drew on. One bright spring day, when primroses scattered their gold along the hedgerows, a baby was born next to the hearth where Tegen herself had come into the world.

There were no stars dancing, but the little girl's wide eyes looked up at her Mam with bright amazement.

'You are my finest and best magic,' Tegen said, stroking her child's hair. 'I'll be happy if I never make another spell, you are perfection. I only wish your Da and my Mam could have seen you. They'd have loved you so much,' her voice caught in her throat. 'And they'd have been so proud.'

At sunset, Clesek came to see his grandchild. Tegen handed him the sleepy bundle. 'Her name is Gilda,' she said.

He held the baby close to his chest and rocked her. 'She is beautiful. So like your mother – and so like you.' He wiped his eyes.

Gilda's birth left Tegen weary.

Her soul was already scarred from all she had seen and failed to prevent. Night terrors swam the winds around her cottage, whispering that everything was her fault.

When she was strong enough to walk, she stood outside and looked up at the stars. 'I will dance. Goban promised the Goddess would protect me. Perhaps she'll speak to me like she used to?'

You have no right to dance, the demon sneered. *You lost faith in your goddess, why would she listen now? She is going to take your baby from you. You cannot trust her.*

The icy wind blew. Tegen shivered and went back inside.

That night, the dreams began.

At first they were simple nightmares of battles, the fires of Camulodunum, the dead prisoners in the grove, the crucified women …

Then came the golem, huge, oozing fire and smoke, its eyes glowing scarlet … And just as she had dreamed before, it opened a gaping maw.

But this time it spoke: *You have been puny and weak. It is not too late to join with me. You will become magnificent and I will make sure you keep your child.*

Tegen woke sweating and shivering. She had been so careful not to give it a mouth.

Despair ate her soul. Her dark hair fell out in handfuls. She grew thin, and sometimes Gilda needed goat's milk on a spoon.

On Beltane morning, Tegen made wreaths of hawthorn for Ula, Claudia and herself, then she gave Kieran a crown of pale golden oak leaves woven with sprigs of black-budded ash. Lastly she tucked a spray of the musty, milky blossom into Gilda's shawl.

'I must find someone to bless you, to protect you from

the demon,' Tegen whispered. 'If there are any druids left in Britain, they'll come to the spring fair. I won't let evil reach you – I swear I won't.'

Then she led the way down the winding path to the meadows between the village and the Winter Seas where the Beltane fair was in full swing.

It was here she had danced for the first time and been given her green silk shawl. On that day, she had begun her journey into magic. Witton had seen her power and been frightened of it.

It was at Beltane she had married Tonn.

Leaving the others to enjoy the juggling displays and the stalls selling spiced cakes and trinkets, Tegen carried Gilda to an oak stump where Witton used to sit. Tegen pushed aside the swathes of ivy. 'This is my seat now,' she said.

But the wood was rotting. There were no druids. Not even any half-trained bards croaking badly rhyming songs to entertain the crowds.

Tegen wandered between the stalls, but the people fell silent or drew back as she approached.

With a heart of lead, she took her baby up the small hill to Witton's old roundhouse, now sagging with rotten thatch and cracked walls. She pushed open the door and went inside. The smell of damp and decay made her cough. Shafts of spring sunlight shed gold on the mouldy sheepskins that had once been the druid's bed. The hearth was desolate and black.

Amongst the ashes lay a few peeled sticks arranged in

patterns. Tegen picked them up and examined them. They weren't ogham, but she sensed they had important meanings.

So, at least one druid had been here since she had left, but was it before or after the slaughter of Mona? Was he or she still alive?

Perched on the same stool she had used when Witton pronounced her Star Dancer, Tegen buried her face in her baby's shawl and cried.

She did not hear the soft footfall behind her. Her eyes were so swollen she did not see the edge of a long, white woollen robe, or a sandaled foot.

'Can I help?' asked a deep voice with a heavy accent.

Tegen looked up. A thin, old man with dark skin drew up another stool and sat beside her.

'Who are you? What are you doing in my house?' Tegen snapped, then felt guilty for being so rude. It hadn't been 'her' house for a very long time.

The man smiled and bowed his head politely. 'Forgive intrusion. I thought here deserted. I stranger. My name Josephus. I live with friends on Tor-hill. I am see celebrations here. I interested your druids, so I am come learn from these remains.' He swept a long hand around the room. 'Druids seems gone, I think?'

Wide eyed, Tegen stared at him. Her hand covered the Watching Woman's stars on her right cheek.

Josephus rose from his stool. 'Please, forgive.' He bowed slightly. 'I go?'

'No ... wait,' Tegen dried her nose and eyes on her sleeve-rag and sniffed. Cuddling Gilda tightly, she looked up into the man's calm, dark eyes. 'You say you live on the Tor? So you must be a druid too? You dress like one – you *feel* like one.'

Josephus put his head to one side. 'You might say yes. But I come from far land. My ways of doings am different from yours, but I love all.' He helped her stand. 'I like see goings-on outside. You honour with me accompanying?'

Tegen smiled at his awkward words and old-fashioned courtesy, but she did not want excitement.

Gilda wriggled and whimpered. 'Thank you, but I'll stay here, my baby needs feeding,' she said.

'Can I holding her?' Josephus asked gently. 'What name is?'

Tegen hesitated while she listened to his spirit. He felt strong and true. 'She is called Gilda. Can ... can you give a strong blessing? One that will really protect her?'

Josephus smiled. 'I can.'

And she entrusted her darling to the old man's open arms.

Humming a lullaby, he cradled Gilda until she was quiet, then he laid his hand on her head and spoke in foreign words.

His blessing rippled gold and white light over Gilda's tiny body. Then he handed her back, still faintly aglow in the hut's dingy light.

'Thank you,' Tegen murmured, and he left.

Six moons later, Ula married Derren. Her own father had been a potter in Gaul and she soon became part of the family business. Kieran and Derren worked on the new roundhouse together and Claudia painted the walls with exotic designs from her mother's tribe. They handfasted at the time of golden leaves, Ula's dress already stretched over her swollen belly.

As the sun set, the couple were escorted to their new home with drums and whistles to scare away demons, Tegen sat with Gilda on her lap, watching Ula's happy face lit by torchlight. The red scars under her fringe had faded. 'Their future will be good,' she told Gilda who gurgled and reached for a firefly glowing in the grass.

At that moment, Claudia and Kieran came running up to Tegen and flung themselves down, pleasantly drunk and full of laughter. 'I am really happy for the first time in my life!' Claudia announced. Then springing up again, she hauled Kieran to his feet. 'Dance with me!'

'There's no music,' he objected.

'I hear crickets!' Claudia hiccoughed, swinging him around until they both fell in a heap at Tegen's side.

Claudia grabbed her fingers and kissed them. 'Thank you so much for rescuing me, I was never really happy as a Roman lady. I have too much of my mother's Celtic blood in my veins. If it hadn't been for Ula, I'd never have survived Camulodunum. She insisted I fled with Owein. She kept me going all the time we were hiding in that stinking waggon. You once said she'd save my life. I thought you meant she'd do something big and heroic, but it was in simple things like making sure I ate and laughed.'

'She's no less a hero!' Tegen replied.

'Oh I know, especially as I was so awful! That's why I'm so happy for her. I could stay here forever! I want to dance again!' She rolled over in the long grass and kicked her feet towards the stars.

'You won't though,' Tegen said.

'Won't what?'

'Stay here forever, I have seen it.'

Claudia sat up, wide-eyed. 'Where will I go?'

'Somewhere green – with hills.'

'What about me?' Kieran asked.

'You will become a bard in a foreign land.'

Kieran pushed Tegen playfully. 'Don't be daft!'

'You'll believe me when it happens. Only Ula and Derren will stay here, the rest of us must leave – soon. Trouble is brewing.'

'What sort of trouble?' Kieran frowned.

Tegen stroked Gilda's dark curls. 'Suetonius is looking for me, and he's getting close.'

3. THE TOR

Winter came. At first the Romans at the mines left the local people alone, only appearing in the villages to collect taxes or occasionally to search for a thief or vandal.

But beyond the Winter Seas, there was hunger because farmers had fought rather than sown crops. The old ways were lost; the Goddess was no longer worshipped properly.

The Romans demanded more than the people could afford. Reprisals and vengeance killings multiplied.

Despite the hardships, Gilda blossomed. As she grew, so Tegen withered under the weight of her persistent dreams. They clung to her spirit like a cloak of sodden wool.

One night, Tegen threw off her sheepskins. Dripping with sweat, she coughed and struggled to breathe. She opened her eyes in terror.

The golem was leaning over her bed. It opened its fiery mouth, its words crackled:

The master has been patient too long. Tonight you must bow to your new lord.

Tegen screamed, '*Never*! Get out! Get out of my head. Get out of my house. NOW! You don't exist! I destroyed you. You're *nothing*!'

And the creature laughed like snapping wood. Its breath stank of soot.

'*FIRE!*' Kieran yelled from downstairs. 'Tegen? Claudia? Get *out*! The cottage is on fire!'

With Gilda howling under her arm, Tegen scrambled down the ladder into the choking heat and smoke. The hearth was spitting as if loaded with pinecones. Flickering red light licked the walls and billows of smoke.

Tegen looked around. 'Where's my cloak?'

'Forget it! Come ON!' Kieran yelled, opening the door. Icy air blasted inside, flames rose up roaring.

Tegen and Claudia flung themselves outside, just as the roof collapsed with a deafening crash.

'Witch!' screamed a voice. Rough hands grabbed at Tegen's arms.

She clutched Gilda closer. They were surrounded by angry, torch lit faces. Some were yelling, others wielding sticks and knives. 'Where's the witch? Burn her!' they screeched.

Whimpering, Claudia clutched at Tegen. Kieran drew his knife, but there were too many to fight.

Muttering a spell, Tegen drew a pall of thick smoke around herself and her friends. 'Run!' she urged, grabbing what she hoped was Claudia's shoulder.

Cloaked by magic, they slipped between the angry hordes and ran downhill through the dark woods until they came to a hidden hollow. There, they crouched and shivered.

Gilda sobbed and Tegen gave her a finger to suck.

Kieran went a little way back into the trees, and then

returned. 'No one's following, we're safe for the moment.'

'What was that for?' Claudia demanded. 'We haven't hurt anyone.'

Kieran sat next to her. 'I didn't want to say anything, not with everyone being so happy about the wedding an'all. There's been rumours in the village about Tegen being a witch … Something to do with raising a demon in a cave and drowning a lot of people?'

'There was a flood, but it wasn't me who summoned the demon,' Tegen replied quietly. 'But why a fire, and why tonight?'

Kieran sighed and buried his head between his knees. 'I had no idea it'd come to this, honest,' he said at last. 'They say in the village that there's Roman money being offered for you.'

Gilda snuffled unhappily. Tegen cuddled her, grateful for her damp warmth. 'Perhaps they thought it was easier to kill me than capture me alive?'

Kieran nodded. 'Maybe. They'd do anything not to have them bloody Romans in the village. Easier to hand over a corpse than risk being fried by one of your spells. But I didn't think they'd do this, I thought it was all talk. Sorry, I should have said something.'

'And I should have guessed.' Tegen hesitated. 'Kieran, can you find a boat?'

'Why?'

Tegen looked back towards her old home, where flames still painted the night. 'We can't stay here. They'll scour the woods when it gets light. I want to go to the Tor – to the new druids. I think I'll be safe there while I think what to do next.'

Kieran scrambled to his feet. 'I'll go to Ula's first and borrow a couple of cloaks and some food. You hide, and when you hear me call like a heron three times, come to the water's edge and answer like an owl.'

'Thank you,' Tegen replied, and Claudia jumped to her feet and hugged him.

A short while later, when dawn was little more than a smudge of light in the east, a harsh voice cried three times.

Clutching Gilda, Tegen made her way through the squashy mud to the water's edge, Claudia slipping and cursing behind her.

With wet shoes and shivering badly, Tegen hooted back.

The sound of a paddle's steady splash veered towards them.

Tegen hooted once more. 'Over here, you've gone too far,' she called softly.

The coracle turned, and soon Kieran was steering the little boat towards the shore. He splashed into the water and dragged the boat across the mud. 'Sorry, it's too shallow; you'll have to wade. Take my hand.'

Claudia lifted her skirt and stepped into the chilly water with a shudder.

When she had clambered in and settled herself down, Tegen passed Gilda across to her, then she took her place.

Kieran bent his back and pushed the boat into deeper water. 'It's getting light, hurry, try and get behind one of the little islands before the sun comes up or they'll see you and be after you.'

Tegen nodded and picked up the paddle.

'Aren't you coming?' Claudia asked.

'No room,' he answered tersely. 'I'll hide at Ula's for a couple of days. With any luck they'll think Tegen is dead and everything will blow over very quickly. The Romans can't go after someone who's just ash.'

As the boat span across the winter seas, Tegen wove a blessing and sent it after Kieran. 'Come and see us soon. Ask for the house of Josephus.'

All morning, they paddled across the marshy seas, keeping out of sight behind sedge-covered islets. It was almost noon when they edged the boat around the tip of a scrub-covered promontory that looked like an enormous sleeping pig. On the far side, the afternoon sun caught on a long wooden wharf where two ships were moored.

One was wide and laden with bulging sacks. Only a large brown dog was on board, watching imperiously from his throne of stinking, uncured skins.

The other had high, gaudily painted prows. A man was striding the narrow central deck shouting orders to a dozen slaves. Their manacles clanked as they struggled to get their long oars into position.

The rest of the dock was empty, apart from an old

watchman dozing by a brazier.

'I thought this was a sacred place,' Tegen said, 'it looks more like a trading post.'

Claudia shrugged. 'I don't care what it is – I have to get out of this wind and find something to eat. Gilda is frozen too.'

With a few more strokes, Tegen brought the coracle alongside the jetty. She gripped the slimy planks and heaved herself up. Claudia tossed her a rope which she looped around a wooden post and made fast.

Tegen rubbed her stiff, blistered fingers, then took Gilda while Claudia scrambled out of the boat. Together they made their way up a narrow zigzagging path that climbed the steep slope of the promontory. Their wet boots slipped on the greasy mud and the wind slammed their backs as they struggled on. At the top, they paused to catch their breath. Ten or fifteen arrow-shots to their right, a swathe of woodland skirted the steep sided Tor, which rose dramatically to a forlorn crag at the top.

'I longed to climb up there when I was a child.' Tegen said, then she swung around to survey the view. Then she laughed. 'I don't believe it!' she exclaimed, running to where a small thorn tree was in full blossom, its creamy flowers nodding between sparse green leaves. 'Is this a sign that the Goddess *is* still alive in the Land?' Pulling a few red threads from her cloak, she bound them around a spindly branch in offering.

The blossom bowed merrily in response.

315

Claudia staggered and slipped as she joined Tegen. 'Who cares about a tree?' she grumbled. 'I'm freezing, and what if we get seen? Have you any idea where this man lives?' she demanded between chattering teeth.

'No, but there's only one path, so we'll take that.'

The girls walked through the newly built settlement. A small stream trickled down the main street, with shops and alehouses on either side. A woman was selling turnips and leeks from a basket, while her son juggled green apples. A couple of farmers strode down the road whacking sticks at a flock of goats. From the other direction a gaggle of geese waddled and hissed, chased by noisy children.

Tegen bought a pot of milk for Gilda and asked directions, then they trudged uphill past a scattering of small huts huddled together as if for warmth. At last they came to a cress-filled water meadow below a small coombe with a lonely cottage.

The wind blew colder as heavy yellowish clouds piled in the northern sky.

'Are you sure about these druids?' Claudia asked through chattering teeth. 'I've heard people saying they're foreign. They might be Romans.'

Tegen squeezed her hand. 'If they can make that tree bloom on a winter's day, then they might just be capable of miracles. Who else can we turn to? The man I met was kind; I think they are very like druids. We will be safe, and soon you will go to a green land – and so will my Gilda. I have seen it.'

But where will I be? Tegen wondered silently, sniffing back tears.

The golem's threat was as raw and awful by day as it was by night.

Tegen whispered into Gilda's ear, 'You will be safe, but I must face my fears and be ready for whatever happens next.'

The baby looked up at her Mam and smiled, blowing bubbles through her snotty nose.

Tegen kissed her. 'And above all, you must be kept safe, my darling,' she added under her breath. She longed for Josephus's soft lights to flow over them both. If only he could wash her pain away – and protect her baby.

They reached the whitewashed cottage. Smoke seeped through the thatch, and inside, someone was singing. Tegen knocked hard on the plank door.

A tall man with dark skin and a kindly smile opened it. His long white robe tugged in the gale.

'Hello Josephus,' Tegen said. 'We need help. May we come in?'

4. REFUGE

'Tegen and Gilda!' Josephus exclaimed. 'You and friend welcome.' He ushered them into the gentle darkness of the little hut. 'I thought I hear voices. Come. What bitter day! I have plenty eating.' He gestured towards a pot of vegetable stew and flatbread baking on the central hearth.

Josephus shut the door against the winter's raging. The girls found stools while the old man dished up food. Then he took Gilda and fed her bread dipped in gravy.

'How this old man serve you?' he asked as they ate.

'I am being hunted, Tegen explained, 'we need somewhere to hide, until I can make – arrangements.'

Josephus considered Tegen keenly. 'Is all?' he asked simply. His question searched out her soul, as if he knew she was suffering.

Tegen wanted to tell him, she *needed* to tell someone. 'And ... and I'm having bad dreams.'

'Ah.' Josephus reached out for Tegen's fingers. 'I very sorry you dreamings have. We talking later, yes?'

Tegen fought the lump swelling in her throat. She nodded silently. At last she replied, 'There was a fire last night. Some people think I'm a witch, and they want to kill me – or sell me to the Romans. And there's someone who hates me ... Someone important.'

318

'And you afraid. I understand.'

'No, not exactly,' Tegen took her sleeping daughter from Josephus. 'I'm not afraid of the man, it's just I think I may have to give up my daughter to be free to fight him … and I think I'll die of grief if she's not with me. I need somewhere quiet to think – and to be certain what to do.'

She raised an eyebrow at the old man. 'Is that possible?' she asked. 'Do you have somewhere we can stay?'

'I take you to my sister-house. She makes you warm and snug. My home not excellent for lady visitors. She kind lady, will help with gladness.'

The following morning, Tegen left Gilda with Claudia, and went alone to Josephus's hut.

His sister Marah was with him, and together they listened as Tegen told of her birth, her sparse training, her marriage to Griff and how he died a hero when the demon was raised in the caves. She described Admidios the Shadow Walker and how he murdered King Eiser. With pride in her voice she told how Owein and Sabrina had fought to defend Britain.

As the afternoon wore on, she found the words to tell of Étain and her mirror magic, Tonn and his unfailing love, his self-sacrifice and its pointlessness.

Josephus and Marah shared their food and clouds gathered. While she described Boudica and her vile cruelty, the skies wept.

By the time the sun was setting, Tegen had torn at the

scar on her finger until it bled, she had told all about the golem and the disastrous battle with Suetonius.

'I stupidly thought that when the fighting finished, that the hatred and vengeance would stop too,' Tegen explained. 'But it's getting worse, my own people are suffering because of me. I've seen in the fire that my child must go over the seas to Ériu, but without me. My dreams say that if I join with the demon that pursues me, I may keep her.' Tegen swallowed hard.

'You torn in half.' Marah touched her hand. 'Poor child.'

'I must let Gilda go – but what if I refuse?' Tegen wiped a tear away. 'But what if I let her go and I still fail? I'll have lost the most precious love I have. Bran told me not to be afraid of fear, but this is too big. I'm not strong enough. I'm about to fail my destiny.'

'And what destiny is yours?' the old man asked kindly.

Tegen stared into the flames dancing on the hearth. 'When I was younger, I thought I had to make difficult spells to throw out the Romans, but they are only people, like us. They aren't the enemy.'

Marah wrapped a piece of rag around Tegen's bleeding finger.

Josephus thought for a moment. 'So, who is enemy, you thinking?'

'The enemy is the demon that pursues me – hatred and vengeance.' Tegen thumped her knee. 'But it's too strong, it's already destroyed the Spirit of Britain. Now it's sworn to come at Imbolg and destroy Gilda and all I love.'

She sighed. 'I don't know how to stand against that.'

Josephus and Marah exchanged glances. 'We had friend, one time,' Marah began, 'he thought save his country from Romans. They grow strong. He fought hate and vengeance also.'

'What happened?' Tegen asked, eyes wide.

'The Romans kill him dead,' Josephus replied simply.

Marah nodded slowly. 'Our people betray. Cruel when he do only good things.'

'But he not fail,' Josephus added. 'You not know what waves you make when your ship-wake pass by.'

Tegen leaned on her elbow and sipped at a chamomile tisane. 'How do you mean?'

'Do what best you can, then good things happen. Maybe slow, but they come.' Josephus reached over to the quern where a few grains of barley lay scattered. 'Tell me please – you plant this to grow the nettles?'

Tegen frowned. 'Of course not. You get more barley.'

The old man tapped the side of his nose conspiratorially. 'Here big secret. You plant love-seeds and they never bloom into hate-flowers. No love-seed ever dies. It may sleep long time. Young plant may be boot-trodden, but it always spring hope somewhere.'

'So, you think if I trust my destiny, and let Gilda go when the time comes – then all will be well?'

Marah bowed her head over her hands, then said, 'One day, yes. Is true.'

The room fell silent except for the crackle of the flames

on the hearth and Gilda's soft snuffles.

Then Josephus laughed. 'I talk much. Marah is face-making at me. I go, you rest.' He leaned over and kissed Tegen's head. 'Why you think when clouds come, sun go away?'

Tegen frowned. 'But it doesn't.'

'Nor your Lady go away. Just no see her. Your Time of Stone now yes? Clouds and snow and oh so much rain?' Josephus shivered. 'Land of mists. But Land not dead, just wait spirit come to make green.'

Tegen remembered she had used almost exactly the same image to comfort Witton when he was ill. She nodded. 'Thank you.'

Josephus pressed a barleycorn into her hand and closed her fingers over it.

And that night she did not dream.

The morning before Imbolg, Kieran arrived at Marah's hut. His face was taut and he paced up and down by the fire, chewing his lip.

'Sit still, won't you?' Claudia demanded. 'Your pacing is making me edgy too.' She turned the dough she was kneading and pummelled it extra hard.

Kieran hesitated and scowled at his boots.

Tegen grabbed his arm and swung him to face her. 'What's up? You're like a wild cat in a cage. Sit down and stop fretting. Tell me what's wrong.' She dumped Gilda in Kieran's arms. 'I'll give you some bread and milk. You can feed her for me. Whatever it is, it can't be so bad you can't tell me.'

Kieran perched on the edge of the bed and absently tore fragments off the bannock, then ate them himself, making Gilda wail.

'Give her back then,' Tegen huffed. 'But what's the matter?'

Kieran finished the bread and wiped his hands on his trousers. 'You're not going to like it ...'

'Like what?' Tegen and Claudia chorused.

He paused, took a deep breath and said, 'Tegen, you've got to get away. Today. Now.'

'Why?' Claudia demanded.

'Surely Suetonius isn't still looking for me?' Tegen asked.

'He's got soldiers and spies after you everywhere. But worse than that, there's cattle disease on the hills, the stored grain's gone mouldy and people have got rye-madness. They're looking for someone to blame. People are saying that you're still alive and stirring things up from here.' He kicked at the hearthstones with his heel. 'Your Da and I – we – we think you ought to go back to Ériu.' He gripped her hands and looked earnestly into her eyes. 'Please go, now's your chance to be happy!'

Tegen's breath caught in her throat. 'But how can we get there? Boats are expensive.'

Kieran twisted his hands together. 'Don't be cross Tegen. Your Da and me, well, we've hired a currach see?

It's waiting down at the wharf.'

Tegen rolled her eyes. 'I think I'd rather walk than go to sea again.'

'You're not taking this seriously,' Kieran scowled. 'Gilda will be safe with Tonn's people – so will you.'

Tegen watched her little girl rolling on the hard earth floor with a puppy she'd adopted. Her own home, her own hearth, Bran had promised, but it'd never be home without Gilda …

'I'd like to go,' Claudia interrupted. 'You said I'd go to a green land with hills, is that what Ériu is like?'

Tegen stared into the hearth-flames and searched for patterns. 'Yes Claudia, it's just like that, and you must go. You must take Gilda and look after her because … because I'm not coming yet.'

Lost in his own thoughts, Kieran's eyes brightened. 'And is this my chance to become a bard in a foreign land? What do you think? A whole new life for us all, see?' He tapped a bright rhythm with a stick on a cooking pot.

Tegen snatched the stick away. 'What about my Da?'

'Your Da says he's too old for travelling,' Kieran said. 'But he sends you and Gilda his blessings.'

Tegen's throat tightened. 'What about Ula?' she whispered.

'She's happy; everyone in the village loves her. They'll defend a runaway slave with their lives.' Kieran squeezed Tegen hand. 'Have a think, but you've got to hurry. The waters ain't very deep this year. We must get past them marshes before sunset.'

Tegen sat quietly and said nothing.

Kieran hugged her. 'Cheer up. Do you remember you and Brigid saying time weren't right for me to go to Ériu? I made a fuss, but you were right. This time you've got to trust me. Them hills is swarming with soldiers, and the people are hungry. Someone'll crack for silver. Bound to. And if they don't get you now, they'll be here soon. You'll be caught, and Josephus and his friends'll be killed just for looking after you.'

Tegen's head ached. She'd be safe from Suetonius in Ériu, but the demon would follow her. On the other hand, there'd be friends and druids to guard them. Staying on the Tor would endanger Josephus and Marah.

This was it: the time had come for her to be the Star Dancer – without Gilda.

Tegen gulped. 'Tomorrow maybe?'

Kieran gripped her shoulders. 'No. It's got to be now. The captain won't wait.'

A knock at the door made Tegen jump. Josephus was standing on the threshold. 'You come walk with me?' he asked simply. 'Marah has made cakes for Gilda.' He shot a glance at Kieran. 'And your-ever hungry friend too, I think?'

The thought of fresh air and Josephus' counsel sounded good. She glanced at Kieran.

'I'll wait here for one hand span of the sun,' he warned. 'Then I'm off.'

Claudia picked up Gilda and they headed for the smells of baking.

Together Tegen and the old man strolled through the woods and over the lower slopes of the great hill. At last, in his soft, rich accent he asked, 'You got bad news?'

'Yes. My enemy is getting close. Kieran thinks I should leave – now.'

'Us protect you. No fear for you.' He took her hand and squeezed it.

'But they will kill you and Marah, and all your friends, so I must go – to go to a place I love – across the sea. It's called Ériu.'

Jospehus nodded silently.

The long green grass swished around Tegen's skirt. At last, she said, 'I may outrun the Romans, but I fear the demon will always find me – and Gilda. The time has come for me to lose my daughter.'

Josephus stroked his white beard. 'Druids say things turn, is going round and round forever?' He raised an eyebrow in her direction. 'Same pattern?'

'There comes a time of change,' Tegen explained, 'when the elements have done their work. It's called the Time of Spirit, when all good guardians work as one. It brings things together. Human souls have to face the past and make sense of the pattern. If they succeed, then the circle becomes a spiral and they step up to a new level. It's like changing key in music.'

'And when Spirit Time comes, there no point to stick in old pattern? We open new ideas. Maybe new wonders too? Your destiny bigger and wider than you guess.' He spread his arms wide. 'Like skies.'

Then he turned to Tegen. 'You still got barleycorn?'

She nodded and took it from her pouch. 'I understand,' she replied softly. 'It's time to plant the love-seed and not be afraid.'

'This is your Imbolg. Time for hope.' Josephus patted her back. 'We go back, your Kieran friend got feet that itch, yes?'

'Hurry, quick-quick.' Marah was running across the meadow to meet Tegen and Josephus. 'Your friend Kieran has Gilda and gone help Claudia pack. You eat.'

She almost dragged Tegen into Josephus's hut. Her shaking hands spilled the soup she served.

'What's matter, Marah?' asked her brother gently.

She looked askance at Tegen and hesitated. 'Just now … men with swords come. Looking for witch-girl with black hair. *British mens.*'

Tegen froze. The new druids had all taken vows never to lie. 'What did you tell them?'

Marah's face creased in merriment. 'Not worry. I tell them silly and must use eyes. You not here. I give ale and they go. But …' she glanced across at Josephus, 'Some tongues will wag for silver pieces.'

Josephus ground his teeth. 'Trouble comes quick.'

Tegen absently took a spoonful of Marah's pottage, then put the bowl on the floor.

'You must eat!' Marah scolded. You go long-long way tonight.'

Tegen ignored her.

'You no like?'

Tegen shook her head. 'No, it's delicious, but *look*!' Pictures were forming in the fire. She dug her nails into her palms as she saw a tall man with a badly scarred face and wearing Roman armour. He was carrying a flaming torch, and smirking with pleasure as he reached up, setting fire to a crumbling old roundhouse on a small hill. The wind whipped the flames into a furnace. Tegen held her breath as she watched the walls fall and the thatch collapse sending a frenzy of sparks whirling into the sky.

The fire raged and more and more images tumbled in on one another. Terrified villagers, women, children, hauled from their homes. Goats and geese hacked to death.

Fire. Swords. Blood. Screams.

'No!' Tegen gasped as she saw Derren corralled with other men in a pigpen. Amongst the women, heavily pregnant Ula wept and begged for him to be spared.

She could hear the weeping and smell the smoke. This was not mere imagination.

Tegen grabbed her cloak. 'Kieran's right. I must go. *Now*. I might not be too late.' She kissed Marah and Josephus and ran outside.

Marah leaped up and called after her. 'Men gone, you no

rushing now?'

Pulling her hood tightly around her head, Tegen turned back. 'It's Suetonius, he's at my village, I don't know if it's about to happen, or if it's all over, but he's going to kill everyone at home unless I stop him.'

'But how you can?' Marah's dark eyes were wretched with worry.

'I don't know, but I must try!'

5.   SPIRIT-TIME

Tegen stopped to catch her breath as she reached her little roundhouse. By her feet, snowdrops were nodding in the wind.

'Today is Imbolg – my birthday,' she whispered. 'It's the day Huval said I'll come into my full strength, but I don't feel very strong. I cannot go to Ériu, but Gilda must.

'It is time to face the demon and make it stop!'

The air tasted of early spring. There had to be hope.

'Lord Bran,' she prayed, 'it is time to keep your word and give me strength. Lady Brigid, send me your boat as you did before. Goban, take my baby home.' She imagined a ship with a large sail flying safely across the waters to Ériu. 'Let it be so.'

Inside the roundhouse, Claudia's voice shrieked and wailed. 'I can't do this! Why did Ula stay behind? This is her job! I'm not standing for it!'

Tegen peered inside and watched Claudia stuffing bags randomly with shawls, cooking pots, combs and sacks of beans.

Kieran was close behind her, pulling everything out again. 'No Claudia, we don't need cooking gear, and what good are dried beans on a boat?'

Gilda was sitting on the bed cuddling her puppy's neck until the whites of his eyes bulged.

Claudia span around as Tegen walked in. 'This is impossible!' she howled, flinging a spindle onto the floor. 'Kieran says we have to pack, but everything I put in, he takes out again!' She swiped at his head with an iron ladle.

He ducked. 'She's packing all the wrong stuff – I keep *telling* her what we need!' he bellowed back.

Tegen held up her hands. Everyone fell silent. 'We'll just take clothes,' she said quietly. Then opening her pouch she pulled out some coins. 'Kieran and I will pack, Claudia, please go and buy bread, ale and dried meat. We'll meet beyond the village, by the tree with winter flowers.'

Throwing Kieran a look of scorn, Claudia flounced out of the roundhouse yelling '*Slave!*' over her shoulder.

Tegen folded Claudia and Gilda's clothes and stuffed them into a sack. Lastly she added Tonn's stone egg and the blue glass necklace he had given her for their handfasting.

Kieran scooped up Gilda and kissed her dark hair. 'We're off to see your Grandma, what do you think of that?'

Gilda blew him a raspberry and giggled.

His eyes had a faraway look. 'Brigid promised I'd go to Ériu one day. I can't wait to see Tara and the Lia Fail and to meet queen Étain.'

'Good, we must hurry. That's everything packed.' Tegen swung a bundle over her shoulder and tied it on. 'Ready?'

Kieran hauled the biggest basket onto his back. 'I am. That was so much easier without Claudia.'

'She can't help it,' Tegen sighed. 'Poor girl, she was brought up with Ula doing everything for her. Try and be patient.'

Wrapping Gilda in a thick shawl, Tegen carried her into the morning air and shut the door. The black puppy trotted alongside, his tail wagging.

'Shoo!' Tegen flapped at him.

He sat, with drooping ears. Seeing he wasn't following, Gilda began to wail.

'Oh very well, come on then. But only if there's room,' Tegen warned, and they set off.

Marah and Josephus were waiting for them by the bridge. 'Oh, God bless you and make many smilings on you,' Marah sobbed, taking Gilda for one last cuddle.

Josephus nodded quietly. 'He always be with you, whatever name you use.' He kissed Tegen's cheek and pressed a bag of nuts into Kieran's bag.

Then holding hands, Josephus and Marah sang a hymn, and waved.

'Thank you for everything,' Tegen called out. Then with lumps in their throats, the travellers strode away between the vegetable gardens, and through the village to the long hill like a pig's back that sheltered the shipping jetty.

Claudia called to them from the top of the path, bundles of food and leather bottles slung over her shoulders. 'The boat's waiting!' she called out. 'The captain says we must hurry because of the tides.'

Tegen nodded. 'Just one last thing,' she said, leading her friends to the little thorn tree that still bore a few milky blossoms.

Tegen cut four twigs. She put one under her own cloak pin, gave one to Claudia, and tucked a sprig inside the baby's shawl. The last piece, she handed to Kieran. 'Bind it to the top of your staff, it will keep you safe wherever you go.'

He looked at it critically, 'Here, is this some of Josephus's magic?'

'Yes, he had a staff of that thorn.' She rolled her twig between her fingers until she found one white and green bud, like a minute globe. 'When he landed here, the rod's heel sank in the mud. The top sprang into leaf and flower, even though it was midwinter. That's how he knew that he and his companions must stay. It is good magic.'

Kieran pushed the blossom away. 'Don't want any foreign muck, ta.' He wiped his hands down the side of his breeches.

Tegen pursed her lips and scowled. '*All* our ideas come from other places, other times. We mix them together to make the best, strongest magic we know. You must *never* scorn anything for being different – you'll miss something sent to help you and that'd insult the Goddess!' She thrust the leaves at him again. 'You'll find many things not to your taste in Ériu. If you can't trust a simple magic like this, how will you survive in a new land?'

'I'll come home!' he protested, clutching at his bags.

'No. You won't.' Tegen replied. 'Not ever.'

Scowling, Kieran snatched the twig, rammed it into a crack at the top of his staff, then bound it tight with a thread from his cloak.

Holding Gilda tightly, Tegen led the way down to the jetty where a currach was moored between two Roman trading vessels.

Midships, a tall, leather-clad man was readying the sails.

'Hello,' Tegen called out. 'We're here.'

The captain ducked the boom and reached out to squeeze Tegen's hand. 'Merrily met, Star Dancer.'

'Goban?' Tegen gasped. 'I thought you'd just send someone – but it's you!'

'Whom else would Brigid trust with her own boat?' he laughed, pointing at a small bundle of rowan twigs and berries tied to the prow. 'Now, we must hurry. Those who want to harm you are hot on your heels, I smell them in the wind.' He reached out to help the travellers aboard. Kieran tossed the bundles into the bottom and Gilda's little dog leapt straight in after them. The boat rocked as they found their places.

Just then, a man's voice yelled, 'Oi you! Get back here, *witch*!'

Ignoring the two figures bounding down the steep hillside above, Kieran cast off. He leaped into the bows and grabbed an oar to push them away from the wharf.

Goban leaned on the tiller, the sails cracked and filled, the boat slid away from its mooring and out into the main channel.

'Damn her, she's getting away!'

A spear whizzed through the air and thudded into the

planking of the bow. Kieran leaned over to wrench it out.

'Leave it!' Goban roared. 'Get it out once we're safely away. 'Hold the sheet, pull hard, keep the sails taut.'

Midstream, they caught a stiff breeze and the boat flew into the middle of the grey choppy seas.

The men thundered onto the wharf and upturned a small coracle. Within moments they had splashed it into the water. Paddling urgently, they were gaining on the currach.

Tegen clambered over bundles and baskets, making her way to the stern where she knelt beside Goban. 'Please, before you go to Ériu, take me back to my village. I need to face Suetonius. He's about to murder everyone. Can you wait for me? Somewhere out of sight?'

He shook his head and leaned on the tiller. 'I cannot take you to your village, Star Dancer.'

'But ...' she began.

'Listen, the men following us are being propelled by your demon.'

Tegen glanced over her shoulder. The coracle was splashing towards them at amazing speed. The men worked the paddles manically, eyes bulging and jaws set.

'Can't you and I join our magic together?' Tegen asked.

Keeping his eyes intently on the sails, Goban replied, 'No. The tide is too low. I couldn't land this boat until evening, even if all was well. I'll bring you to the trackway that crosses the marsh. It'll take you home. Your friends have stabled Epona well, I will call her and she will be waiting for you. Now is the Time of Spirit. You must do what only you can do. You have the Lady's blessing.'

Goban pulled the tiller back. Water slapped noisily at the hull as the boat swung to starboard. Ahead lay the rough line of the wooden trackway and they were speeding urgently towards it.

'What are you doing?' yelled Kieran from the bows. 'Captain, you're going to crash her!'

'I'm getting off, here,' Tegen replied. 'I'm going back to my village.'

'But you can't, you've got to come!' Kieran grabbed her cloak.

She tugged herself free. 'No. I … I've got to go.' Tegen's throat tightened. Her breath came harsh and fast. 'I'll try and join you – later. I hope.'

'But you can't!' he protested.

Tegen looked back at Goban.

He smiled, his dark eyes kind. 'Death brings life and life brings death. Sacrifice with love creates hope, so it goes.'

'I remember,' she whispered.

He turned the tiller so the boat came alongside the planks and poles that spanned the marshy waters. He kissed her hand and squeezed it. A warm glow filled Tegen's soul. 'Oh, by the way, you dropped this.' He slipped a cold iron ring over her bleeding finger.

She traced the simple inscribed design of sacred ogham. 'But I lost that in the sea, how …?'

Goban ignored her. 'Slacken the sail!' he bellowed.

With a scowl, Kieran obeyed. The heavy leather sagged

and the bow knocked against the planks of the trackway.

Tegen clambered forward.

Gilda held her arms out and Tegen hugged her. 'Be good,' she whispered through choking tears. Claudia held her hands briefly and Kieran bowed his head for a blessing.

Then Tegen sprang onto the wobbly walkway.

'Take Gilda to Queen Étain of Tara, in Ériu. Show the queen Gilda's blue glass necklace, it will prove she is Tonn's child.'

'Farewell, all shall be well!' Goban called out.

'And all manner of things shall be well,' Tegen replied, then raising her hands she sent a spell for good weather and fair winds. 'I'll see you all soon – I hope,' she whispered.

Goban took a deep breath and blew. The dark sail filled and they sped towards the open sea.

As Tegen ran across the wobbly wooden struts towards her village, a voice yelled behind her.

'There she is! Ignore the currach! Get *her*!'

She turned. Her pursuers were scarcely an arrow shot away.

The two men paddled with demonic fury, their eyes bulging and their teeth bared. Closer and closer they swept, their bow wave lapping the wooden track.

Tegen turned and sprinted.

6. THE TRACKWAY

The planking creaked and wobbled under Tegen's pounding feet. Slipping and skidding on the slimy wood, she slowed her pace.

The small boat splashed alongside – almost within arm's reach.

Out of breath and with a stitch growing in her side, Tegen turned and raised a spell to tip the boat and drown the men.

But that wasn't the way, and she knew it.

Remembering how Goban blew up a wind, she did the same.

The sudden squall hit the little craft, spinning it across the waves.

'Taranis curse your blood!' yelled one of the men.

As Tegen ran out of breath they paddled again, coming faster than ever.

Tegen wove herself a spirit shield and ran on over silvery pools and channels.

Beneath her boots, the sodden wood split and crumbled. She came to a stretch where the planks were rotted away. Tegen measured the distance and leaped. She landed, missed and slid into sucking mud. Grabbing an upright post, she hauled herself out. Her wet boots squelched and slipped worse than ever.

Behind her, the splashing and yelling was getting closer.

Just ahead, the walkway rose onto a muddy islet covered with brambles and rough willows. Tegen clambered to the top and looked around. The waters were shallow and reedy. The coracle could not get close. She bent over and tried to catch her breath, easing the pain in her ribs.

Crossing to the far side of the islet, she looked across to her village nestling beneath the looming hills. There was no sign of smoke yet, but Suetonius was there. She could sense him.

Maybe she was a bargaining counter? Her capture in exchange for the village?

'Not that I can see Suetonius missing the chance of a good slaughter,' she muttered wryly.

Then, to her horror, she saw the men had paddled ahead. They were standing on the last stretch of trackway, waiting to catch her, scarcely a stone's throw from land.

Tegen shielded her eyes from the afternoon sun and squinted. Light glinted on long knives in their hands. She pursed her lips. There's no way around them, she thought. If I jump in the water they'll simply haul me out.

For a moment, Tegen was surprised at how calm she felt, but with Goban's ring warm on her finger, and his kiss on her cheek, she was not afraid.

'I'll think of something,' she promised herself, stepping onto the final stretch of wooden track. This part was made from tightly woven hurdles laid over sucking marsh. On both sides, the water was lapping and swirling. The tide was turning.

Just a short way ahead, the men waited, grinning through plaited beards.

Sprinting forwards, the taller man yelled, 'Come here girly, we ain't gonna hurt you. Need you alive, see?'

Under her breath, Tegen muttered,

'Slip and slime, this trackway's mine.

Slime and slip, have a good trip!'

She clicked her fingers. The next plank tipped and the man slid sideways.

'*Shit!*' he bellowed, splashing into the water. Moments later he re-emerged, spitting mud. 'You bitch, I'll kill you for that!'

His companion stretched out a hand.

'Leave me, get *her!*' he screeched, waving his fist.

The second man nodded, then crept forward, dagger in hand, eyes intent on his quarry. His lips were moving silently.

Tegen narrowed her eyes and strengthened her spirit shield.

Just then she heard a frantic neighing. Glancing ahead, she glimpsed Epona at the end of the track, pawing at the ground. Goban had been as good as his word and sent the Lady's horse to her aid.

'Don't fret old friend,' Tegen murmured, 'I'm coming.'

The man finished his spell, and with a grin of triumph, he set all the planks and hurdles shaking.

Raising her hand, Tegen sent the spell careering back. The wooden path shivered and creaked. Stakes and posts

340

popped, splinters span into the air, stinking mud heaved and gurgled.

The trackway was gone and both men were now chest deep in the water. But they were laughing! 'We got you good and proper now girly!' one taunted. 'How you gonna get away from us now, eh?'

The second man turned and gave an ear-splitting whistle. Far across the meadows, Tegen saw a group of men sprinting towards them. It was only a matter of time until someone found another coracle and rope and …

Putting her own fingers in her mouth, Tegen whistled louder.

Epona whinnied and sprang into the water.

Then Tegen's heart sank; there was neither saddle nor bridle. 'Never mind, I rode like this as a child. I can do it again – I just have to hold on tight.'

As Epona came within reach, Tegen curled her fingers in the mare's thick mane and swung onto her back.

With wild arcs of spray, Epona splashed her way ashore, then stopped.

Guessing what was coming, Tegen clung on with every muscle as the horse lowered her head and shook herself dry.

'Come on Epona, to the village,' Tegen urged. 'You'll dry as you run.'

The mare flared her nostrils and broke into a trot. Under Tegen's knees, her strong shoulders and flanks rippled as she gathered into a canter across the meadows, away from the men in the water and their furious friends.

The thundering rhythm of Epona's hooves pounded into a full gallop.

Tegen lowered her head and clung on.

The rough ground rose steeply to meet the wooded mouth of the valley. There, on a small hillock, stood the decrepit remains of Witton's old roundhouse.

As Tegen drew close, she smelled smoke. She looked up. Flames cracked and spat through the rotten thatch, the roof fell in, sending sparks flying into the autumn air.

Just then, a tall black stallion trotted from behind the mound. On his back sat an upright figure in a roman crested helmet and eagle-embossed breastplate. He turned his face towards Tegen. A dark scar ran down his right cheek.

'Woah, steady girl.' Tegen slowed Epona to a trot.

The man stopped and threw aside the torch in his hand. His stare spread into a cruel smile of recognition. Without speaking, he turned his mount back towards the village.

Heart thudding, Tegen straightened her back and followed.

Somewhere close by, people screamed and shouted, children wailed and dogs barked. Step by step, the noise swelled.

Tegen rounded the mound. The village palisade stretched before her. Every detail she had seen in the fire was true. The gates were pulled off their hinges. Inside the fence, terrified women and children huddled together.

Swords drawn, soldiers corralled the men into a pigpen.

The air smelled of salt-sweet blood.

The mare danced sideways. 'Come on girl,' Tegen urged, squeezing Epona's flanks. 'You're safe with me. I just want to see ...'

She rode towards the village. Between the roundhouses slimy corpses of goats and geese were strewn around – all hacked and bloody.

Suetonius rode to Tegen's side. He pointed at the carrion. 'I think your people understand what will happen to them if you don't co-operate.'

'Tegen!' Ula yelled, 'They've got Derren, and your Da!'

A soldier slapped Ula's face.

'You know her?' Suetonius smirked. 'Bring the woman.'

The man yanked Ula forward. She sagged and stumbled. Her belly was huge.

Tegen guessed her baby could come any moment. She twisted her fingers more tightly in Epona's mane. 'Ready?' she whispered.

Epona tossed her head and nickered.

Drawing herself tall, Tegen wove a fresh spirit shield. 'Your quarrel is with me. Let her go,' she ordered loudly.

Suetonius ground his teeth. 'Surrender, or the villagers will die. One by one. This woman first.' His accent was thick, but his meaning was clear. He nodded and soldiers pressed their swords against their captive's necks.

Women screamed. Men swore.

Tegen's eyes flashed fire. 'Stop!'

7.   BAREBACK

Silence fell, every eye turned.

Epona shifted nervously.

Tegen laid a reassuring hand on the mare's withers. Her mouth was dry and her heart pounded. 'Let them go Suetonius Paulinus. I agree, I will surrender'

Suetonius smirked.

'But only if you catch me!' Tegen taunted as she kicked Epona smartly. The horse sprang straight into a gallop, bounding away from the village and uphill through the woods.

Tegen flattened her body over Epona's back, willing herself to become one with the mare, muscle by muscle, and bone by bone.

Screwing up her eyes in delight, Tegen pressed her face beside the mare's neck and whispered, 'To the caves!' In her mind she imagined the path the funeral processions took: the stony climb beside the stream, crossing it twice, then the steep stretch through the rocky coombe, ending by the great yew tree that guarded the entrance to Tir na nÓg.

'Can you see the way, Epona? Take me there!'

The mare put back her ears and bolted.

Together they galloped – a single being – bound by thrill and terror.

Epona's iron shoes sparked as she sprang up the path. Twigs and boughs scraped her flanks. Her coat was soon sticky with sweaty froth and her mane whipped at Tegen's face, twisting painfully with her hair.

Low branches caught Tegen's cloak and legs. Her back hurt, her eyes watered, her face and hands smarted, her legs screamed with effort. But she held on, clenching her knees tightly, yet letting her body flow as one with Epona's.

On. On.

With a sudden bunching in Epona's quarters, she leaped.

The lurch left Tegen's stomach behind.

The mare landed with a crunch of wet gravel and surged ahead. Tegen bit her tongue painfully and yelped as she slithered forward. She must not fall! Somehow she shoved herself upright and eased once more into the flow of Epona's strides.

That's the first stream crossing, she told herself.

Suddenly she thought she saw Derowen, blocking the path ahead. She was dressed in blue with her hair combed loose, as she had for Gilda's funeral.

As Tegen approached, Derowen spread her hands

Tegen sat up to slow Epona, but the mare ignored the signal and smashed through the vision. Pebbles and mud sprayed from her hooves as she pounded up the twisting track.

With another sharp turn and bunching muscles, Epona leaped the stream once more. Tegen's stomach twisted, but she was ready for the landing this time.

Shouts and thudding hooves from behind ripped at

Tegen's concentration. She lurched sideways and almost fell. In one spongy bounce, the mare slowed. Tegen hauled herself back up and glanced over her shoulder.

Suetonius thundered in, his huge stallion wide-eyed and foaming with sweat. Steam snorted from red nostrils. Suetonius rose in his saddle and lashed at his horse, urging it closer.

More shouts came from below as five more horses leaped the stream and stormed along the path.

Epona swung abruptly aside, powering up a steep bank between the trees.

'Where're we going? This isn't the way!' Tegen shouted, flattening herself onto Epona's back.

The mare's whole body heaved and worked as she lumbered higher. More branches scratched and scraped along her back. Epona slowed, her sides heaving, legs shaking.

Incoherent yells and curses made Tegen take another look.

Suetonius had tried to follow her, but both he and his stallion were snagged in the embrace of a holly tree. The general was ignominiously caught by his cloak and breeches. Under him, his horse struggled to free its mane. Behind him his men were hacking at the prickly branches, but the more they cut, the closer the other trees seemed to be crowding, their bare branches reaching down like clawed fingers.

'A blessing on these woods,' Tegen laughed. She stroked

Epona's neck. 'Well done. You are truly magical. Can we get to the caves ahead of them from here?'

Epona tossed her head and shook herself. Tegen slid from her back. 'You're right, it's easier if we walk,' she said. 'You deserve a rest anyway.' She tried to stand, but her back and legs had seized up and her knees gave way.

After a few moments' rest against a tree, Tegen led Epona onwards. Walking eased her stiffness as they picked their way between boulders, brooks, tangled coppices and hanging ivy.

Epona chose a badger track that wound into a deep valley with ivy and fern-clad rocks towering on all sides. She trotted ahead, neck stretched out, ears flicking and hoof beats echoing. At last she slowed, and stood in a small patch of sunlight. There she stood quietly, enjoying the rest and warmth, swishing her tail.

White bathed in gold. The Goddess's horse.

Using a fallen tree, Tegen climbed shakily onto Epona's back once more. 'One last ride my beauty. Take me to the other side, then you'll be free.'

To their left was the dark, open mouth of the funeral caves, guarded by the writhing-branched yew tree. Ahead was the rushing stream that flowed from Tir na nÓg. To their right was the forest path.

From that direction came the muffled thunder of approaching hooves and shouting men.

Epona splashed through the stream and trotted towards the cave mouth. There, Tegen slipped to the ground for the last time. She rubbed and kissed her horse's velvet nose. 'I don't know if I shall ever see you again, Epona. But thank you for everything. My blessings go with you. Good bye!'

Epona stamped and huffed warm hay-breath into Tegen's face. With a snort and a twitch of her ears, she swung around and walked away between the trees.

Before Tegen could wipe her tears, Suetonius and his men galloped into the coombe and leaped the stream, hooves clattering noisily as the horses landed on the wet rocks.

Tegen stepped back as the tall, long-necked mounts closed in around her.

With a soft hush, the men drew their pugios. Sharp blades glinted in the shafts of late sunlight.

Tegen stroked Goban's ring. The iron was cool. 'All shall be well, and all manner of things shall be well,' she whispered to herself.

'Shut your spells up!' Suetonius sneered as he dismounted.

'No spells,' Tegen replied calmly.

Suetonius touched his scar with his free hand, and with the other, he raised his blade to Tegen's neck.

She did not flinch.

At a nod from their general, five soldiers dismounted and closed in around Tegen. Their eyes were bright and cruel. What could an unarmed girl do against them?

Jumping onto a rock, Tegen spread her hands. 'Here I am. Come and get me.'

8.   TORMENT

Suetonius stepped towards her, his white teeth bright. He bent his knees, moving stealthily, as if closing in on a wounded bear.

'I'm unarmed. You're not afraid are you?' Tegen challenged.

Suetonius pursed his lips and took another step. *That's her, that's her!* the voice in his head persisted. *Get her now!*

Tegen jumped off the boulder and placed a hand on the bough of the great yew tree. 'Lord Gwyn, let me in, give me safe passage I beg you,' she prayed. 'And take this demon back where it belongs. If we humans don't have hope, you gods are nothing.'

The dark green silence of the tree welcomed her. Stooping, she picked up a dead branch and ran into the darkness.

The cave was damp and cool. Tegen's feet slipped on the wet rocks underfoot. She closed her hand around Goban's iron ring. It was getting hot. But she had nothing to fear; she knew the way into the caves and she had walked in Tir na nÓg before. She was a friend to the spirits of rock and water. They would protect her soul, whatever happened to her body.

This was the womb of rebirth.

She made her way further into the dark, her left hand tracing the well-worn pattern of rocks that guided mourners to the resting place of the dead.

Behind her, she heard Suetonius yelling at his men.

They haven't got a torch or anything to make one with, she chuckled.

She willed fire to the end of her yew branch. Flames leaped.

Suetonius winced.

'Scared?' she taunted, 'then follow my light.'

'... light ... light ... light,' her voice echoed back over the drip-drip of the wet cave walls.

'Bitch-itch-itch!' A man's voice yelled behind her.

'Scum-um-um!'

'Slave-ave-ave!'

More and more voices echoed until it seemed as if a thousand men were behind her, but Tegen smiled. It was just voices, pretending to be bigger than they were.

Suetonius led his men, their hob-nailed boots striking the rock, with cold, precise rhythm that echoed and re-echoed into the clattering of a thousand boots. Sparks flew in the darkness. Slipping. Sliding. Swearing. The shouts became fearful.

Down over rocks and mud shoots Tegen led them, past stone waterfalls and pale bony fingers and giant's tears.

Down into the ever-hungry gullet of Tir na nÓg.

Holding the torch high, Tegen splashed through shallow pools of ice-cold water. At last she came to a twisting stalagmite that grew like a massive stone tree, pale and gleaming into the darkness above. For a moment she paused. As the men clattered noisily behind her she called out, 'Careful, it's low here.'

'Here-ere-ere,' her voice continued on into the darkness.

She ducked under the sharp overhang and crawled along a narrow passageway, chuckling as helmets clanked and skulls cracked behind her.

At last she came to a wide space where the echo of her soft-soled boots whispered into the towering rock dome above. At her feet spread a black lake. Here old Gilda had been sent to her rest, as had Witton, and probably her mother too. Tegen held her torch high to see the low lintel of the next cave where the bodies were sent. 'May you all be born again soon,' she whispered.

Here too, her beloved Griff had died helping others. Here she had danced for the Lady to quell the floods and to send the demon back.

She heard the approaching footsteps and whispers – but did not run.

'Got her!' Rough hands grabbed at Tegen's cloak.

She loosened the pin and blew out her torch.

'What the-the-the?' yelled Suetonius.

'Got her-her-her!' shouted a soldier.

'That's *me-me-me*, you moron!'

'I'm here,' Tegen replied softly, stepping away. She clicked her fingers and fire returned to the yew branch.

In the flickering light, six wide-eyed faces snarled at her.

Before they could take a step, Tegen held up her hand. 'Stop!' she commanded. 'I know you understand British, so listen. I don't need a light in these caves. I've come here since I was a child. There are many treacherous cracks and gullies. Without a light, you are all dead men.'

Suetonius and his officers looked at each other nervously.

'I will give you this torch,' she held it out.

Suetonius grabbed for it, but Tegen snatched it back.

'This Land is sacred – the body of the Goddess. Her bones are all around you, her hair is our forests and her blood is our seas and streams.'

Soft footfalls echoed as two men sidled around Tegen, closing in on her.

Undaunted, Tegen rolled the tiny barleycorn between her fingers. 'It is time for forgiveness and healing. If you swear to stop revenge attacks on my people and let us live in peace, the torch will lead you out safely. If you don't agree, I will still give you the light … But the fire will go out. You and your men will grope your way back.'

Suetonius narrowed his eyes and snatched the burning stick. 'I don't make bargains with witch girls.'

A howling wind blasted from nowhere. The torch went out, leaving only sour smoke.

After a long, heart-thudding moment, Suetonius called into the darkness, 'Slave, where are you? Here she is, come and get her. I've kept my part of the bargain, now you keep yours. Get me out of here, make me Emperor.'

With a thundering roar, the cavern shook. Violent lights swirled. Boulders tumbled.

Suetonius and his men cowered.

Fool, she's stronger than before. You've done nothing! roared the demon in Suetonius's head.

More stones clattered, echoing louder and louder.

'Mithras, save us!' the men begged, sinking to their knees.

Only Suetonius stood his ground. 'Slave!' he yelled at the mayhem, 'You promised!'

*No. **You** promised.*

Suetonius strode to where he thought Tegen stood. Over the roaring chaos he bellowed, 'When I get out, your whole village will die. In fact I will kill every damn Briton I ever meet.'

From somewhere behind him, Tegen laughed. 'I don't think so,' she said, raising her arms.

The earthquake subsided.

With a whispered word, Tegen re-lit the yew branch in Suetonius's hand. 'I told you, the fire will only burn if you cease to bully and murder innocent people.

Growling, Suetonius held out the torch and swung around. 'Where are you?' he demanded.

From the dancing shadows, Tegen's voice floated back. 'I have made a spell to bring you and your men safely out of these caves. But without the protection of my fire, the demon will torment you all the way. I cannot promise what state you'll be in at the end.'

Suetonius snarled, searching every dancing shadow for his quarry.

'I'm here,' she called out.

Lifting the flame high, he span on his heel.

Tegen was sitting calmly on a low mound in the middle of the cavern. 'So – what is your answer?' she asked softly. 'Will you allow the Time of Spirit to heal our peoples?'

'Never!' Suetonius flung the brand to the ground. It sizzled and the cave felt darker than ever.

Once more the howling, creaking and cracking of rocks began.

'I should hurry,' Tegen called out calmly, as the demon's tormenting, swirling lights began once more.

And six men fled screaming.

The last echoes of terrified men and their clattering boots faded, but Tegen was not alone.

You could have been magnificent with me, the demon's voice whispered inside Tegen's head.

'Magnificent like Boudica?' she replied.

More so!

So ... like Suetonius?

With me as your guide, you could have ruled the world!

'But I don't want to rule the world,' she said. 'Go back to the depths of Tir na nÓg where you belong and leave me alone.'

Ha! Make me.

Tegen took a deep breath and said, 'Demon, I reject you. The Time of Spirit is here.'

The cave filled with eerie lights that flashed and

exploded with ear-splitting cracks. The rocks shook.

Tegen stumbled to the ground. Unafraid she got to her feet.

Cold winds howled, the river rose and splashed at Tegen's knees. Faces of those she had loved and hated swirled around her, calling, begging, cajoling, threatening.

She dismissed them with a wave of her hand. 'These are just nightmares. They are nothing.'

As the noise whimpered to nothingness, Tegen called out, 'Now it's my turn to do a spell.' She dropped her barleycorn into the receding water. 'Float downstream, take root where you're needed.'

One seed? You'll defy me with that? Sneered the demon.

'It's enough,' Tegen replied. 'However you curse our world in the years to come, there will always be hope and reconciliation. That is my magic. So will it be.'

You'll soon come snivelling back to me begging for my power and glory.

'No, I won't. That was my final spell. My magic is finished. I am of no use to you.' She brushed off her hands. 'Look – my power has all gone.'

No! the demon gasped. *No ... no ... no ...*

The cave flashed with white, searing light, then there was ... nothing.

Tegen stood quite still in the absolute darkness, listening to the cool, drip-dripping silence.

9.   STAR DANCE

Without bothering to make any sort of fire or light, Tegen stood on her toes and swung around, bowing in turn to each to the spirits of earth, air, fire and water. Lastly, she knelt to the spirit of goodness that was her guiding star, the only light she needed.

Somewhere, high above the hillside, stars twinkled. The Watching Woman's constellation was shining for her, even in the depths of the earth.

With a shout of joy, Tegen sprang to her feet and danced.

The little drummer boy she had first heard as a child, stood close by her side once more. He was beating out a joyous heart-rhythm as he had that Beltane morning in the meadows. The sun shone and Griff laughed and clapped as he watched her dance.

Then Tonn was swinging her around in his arms. He was her Green Man as together they leaped their wedding fire.

In the snow, under the waves, on top of Cadair Idris – in the dark in Tonn's loving embrace. All the steps and songs and music she had ever known came whirling together into one triumphant silver spiral that twisted up into the night sky.

After a few moments, Tegen heard the soft pat-pat of a

second pair of feet, following her patterns and swaying in perfect time with her.

Arms encircled her. Arms she had not forgotten. Arms she loved.

Tegen leaned her face into Tonn's chest and smelled his skin. Thyme and grass, wood smoke and wind.

'You're really here?' she breathed.

He kissed her hair. 'I am.'

Then another hand took hers. Sticky. Strong. Squeezing her fingers with love.

'Griff?' she gasped. His heavy boots thudded in steady time with hers.

The cavern had gone. She was dancing with the two men she loved most, on a hillside in open starlight.

The three of them circled around a rowan tree; its berries tiny sparks of merry flames.

Tegen stopped to catch her breath. She looked from Tonn to Griff.

'Am I dead?' she croaked huskily.

'No,' Tonn replied, gently kissing her lips. 'Not yet.'

'But you ...?'

'Goban says we gotta come,' Griff replied. Then taking her hand, he led her away from the fire-tree towards a little boat, rocking on an obsidian lake. A small bundle of brightly berried rowan twigs was tied to the bow.

'This is Brigid's boat, isn't it?' Tegen asked, 'I thought it was on its way to Ériu?

Tonn helped Tegen and Griff in. 'She sent it back for

you,' he replied. Then both men took paddles and with steady rhythmic splashes, they moved smoothly across the water, sending the reflected stars rippling away under the currach's bows.

Tegen rubbed her eyes. 'Are you – *is* this real?'

Griff nodded so hard he rocked the little boat. 'Oh yes. Goban says Tegen need help-quickly.' He grinned. 'Luvs yer Tegen, alwus will. Gotta help Tegen.' And he kissed her cheek.

She blew her nose on her sleeve and wiped her eyes.

The rowan twigs sparkled brightly, sending flickering golden light over Tonn's eyes and beard. He laid his paddle aside and cradled Tegen's face in his hands. 'We're taking you home, beloved.'

Tegen's eyes widened. 'Can I die if I want to, and be with you and Griff until we are reborn?'

Tonn nodded and pointed to the west. 'If we go that way, we will all be together until the Lady calls us to go back and work for her again.'

Tegen bit her lip. 'And ... where else might I be allowed to go?'

The boat swept in a wide circle. Above, the stars span in a silver arc. 'Anywhere you like,' Tonn replied. 'Bran promised you peace and a home. Your work is finished, it's time to choose your reward.'

'But what about Suetonius?'

'He climbed out of the caves two days after you left. Quite mad. He and his cohort have been sent back to Rome.

There's a new governor of Britain now. I think things will change for the better. Your barleycorn has taken root. There will be healing, for a while.'

'What do you mean, "two days after I left"?' Tegen asked.

'Time in Tir na nÓg is different,' Tonn explained.

'I understand … And our little Gilda? Where is she?'

'Our beautiful daughter is safe in Tara with my mother, being cosseted and fed on honey cakes. She misses you.' Tonn's eyes clouded.

Tegen's breath caught in her throat. 'I want, I so want to be with you – and Griff for ever – I love you both so much, but I think …'

'You think our baby girl needs her Mam? So do I. Go back to her and we'll be watching over you both, I swear. And what seems to be long years to you, are nothing to us in Tir na nÓg. We'll all be together again one day.'

'What do you think Griff?'

Griff nodded cheerfully. 'Loves yer Tegen. Miss yous, but I'll allus be waitin' for yous. 'Ere, this is for little baba. From uncle Griff.' He pressed a roughly carved little doll in Tegen's hand. 'Give her a kiss from me, will yus?'

Tegen took the toy and put it into her pouch. 'I will.' She reached out and hugged her beloved Tonn and Griff until her back and neck almost cracked. Kisses, tears and love twisted them together in an unbreakable knot.

'Almost home,' Tonn said at last, easing himself out of Tegen's grasp.

The boat glided down a narrow stone gully with morning light ahead. The smell of young grass and blossom filled Tegen's lungs. She heard birdsong, goats bleating and children laughing. 'But – but it's spring …' she looked around, bemused. 'It was Imbolg when I went into the caves.'

'A little time has passed in your world, but all is well. Indeed, because of you, all manner of things shall be well.'

The boat grounded. Tonn stepped out and held it steady. 'You'll have to wade from here, beloved. It isn't far.' He held her and kissed her one last time.

As they stood, the sunlight shifted and fell on his dear face, and he faded.

'No!' Tegen gasped. 'You can't leave me – not again.'

She ran into the tunnel once more. In the gloom, she glimpsed Griff waving to her from the back of the little boat. 'Bye byes Tegen. Will you makes me some honey cakes? I miss 'em big missin.'

Tegen stood unsteadily, then pulled herself together. 'Look under a yew tree at Samhain, Griff. I'll make you a whole plateful, every year, I promise.'

Turning her back on the darkness, she splashed through the stream as it trickled out of a wide crack in a grassy hillside.

Nodding over the sunlit entrance was a rowan tree in full blossom. Next to it a musty hawthorn spread its frothy cream.

Tegen turned the ring on her finger and touched the

spreading flowers. Bowing her head, she said, 'Thank you Lady, for everything – and I'm sorry I doubted you.'

Then pulling off her sodden boots, she ran uphill and through the busy streets of Tara to the Ráth of Grainne where she had once lived. Leaning breathlessly on the roundhouse doorpost, she called out, 'Gilda! Gilda, I'm home!'

A tiny child with a mop of dark curls crawled merrily across the floor and looked up at Tegen with big green eyes. 'Ma-ma-*Mam*!' she cooed.

Tegen scooped up her baby and kissed her cheek. 'Your Mam's come home now – for always.'

★

WHO'S WHO IN TEGEN'S WORLD

DRUIDS

Bronnen and Dallel – Senior druids at Sinodun. They help Tegen in her quest and teach her to Fire Walk in Tir na nÓg.

Enid – Gronw's apprentice. At first she is Tegen's friend, but when she has to undergo a gruelling winter ritual, she learns to hate.

Gorgans – An albino who longs to be a warrior but can't bear sunlight. Addicted to power, he becomes a druid. He wants to be the Star Dancer, and sets out to destroy Tegen with Derowen's help.

Gronw – the Chief Druid of the people of Bera. He is very wise and he mentors Tegen by teaching her to question everything.

Huval – A kindly druid who takes over Tegen's mentoring when Witton dies.

Moryn – The self-appointed leader of the druids after the slaughter on Mona. He sends Tegen to become Boudica's Battle druid.

Owein – An ovate (second stage druid), a little older than Tegen. He is secretly the son of Cara (Caractacus) the British warlord who almost defeated the Romans. He was raised in Rome by his uncle Admidios, to become a puppet king acceptable to both sides. An accident left him disabled, excluding him from kingship by British law. He is a natural diplomat who can see that if the Romans can't be got rid of, then a humane co-existence must be worked out. He is engaged to Sabrina, then believing she is dead, to Claudia Metella, both times to create political alliances.

Tegen – A British girl born during a meteorite shower that seemed to come from Cassiopeia in about 43AD, just as the Romans were invading. These 'Dancing Stars' are seen as a sign that a great druid has been born who can save the British people.

Witton – The elderly chief druid of the Winter Seas, (the Somerset Levels). He recognises Tegen's powers and begins to mentor her.

*

WITCHES, SHADOW WALKERS AND 'WISE ONES' *Not trained as druids, but with magical abilities – for good or evil.*

Admidios: A minor British king who sided with the Romans very early on. He betrayed his brother Cara, and stole baby Owein as a 'gift' for the Emperor Caligula, hoping to buy favour. When Caligula died, Admidios was ignored by his successor, Claudius. Admidios's lust for power turned him into a 'Shadow Walker,' a black magician in league with the demon. Derowen the Raven is his familiar.

Aodh – A spell-caster, a worker of dark magic. The brother of Addedomaros.

Derowen: A failed druid, who resorts to black magic to control and destroy. She raises the cave demon, and is killed by it, but even after her death, she still hunts Tegen. In Fire Dreamer, she takes the form of a raven.

Gilda: She gave up her druid training for love, but was cheated by Derowen. She is a 'wise woman', a white witch who uses herbalism and kindly magic. She was Tegen's midwife and always believed in her. Derowen tricked Tegen into killing Gilda. Tegen names her child after her.

Griff: He is a 'Gifted One', who has psychic power and wise insights. He is Derowen's secret son whom she abandoned because he had Downs Syndrome. A foundling, he became Tegen's foster brother, and for political reasons, Griff and Tegen are handfasted. They care deeply for each other, and Tegen is devastated when Griff dies in the floods caused by the cave demon.

*

SPIRITUAL BEINGS

The Demon:
A creature from the Otherworld, the essence of evil and chaos, serving only itself. When Derowen's spells in the funeral caves open the way between the worlds, the demon seizes the chance to wreck havoc. He seeks to possess Tegen and use her magical powers to rule humanity.

Gods and Goddesses: *note: The ancient Celts did not have a set pantheon of deities, they varied locally.*

Andraste: A war goddess worshipped by Boudica

Bera: Another aspect of the Watching Woman, the goddess of cereals and growth, the mother of Goban and Brigid.

Brigid: Another form of the Watching Woman, and Goban's sister, with special care for blacksmiths, poets and midwives.

Bran the Blessed – A mythical Lord of the Britons who made the Cauldron of Re-birth and gave his life to rescue his people and his sister. His head was buried on the White

Hill of Lundein (where the Tower of London now stands) to protect the Land for ever and to give wisdom to all who sought it.

Goban – A smith god who gives Tegen an iron ring of protection. He becomes the Samhain sacrifice to bring fruitfulness to the land for the following year. His belief in re-birth is absolute, and his loving determination to ensure that life goes on, moves Tegen deeply.

Old Ones / Hill People – Small nomadic people with earth magic. See Y Tylwyth Teg.

The Lady – Another name for Tegen's goddess (See Watching Woman).

Sul: the goddess of Bath's Hot springs. (Sul's Land)

Skatha – her name means darkness or shadow, an underworld goddess of war.

The Watching Woman – Tegen worships a benevolent earth goddess with many aspects and incarnations. Her star sign we now call Cassiopeia, Tegen calls it the Watching Woman because it can be seen all year.

Taranis – A Celtic god of thunder and storms.

Y Tylwyth Teg – Traditionally Welsh fairy folk, used here as the Welsh names for the Old Ones.

★

KINGS, QUEENS AND COMMONERS
(R) = Real people

Addedomaros – King of the Trinovantes (Colchester and Suffolk)

Boudica – (R) The wife of Prasutagus (R), King of the pro-Roman Iceni tribe. When Prasutagus died in circa AD 59 or 60, he bequeathed half his kingdom to the Emperor Nero, and the other half to his daughters. Nero commanded that the whole kingdom be seized, Boudica flogged and the daughters raped (possibly by slaves). Enraged by the insult, Boudica led the Iceni people, along with their neighbours the Trinovantes, in rebellion. As Suetonius Paulinus was away, subduing the people of Mona (Anglesey) there was almost no opposition.

Daig – A chieftain of the Trinovantes

King Eiser – King of the Catuvellauni. He is spearheading the campaign to destroy the Romans, so Admidios and Derowen murder him with black magic. This murder brings Tegen into a new level of magic and precipitates the events of Wave Hunter.

Kieran – A son of a salt-trader and a Silure warrior. Brought up by his abusive aunt and a weak mother, he is resentful, wary and bitter. He becomes Admidios' slave in lieu of unpaid taxes. Tegen befriends him and he helps her defeat the Shadow Walker. He receives the gift of poetry when he spends the night on Cadair Idris, becomes a bard and a Silure Warrior like his father.

Oriana and Megan – Imagined names for Boudica's daughters, raped by Roman soldiers or slaves as punishment for inheriting half of their father's kingdom.

Princess (Later Queen) Sabrina – The only surviving child of Eiser, King of the Dobunni tribe. A warrior at heart, Sabrina had no wish to be queen. Impulsive and passionately anti-Roman, she leads her people into a Roman trap and is sold as a gladiatrix (female gladiator).

She and Owein were betrothed as a political match, but neither wanted it. Eventually she is freed and she joins Boudica's rebellion.

Venutius – (R) King of the Brigantes tribe (roughly Yorkshire). Venutius was initially pro-Roman but his wife, Cartimandua betrayed the rebel king Caractacus to Rome. Later Venutius and Cartimandua divorced and it is possible he joined Boudica in her revolt.

*

ROMANS

Claudia Prima Metella – only surviving child of Julius Claudius Metellus and a Gaulish slave woman. Widowed when her husband died at the battle of Mona, now betrothed to Owein (Sextus) ap Caractacus, a political marriage.

Gaius Suetonius Paulinus: – (R) A Roman general who became Governor of Britain in AD 59, quickly gaining a reputation for unnecessary cruelty and savagery, especially in Wales. In Fire Dreamer, Tegen tricked him and burned him with magical flames, exacerbating his hatred of the British, and of druids in particular. The real Suetonius ordered the massacre of the druids on Mona (Anglesey) in AD 60, and led the campaign against Boudica in AD 61. Afterwards, he was the subject of an enquiry for his unnecessary cruelty and recalled to Rome to be replaced by the more moderate Publius Petronius Turpilianus. After a not very glorious career, Suetonius was accused of treachery and faded into obscurity.

Julius Claudius Metellus – A Roman general, father of Claudia Prima Metella

Poenius Postumus – (R) The Roman chief of staff in Isca Dumnoniorum (Exeter) who refused to come to help

Suetonius when ordered to do so. Afterwards he fell on his sword for shame: his men did not share in the loot and the glory and he had disobeyed a direct command.

Ula – Claudia's Gaulish slave

★

HISTORICAL AND MADE-UP NAMES USED FOR REAL PLACES
Maps of Tegen's journeys are available on www.bethwebb.co.uk

Bagendun – Bagendon
Bara's stronghold – Barbury Castle, on the Ridgeway
Boudica's marsh stronghold – Stonea Camp, Fens
Boudica's palace – Thetford, Norfolk
Boudica's mustering space – Gallows Hill, Fison's Way, Thetford
Boudica's final battle – somewhere along Watling Street (now the A5), probably Mancetter (Warwickshire) or High Cross, Leicestershire
Brigid's smithy – the village of Tywyn, Gwynedd
Cadair Idris – part of the Snowdonia range in north Wales
Camulodunum – Colchester
Corinium – Cirencester
Diva – Chester
Dorcic – Dorchester on Thames
Ériu – Ireland
Funeral caves – Wookey Hole in Somerset
Hill of Gold, Silver and Tin – Alderly Edge
Hill of the King – Silbury Hill
House of Bera – Castell y Bere in Gwynedd
Isca Dumnoniorum – Roman Exeter
Lindum / Colonia Lindensium - Lincoln
Lundein – the White Hill, now the Tower of London
Londinium – built north of the river Thames between Ludgate and Aldgate.
Mona/Ynys Môn – Anglesey, Wales

Rearing River – the River Severn at Frampton on Severn
Sinodun – Wittenham Clumps
Stone Forest – Avebury stone circle
Sul's Land – Bath
Tal y Llyn – a lake at the top of Cadair Idris Tara – Tara in Meath, Ireland
Tamesis – the Thames (Tegen and Owein join it at Streatley)
Tara – The Hill of Tara, Ireland, once the seat of the High Kings
Tegen's Home Village – near modern day Wookey Village, Somerset
The ruined stronghold (Fire Dreamer) – Liddington Castle, on the Ridgeway
The first Wight-Barrow (Fire Dreamer) – West Kennet Long Barrow
The second Wight-Barrow (Fire Dreamer) – Wayland's Smithy, Uffington Castle
Tor – Glastonbury village and Tor.
White Horse – the White Horse of Uffington on the Ridgeway
Winter Seas – the Somerset Levels
Verulamium – St Albans
Y Fenni – Abergavenny

★

ANCIENT NAMES FOR SEASONS AND FESTIVALS
Pronunciation varies, guides can be found on the internet.

Imbolg – Feb 2nd. Now St Brigid's day, previously the first day of spring, a festival of the goddess Brigid, and Tegen's birthday.

Beltane – Early May (usually the 1st). A fire festival to celebrate the coming fertility of the summer. Marriages are often contracted and blossom of the hawthorn or May tree is highly prized.

Lughnasadh – Early August, the beginning of harvest, and dedicated to the god Lugh (strength and sunlight).

Samhain – Oct 31st – Nov 1st. We now call this Hallowe'en / All Saint's Day. It marks the last of the harvest, and is the festival of death, when the spirits of the departed visit the world to make sure they are remembered. Cakes and drinks are left out for the ancestors. It's also the end of the ancient year and diseased and unwanted things are burned to start the New Year clean and fresh – we now have 'bonfires'!

Equinoxes – When the days and nights are of equal length (March 21st and September 21st)

Solstices – Midsummer and midwinter's day (Dec 21st and June 21st)

★

GLOSSARY OF UNUSUAL TERMS

Clamp – A heap of wood covered with turf and slowly burned to make charcoal.

Glamour – A spell that conceals the true nature of something.

Gladius – A Roman short stabbing sword (plural Gladii)

Land – When land is spelled with a capital L, it describes the ancient belief that the ground itself is body of the Goddess and is therefore sacred.

Oppidum (*pl Oppida*) – a large defended settlement.

Pugio – Roman dagger

Withy / withies: long flexible young sticks, usually willow, used for basket making, thatching and wattle and daub walls.

Wight-barrow – a long barrow (Bronze Age funeral mound). Tegen believes that sleeping in them means the ancestors give her dreams.

*

Book one: **Star Dancer, the book of Air**

Book two: **Fire Dreamer, the book of Fire**

Book three: **Wave Hunter, the book of Water**

Book four: **Stone Keeper, the book of Stone**

Available from all good bookshops.
Also available on Kindle.

To read the opening chapters of Beth Webb's books, or to
find out more about how she researched and wrote
this series, log onto:
www.bethwebb.co.uk

you can also find Beth on
http://www.facebook.com/bethwebbauthor
Twitter@webbfooted.

*

Beth Webb lives in Somerset, England, not far from the Mendip hills and levels (Winter Seas) of Tegen's home. The Star Dancer stories are a carefully researched mixture of history and myth, richly spiced with magical imagination.
The druids were (and are) real, and the Roman Invasion of CE 43 as described in Fire Dreamer, Wave Hunter and Stone Keeper, was all too real as well.

For more information about Beth, her other books and her top writing tips, go to:
www.bethwebb.co.uk

*

www.marchhamilton.com

MHM Publishing